TEMPTED BY HER ISLAND MILLIONAIRE

NINA SINGH

THE CAPTAIN'S BABY BARGAIN

MERLINE LOVELACE

This book is produced from independently certified FSC™ paper to ensure responsible forest management.

For more information visit: www.harpercollins.co.uk/green

Printed and bound in Spain
by CPI, Barcelona

MILLS & BOON

First Published in Great Britain 2018
by Mills & Boon, an imprint of HarperCollinsPublishers,
1 London Bridge Street, London, SE1 9GF

Tempted by Her Island Millionaire © 2018 Nilay Nina Singh
The Captain's Baby Bargain © 2018 Merline Lovelace

ISBN: 978-0-263-26511-8

38-0718

MIX
Paper from
responsible sources
FSC
www.fsc.org
FSC® C007454

LANCASHIRE COUNTY LIBRARY	
3011813668139 6	
Askews & Holts	05-Jul-2018
AF AFR	£5.99
CLO	

TEMPTED BY HER ISLAND MILLIONAIRE

NINA SINGH

For my dear husband.
That was quite an impressive anniversary gift, hon.

And for my children.
Thank you for enduring bitter cold atop
a volcano, waiting for a sunrise with me.

CHAPTER ONE

His sister was starting to get on his nerves.

He loved her more than anyone else on this earth, but she had been pushing the boundaries of that love ever since she'd gotten engaged.

Clint held the cell phone to his ear, only partially listening to her latest panic-stricken rant. He knew better than to try and say anything to calm her down. The last time he'd tried that, he'd gotten an earful of colorful curse words streamed through the line that would have made his construction contractors blush.

He understood, or he was trying hard to anyway. She had a lot on her mind with the wedding fast approaching. In fact, his town car was dropping him off at the airport at this very moment on his way to sunny Maui where Lizzie and her fiancé would be tying the knot in a few short days. Only now she had some sort of pressing issue with a last-minute change, something to do with the catering. An issue she seemed to be taking way out of proportion. He'd simply learn who he had to pay to fix it once he got there. What was one more expense when it came to this wedding?

He'd be sure to take care of it after arrival. Again, he wasn't going to tell her that. Right now, Lizzie just needed to vent.

His sister had always been a bit overly dramatic. But this wedding was taking that penchant to a whole new level and making him wonder, for that matter, exactly how many women had been put on this earth simply to irritate him?

"Anyway, how are you doing? Anything new?" Lizzie surprised him by asking. Rant over somehow. Not that he wasn't grateful.

Did he dare tell her? That he was unexpectedly attending her wedding solo since the huge fallout with Maxine the other day. After she'd finally made one ultimatum too many.

He decided not to risk it. Lizzie would no doubt want the distraction and try to probe for all the details. Not something he wanted to get into right now. He'd tell her once he arrived at the resort.

"I'm doing fine," he answered honestly. In truth, it was a relief to have finally severed the relationship with the up-and-coming actress. Maxine had grown increasingly demanding and pouty over the past several months. The only frustration now was that he'd already paid for all her flights, excursions and accommodations. Not to mention a hefty spa-and-beauty package at the resort. Shameful waste. Though part of him couldn't help but wonder if it was worth it. "About to go check in for my flight as a matter of fact."

"I'll let you go then, big brother." She paused but didn't hang up. He knew what was coming and he appreciated it. But it still made him uneasy every time she did it. "And you know how much it means that you're doing all this for me," she said, her voice nearly breaking. "I mean it. Thank you."

So unnecessary. She was the only family he had. He'd been solely responsible for her since they were both barely teens, so of course, he would take care of her wedding. And anything else that would make up for the unfair lot they'd been dealt growing up. She didn't need to thank him for that. The wedding was just one more thing he considered his duty.

Unfortunately, so was having to listen to her mini breakdowns every time a snag occurred.

"You're welcome, Lizzie," he answered simply, then disconnected.

The morning didn't get any better after he'd checked in for his flight. With precision, he'd arrived with just enough time to answer any urgent emails and go over a new bid, then comfortably board without having to rush. The airline announced a delay before he'd even gotten a chance to pull his tablet out and log on to his company intranet.

Clint cursed under his breath. An hour, at least. As luck would have it, his private jet was being serviced. The timing was beyond inconvenient. Well, he wasn't going to sit here in this loud, crowded gate area. He'd go kill the time at the private executive suite the airport provided for certain clientele. Maybe he'd even get a chance to read a paper in some peace and quiet.

He swiped his card to get past the secure glass door to the exclusive suite and realized quickly that peace and quiet were not in the equation this morning.

This was, without question, one of the most embarrassing experiences of her whole life. Rita wanted to sink into the ground as she stammered to answer the airport employee who was very politely and professionally interrogating her. Not only had the other three people in the suite started to stare, she noticed from the corner of her vision that someone else had just walked in—a tall dark man with a leather briefcase. Wonderful. Yet one more person to witness her abject humiliation.

"I'm terribly sorry, miss. But there's no record of anyone sponsoring you to be in this room," the well-heeled, highly polished attendant repeated. Sheila, according to the gold name tag on her uniform. "I'm afraid you'll have to pay for your breakfast and then leave."

"Oh, um… I don't understand… I was told by my friend who's a member that I'd be allowed to hang out here if I wanted, and the flight was delayed. I just thought—" Her words were an incoherent mess. She'd never been good under pressure. And this haughty woman was making her feel like a piece of mud she was trying to brush off her Louboutins.

The attendant remained silent. Rita couldn't detect one iota of sympathy in her eyes.

Oh, what the hell. The mushroom omelet and mimosa weren't worth the trouble. Though it had to be the most delicious breakfast she'd ever been served.

"Fine, what do I owe you for the breakfast?" She reached for her wallet.

"With the drink, it will be seventy-five dollars."

She nearly dropped her purse when she heard the figure. "Seventy-five dollars?" How could that be? Had they personally flown in the mushrooms straight from Japan and had a master chef prepare the meal?

Sheila merely nodded in such a superior way that Rita knew she wasn't imagining her satisfied smirk of a smile. Satisfaction at her discomfort.

Currently between jobs, Rita had been trying hard to maintain a certain budget. A tight one. The loss of that kind of money had tears springing into her eyes. With shaky fingers, she reached for her credit card, which was already perilously close to the limit as she was about to spend a week in Hawaii. Most of her expenses were taken care of by the wedding party, but she'd still need money for extra meals or souvenirs. Why had she ever walked in here?

Suddenly, a wall in the form of a navy-blue silk shirt appeared in her vision. Someone had stepped between her and the employee, his back to Rita. The newcomer who'd walked in about thirty seconds ago. "Excuse me to interrupt, here. But I'd like to sponsor the young lady as my guest. Please put her breakfast charges on my account."

What?

Great. Now she was getting pity charity from strangers who wanted to pay for her breakfast. "That won't be necessary," she argued to the man's back. Lord, he was broad shouldered. She could see his toned muscles outlined under the finely tailored shirt. It was difficult to get around him to address the attendant.

"I insist," the stranger said to her over his shoulder.

"Certainly, sir. How nice to see you again," the attendant said to him. Rita dared a peek over his shoulder to look at her. It appeared that now Sheila was the one who looked somewhat uncomfortable, she noted with no small degree of satisfaction herself.

Still, she couldn't have random strangers pay for her breakfast. "I said that won't be necessary." She tried to step around him once more.

The man actually stretched his arm out to block her!

Of all the nerve. Granted, he was trying to do something incredibly nice for her but to actually stop her from having any say in the matter was a bit much. Nice or not, he had no right. It wasn't like she really needed his help. The amount would cause a dent in her bank account but she did have the means to pay it.

But it was too late. Sheila flashed him a bright smile, the smirk entirely gone. "I'll take care of it right away, Mr. Fallon."

Mr. Fallon. He turned to her as the attendant walked away. Rita blinked and did a double take as his deep brown eyes met hers. Recognition dawned with a sinking sensation as she realized exactly who he was—the dark hair, the familiar coloring and features.

"I didn't mean to insult you," he told her. "It's just that

I happened to have witnessed that particular employee's pettiness before. I might have to initiate some sort of formal complaint about her with the airport actually."

Oh, no. That wasn't what she wanted at all. "Please don't do that. I don't want to think about someone losing their job because of me."

He quirked an eyebrow in question. "No matter how badly they had it coming?"

She shook her head. "And it's not that I feel insulted."

"No?"

"No, not really." She blew out a breath. "I'm just a bit embarrassed. I wish I'd never walked in here in the first place."

His eyes narrowed on her. Rita couldn't quite read the expression on his face. "I'm actually really glad you did."

A small sensation tingled at the base of her spine. Was he trying to flirt with her now? Yep, definitely the most mortifying thing to ever happen to her. To make the whole thing so much worse, Clinton Fallon had no clue who she was. He didn't even remember her.

Clint wanted to tell the young lady he could relate. It hadn't been that long ago that people like Sheila had talked down to him in the same manner he'd just witnessed her being subjected to. Her embarrassed expression and obviously flustered state when he'd walked in had touched a nerve within him that he'd long since thought was dormant. Apparently, the universe decided he was due for a periodic reminder.

He was glad for it, as he'd just told her. He didn't want to get too complacent or take anything for granted.

"I guess I owe you a thank-you," she was saying.

Guessed? "Uh…you're welcome."

She reached for her carry-on. "I think I'll leave."

Clint stepped in front of her before she got far. Was she

confused? He'd just taken care of the matter so that she could stay. "You no longer have to."

Something flashed behind her eyes. It didn't strike him as gratitude. Far from it. He had offended her. Well, what was he supposed to have done? Let her get tossed out on her behind?

"Nevertheless. I'm not sure I want to stay in here any longer."

"You mentioned your flight was delayed. At least finish your breakfast."

"I'm sure it's cold now," she muttered, then blew out a breath. "I'm sorry. It's just—I've really been looking forward to this trip. And so far it hasn't exactly started off on the most positive note."

"I understand," he told her, a feeling of empathy settling deep within his chest. He did understand. More than she knew.

Rita adjusted her collar and tried to quell the shaking in her stomach. Clinton Fallon was standing before her without any clue as to who she was. Apparently, she hadn't made much of an impression on him all those years ago when she'd been at university with his sister. First, he'd witnessed her abject humiliation by the suite attendant. And now she was going to have to find a way to introduce herself.

Or reintroduce herself as the case may be. By contrast, she couldn't count the number of times she'd thought about him over the years. As if she hadn't felt silly enough about that small fact until this encounter.

She was trying to figure out a way to tell him exactly who she was when he extended his hand. "I'm Clinton—"

"I know who you are," she blurted out without really thinking.

He blinked. "You do?"

A small lump of disappointment settled in her gut. He

really had no inkling, no recollection whatsoever. Why was she surprised? Or even disappointed? People like him didn't take much note of ladies like her.

And exactly what kind of lady was she now? How would she begin to describe herself? Perhaps she could use the term *recent divorcée*. Or *unemployed veterinarian*. Or *failed daughter*. Unfortunately, any one of those could apply.

"Here. Let's give this a try." She removed a hair band from her wrist and quickly tied her thick dark hair in a loose ponytail. Then she removed a pair of thick glasses from her pocket and perched them on her nose.

Clint's only response was a completely blank look. Still nothing.

Rita sighed. Now she was just humiliating herself even more. He had no idea who she was. How often had she thought about him over the years? How often had she wondered where he was and what he was doing?

While he hadn't even given her a second thought, it seemed.

"I went to school with Lizzie," she told him. "You and I met in passing a few times at various school-sponsored family events." She extended her hand. "Rita Paul. I'm actually on my way to your sister's wedding myself."

His smile grew wide as he took it. "I'm sorry. I'm just so bad with faces."

"No need to apologize." Though she did appreciate the effort. An awkward moment passed as they limply shook hands. As if neither could decide who should let go first. Why was she behaving so loopily around this man? Finally, Rita pulled out of his grasp.

"It should have occurred to me that at least one or two of Lizzie's friends would be on this flight," Clint continued. "I'm not used to flying with the airlines. My private aircraft is undergoing some repairs."

"Did you really just say that your jet is in the shop?"

He gave her an embarrassed smile. "I guess I did."

He'd certainly come far. Though again, she wasn't surprised. The man she'd met all those years ago was clearly driven and talented. "You were just starting out in the construction business back when Lizzie and I were in school."

He nodded. "That's correct."

"You've just acquired a company, I believe."

"Correct again. The man I worked for was ready to retire. Said he trusted me more than anyone else to take over. Gave me quite a deal when he sold me the business."

"A deal you clearly made the most of then took to new astronomical heights."

He studied her. "I guess you could say that. Along with some well-placed investments, things have gone pretty well."

What an understatement. The man owned a private jet. She knew he'd single-handedly put his sister through school. No doubt, he was the one paying for this lavish destination wedding.

Clint Fallon represented the epitome of a self-made success story. She'd followed his life for a while in the local papers and news sites after graduating from school. Everyone was fascinated by a self-made man. But then her own life had gone completely awry. Unlike Clint and his string of successes, she'd only managed to accumulate one failure after another. Though heaven knew he'd been handed a much worse set of circumstances.

Well, this was her chance to get away from all that and try to forget. For the next few days anyway. This trip was all about Lizzie and her future husband and the love they shared.

She was trying to come up with a response when the airline announced they were finally boarding. "I should head out to the lobby," she told him. "I'm seated toward the back. I'll be one of the first they call."

But he reached for her arm to stop her from leaving. "Wait. I happen to know the seat next to me is free."

"But I thought this was a full flight. They were asking for volunteers to give up their spots."

"Fairly recent development. I didn't get a chance to update the airline. I was supposed to be, ah…traveling with someone. Their plans fell through at the last minute."

Understanding dawned. Pictures of Clint always showed him with a female companion. Always someone very glamorous and beautiful. None seemed to last for more than a few news cycles. The timing of his latest breakup appeared fairly inconvenient. He was going stag to his own sister's wedding.

"You can sit with me up in first class."

She had to decline. He'd already done more than enough by paying for her breakfast and vouching for her to stay in the lounge. "I appreciate that. But it's not necessary."

He blinked at her. "I could use the company," he countered, then pulled his phone out of his pocket. "It'll just take me a second."

Before she knew what he was up to, he was quickly on the phone with the airlines. Clearly, he had some kind of executive direct line that reached an employee right away.

Clint wasn't terribly good at reading her frustrated vibe.

He was already ending the call before she could protest any further. "You're all set. We can board together."

Rita clamped down on her annoyance. If she said anything further she would merely sound petulant and ungrateful. Never mind that she was trying to feel more in charge of herself, more in control of her life. This flight had literally been the first travel ticket she'd purchased for herself, paid for completely on her own. And Clint Fallon had just given it away and upgraded her to first class.

She knew it was illogical of her to be angry or to feel slighted. Clint had no idea of her circumstances. Or the silly symbolic meaning she'd put behind the whole trip.

Rita herself had only actually just now realized how much it meant to her.

It appeared Rita had not taken him seriously when he'd said he could use some company on the flight. Despite sitting right next to him, she'd barely spoken two words. The complete opposite of what he knew would have happened with Maxie. She would have no doubt talked his ear off about everything from her latest gig to the spa treatment she'd been scheduled for.

Something between the two extremes would have been nice.

He should have taken the opportunity to get some work done. But he'd found himself distracted by the delicate rose scent of her perfume. Her jet-black hair brushed against his shoulder when she shifted in her seat and he'd had to resist the urge to ask her if he could run his fingers through the thick silky strands.

How uncharacteristic of him.

Now, several hours later, she was just as quiet. They were finally approaching the Grande Maui resort in Kaanapali. And he was experiencing yet another silent ride. The woman had no interest in speaking to him.

The vehicle finally came to a stop and they both exited, then waited as the young driver pulled their bags out of the rear trunk.

He heard Lizzie's excited voice from behind before he could even reach for his luggage.

"You're here!" his sister shouted, her voice breathy with excitement. He found himself bear-hugged in her skinny arms a short second later. She noticed Rita standing next to them when she finally let go. "You're here too." Lizzie glanced at the town car. "You two came together?"

She didn't wait for an answer as she took Rita in her arms next. Clint watched as the two women also embraced, Rita's dark hair and olive skin a complete contrast to his sister's red coloring and fair complexion. There was true affection in their tight hug.

"I ran into Rita at the airport," he answered his sister over their heads.

"Oh, how fortunate," Lizzie exclaimed as they finally pulled apart.

"Yes. Very lucky for me," Rita began. "He paid for my breakfast, saved me from a very embarrassing situation at the executive lounge, then upgraded me to first class."

If she actually felt lucky about any of that, her tone distinctly said otherwise. Was she mad at him? Whatever for? The thought tugged at him. Usually, the women in his life made it more than clear whatever his transgressions against them might be. Maybe he was interpreting her tiredness after a long flight for sarcasm. Or perhaps he was hearing things; the large gushing stone fountain behind them was pretty loud after all.

"You'll both have to tell me exactly how you ran into each other," Lizzie said and peeked inside the still-waiting car. "But where's Maxie?"

Both ladies turned to him, awaiting his answer. He bit back a curse. This wasn't something he wanted to get into in front of Rita Paul. Though he'd be hard-pressed to say why that was so.

"Change of plans. I'll be unaccompanied on this trip," he told his sister, hoping beyond any real expectation that she'd let the matter drop.

She didn't. Lizzie's eyes grew wide and a huge grin spread across her lips. "I heard nothing of this change."

"Things didn't work out." And that's all he wanted to say on the matter.

His sister's smile grew wider. "You don't say!"

She'd never really taken to Maxie. Not that there'd been anyone he'd been with so far that she'd approved of. His sister kept telling him the women he dated were far too shallow.

Little did Lizzie know, at this point in his life, he wanted shallow. Particularly now, when he was no longer solely responsible for his sister.

Rita glanced from one of them to the other. Suddenly, Lizzie clamped a hand over her mouth; the smile completely disintegrated. "Oh, Rita, I don't mean to be insensitive. I'm so sorry things didn't work out between you and Jay."

A flash of regret seemed to pass through Rita's eyes, but it was gone in an instant. "It wasn't meant to be. Let's just focus on celebrating you and Jonathon."

"I missed you." The two women linked arms, then slowly started to walk toward the front desk. Clint hovered behind, tipping the bell steward who loaded their luggage onto a cart. His gaze remained on Rita as she walked away. He didn't know the woman from a passing acquaintance but he felt… He couldn't even describe what he felt.

He'd met her years ago and had somehow forgotten her. Which seemed unbelievable given his reaction to her now.

She was one of his sister's close friends. A bridesmaid in her wedding. Based on their conversation just now, she'd clearly just come out of what sounded like a serious relationship.

The last thing he wanted was any kind of meaningful relationship himself. Not for several years. He'd done all he could for his sister. She was a grown, educated, about-to-be-married woman. He intended this next period of his life to be all about his growing business and doing all the things he hadn't been able to do after he and Lizzie had been orphaned when he was merely sixteen. His sister had only been fourteen.

Lizzie turned and gave him a questioning look. He read it as "Hurry up, already." For the younger sibling, she could certainly be quite bossy, Clint thought as he strolled to where they now stood by the check-in desk.

"This is the man whose credit card is covering all these charges," Lizzie told the desk clerk as she pointed at him. "Including the expanded catering menu we discussed earlier."

The gentleman handed him a key card. "Mr. Fallon. Welcome. Your suite is ready and waiting for you. You'll find a chilled bottle of champagne and a basket of fruit."

Lizzie clapped her hands and turned to him. "Excellent, Rita and I will be snagging that champagne from you, big brother."

"Is that so? And why should I relinquish it to you two?"

Lizzie huffed with impatience, as if the answer should be obvious. "Because us girls are celebrating. More than just my upcoming nuptials."

"Fine. Consider it yours." He knew he could be too indulgent with her sometimes. But this was her wedding. "What else will you two be celebrating then?"

She draped her arm around Rita's shoulders. "We are also celebrating this young lady's newly found freedom."

Rita's eyes flickered downward. She looked far from celebratory at the moment.

Clint signed the paperwork he'd been handed and watched as the two women slowly made their way down the hall.

So who exactly was Jay? And was there any chance Rita was still hung up on him?

But there was no denying the real, much bigger question— why did Clint want to know so badly?

CHAPTER TWO

Her divorce was hardly a cause for celebration.

Rita was just getting used to the idea that she was single again. The breakup had been her idea. She'd been the one who wanted out of her marriage. Still, it wasn't something she wanted to party over. Jay hadn't been a bad person. He hadn't even been a bad husband. In fact, he'd make some-one else a fitting spouse one day. Just not her.

But Lizzie's heart was in the right place. So Rita fig-ured she'd drink Clint's champagne with her. Speaking of, she hadn't missed Clint's curious glance in her direc-tion when Lizzie had spoken of her breakup. Now, as they passed through the open-air lobby on the way to his suite, she could feel his intense gaze on her back. The knowledge sent a tingle of awareness along the surface of her skin.

Cut it out.

She was simply reacting to seeing her crush again after all these years. And that's all Clint had ever been: a crush.

"And it all starts tonight!" Lizzie chimed with excite-ment.

Rita was paying just enough attention to know Lizzie was rambling on about the various sightseeing tours and excursions planned for the wedding party. Apparently, it all kicked off with a traditional Hawaiian luau this evening.

Good thing one of them was talking; God bless her old friend for never being at a loss for words, as Rita wasn't feeling particularly chatty. Heaven knew she hadn't said much to Clint on the plane ride over. But what would she have talked about? Her stalled career? Her failed marriage? And she certainly didn't want to get into her currently very strained relationship with her parents.

At least she wasn't the only one here alone. Clint was also without a plus-one. Looked like they both were leaving some part of their pasts behind.

They finally reached his door and Clint used his card to let them in. Rita had to bite down a gasp as she stepped inside. His suite was the size of a small apartment. A wall of glass stood opposite them, the view a spectacular one of the ocean and the island mountain in the distance. Pity the woman who was supposed to be here and was now missing out on all this.

Among the other things she was missing out on.

Rita couldn't help but study Clint as he walked to the veranda and pulled the sliding door open. She'd certainly had good taste all those years ago when she'd first started crushing on the man. Tall and lean, he seemed to be quite fit. And he had the most striking facial features. Where his sister was fair with a patrician nose, Clint had more the look of a well-mixed genealogy. Lizzie had mentioned once that there was some Asian blood in their family ancestry. Though those genes hadn't found his sister, Clint clearly had what would be described as such characteristics. Overall, it made for a dashing, exotic look that definitely made him stand out in a crowd.

"They gave you the good stuff," Lizzie said as she pulled a green glass bottle out of the ice bucket.

"And I'm giving it to you two," Clint replied.

"I suppose we can let you have a glass. Not a big one though." Lizzie pinched her fingers in a demonstration of how much his pour would be. "We probably shouldn't have too much right now anyway. There'll be plenty of food and drink at the luau later this evening," she said, then glanced at Rita as if looking for agreement.

"Right."

"By the way—" Lizzie addressed her brother "—Tessa Campbell has been asking about you since she arrived. She happens to be your roommate, Rita."

Clint gave her a distracted nod as he stood staring at the majestic view in front of them. "Which one was she again?"

Lizzie gave an exaggerated roll of her eyes in Rita's direction, the effect so comical it made her giggle. "How can you not remember?" she asked her brother as she gave him the bottle to uncork. "She's been hitting on you since the tenth grade. Wait till she finds out you're here alone."

He actually groaned. "Now I remember. What are the chances I'll be able to avoid her?"

"Slim to none," his sister replied. "She is a member of the wedding party after all."

"Great."

Clint's tone held every hint of resignation. He was a man used to such attention. She wasn't surprised. It was all merely an annoyance for him. He deftly uncorked the bottle with a pop and grabbed two flutes off the serving table then began pouring. Tiny florescent bubbles floated through the air. He handed each of them a glass.

Lizzie suddenly let out a laugh that had her snorting bubbly champagne through her nose. The sight, in turn, made Rita laugh.

"What's so funny?" Clint wanted to know.

Lizzie rubbed the tip of her nose. "I just had an image of you ducking behind palm trees during the luau when you saw Tessa approaching."

Rita laughed harder at the visual that invoked. Clint glanced from one to the other, a resigned expression on his face. "I'm glad you two find this so amusing."

"I'm sorry," Rita told him but she couldn't seem to stop one last giggle. When was the last time she'd really laughed? The past few months had been an emotional hailstorm. She was so glad to be here, finally able to get away. To have it be for such a happy occasion was just icing on the cake. This chance to step back from her troubles for a while was exactly what she needed right now.

But then Clint focused those dark chestnut-brown eyes on her, his lips curved into a smile. She had to suck in a breath just as her stomach did a dive straight to her toes. Perhaps she'd found trouble yet again.

Clint's intention to get some rest before the luau with a quick nap was not going well. Every time he started to drift off, a set of dark brown eyes framed by silky jet-black hair sprang into his mind's eye and jolted him awake. What was wrong with him?

He was simply here to see his sister married off and to give her away. Not to explore a wayward attraction to a friend of hers.

A glance at the wall clock across the room told him the shuttle to take them into town for tonight's festivities would be arriving right about now. He had to get going. Lizzie didn't tolerate lateness. Not even from the big brother who was paying for this whole shindig. He didn't mind. Somehow his sister had escaped the cynicism spouted by their grandmother all those years. Bless her for it.

Maybe Lizzie would prove him and his grandmother wrong and make her marriage work. Maybe she'd be the one to break the Fallon chain of doomed relationships.

Lord knew, he wasn't going to be the one to try.

If that made him cynical, so be it. At least Lizzie had found love. Or what she thought was love. But then she'd always been the dreamer. While he'd had to be the responsible, serious one. He'd had no choice. With both parents gone and only an elderly, bitter matron in charge of them, the burden of responsibility had fallen solely on his shoulders.

He figured he'd done okay. They both had, he and his sister. Hokey as it sounded, he'd have to say he was proud of the woman his sister had become. And happy for her that she'd found someone. Jonathon was a good man. He'd make Lizzie a good husband. Someday, he'd make a good father.

Not that Clint was in any kind of hurry to become an uncle, he mused as he walked to the bathroom and turned on the shower. It would have to be a short one. Officially, Clint was the main host of this wedding. He couldn't be missing shuttles and ending up running late to the events. That also meant he had to be very cordial and very polite to every one of their guests.

So it galled him that there was only one in particular he was thinking of right now, wondering if they'd be seated anywhere near each other. Or maybe even together. He didn't know the full wedding party details; he had left Lizzie and Jonathon pretty much to their own devices when it came to planning.

Now he wished he'd been more involved. It might have avoided the whole fiasco at the airport when he couldn't even remember who Rita was. That had been wildly embarrassing. Had he apologized to her? He couldn't recall. If he didn't run into her tonight, he'd have to make it a point to find her and do so.

Right. And that would be the only reason for him to want to seek her out.

Damn it. Why couldn't he stop thinking about her?

Shutting off the water and toweling off, Clint realized he barely had time to make it downstairs in time for the shuttle bus. Throwing on a pair of khaki shorts and a Hawaiian shirt, he didn't bother to button it as he ran toward the hallway stairs that led to the lobby. Waiting for the elevator would be too risky.

In his hurry, Clint realized too late that someone else was on the stairway making their way down. The crash was unavoidable. Unable to stop himself at the speed he was going, he collided hard with an unsuspecting, soft body. He just barely managed to catch her in his arms and avoid what was sure to be a harrowing tumble down several sets of steps.

Turned out he wouldn't have to go looking for Rita after all.

"Oh, my—" Her words cut off as chocolate-brown eyes blinked at him with shock. Her gaze drooped down to his bare chest for a split second before snapping back up to his face.

"I'm so sorry," he began. "Are you all right?"

She blinked once more. "You're not even dressed."

Clint made himself release her in order to pull his shirt together. He began hastily buttoning. "Yeah, part of the reason for my rush. I'm running a little late."

"I guess *running* would be the operative word."

"And *colliding*. Don't forget *colliding*. You never answered my question."

"Question?"

"Are you all right? I didn't hurt you, did I?"

"I'm fine, just a little startled." She adjusted the hem of her sundress, which had shifted somewhat as a result of their collision. And what a pretty dress it was, a shiny number with thin straps that rested delicately on her toned shoulders. The navy blue of the fabric brought out the deep, rich hue of her silky, smooth skin.

Had he ever noticed a woman's dress before? Or how it brought out the color of her skin?

"I'm really sorry, Rita." To think, he'd intended earlier to apologize to her for something completely different: forgetting who she was. His mea culpas when it came to her were accumulating.

"Why are you taking the stairs?" he asked her. "Aren't you on a much higher floor?"

She shrugged. "I always take the stairs. It's better for you."

Well, she certainly was fit. And that dress made no bare bones about it. It showed off her long, toned legs and narrow waist.

This was getting ridiculous. He'd nearly caused her to wipe out down the stairs for heaven's sake. Not to mention he'd hauled her against his bare chest to keep her from falling. And now he couldn't stop ogling her. In a deserted stairway, no less.

"We should probably get down there," he said and motioned for her to go ahead down the final flight of steps. As he followed, he forced himself not to look at her shapely, rounded behind. Though it wasn't easy.

There was a whole pig twisting around on a spit. Head and hooves and all. Rita couldn't bear to look at the sight another second. She wasn't a strict vegetarian by any means. But her profession as a veterinarian made such a scene difficult to watch. In fact, she felt a bit queasy.

The rest of the crowd stood next to the open fire pit, oohing and aahing at the large animal about to be served as their dinner. A crowd that included the entire wedding party. She walked toward the water, away from the buffet area where the rest of the feast was being set up.

The party faced the sea, with a majestic view of the mountains on one side and crystal-blue water as far as the eye could see on the other. Banana-leaf-covered cabanas surrounded a large stage area in the center. Tables and tables of various dishes were already being set up.

Clint Fallon had spared no expense for his sister's wedding. Rita nudged the sand at her feet with her sandaled toe. She glanced over to where he stood with the rest of the crowd. Lizzie had been right about Tessa Campbell wanting to corner him. The woman had made a beeline to Clint's side as soon as they'd exited the shuttle bus. She'd been within two feet of him ever since. Several times, when Rita had ventured to look their way, Tessa had her hand on his arm or his shoulder. She'd definitely dominated his full attention so far.

Though Rita got the distinct feeling Clint was merely being polite. Actually, Clint looked somewhat uncomfortable with the constant touching.

Not that it would bother her if there was anything more than that developing between them. And the frustration she felt at that thought wasn't something she was going to dwell on. She thought of their near disaster on the stairs earlier. Like she'd fallen against a hard wall of pure male. She rubbed her cheek where it had landed against his bare chest when he'd barreled into her. Lord, he'd felt solid.

"Thought you'd taken off." A masculine voice sounded behind her and made her jump. Clint. Rita turned to find him no more than a few feet behind her, as if her thoughts had conjured him.

"Just wanted to admire the water for a bit."

He came to stand beside her, both of them facing the coastline. "You find it a much more palatable view than the one back there over by the fire pit."

He was an observant one. "Yes, well, there's that too." He must have been watching her. So maybe Tessa didn't have so much of his attention after all. "Was it that obvious?"

He smiled. "Your disdain was clear."

Oh, no. She hoped she wasn't coming off in that way. As if she were turning her nose up at the chosen venue or choice of entertainment. Sometimes her shyness was known to come off as a haughtiness. It had gotten her into trouble more than once. "It's just that when you spend your days taking care of animals, seeing one spinning above a fire pit that way is a little off-putting."

Something shifted behind Clint's eyes. Then he actually thwacked himself in the forehead with the palm of his hand. "It's you!"

"I beg your pardon?"

"Sarita. With the neon purple hair. Lizzie's roommate off and on during her school days. You were studying to be a veterinarian."

Ah, so now he was finally remembering. Took him long enough. "Wow, that didn't take you long at all," she said, her voice dripping with sarcasm.

He had the decency to duck his head as if chagrined. "I've been meaning to apologize for that." He spread his hands. "But you gotta cut me some slack. You never looked the same those few times I saw you. I mean, was your hair ever the same color?"

She had to give him that. Her puny attempts at college-girl rebellion centered around changing her hair constantly. Her father absolutely hated it. Which was the point, wasn't it? Still, Clint could have registered some recognition before now.

"And Rita's not your name," he declared. "That threw me off too."

"It's a shortened version of my name. As is yours."

He pursed his lips, as if that thought hadn't occurred to him. "I suppose you're right."

He supposed? Of course, she was right. Clint was short

for Clinton. How was that any different than shortening
Sarita to Rita? She didn't get a chance to ask as they were
interrupted.

"There you are! I lost track of you." Tessa ran up to
Clint and wagged her finger at him.

Clint actually groaned out loud. Tessa didn't notice.
Or she didn't really care. Then he shocked her by placing
both his hands around Rita's waist. *That* Tessa definitely
noticed. Her eyes grew wide with shock. And annoyance.

"I was just looking for Sarita. We ran into each other
at the airport and I've been meaning to catch up with her
ever since."

He was? Or was he just trying to use her to deflect
Tessa's attentions? She wasn't sure how she felt about that
last possibility. But when she glanced his way, his eyes
implored her to go along.

His expression was so desperate, she almost felt sorry
for him for a split second. "Yes, I'm hoping to hear about
what Clint's been up to all these years since we've last
seen each other."

Tessa would not be deterred. She crooked her hand into
Clint's elbow. "Well, we can't have you two off by your-
selves. This is a party after all."

"You know, you're absolutely right," Clint agreed with a
wide smile that almost seemed genuine, even as he gently
pulled his arm free. "We'll just be another minute."

Tessa's face fell. It was the first time Rita had actually
observed such a physical embodiment of that expression.
Tessa cleared her throat. "All right then. Don't take too
long," she added before walking away.

"Very smooth, Mr. Fallon."

"What do you mean?"

"I mean the way you dismissed her while somehow
agreeing with her. Very, very smooth."

"I told her the truth. I really do want to hear more about you. What better time than tonight? In this wonderful setting?"

She couldn't read too much into that comment. "Now that you finally remember who I am?"

He started to object but then apparently thought better of it. "And yes, I could use a break from Tessa, sweet as she is. Just stay by my side throughout the night and maybe she'll leave me alone."

"So I'm supposed to let you utilize our newly rediscovered friendship to allow you to avoid a potential suitor?"

He grabbed his chest in mock outrage. "That's only the secondary motive, remember?"

"Why?"

"Why what?"

"Why would I agree to do that?"

He quirked an eyebrow. "Because you can't resist my charm?"

Rita gave him a thumbs-down. "Try again."

"Because you've taken pity on me?"

This time she shook her head.

"Come on," he pleaded. "Just for tonight. So that I can maybe relax and enjoy this amazing dinner and the traditional performance."

She supposed he did at least have a right to that. Given that it was his sister's wedding they were all here for. Besides, she'd been thankful to Clint so many times in the past. Like when he'd bought his sister the car they'd both used to get from their off-campus dorm to their classes in the dead of winter. Or during junior year when their preferred choice of housing had fallen through and he'd pulled all sorts of strings to get them a place to stay.

Just admit that the prospect of spending the evening with him isn't exactly a turnoff.

She gave him a nonchalant shrug. "Why not?"

Somehow, against her better judgment, she'd just agreed to spend the evening close by Clint's side.

"I take it you won't be indulging in the main course," Clint said as he escorted Rita toward the numerous buffet tables laden with island food. So far, she was being a good sport about their earlier agreement to help him keep Tessa at bay. She'd stayed by his side and made sure to keep the conversation going between the two of them. Just generally staying in his company which he was enjoying way more than he should.

Truth be told, he hadn't been expecting to get much pleasure out of this evening. He wasn't exactly a luau type. Thanks to Rita, however, the evening was so far turning out quite differently than he'd imagined. In a very pleasant way.

The way the other woman was shooting daggers at him from across the serving area made it clear she'd noticed the camaraderie between them.

"You would be correct," Rita responded as they reached the first table.

Sarita. No wonder he hadn't recognized her. He could hardly be faulted for not realizing at first glance that she was the bespectacled, purple-haired, shy girl he'd see occasionally when he visited Lizzie at school. Hard to believe this was the same woman standing before him now.

"It's not like I'll go hungry," she added, breaking into his thoughts and motioning to the massive number of dishes laid out before them. He didn't even recognize half the plates. Tropical fruit, various pulled meats, grilled vegetables. In the center of every table sat a bowling-ball-sized bowl of some kind of pinkish pudding-like substance.

"Any idea what that is?" he asked her.

"I believe it's what's known as poi."

"Pa—what, now?"

She laughed as she handed him an empty plate, then grabbed one for herself. "Based on some reading I've done, it's made from some kind of native plant. It's supposed to be full of essential vitamins and minerals. It's supposed to be very good for you. Particularly for—" she paused midsentence "—um… Never mind."

Judging by the way she suddenly ducked her head, something had clearly made her uncomfortable.

"What were you going to say?"

"Nothing. Just an article I read."

"I'm a little hurt that you aren't willing to educate me. Perfectly okay that I'll remain woefully ignorant about whatever this *pwah* is."

She granted him a small laugh. "Poi. It's just very popular with the men in particular."

"Yeah, why's that?"

They both reached for the same serving spoon and the brush of her fingers against his sent a spark of awareness down to his center. Suddenly, he realized what she was referring to. The poi must be considered to lend some kind of boost to male performance.

She quickly pulled her hand away.

"I think I figured it out." He reached for the next item. "Not that someone like me would be concerned about that."

Why the hell had he just said that?

Damn it, now the air between them was awkward and strained. When they'd been having such a relaxed conversation earlier.

"That was just a joke," he said by way of explanation.

"Does that mean it's not true? That you could perhaps use the poi?"

"What? No! I mean, yes. I mean, of course it's true."

Saints above. It was like he didn't even know how to speak around this woman.

She popped a pineapple chunk into her mouth and winked at him with bemusement. He had to remind himself to breathe.

"Ha, ha."

Just to be funny, he scooped a ridiculous amount of the poi and dropped it in the center of his plate.

The show was just starting as they took their seats. He stole a glance at Rita next to him as she watched. She seemed thoroughly entranced by the story the performers were enacting on the stage. Tales about native islanders leaving their home to find more hospitable islands. Kings and queens leading their people to new lands, the culture and customs that they brought with them and how they mixed with inhabitants already living there.

Rita looked like she could be one of those queens. Or a regal princess adjusting to life on a new island. Her sundress swayed softly in the breeze. The glow of the lit torches brought out the dark golden specks of her eyes. Rather than wearing the flower lei they'd received upon arrival around her neck, she'd loosely wrapped it around the crown of her head. The overall effect was mesmerizing.

So much so that Clint barely noticed when the story depiction part of the show was over and the hula dancing had begun. Rhythmic drums filled the air as the dancers bounced to the music, their hips moving in ways that seemed to defy anatomical possibility. The dancers then formed a circle around the tables. Lizzie and Jonathon sat at the table next to them. The woman onstage spoke into her microphone. "I understand there are a bride and groom here celebrating with us."

One of the dancers extended a hand to Lizzie, who took it and then stood from the table. Jonathon stood as well with another dancer leading him by the elbow. All four started making their way toward the stage. Various other couples in the dining area were similarly led.

"Please come participate with us in a traditional celebratory dance," the woman said into the mic.

On her way to the stage, Lizzie suddenly stopped behind him. "Come on, big brother. I don't want you to miss out on this." She grabbed him by the crook of the elbow and pulled.

"Oh, no, you don't. I am not a dancer."

"Tonight you are." She tugged on his arm until he had no choice but to stand.

His sister wanted him to dance. Onstage. A traditional Hawaiian hula. Well, he wasn't going down alone.

"Rita? Care to join us?"

Her jaw fell. "Uh… I'll sit this one out."

"Come on. Don't make me suffer this alone." Before he could finish the sentence, the female dancer behind him took Rita by the hand and made her stand. Essentially making the decision for her. Clint decided he'd be forever indebted to the woman. They made their way toward the stage.

Once there, he found himself thrust in Rita's direction as everyone coupled up to dance, the women in front of the men. A dancer in the front led them, instructing how to move the hips just so. Rita did as instructed. And she seemed to have quite a knack for it. Her hips moved in swift circles in front of him and he thought perhaps his lungs would stop functioning.

Sweet heavens, perhaps he shouldn't have had any of the poi. Not that it would have made any kind of difference.

The early-morning jog along the beach was supposed to clear his head. But images from the previous evening kept invading Clint's mind as he ran at a punishing pace along the water. Rita's smile as she was teasing him about the local delicacy. The way she'd tried to avoid looking at the main dish.

How her hips had moved as she danced in front of him.

So he thought he must have been imaging it when he looked toward the horizon and saw her in the water climbing onto a surfboard, assisted by a tan, blond man. She appeared to be taking a surfing lesson. The man grabbed her about the waist as he held her steady on the waves.

How many times last night had his fingers itched to do the same thing? He couldn't count the number of times he'd awoken after midnight from a dream that prominently featured a dark-haired beauty with a flower lei adorning her head.

He watched her laugh as she toppled off the board and splashed in the water once more. The instructor immediately grabbed her and assisted her back on. Clint suddenly felt an irrationally intense dislike for the man.

This had to stop. He couldn't be having these thoughts. About her or anyone else. He didn't need any kind of disruption in his life right now. Didn't have time for it. He certainly didn't have the time or the inclination for a serious relationship with anyone, let alone a woman like Rita. She deserved nothing less than total commitment. Something he wasn't sure he'd ever be willing to give.

Good thing there were no group activities planned for today. He could use the time to clear his head. The next outing on the agenda wasn't until after midnight tonight, when they'd be picked up to go to Haleakala to see the sunrise atop the volcanic crater. He'd be sure to steer clear of her then.

You Fallon men have no idea how to fall in love without completely sacrificing your souls.

His grandmother was right. Not that he had any kind of notion that he was falling for Rita. It was simply the romantic mood of this wedding and the sensuous setting of the tropical island. Still, he would have to make sure not to let silly whims get the better of him from now on. Asking Rita to pretend they were interested in getting to know each other better had been a mistake. He would have been better off just dodging Tessa's advances.

Much better off than what he was feeling now.

CHAPTER THREE

IF HER TEETH chattered any harder, Rita was sure to crack
a molar. Given that they were supposed to be in one of
the warmest climes on the planet, she hadn't expected it
to be this chilly at any point during this trip. But being on
top of one of the world's tallest volcanos, it made sense if
one thought about it. Especially at about four thirty in the
morning. Well, that particular bit of wisdom wasn't doing
her any good at the moment.

Their tour bus driver said they had to get here this early
or all the viewing spots would completely fill up. If she'd
known about the biting chill, she might have argued to take
the risk. People around her were bundled up in coats and
scarves. A few had thick, plush blankets. Even members
of the wedding party had somehow come prepared. Had
they received some kind of memo she hadn't?

Probably not, Rita thought and hugged her sweatshirt
tighter around herself. They had just somehow planned
better than she had. Story of her life. It wasn't even a terribly thick sweatshirt.

She heard a shuffling behind her and turned to find
Clint approaching. She knew it was him, though it was
somewhat hard to see in the predawn darkness. He had
a thick leather jacket on. Yet another person better prepared than she.

"You're shivering," he stated, noting the obvious.

"Ye-e-es. I—I a-a-am." Okay, so the stutter was a bit exaggerated. But not by much. Her lips were practically flapping together from the cold.

He started shrugging off his coat. "Here, take this."

She stopped him with a hand to his chest. "No way. I am not that s-selfish." The cold stutter made the word sound like she'd said *shellfish* and she had to stifle a laugh.

"I don't know you very well, but that's the last term I would use to describe you."

The words took her aback. In fact, she'd heard herself described that way countless times over the last several months. By people she cared for the most. When all she'd wanted to do was find her own way and discover what made her happy. Correction, she'd wanted to discover what made her *feel*.

Though she didn't want to examine exactly what it was she was feeling right now. Neither did she want to admit that she'd been hoping Clint would find her at some point on top of this mountain.

"I can't take your coat," she insisted through the chattering.

"Well, I can't take watching you succumb to frostbite."

Before she knew what he was up to, he'd stepped behind her and enveloped her in his embrace, the coat wrapped around them both. "Here. In the interest of compromise."

A cocoon of heat suddenly surrounded her, along with his woodsy masculine scent. In her desire for warmth, she didn't bother to stop him or step away. Right. Like that was the only desire driving her at the moment.

"This is supposed to be one of the most spectacular sunrises on the earth. You don't want to turn into a frozen popsicle before you get to see it, do you?"

"I suppose not." She resisted the urge to snuggle her back closer to his chest. "Thank you."

He shrugged against her. "It's the least I can do. After the way you helped me the other night."

"Ah, you mean your evasion mission."

"It seems to have worked. Ms. Campbell seems to be wrapped around one of the other groomsmen at this very moment."

The way he was wrapped around her. "I'm sure she's simply trying to stay warm too."

"No doubt."

"She wasn't terribly happy with me that night after the luau when she came in," she told him, remembering the slamming of the suite door as she was brushing her teeth. Rita had felt somewhat guilty. She had nothing against Tessa; they'd actually been study partners for some core subjects back in school. "I got a bit of the silent treatment before we both retired for the night."

"I think she may forgive you pretty soon. If she hasn't already. Judging by how she's moved on and all."

"I hope so. She did say one thing that night though."

She felt his warm breath against her cheek when he responded. "What's that?"

"She mentioned being surprised you were alone to begin with."

"So you guys were talking about me."

Uh-oh. "I won't deny it. Tessa said there had to be a story to explain why you were here stag at your own sister's wedding."

"Not really. Just one argument too many. Considering it wasn't a serious relationship, this seemed as good a time as any to end things. Rather than pretend during an island wedding full of activities. Some things simply aren't meant to be."

"I see. So it was mutual?" Rita wanted to bite her tongue as soon as the words left her mouth. She was giving Clint every indication that she was interested in his personal life. When she had absolutely no reason to be. No *logical* reason. She had to be careful. It would behoove her to be more guarded about such things, now that she was single again. "I'm sorry. It's not really any of my concern."

He remained silent at that. A strong gust of wind suddenly whipped through the air and she reflexively nestled closer against him.

Mistake.

A current of electricity shot through her core. She was no prude; she'd been a married woman for heaven's sake. But being in Clint's arms was triggering a reaction she hadn't been expecting. One she couldn't relate to anything else.

She'd loved Jay. She really had. But she couldn't recall feeling an electric jolt in the pit of her stomach when he held her. Not like she was feeling this very moment.

"What about you?" Clint surprised her by asking.

"Me?"

"If I recall, Lizzie mentioned a couple of years back attending a traditional Indian wedding. I believe you were the bride."

"You would be correct."

"But you're here alone."

"It's like you said, some things simply aren't meant to be."

He was silent for a moment, then she heard him take a deep breath. "I'm sorry."

"For?"

She felt his arms tighten around her. Sympathy? She certainly hoped not. "It's one thing when a short-term, frivolous relationship ends. A marriage failing is a bit more life altering."

He had no idea. The end of her marriage was only part of it. Someone like Clint would never understand. He could never grasp how someone like her had never truly felt untethered. She was a daughter first. Then a wife. Her identity had always been tied to someone else.

She'd never felt like just Rita. Just herself.

No, she wouldn't even bother to explain. There would be no point.

"Was it one particular thing?" he asked above her head. "That led to your split, I mean."

His question wasn't as simple as it appeared on the surface. There were so many particular smaller issues. And one major underlying one. "Yes. And no." It was the most honest answer she could give.

"So you're saying it's complicated."

She could repeat her answer and be correct once again. "Only in that we wanted different things." Things she was in no way ready for. While Jay wanted them more than anything. Things like a family, children, a house. Things she wouldn't be able to walk away from and then it would be too late, making her stay for all the wrong reasons. "So yes, in that way it was complicated."

She couldn't get into any more than that, despite Clint's charm and the effect he was having on her when he held her this way. How could she explain something that she hadn't fully grasped herself yet?

And what about him? What exactly was his story? The way he'd talked earlier about his relationships sounded as if he expected them all to come with predetermined expiration dates.

She was trying to come up with a way to ask when a small sliver of reddish-orange light broke through the surface of the clouds in the distance. The sun was finally beginning to rise. A collective hush suddenly fell over the murmuring crowd. In slow motion they all watched as more and more streaks of breathtaking hues of red broke over the sky.

The scene took her breath away. Any hint of her earlier

cold or discomfort was completely forgotten. This view, this image would stay with her forever.

As would the thought that she was unexplainably happy that she'd been able to share it with Clint. While he held her in his arms.

The woman pulled at him like a magnet. Clint had fully intended to stay away from her on this trip. He really had. But then he'd seen her shivering in the dark with nothing but a flimsy, hooded sweatshirt and some type of thin fleece headband. The windchill up here had to be below freezing at the least. How was he supposed to walk away?

He wasn't made of stone after all.

Now he was beyond happy that he'd ignored the warnings in his head and gone to her. He couldn't imagine taking in this scene any other way. Tomorrow he might think differently. But right now, watching the brilliant colors slowly explode across the dawn sky above the crater, he was more content than he could ever remember.

Spiritual. It was the one word that came to mind. The most spiritual thing he'd experienced in all his years. And he had the pleasure of doing so with the extraordinary woman who happened to be in his arms.

A few feet away, an elderly gentleman with long white hair dressed in traditional native garb began chanting.

"It's a prayer and salutation to the sun," Rita whispered below his ear. The chanter's deep, rich voice added yet another magical element to the extraordinary moment. Clint allowed himself to simply relax, to simply take in the majesty surrounding him. Rita was breathing steadily and deeply against his chest.

They remained that way several moments even after the sacred chant ended.

"That was amazing." Rita finally broke the silence but

made no effort to move out of his embrace. And he couldn't remember when he'd ever felt so at peace, so serene.

The sound of someone clearing their throat behind them made them both jump. Clint turned to see his sister and her groom both staring with their mouths agape. Reluctantly, he pulled his arms away and let Rita go.

"I was really cold," Rita offered by way of explanation.

Lizzie blinked, then focused her intense gaze on her brother's face.

"She was shivering."

"Right" was Lizzie's only response but she dragged out the word so long it was almost comical. His soon-to-be brother-in-law made a dramatic gesture of coughing into his hand in order to hide his laugh.

Rita adjusted her top and stepped away. "That was quite an amazing sight to behold."

Clint had to tighten his fists to keep from reaching for her again. As silly as that notion was under their current circumstances. But he couldn't deny that his fingers itched to do that very thing.

"Uh-huh. Sure was." Lizzie's double meaning was as clear as the new dawn sky behind them. He'd have to set the record straight with her at some point. Explain to her that he had no long-term sights on her school friend.

She really should know him better than that.

"So anyway," Jonathon finally said, "there's some hot chocolate and coffee waiting on the tour bus. The van with all the bikes is up here now. We'll be heading out shortly to ride." He tugged on his fiancée's hand. Lizzie finally moved and they both walked away.

Though Lizzie shot one more questioning look at him as they left.

"I'd almost forgotten," Rita said, not meeting his gaze. "About the biking."

Part of this excursion was to be a group bike ride back

down the mountain. Apparently, it was the thing to do when you came up here.

"All part of the adventure."

Rita bit down on her lip and glanced up at the road ahead. "I might have to skip that part of the experience."

That took him aback. "Whatever for? Can you ride?"

She nodded. "Yes, of course. But I've never actually ridden down a high, rugged mountain before."

He shrugged. "I'm guessing very few of us have."

She didn't respond.

"What will you do instead?" he asked her, suddenly beyond disappointed that she wouldn't be participating.

"I'll just ride down with the driver in the van."

He gave her a shrug. "I'm going to skip riding too then. I'll just drive down in the van with you."

"What? No. Why would you do that?"

"Well, I'm certainly not going to let you sit by yourself in the back of a van following the rest of us down as we ride. It's just not in my nature."

Her eyes clouded with concern. "I don't want to be the reason you miss out on this, Clint."

"Then reconsider. Come on, it will be fun."

Rita glanced at the road once more, apprehension clear in her expression.

"We'll go nice and slow."

She let out a deep sigh and rubbed her forehead. "All right. If you insist."

Clint couldn't help his smile of relief. He really hadn't been looking forward to the idea of being stuck in a van as everybody else got to enjoy the outdoor weather and mountainside sights. Not to mention, he figured he could use the physical exertion right about now.

Clint seemed to be exerting himself far more than the rest of them. Rita glanced behind her to check him once again.

He was barely keeping up with the group. She was glad he'd talked her into going. She wasn't even sure why she had hesitated back there. Bike riding wasn't a new experience for her. And she'd always been pretty adventurous. Though something had changed within her since the divorce, something that made her second-guess her decisions as well as her abilities. She'd have to work on that.

Now there was no denying that the fresh air and the physical activity were serving to clear her head and invigorate her spirit.

But Clint seemed to be struggling behind her. Despite pedaling furiously and clearly straining, he seemed to consistently lag behind them all.

That made no sense whatsoever; the man was clearly fit. He appeared that way. Though, she'd have to admit, she'd seen more than her fair share of large muscular dogs like pit bulls and Dobermans who lacked stamina and energy.

Great. Now she was comparing the man to various breeds of canine.

Still, it was quite surprising. Especially considering they were going downhill and all. He didn't strike her as the type to fall behind when it came to anything. Let alone a physical activity. But hey, looks are deceiving. She knew that firsthand.

He'd certainly felt lean and muscular earlier this morning. Her mind darted back to the feeling of being held in his arms, snuggled against his chest. *Stop it.* Blinking the images away, she took the next turn perilously close to the edge. She didn't dare look over the side. They'd been given a full safety and precaution lecture, but nothing could have adequately prepared her for just how harrowing a ride this would be.

She really just needed to focus on her own ride and staying steady on the path.

A gurgle of laughter floated over to her from the front

of the procession. She looked ahead to where Lizzie and Jonathon rode next to each other. They'd made some kind of game of trying to grab each other's hands, then letting go and quickly pedaling back to single file when the path became too narrow. How long the guide would let that continue was anybody's guess. But they seemed to be having a delightful time of it in the meantime.

Had she and Jay ever been that playful with each other? Had they ever shared such boisterous laughter? If so, she'd be hard-pressed to recall it.

That's what happened when you married out of a sense of loyalty rather than any kind of love or affection.

Clint had brought up her wedding. She hadn't thought about that day in ages. Though it had been a joyous occasion, she felt as though she'd sleepwalked throughout the entire ceremony and the events leading up to it. Her father had seemed so happy. Her mother the same simply by extension. A description that could pretty much summarize her parents' whole relationship.

Their families having been friends for years—since her father had immigrated—she and Jay had been thrust together pretty much their whole lives. He'd actually declared to her in third grade that he would take her as his wife. She'd stuck her tongue out at him.

And though her mom was as American as apple pie, Anna Paul had never questioned any of it. Again, another depiction that could define her mother's marriage to her father.

A grunt of noise behind her pulled her out of her thoughts. With a start, she realized it was Clint still straining to keep up. He'd broken out in a sheen of sweat. Was he ill?

A flash of concern shot through her chest. What if he wasn't feeling well? Maybe he was coming down with something. Luckily, the guide chose that moment to yell out that they'd be stopping for a water break at a rest area a few yards away.

Moments later, they had come to a complete stop.

"Are you okay?" she asked Clint when he finally pulled up next to her and disembarked from the bike.

"Must be the mountain air." He was as red as the sunset they'd just witnessed. "The brochure mentioned it might affect some people more than others."

"Maybe you should stop. Ask the guide to have the van come for you." No man she knew would go for that. They would take it as an insult to their very masculinity. But it was worth a try to make the suggestion.

"Maybe." To her surprise, Clint didn't immediately shoot down the idea.

Glancing over at his bike, Rita realized there was some kind of lever along the rails of his rear tire. One that wasn't there on hers. "Something's not right," she told him.

"What do you mean?"

"My back wheel looks different than yours."

He examined his bike, then studied hers. "You're right. Your bike's been running smooth?" he asked.

She nodded in reply. He bent and flipped some sort of gage on his back wheel. Something snapped in response on the bike's handlebars. Right then the guide came to stand next to them.

"Sorry, man. Mechanical malfunction. Looks like your brake was engaged this whole time."

Rita couldn't help it. Though she almost hated herself, she just couldn't help the bubble of laughter that erupted from deep within her chest.

"Oh, you think that's funny, do you?" Clint asked. But he wasn't trying to hide his own smile when he said it.

"I'm afraid so. I think it's hilarious."

Again surprising her, he threw his head back and laughed out loud himself.

Clint cursed out loud through his laughter. "Thank goodness you came along. Or I would have struggled with an engaged brake the whole time." He shook his head. "I can't believe it didn't occur to me to check that."

So the man could laugh at himself and didn't consider himself infallible. It was a novel experience for Rita to witness. She'd thought earlier about the lack of laughter between her and Jay. And here was yet another complete difference between the man before her now and the man she'd married. Jay would be taking the guide's name and information, making plans to call his superiors to complain about the oversight.

Enough. This wasn't some kind of schoolyard competition. She had to stop comparing this man she barely knew to her ex-husband.

Jay had been good to her. Even if some of his actions had felt patronizing and made her feel small, his heart had always been in the right place.

She really had no right to judge him so unfairly. Especially not after what she'd done to the man.

CHAPTER FOUR

TESSA WAS ALREADY in the shower when Rita got back to their room. And by the sound of things, she wasn't in there alone. Rita had to smile. Was there ever a time she herself had been that carefree? That determined to just go after what she wanted and just enjoy her life?

No, she never had. Maybe someday she'd reach that level of lightheartedness. Considering the way she'd grown up, it was going to take some time and some work.

As if on cue, her cell vibrated where she'd thrown it on the bed. A picture of her mother holding their shih tzu appeared on the small screen.

Opening the glass sliding door and stepping onto the balcony, she clicked on to answer the call. "Hey, Ma."

A family with three small children was playing some kind of tossing game in the yard right below their room. The gleam of the ocean shimmered in the distance. She tried to focus on those images rather than the expression that was sure to be on her mother's face an ocean away.

"Hello, dear. I finally got tired of waiting for you to call." Of course, the impetus was on her to be the first one to call. As always.

"Things have been very busy. Lizzie's packed a lot of activities into the schedule."

Rita could hear the notes of some bouncy hip-hop tune

in the background. For as straitlaced and matronly as her mother was, she had some very eclectic tastes in music. Much to her father's chagrin. In so many ways, they were complete opposites. Maybe that was the secret of their success.

"How is dear Lizzie?" her mother asked. "Any wedding jitters?"

Rita thought about their playfulness during the bike ride. On the contrary, Lizzie and Jonathon seemed like they couldn't wait to tie the knot. "I haven't noticed any."

"Good. That's good to hear. I hope the two of them can make it work." The words *unlike you* hung unspoken in the air.

Rita bit back the response that popped into her head. Lizzie and Jonathon were so very different than she and Jay. For one, they'd actually chosen each other. "I think they will. All signs point in that direction."

"Good," her mom repeated. An awkward silence ensued in which all Rita could hear were some very racy lyrics about going to "da club." There was no way her father was home. Else he was on a completely different floor or puttering around in his garden outside.

"Jay came by the other day," her mother suddenly announced. "He asked about you."

A pang of sensation stirred within her chest. They had no business being married, but she missed Jay. She really did. One of the hardest things about the divorce was the fact that she'd felt like she lost a lifelong friend. Maybe over time they could become close that way once more. Another endeavor that was sure to take time, if it was possible at all.

"How is he doing?"

"He still seems quite morose, to be honest." A heavy pause followed which Rita figured she was supposed to fill. But what could she say to that? They'd gone over this before. The notion that perhaps Rita had been too hasty to end her marriage. Jay had pleaded with her to keep trying, claimed complete shock that she was ready to walk out. But she'd held firm. No reason to draw out the inevitable after all. Her husband showed no inclination to change. And she didn't know how.

Finally, her mother relented. After a long sigh, she continued, "His research is going well, at least. Said he was close to another patent. I get the impression he's thrown himself deeply into his work."

That made sense. There were times she hadn't seen him for days at a time. He'd disappear into the lab early and come home late. A slight wave of guilt hit her when she recalled how she'd mostly felt relieved those days, relishing the solitude and having the town house to herself. Jay had a very large personality. When he was around, there was no solitude to be found. "I'm glad he's doing well. On the professional front anyway. I know the rest will follow for him."

She heard her mother take a deep breath. "And what about you, love? Are you really doing well?"

She was. This trip away was exactly what she needed. Seeing Lizzie again, enjoying the majestic beauty of the island. Simply being in an environment so different from home, not to mention all the activities. She really hadn't anticipated enjoying a group bike ride down a rugged mountain. Clint had convinced her otherwise.

Clint. She couldn't deny she was enjoying his company. Perhaps more than she should have.

"Yes, Mom. I'm having a lot of fun here."

"Of course, you are, dear. But what about after?"

"After?"

"You're in paradise now, sweetie. What happens when you return and reality descends? I don't want you to regret your decisions. Now that it's too late to rectify any mistakes."

There was that word again. Some of the most important decisions she'd made in her life were ones her parents considered as her mistakes.

Rita rubbed her temple. Was it too much to ask just to live day by day? Did she always have to be focused on some future point off in the distance? "I'll be too busy to wallow, Ma. I have a lot to do when I get back."

For one, she'd have to look for another job. Perhaps she might finally find somewhere she could really make a difference. Although she loved the animals, she'd had her fill of the bureaucracy and constant focus on profit margins at her last position. She'd only taken the job to make Jay happy. Well, as happy as he was going to be when it came to her career.

"Your dad's threatening to retire. Again." Her mom suddenly changed the topic.

Speaking of people she missed. Though she'd seen her father plenty of times since the divorce, there seemed to be so much emotional distance between them now. Even more so than usual. "I'll believe it when I see it," she responded with a smile. Dad made that claim once or twice a year. Usually around wintertime, when he dreaded facing driving in the snow to his downtown office.

"He misses you." Rita sucked in a breath at her mother's words. The woman had always been very astute. And straightforward.

"I miss him too, Ma." She felt her eyes moisten with tears as she continued, "But I know I've disappointed him. Again."

"Oh, honey. He's your father."

"I think we'll just need some time. To find our way again with each other. I'm sure it will happen."

Sometimes, it was best just to tell her mother what she wanted to hear.

* * *

Clint watched from his balcony as a solitary figure made her way toward the water, strolling slowly, her head down. Even from this distance, there was no mistaking who it was. Rita. The slump of her shoulders and the drag in her step told him she wasn't exactly enjoying her slow walk along the beach. Something was on her mind.

It was none of his business really. This was one of the rare nights that Lizzie and Jonathon didn't have anything scheduled on an otherwise ridiculously packed itinerary. Good thing too. The excursion planned for tomorrow was a whole-day event: a ride down the Road to Hana, which apparently took several hours as a driver took them around the island and showed them many of the pertinent sights. So tomorrow would be completely spent.

And Clint had work to do. He'd already been away from his office for two straight days; there were a slew of emails waiting for him and several items that needed the CEO's signature.

The wise and prudent thing for him to do would be to pour himself a beer from the minibar, order some room service for dinner and fire up his laptop. But his eyes couldn't tear away from where Rita stood off in the distance. An unfamiliar tingle stirred in his chest. If he didn't know better, he'd think it was concern. Which made absolutely no sense. Aside from Lizzie, he'd never really been personally concerned about anyone's emotional state. Sure, he cared for his employees and made sure to take care of them, particularly the more loyal workers who had been with him from the beginning. It was those employees who deserved some of his attention right now in the form of email responses and returned phone calls. He was too hands-on not to be missed when away from the office.

Plus, as sweet as she was, he really had no business worrying about Rita Paul's mood.

He tore his gaze away from where she stood and turned back into the room. As soon as he booted up his computer, several messages scrolled across the scene. Clint rubbed his eyes. Yeah, it would be a long night of correspondence and directives. So he had to focus, which meant he had to keep his mind from drifting. Without meaning to, he looked up to glance toward the beach once more.

She'd moved. He could no longer see her. Had she gone back to her room? Walked farther along?

Damn. It didn't matter. He had work to do.

Clint clicked on the first message and began to type.

She had to get used to this, Rita thought as she perused the menu she'd been handed. Being a single woman now, she had to get used to dining alone. What better time to start than a beachside seafood restaurant on exotic Maui?

At the table next to her sat a family of five with three young children. As frenzied as the parents looked, they posed a perfect picture of a happy unit. As the mom explained something on the menu to her preteen, her husband slowly rubbed a gentle hand down her back. True affection was clear in his absentminded movements. Rita forced herself to look away. Perhaps she'd have that someday. But that day was far-off.

As painful as it was, moments like this made her realize how right she'd been to end her marriage. She and Jay would never have been that couple sitting next to her right now. He may have loved her, but Jay wasn't the type to ever display affection in public. It seemed such a small thing, but small things sometimes made all the difference. She hadn't been able to explain that to him, or her parents for that matter, without feeling like she was being petty and childish. Rita thought back to the phone call earlier with her mother. Maybe they would never understand. Her ex-husband certainly didn't seem to still.

She found herself eavesdropping on the conversation at the next table. Having settled in with their appetizer as their children colored with fat, stubby crayons, the parents were now discussing the prospect of moving to a larger house. Rita watched as the man listened intently to his wife's thoughts and concerns on the matter. He reassured her they would make the correct decision when the time came. She responded with a small kiss to his cheek.

So different from any major discussion she'd ever had with Jay. In fact, when they were first engaged, her ex-husband had declared unequivocally that he had no intention of moving out of the condo he rented close to the university where he worked. It was understood that she would have to make herself at home at his place. She'd just accepted it. Then she'd been miserable. There'd been nothing overtly wrong with the place, but Rita had never felt like she truly belonged there. Her attempts at redecorating had been met with resistance and resentment.

Jay liked his environment the way it was.

In retrospect, she had to admit that perhaps she should have held her ground, tried harder to exert her desires. But it hadn't seemed worth the effort. Her heart was never quite in it. Pulling her thoughts away from the past and from the conversation she had no business listening in on, she took a sip of her lemon water. No, her marriage had never been a true partnership, not like the one sitting at the next table anyway.

Was there a chance she would find that someday? Would she even have the gumption to risk her heart again? An unbidden image of chestnut-brown eyes and a dashing smile clouded her vision. Rita made herself blink it away and focus on her menu.

She honestly didn't know the answers. In the meantime, it looked like she'd be dining alone for a while.

* * *

He absolutely had to stay here and get some more of these emails answered. Clint stared at the screen until the words became a jumble of blurry swirls in his vision.

Focus.

He'd barely gone through a dozen or so messages. He had no business wondering about Rita and where she'd been heading. He absolutely could not go find her. It made no sense. And he was all about being logical and sensible.

So why did he suddenly stand and grab his shirt and sandals rather than clicking on the reply button of the message he'd been staring at for the past twenty minutes? Why was he out the door, making his way downstairs and outside before he could give it any more thought?

It didn't take long to spot her; she hadn't been moving very quickly after all. Clint watched as she went up to the maître d' podium of an outdoor restaurant, then was led away to one of the outer tables.

She sat down with a smile to the waitress, opened up her menu and seemingly ordered a drink. In a sea of tables, Rita sat by herself. When her drink arrived—some fruity concoction with an umbrella—she just stared at it for several moments. She was the only one eating solitary.

Damn.

This was silly. He couldn't very well just stand here staring at her any longer. How much time had passed anyway? Without allowing himself any further debate, he made his way to where she sat.

So deep in thought, she didn't seem to even hear him approach.

"A lei for your thoughts?" he said, clearly startling her out of her reverie.

"Clint." She gave him such a welcoming, radiant smile that it almost had his knees buckling with pleasure. Then she tucked a strand of hair that was blowing in her face behind her ear. It immediately escaped again from the wind. "I just thought I'd grab a bite."

"Are you waiting for someone?" he asked, though he was pretty sure he knew the answer.

She shook her head. "No, it's just me. What about you?" she asked. "How did you decide to come here?"

He didn't have it in him to lie. "I saw you out here and thought maybe you could use some company. You seem a bit…melancholy. If you don't mind my saying."

She didn't answer right away, instead turning to stare off into the distance. "You're a very observant gentleman, Clint Fallon."

And she was downright beautiful. The sinking sun made her dark hair shimmer around her face; her lashes went on forever over piercing brown eyes. Clint had to suck in a breath and turn away to keep from staring at her.

"Have you eaten? I think I owe you a dinner," she suddenly proclaimed.

"Not yet. But I don't see why you would owe me anything."

"You saved me from certain frostbite early this morning. Remember?"

He'd been right about what he'd witnessed from the balcony. She was definitely nursing some kind of hurt. Her tone sounded down and defeated.

He'd never been accused of being the most attentive listener, but he could certainly lend an ear when he needed to, when the situation called for it. He heard a clear calling right now.

"I don't typically turn down pretty ladies who want to feed me." He pulled out the chair across the table from her and sat down.

A smile tugged at her mouth. "Does that happen to you often?"

"Not often enough."

"I find that hard to believe."

She motioned to the menu that sat in front of him. "This place is supposed to be one of the best eateries in town. The concierge mentioned they have the best *hula* pies on the island."

"Moola pies? Sounds expensive."

Feeble a joke as it was, her smile grew wider. "*Hula* pies."

"What exactly is *hula* pie?"

"You'll have to experience it yourself."

"Thank you for the recommendation, ma'am. I look forward to it."

Sooner than he would have thought, the restaurant started to fill. They'd timed it right; the place was just on the verge of welcoming the evening dinner crowd and gradually becoming busier and busier.

In no time at all, almost every table was full and a line had formed outside the door all the way down to the beach.

"That was lucky. Timing it so that we don't have to wait for a table."

"If you're feeling lucky now, wait till you taste this pie." Her tone was whimsical but the merriment didn't quite reach her eyes.

What in the world could have brought her so down since their bike ride earlier today? He hoped she had grown comfortable enough with him to tell him whatever it was.

The waitress arrived to take their order. Clint ordered the *poke*, apparently some sushi dish that the menu said was the freshest this side of the sea, and a beer.

"I'll have the *hula* pie, please," Rita told her.

"Yes, miss. And for dinner?"

"I'm going with that as my dinner."

The waitress gave her an indulgent wink, then took their menus and left before returning with Clint's drink.

Clint chuckled. "Ice cream, chocolate, coconut and nuts. I suppose that covers most of the food groups."

"Sometimes a girl's just looking to have dessert."

"One of those afternoons?"

"You could say that."

"Please don't tell me my sister's pulling some bridezilla moves and hassling her bridesmaids."

She shook her head. "No, nothing like that. I haven't even seen Lizzie since this morning's bike ride."

"Phew, I didn't want to have to reprimand her at her own wedding."

She gave him a curious look at that statement, then reached for her cocktail. He tried not to focus too closely on her lips when she lifted the cherry and popped it in her mouth. "Just a phone call from back home. I let it affect me more than I should have."

"Must have been one heck of a phone call. You just ordered dessert for dinner. Not that there's anything wrong with that."

"There are people who might not agree with you on that point. They'd see plenty wrong with it."

The ex. She had to be talking about him. Perhaps that had been who her misbegotten call had been with. He clenched his fists on the table and had to take a swig of his beer. The idea that she stayed in touch still with her former husband left a bad taste in his mouth. But again, none of his business.

"Anyone in particular we're talking about?"

She took another sip of her drink, looked out over the horizon at the setting sun. Though the scene held no comparison to the breathtaking visual of the sunrise they'd watched this morning, the sheer magnitude of vibrant color in the Hawaiian sky was a sight to behold.

"Could easily apply to several people actually. People who are very focused on rules and structure and propriety."

Oh, yeah. She definitely had something on her mind. "Nothing wrong with rules and structure," he told her. "As long as those rules serve a purpose and make sense."

"I suppose you're right."

"I think so. I wouldn't be able to run an international construction firm if I didn't adhere to some type of structure and follow it rigidly."

"Run a tight ship, do you?" She asked with a hint of a smile.

No doubt about it. Not when his reputation and livelihood were on the line. The slightest mistake could cost big. Both in terms of dollars and time. Not to mention, the risk to lives if proper safety protocols weren't followed. When it came to his company, Clint kept as much as feasible under his tight control. Down to the specific types of screws and nails to be used at all of his sites. "I have to run a tight ship. A lot can go wrong on a construction site. Especially when you're talking tall buildings. Can't leave anything to chance."

She chuckled at that and started fidgeting with her napkin. "You sound very much like someone else I know. That's a favorite phrase of his." Raising her glass in a mock salute, she cleared her throat. "You can't leave anything to chance." Her tone was exaggeratingly deep.

"Sounds like a wise man. Want to tell me who you might be referring to?" Though he could guess. It didn't take a mind reading ability to figure who she meant.

"I will tell you. Probably because I've had half of this very strong drink on an empty stomach."

He doubted the fruity cocktail—complete with a paper umbrella—could be that potent. She was clearly a lightweight. "Maybe you should slow down."

"I'm talking about my ex," she said, ignoring his warning. "More than once, he tried to teach me a lesson about why I should be more disciplined and not leave things to chance."

Taught her a lesson? The hair on the back of Clint's neck stood up as a bolt of fury shot through him. His vision blurred. If that pitiful excuse for a man had so much as harmed a hair on her, he'd make it a life goal to find him and do some score settling.

"Rita. Did he hurt you in any way?" he asked steadily through tightly clenched teeth.

She blinked. "What? No. That's not what I mean," she said with a dismissive wave of her hand.

Clint let out the breath that had caught in his throat. "Then what do you mean exactly? About teaching you a lesson?"

"Exactly that. Jay's a medical researcher at a prominent university. He's used to controlling every variable. I'm a bit more carefree. He simply took some pains to show me why his way was right and mine was foolish."

"I don't follow."

She leaned forward on the table, steepled her fingers. "There was the time we were grocery shopping. I walked away down another aisle. I left my purse in the cart. I knew exactly what I was going to get and where it was." She glanced off to the side, as if recalling the exact memory. "When I got back to the cart moments later, my purse was gone."

He was starting to see where this might be going. "Let me guess, he'd warned you repeatedly not to leave your bag unattended."

She raised her glass. "A toast to you for the right answer. I got a scathing lecture about how right he'd been. How reckless and senseless it was of me to walk away from the cart that held my wallet, my keys, my money."

All right. It sounded like it might have been harsh for

her to hear. But many husbands would have reacted the same way.

But Rita's hands were trembling as she recalled the story.

"I was panicked," she continued. "My phone, my license. Everything was in that bag."

"I guess he could have been a bit more understanding." Still, it hardly seemed like an unforgivable reaction. She had been rather careless to leave the purse unattended.

She laughed but it sounded less than jovial. "There's a surprise ending to this story."

"What's that?"

Her fingers tightened on the stem of her glass. "He's the one who'd taken it. He'd walked all the way back to the parking lot and to our car and thrown it in the trunk."

That *was* a surprise ending. Clint had definitely not seen that twist coming. Words failed him. Who would do something like that?

"What happened?" he finally managed to utter.

"After several minutes of panicked searching, during which he coldly stood by and watched by the way, I finally asked for his phone so I could notify the authorities about the theft of my personal belongings. That's when he finally told me he'd had it the whole time."

Clint downed the rest of his beer. He couldn't imagine doing such a thing to another person, especially someone he supposedly loved. It seemed so... *Petty* was the one word that came to mind.

"That was just one example," Rita added, polishing off her drink, as well.

"There was more?"

She nodded. "Little things. He insisted on being in charge of my online passwords because I didn't change them often enough. He kept asking how I planned to be a responsible mother one day if I couldn't keep track of little details such as security codes. So, ultimately, I decided that I wasn't even ready to be a wife. Let alone a mother."

Clint needed another drink. But the waitress was nowhere to be found. To think, this accomplished, intelligent, talented woman before him was thought to be careless and in need of strict guidance by the man she'd married.

"I had to walk away. The controlling became too much," she said on a sigh.

He couldn't help himself. He reached across the table and took her hand in his. "I'd say that behavior sounds a bit beyond controlling." Much more. In fact, the word *belittling* came to mind.

CHAPTER FIVE

HER HEAD POUNDED like a slow hammer when she awoke the next morning. There was a reason she generally tried to stay away from hard liquor. If she'd only stuck with her usual cabernet, she wouldn't be feeling so foolish this morning.

Though she couldn't bring herself to regret a single moment of it. Sitting there with Clint in that restaurant, she could almost pretend she was a regular young adult on an exciting date with a new man. Not a recent divorcée who was just sharing a meal with her friend's brother. Her friend's handsome, charming and beyond alluring brother.

A smile touched her lips when she thought of the joy that had flooded her chest when she'd looked up to find he'd followed her, that she wouldn't have to eat alone after all. A silly girlish giggle escaped her lips before she bit down on it. How foolish of her.

In any case, she should have definitely gone easier on the mixed drinks. But no, she'd had to indulge. And look where it had gotten her. She'd ended up letting her tongue loose and way oversharing with Clint Fallon. A man she had nothing in common with. A man she would probably never see again after this wedding was over.

And in the meantime, she had to spend a whole day with him and the rest of the wedding party in a large van as they traveled the Road to Hana.

He'd caught her at a vulnerable time, she thought as she summoned the elevator—this time unable to face the stairs—to take her down to the front entrance where the shuttle would be picking everyone up. Phone calls from her mother tended to put her in such a state. She'd simply meant to take a walk along the beach to shake off the doldrums of her conversation, then check out the restaurant she'd heard so much about since arriving.

But then he'd shown up.

Rita stepped into the glass elevator and watched the scenery outside as the unit began to descend to the first-floor lobby. There was no denying her immediate reaction upon seeing him last night though. There was no denying her reaction to him in general.

The truth was, a wave of pleasure had bloomed in her chest when she'd seen him arrive to eat with her last night. Electricity had crackled between them all during dinner, even after she'd overconfided.

And how foolish was that? They were from two different worlds. He'd accomplished so much and her life was in complete shambles. Before she could even think about any kind of attempt at a relationship, she had to repair everything that had gone so wrong these past couple of years.

Starting with repairing the relationship with her father.

The only sound thing to do today would be to avoid Clint Fallon altogether. She would appreciate the sights, take lots of photos, talk to everybody else and try to enjoy herself. With a sigh of relief about her decision, she stepped outside through the sliding doors of the front hotel entrance.

The bus was almost completely full by the time she got on. She passed Lizzie and Jonathon in the front row. They were too engrossed with each other to take any notice of her. Seat after seat was taken.

The only one she didn't see yet was Clint. Rita con-

tinued slowly making her way to the back of the bus.
Tessa smiled at her from one of the middle seats, next
to a groomsman Rita didn't know by name. Probably the
shower buddy from the other night. Still no Clint. There
was definitely a pattern. Every seat held a man/woman
pairing. Looked like there was a lot of hooking up going
on.

Oh, great, she could see where this was headed.

There were times Rita was sure the universe was simply laughing at her. This was clearly one of those times.

She found Clint in the final row. With the only open
spot left on the bus next to him. He scooted over and gestured for her to sit. Like she had a choice. "Looks like everyone has paired up," he said as he scooted over. "Kind
of leaves you and I as odd men out."

Which essentially had the effect of pairing them up as
well, Rita thought, trying not to groan out loud.

So much for the Fallon-avoidance plan.

Within an hour, they'd reached their first stop. Somehow, the day had grown cloudy with a slight mist of rain.
The change in weather did nothing to diminish the sight
however. They were on top of a lookout that showcased
several majestic waterfalls.

The pairing on the bus didn't disperse as everyone exited the vehicle. Several of the couples held hands. More
than a few relationships had apparently formed over the
short time they'd been in Hawaii.

She walked over to one of the railings and leaned on
the metal, simply taking in the view. Sure enough, Clint
appeared beside her within moments. He leaned over the
banister, as well.

"If you want some alone time, just let me know."

She couldn't even be sure if that's what she wanted.
Her emotions and feelings were just a mishmash of confusion right now.

"But it seems a shame not to share the beauty of this experience with someone else," Clint added.

He was right, of course. This was silly. They were both adults. They might even be considered friends.

She gave him a slight smile, not turning away from the view. "I thought maybe you'd be tired of my rambling. I did somewhat talk your ear off last night."

"Do you really believe that?"

No, she didn't. Clint was genuine and attentive. He'd listened to her and sympathized last night. Not once had she felt a hint of judgment on his part. Exactly what someone would want if they were looking for a confidant.

She hadn't realized how much she needed that, just to have someone listen. Without any criticism, unlike her parents whenever the matter came up. Her girlfriends were all too quick to try to reassure her that the divorce was for the best, just like Lizzie had the day of arrival. Hard to believe Clint Fallon was the first person to give her a chance to finally get some of the turmoil off her chest. It was more than just the drink. She'd found Clint surprisingly easy to talk to, to confide in.

Still, thinking back on the exchange now, she felt raw and exposed. "I didn't mean to share that much," she admitted.

He waited a while before answering. "I'm really glad you did."

Clint resisted the urge to gently nudge Rita's head onto his shoulder. She'd fallen asleep as they drove to their next stop on the tour. She didn't look terribly comfortable with her head bent at an odd angle against the seat. He wasn't sure how she'd react, given how regretful she seemed about their time together last night at dinner. She couldn't think he thought any less of her because of what she'd told him about her failed marriage. If anything, he'd been struck by her strength and resilience in the face of such a situation. Someone should have really told her that at some point.

He was spared further internal debate about moving her when they finally reached their next destination: one of the Seven Sacred Pools of 'Ohe'o. He gave Rita a soft tap on the shoulder to wake her up. She opened her eyes with a start.

"Sorry. But we're here. I didn't think you'd want to sleep through the Seven Sacred Pools visit."

Rubbing her eyes, she stood and stretched out her legs. The innocent gesture sent a bolt of awareness through him. He gave himself a mental snap. Resilient or not, the woman was reeling from a broken relationship. He had no business staring at and appreciating her legs. Shapely and alluring as they may be.

"Thanks. Guess I was more tired than I realized. Did I miss anything along the ride?"

Clint shook his head, then stood to join her in the aisle of the van. "Only an interesting dissertation about lava tunnels from our expert tour guide/driver. He seems to know quite a bit. Both about the geography and folklore. Said he was born and raised on Maui." Okay, he was clearly rambling. But they'd already had a few moments of awkwardness between them so far this morning. He found himself missing the easy camaraderie of the previous evening. It couldn't have been totally alcohol driven, could it?

"You'll have to fill me in on the rest at some point," she said as they exited the van.

This was one of the spots they'd been told to pack bathing suits for. A lush green mountainside with several small waterfalls surrounded a pool of crystal-blue water. It was apparently one of the most popular spots for tourists to take a dip in. A few of the visitors already there were jumping into the water off some of the lower cliffs.

"This is one of the seven legendary pools," their tour

guide and driver said to their quickly dispersing crowd, raising his voice to be heard. "It is said that a dip in these pools will lead to good fortune and the finding of true love." He scanned the wedding party. Several couples were already in the water, giggling and splashing around. Tessa had jumped onto her groomsman's back as he playfully ducked under the water to get her wet. Jonathon had his arms wrapped around Lizzie's waist as they waded into the pool.

"Then again, it looks like you all might not need it," the tour guide added with a light chuckle.

A heady idea suddenly occurred to Clint. He turned to Rita standing next to him. "Would you like to come with me?"

She gave him a questioning look. "To swim?"

"Sort of. I think we should try jumping off a cliff."

Rita was determined to make the best of the way this day was turning out. Clearly, she and Clint were the only people in the wedding party who hadn't hooked up, so to speak. Well, good for them. As for her, she was going to make the most of this adventure, enjoy the company of the man saddled with her for now and try to just enjoy herself in general.

Though she hadn't exactly planned to start with a jump into a deep pool of water off a rocky cliff. Some of which didn't seem terribly high, but still.

"Are you with me?" he asked her. "You can swim, right?"

"It's not the swimming part that I'm grappling with."

"Come on. It'll be fun. I'll lead the way and stay with you the whole time." With that, he took her hand and they started making their way along the slippery, wet rocks surrounding the edge of the water. She'd never seen such greenery, such lush plant life. She'd never cliff jumped before.

But despite her apprehension, she'd be a fool to miss out on any of this. If just for today, she was going to forget about the shambles her life had become, forget about the depressing phone call with her mother yesterday and try to fully immerse herself in this adventure.

To his credit, Clint kept to his word and steadied her the whole way up. If he would do a cliff jump with her, he'd probably follow her anywhere. Pretty soon, they found themselves perched on the precipice of a jutting boulder along the side of the mountain about ten feet above the water.

"Is this a good spot?" Clint asked.

"Well, I'm not going up any farther, if that's what you mean." Though now she was looking down, she wasn't quite sure even this was too high.

Clint chuckled. "We can jump in together, if you'd like," he said, taking her hand once more. Her fingers reflexively curled around his. She'd been trying not to look at him too closely after he'd taken his shirt off earlier. The man was fit. A solid chest, taught, defined muscles, skin already a deep rich tan.

"Are you having second thoughts about this?"

More like I'm having unwanted thoughts about you.

She shook her head. "I think maybe we should just jump before I start to though."

"You're sure you're comfortable in the water?"

"Oh, yes." The water part wasn't the issue. It was the whole launching herself off a cliff thing. How in the world had she allowed herself to get talked into this? Why did she get the impression she wouldn't even be attempting it if Clint wasn't by her side? And what exactly did that mean for her mental state when it came to him?

This was so not the time to contemplate it.

"In that case—" He didn't finish, just tugged her along with him as they both jumped off.

Rita felt herself hit the water with a resounding splash. Exhilaration pumped through her veins as she broke the surface, laughter erupting in her throat.

Clint still held on to her hand.

"That was amazing."

"Hope I didn't take you by surprise, tugging you in like that."

"Oh, but you did." She playfully splashed him. "And you don't regret it at all, do you?"

He laughed in return. "Figured you didn't need too much time to think about it."

She dived under the surface, allowing the coolness of the water to refresh her both in body and spirit. If she had to work hard to have fun and forget her troubles for a while, then so be it. Though she had to admit, having Clint around was making the endeavor easier than it otherwise would have been. Too easy.

All too soon, the guide signaled that their party should probably start toweling off and return to the van. Reluctantly, Rita followed as Clint guided her toward the edge of the pool and helped her out. Their guide handed them thick towels.

"Thanks for doing that with me." Clint rubbed the towel around his head to dry off his hair. The strands were a mess of spikes around his head when he was done. Somehow the look did nothing to diminish the rugged handsomeness of his face. The wetness turned his locks from a dark brown to jet-black that brought out the golden specks in his eyes.

Rita looked away and focused on getting herself dry. But she couldn't hide the shiver than ran over her skin, only partially due to the chill of being wet. The sun had poked through a thick cloud while they'd been swimming but it was still somewhat overcast.

"Here." Clint stepped over to her and draped his towel over her shoulders.

"Thanks—you keep helping me to stay warm, it seems."
Not to mention, the exciting things he'd been convincing
her to try. As if something happened to her cautious inhi-
bitions around this man.

The clap of the guide to summon them cut off Clint's
response. He followed her to the van and they both got
on board.

"You may be wondering why these pools are full of
fresh water when they touch the sea," the guide began,
using a microphone to address his many passengers. Part
of the experience of the tour was a continuing commen-
tary about the island and the sites they were visiting. Rita
found it charming. The driver was personable and well-
spoken, a good fit for the job he was in. "There are many
theories, some more scientific than others."

"We want to hear one of the nonscientific theories,"
Lizzie declared from the front and Rita saw Jonathon give
her shoulders an indulgent squeeze. A collective shout of
agreement chorused from the others.

"Anything for the customer," the guide said into his
mic. "There's a particularly sad legend about a princess
and her lost love."

Rita settled back into her seat; Clint's warmth next to
her and the deep voice of the driver lulled her into a med-
itative state of relaxation that she more than welcomed.

The man proceeded to tell a wrenching story that had
to be based on at least some truth—that thought made her
heart ache—about a princess who fell deeply in love with
one of her guards. But she was honor and duty bound to
marry a prince from another neighboring native tribe, one
her father had picked for her.

The princess turned her back on her true love in order to
perform her expected duties and married a man she didn't
care for. He turned out to be cruel and vicious. In a fit of
rage and jealousy, he killed the princess when he thought

she was being unfaithful. He had incorrectly mistaken one of her handmaidens for another man as both male and female islanders wore their hair long past their hips. Finding out about his error made him irrationally even angrier.

So just for good measure, he searched out the man who had first claimed the princess's heart and brutally murdered him, as well.

"So every night, the ghost of the poor princess sheds enough fresh tears into the pools to flood out all the salt water." With that, the guide rehung his mic into its slot on the dashboard.

A quietness settled over the cabin of the van. The overall mood had definitely turned to the somber side.

Rita knew it was simply a story, most likely based on generations of native folklore. But the lesson and theme was a universal one and she found herself instinctively nestling closer to the man sitting next to her.

"Next stop is Black Sand Beach." The driver's voice crackled through the vehicle's intercom system and pulled Rita out of her thoughts. She'd been thinking about the sorrowful story of the princess since they'd left the last location.

"Ready for the next adventure?" Clint asked as they pulled to a stop. Another breathtaking scene of visual magic greeted them when they disembarked.

A wide pathway led to a steep stairway that took them down to a beach unlike any she'd seen before.

The sand, the pebbles, the boulders that met the crashing waves were all completely black. As if some divine hand had taken a tub of ebony paint and brushed wide strokes over the entire area.

"Amazing, isn't it?" Clint asked her.

"I don't have the words." She turned to him. "Thank you for this. Really. I would have never seen any of this if it hadn't been for you. And Lizzie."

He ducked his head like a small boy almost. She'd embarrassed him. "More so Lizzie. She and Jonathon coordinated with a planner and booked every tour and excursion."

He wasn't going to take any of the credit, even if he was bankrolling the whole thing. As far as big brothers went, Lizzie had hit the jackpot.

"There's a cave over there." Clint changed the subject before she could say any more about his part in all the wonder they were experiencing. "I say we go explore."

Without waiting for an answer. He pulled her behind him and led her into the mouth of a cavern. Not that she would have said no in any case.

It was like stepping into another dimension. All the noises outside went suddenly mute. Other than the opening, the area around them was pitch-black. The walls shimmered with moisture. A sudden cold wetness ran over her sandaled feet. The unexpected sensation jolted her; she lost her balance and startled to topple backward.

A set of steel-hard arms immediately wrapped around her waist and pulled her upright. She found herself hauled against a hard, broad chest.

"We've got to stop meeting like this," Clint said hoarsely against her ear. The heat of his breath sent a tingle along her skin. It would be so easy to turn to him, to totally succumb to the warmth and security of his embrace.

"You seem to keep rescuing me. Starting at the airport."

She felt him chuckle more than she heard it. "You're hardly the type of woman who needs rescuing, Rita."

Did he really mean that? Did he see her that way? As someone strong? Independent?

She felt heady at the thought. So many times in her life, the people she loved the most made sure to point out all the ways she was *less*. So often, Rita had spent all her energy trying to simply prove them wrong. But this man before her now seemed to think otherwise, he seemed to see her as *more*. It was a new experience.

A peal of laughter from outside the cave spiked through the air and pulled her back to reality.

"We should go with the others," she said.

Clint hesitated a beat but slowly let her go. "Yeah, you're right."

Rita sucked in a breath of air as she followed and gave herself a mental shake. She had to keep her bearings about her. The exotic location and all the excitement was making her act with uncharacteristic recklessness. For one insane moment, she'd thought about kissing him. Her fingers went to her lips as she wondered what that might have felt like, what he might have tasted like.

No. She had to accept that this was part of some dreamlike fantasy that she was unlikely to encounter again. Reality would return soon enough and she had to be ready for it.

But she would never forget the things he'd said to her, the way he'd made her feel for the brief moment when it was just the two of them in this empty cave. She reached down and picked up one of the small black rocks from the ground. Turning it in the palm of her hand, she slipped it into the pocket of her jean shorts.

No, she would never forget standing in a tight, dark cave with Clint nor the feelings the close proximity elicited within her. But she wanted a memento nevertheless.

CHAPTER SIX

CLINT DESPERATELY WANTED a shower. Preferably a cold one. The colder the better. Then he was going to find an aged bottle of fine bourbon and spend the night on his balcony drinking and willing away the thoughts that were sure to plague him after the day he'd just spent.

With Rita.

He would have to try hard not to think about all the times her leg had brushed along his in the seat during the drive. All the times the car had gone around a curve and her delicious, supple body had slid up against him.

And he absolutely could not think about the way she'd felt in his arms after they'd jumped into the sacred pool together. She'd almost said no to that. Just as she'd originally balked at the bike ride. Rita must have taken quite a hit to her confidence these past few months. She just needed a nudge to show her how capable and competent she was. A small hint of pride sparked in his chest that he'd been the one she'd allowed in enough to do so.

He'd wanted so badly to kiss her in that secluded cave. He could imagine even now how she would taste.

It was going to be a hell of a night.

Right now, they were all spilling into the lobby after several hours spent seeing the sights and attractions along the Road to Hana. It had been a long day. Fun but tiring. The kind of day that would normally end for him with a cold drink in his hand and a warm body in his bed. An unbidden image of dark chocolate eyes and silky black hair popped into his mind before he pushed it away.

He'd had way too much fun with Rita. Every stop made more enjoyable with her accompanying him. So much so that he didn't want it to end. But it would have to. If she was anyone else, he'd ask her to join him on that balcony. To share that drink with him and let the rest of the evening take its natural course.

But no. Not this time. Not with this woman.

He didn't do long-term relationships and she wasn't the kind to have a fling with. Especially considering she was still licking her wounds after a recent divorce.

Oh, and there was also that whole thing about her being a close friend of his younger sister's. There were all sorts of ways a careless move with Rita could get messy and complicated.

Logic dictated that he simply bid her good-night and hope he'd see her again tomorrow morning. He turned to do just that but was abruptly cut off by Lizzie's angry shriek from across the lobby.

"How could you say something like that?" she demanded of her fiancé, her cheeks blazing red with fury. "You can be such an ass sometimes."

"What did you just call me?" For his part, Jonathon looked equally as enraged.

"You heard me."

Clint debated going over there to pull one or the other to the side. They'd started to attract the attention of other guests. The night manager behind the desk looked as if he was trying to decide the same thing. The man had gone pale and swallowed hard.

"I would hate to have to burden you with an ass for a husband," Jonathon fired back.

Lizzie's eyes narrowed on Jonathon's face. "What's that

supposed to mean? What exactly is it that you're trying to say?"

Clint uttered a curse under his breath. He really wished she hadn't asked him that. Jonathon's reply was exactly what he'd feared it might be.

This did not bode well.

"Maybe this is a mistake, Lizzie," Jonathon bit out through clenched teeth. "Maybe we should call off the whole thing."

Lizzie's gasp of horror was audible; she visibly bit back a sob. Clint started forward but felt a small hand grab him about the wrist. He turned to see Rita shaking her head slowly at him, a clear warning in her eyes.

His sister brushed past him as she fled the lobby. Jonathon stomped off in the opposite direction, leaving everyone else in the lobby staring agape.

Several bridesmaids and groomsmen turned to him, as if awaiting some sort of explanation. Like he had any idea what had set the whole argument off. Last he'd seen, the two had been all over each other on the bus.

"Show's over, folks," he said to the collective crowd. Several moments passed but eventually, one by one, everyone started to disperse.

All except for Rita.

She cleared her throat next to him. "I hope you understand why I stopped you from going to them."

He sighed. "Yes. You were right. Nothing would have been gained by me getting in the middle of that." He turned to look her straight in the eye. "I owe you a thank-you for averting it." He could have very well made things much worse. Though it looked bad enough already.

"They probably both just need some time," Rita said. "Weddings can be really stressful. Once they've had a chance to cool off, I'm sure they'll both be ready to make up."

He certainly hoped so. Otherwise, he'd have a huge

mess on his hands. All the pending arrivals would need to be notified. Contracts would need to be canceled. There was no way he'd see any kind of refund for anything. Not at this late stage.

Not that any of that mattered. Lizzie would be miserable and that tugged at his heart. She deserved to be happy.

The manager appeared by them, his cheeks a slight pink. "Any way I may be of service, Mr. Fallon?"

"Yes, please. Send a bottle of your house merlot and some snacks to my sister's room. Please add a card that says she knows where to find me if she needs."

"Right away, sir."

Clint turned to see Rita eyeing him, a curious glint in her expression. "What?" he asked.

She shook her head. A soft smile graced her lips. "I think you could use a drink yourself. Can I interest you in joining me for one?"

All his earlier intentions of avoidance fled in that very instant. Nothing in the world could have possessed him to turn her down in that moment, not when she was looking at him like that.

"I'd be very interested," he told her, ignoring the cry of warning in his head.

The moon cast silver light on the sand next to their table at the outdoor bar of the resort. Foamy waves crashed against land a few feet away from where they sat. Rita ran her finger around the rim of her wineglass. She didn't really want the drink, felt tired down to her bones after the day they'd just had.

There was no denying that Lizzie and Jonathon's argument had shaken her. They'd seemed so happy together just a few short hours ago. The thought of the two of them breaking up just before their wedding was almost too much to bear. There was no way she would be able to fall asleep with all that on her mind.

Plus, she had to admit she didn't want to say goodbye to Clint just yet. There was nothing scheduled for tomorrow. No excursions, no meals with the wedding party.

She realized she dreaded the idea that the whole day might go by without seeing him. That thought sent a surge of guilt through her chest. She should be worrying about her friend and the possibility her engagement may have ended just days before she was due to be married. Instead, here Rita sat, overly concerned about spending time with that friend's brother.

What was it about this particular man that called to her so strongly? Her friends had warned about being on the rebound and falling too quickly for someone. But this didn't feel like a rebound scenario. Not that she could really know for sure. All of this was so new to her.

She hadn't really dated anyone seriously. And as soon as she was old enough, her father had subtly pushed her toward Jay in so many nuanced and not-so-nuanced ways.

If ever there was someone who should tread carefully when it came to the opposite sex, she would be the poster child.

"I wonder what triggered that whole thing," Clint said after taking a small sip from his drink. The thick amber liquid in his glass told her it was something strong which would probably make a lightweight like her gag if she tried it.

"Lizzie and Jonathon's argument, you mean?"

He nodded. "I'm guessing it was something she was being stubborn about. She can be a little self-centered." He sighed and looked out toward ocean. In the distance the water looked as black as the cave they'd been in earlier. The cave where she'd fallen into Clint's strong arms when he'd caught her before she could fall.

Don't go there.

"I blame myself for that," he added. "For how stubborn and self-centered my little sister can be."

"I think you're giving yourself too much credit. Or fault, in this case."

He shrugged. "Maybe. But I was the one responsible for her."

"You're not that much older than her, Clint."

"That may be so. But after our parents died, there was no one else."

Rita knew a bit about their struggles as teens after the passing of their mom and dad. They'd been sent to live with a maternal grandmother who was way past the age of being able to care for two grieving and active teenagers. Lizzie hadn't really talked about it much at school, but there'd been enough times when she'd opened up.

From what Rita understood, Clint had started working as soon as he was of age to help care for himself and his sister. By the time Rita had met her, Lizzie's brother was already on his way to becoming a multimillionaire tycoon with his own construction firm with satellites all over the nation.

Quite extraordinary if one thought about it.

"Oh, Clint," she began, unable to keep the sudden emotion out of her voice. "You had to grow up pretty fast, didn't you?"

He looked off into the distance toward the water. "Not by choice."

He was so wrong about that. "You did have a choice. You could have left Lizzie to her own devices. Or tried to get your grandmother to step up."

He laughed at the idea. "Yeah. That wasn't going to happen. It was clear within months of us moving in with her."

"What do you mean?"

"Nothing specific. Just that money was always tight.

My parents didn't exactly save for a rainy day. Too busy spending it all on their travels and adventures. What little they left, my grandmother put away. Never let us touch it. We were in a new school, the kids ready to pounce at our clear disadvantages. The girls were particularly hard on Lizzie. For having to wear the same clothing and shoes to school almost every day."

"What did you do?"

He rubbed a hand down his face. "It's not important."

She leaned closer across the table. "Please tell me."

He hesitated so long, Rita thought he might not answer. Finally, he let out a deep sigh. "What could I do? I got several odd jobs so that we could have some kind of spending money. It wasn't much, just tips from busing tables at a restaurant and lawn mowing money. But it was something."

She thought of the boy he must have been, the sheer effort and discipline it must have taken for him to rise to where he was.

An urge to go to him, wrap her arms around his shoulders to comfort and soothe him almost overwhelmed her. She fought it. Hard.

"Thanks again for making sure I didn't get in the middle of their argument," he told her. "I wasn't even sure what I would have said. Or which one of them I would have said it to."

"It never works out well when a third party tries to intervene in a relationship."

Clint didn't say anything for several beats, just studied her face. "You sound like you're speaking from experience."

She allowed herself a laugh that held no real humor. "I suppose I am. To this day, both my parents seem to think I was the one who managed to ruin a good marriage. My mom is a bit more vocal about it but my father's feelings have been made clear, as well. Many times."

He reached for her hand across the table and held it tightly in his. The warmth of his skin sent a tingling sensation up her arm and straight to her heart. "I'm sorry you had to deal with that, Rita. You deserve so much more."

"Thank you for that." She ducked her head. "I wouldn't want either Lizzie or Jonathon to feel that way. Not even for a moment."

He gave her hand another squeeze before slowly letting it go.

"I just hope they figure it out soon." He let out a small chuckle and rubbed a hand down his face. "Who knows. Maybe this is happening because someone didn't pay heed to the curse our tour guide warned us about."

"Curse? I didn't hear anything about a curse." Just that terribly sad story about the heartbroken princess who'd tried to do right by her family and tribe only to be murdered.

Clint polished off his drink. "You might have been sleeping. He said nothing should be removed from any of the beaches we visited. Not even so much as a pebble. Or it would lead to doom and bad luck."

Rita felt a slow sinking in her chest. She'd taken that small rock. But surely it was just a silly superstitious story. She'd simply wanted a small souvenir.

Her small transgression could absolutely *not* be the reason the bride and groom were fighting at this very moment. And threatening to call off the wedding.

"It sounds like mere superstition," Rita said, voicing her thoughts, just as their waitress appeared. "Island folklore."

Their server smiled at them. "What folk story are you referring to?" The young lady asked with a friendly smile. Her name tag said Tanna in curly black lettering. "I come from several generations of native Hawaiians. I may know it."

"The superstition that says removing anything from Black Sand Beach will result in misfortune."

Tanna shook her head vehemently. "Oh, no. That one's real. Those beaches are sacred. Nothing is to be removed. It's absolutely bad luck."

Rita felt her stomach drop. This was just silly. She hadn't even known she was doing anything wrong!

Tanna continued, "It is very easy to anger the spirits. Every pebble, every rock, every grain of sand is exactly where it is supposed to be. The slightest intentional human disruption will lead to disorder and make the spirits very unhappy."

"It's like a more eerie version of the butterfly effect," Clint told her.

"What's that?" Tanna wanted to know.

"There's a theory stateside that even the interruption of a butterfly flapping its wings can have a ripple effect and cause devastating changes throughout eternity."

Tanna studied his face for a moment. "That's heavy." Then she eyed them both before continuing, "Can I tell you two something?"

They both nodded as Tanna leaned in and lowered her voice. "This very resort was built on sacred ceremonial ground. My *tutu* keeps imploring me to quit this job. I could tell you stories from guests that would make you want to check out right now." A silence settled in the air between them. Suddenly, Tanna straightened. "Anyway, can I get you anything else?" she asked, indicating Clint's empty glass.

"No, thanks."

Great. Just great. Rita grabbed her still-full goblet and downed the glass of wine she suddenly decided she wanted. As if she didn't have enough on her mind. Now she had to worry that she may have inadvertently jinxed Lizzie's wedding.

A bubble of laughter crawled up her throat as she realized how silly that notion was. Curses. Spirits. She was

essentially a scientist by trade, trained as an animal veterinarian. She didn't believe in anything so fanciful.

But a nagging sensation ran over the back of her neck
as they stood to leave. She could have sworn the breeze
picked up just then, enough to whip a nasty gust of sand
into her face.

Rita punched her pillow for what had to be the hundredth
time in the past two hours. The digital clock next to her
bed read 3:10 a.m. Would she ever get any sleep tonight?
As exhausted as she was, she desperately needed it. But
what her muscles were craving, a sound night of rest, her
mind just didn't seem to be in the mood for. And her mind
could be quite stubborn.

Rather than allowing her to succumb to much-needed
slumber, her mind insisted on replaying the scenes of the
day on a repeat loop. Clint's smile as he pulled her off the
cliff to jump with him. The way he pointed out the glorious mountains in the distance during the drive. How he'd
held her in the cave. Each moment of remembrance sent a
tingle of awareness down her spine.

Oh, and there was also that thoughtful, kind gesture he'd
made to his sister when he'd sent her room service after the
fight. Not to mention, all that he'd shared with her about
the difficulties he and Lizzie had endured growing up.

She had to stop thinking about him.

Only when she forced her mind away from the enig-
matic man who seemed to be haunting her thoughts, it
turned to a disturbing mishmash of angry spirits and a
crying dead princess.

Get a grip, already.

She tossed onto her back with a frustrated sigh and
stared at the blinking light of the fire alarm on the ceiling.
Tessa was breathing evenly in the twin bed next to hers.
Surprisingly, her roommate had made it in alone and at a

decent hour last night. The epic fight between bride and groom that everyone witnessed in the lobby no doubt cast a pall on more than one partygoer's plans.

She counted seventy-five blinks on the alarm, then forced herself to close her eyes. If sleep was going to elude her all night, then she'd just have to stare at the inside of her eyelids for a while. Only now she could see the blinking light in her head, so she started counting again. Some people counted sheep. She got enough of animals during her waking hours. She found other things to count. She made it to eighty this time when she felt the air shift at the foot of her bed. Now she was disrupting her roommate's sleep with her constant tossing and turning.

"Sorry, Tessa. Bad case of insomnia. It's why I'm moving around so much and rustling the sheets."

But the responding mumble from Tessa came from the other side of the room. Where she was apparently still in bed. Rita's eyelids flew open. A shadow moved from the foot of her bed to the side and then to the sliding glass door of the balcony.

Rita's mouth went dry and her heart pounded in her chest. She was not imagining it. Clicking on the small night-light above the headboard, she bolted upright.

Nothing.

There was no one there.

Rita blew out a long sigh of relief. Talk about getting a grip. She was letting all the ghost stories get to her. There was no such thing as a crying princess spirit. There was no such thing as a vengeful one who wanted to keep all his rocks on his beach. Really, she had to stop taking everything people told her to heart. Also, putting an end to any kind of late-night drinking would probably be wise, as well.

Throwing the covers off, she rose out of bed to get a glass of water from the bathroom. A crumpled piece of fabric lay on the floor by the bathroom door. She kicked it aside before realizing what it was.

But it couldn't be.

With dread, Rita bent to pick up the item to make sure. Her mouth went dry when she saw what it was she held. Her jean shorts. The ones with the rock in the pocket. She was one hundred percent certain she'd thrown those in the closet atop her other worn clothing when she'd walked in this evening. In fact, the rock had been completely forgotten after the emotional tug of the fight between Lizzie and Jonathon. She hadn't given it a second thought until all the talk of curses and spirits.

The added weight of the fabric told her it was still in there. Was she losing her mind? Had she pulled it out and forgotten somehow? There had to be a logical explanation.

She'd never been one to entertain superstition. But her father had grown up believing in various gods and guiding spirits. He wasn't terribly traditional but he'd definitely carried over some beliefs with him.

Even as a child, she'd always scoffed at his stories, along with her mother. They were both convinced that he couldn't really believe all the things he was spouting. It all seemed the stuff of fairy tales and lore, though Papa insisted it was all real.

In a stunned daze, Rita made her way back to bed. The night-light was going to stay on for the remainder of the night. One thing was certain, she had lost all hope of getting any sleep.

CHAPTER SEVEN

CLINT FOUND IT impossible to sleep.

Now as a result of a restless, frustrating night he'd started his jog ridiculously early. The term *predawn* came to mind. Rita. She'd been all he could think about. The whole day spent with her yesterday was magical. One he'd never forget. But she'd gone suddenly quiet after their nightcap. He had been about to suggest a walk along the beach when she'd abruptly bidden him good-night and then practically run to the elevator.

Was it something he'd said?

He hadn't meant to get into all that about his grandmother and the loss of his parents. Those weren't topics he normally entertained or liked to talk about. Not with anyone. But the more he got to know Rita, the more he felt able to open up. Even about his childhood. And she'd seemed genuinely interested, asked him to confide in her. Which had been far too easy. He'd never felt so comfortable around a woman, so at ease with just being himself.

But something had definitely spooked her at the end. Served him right. The past was better left behind where it belonged.

Then there was the worry about his sister. He'd not heard from her at all after that little display in the lobby other than a quick text.

Thank you for the wine and chocolate, big brother. Just need some time alone. Time to think.

Women. He would never understand them. It was why he was going to stay single for as long as he could. Perhaps even as long as he lived. A set of dreamy dark chocolate eyes framed by long lashes flashed into his mind. He pounded the sand even harder.

By the time he made it back to the entrance of the hotel lobby, he'd only hammered out a fraction of his frustration. But it was better than nothing. The resort was still quiet. Only maintenance and servicemen were up and about.

So he figured he was seeing things when he spotted Rita at the outside bellhop stand. Clint squinted against the early sun rays. Yeah, it was definitely her. What in the world was she doing out here at this time of morning?

One way to find out.

The bellhop was typing something out for her on his handheld tablet when Clint tapped her on the shoulder. She jumped and clapped a hand to her chest.

"Clint. What are you doing here?"

He made a show of looking down at his workout clothes and lifted the cell phone in his hands, then pointed to the wireless earbuds in his ears.

"Right. How was your run?"

He ignored that. He also tried hard to ignore her shapely, toned legs in the black capri leggings she was wearing. Or the way the white tank beneath her jean jacket came up just above her cleavage.

"Going somewhere?"

"As a matter of fact, I am. I was going to try to text Lizzie later. Both to check in and to see how she was doing."

She was going to text Lizzie. Had no intention of contacting him. Why that thought stung was beyond him. She certainly didn't need to okay her whereabouts with him. Though it would have been nice.

"She told me last night she just wanted some time to think. Alone. Where?"

"Huh?"

"Where are you planning to go?"

She bit down on her lower lip. "I'd rather not say."

The bellhop's gaze bounced from one to the other, as if he was watching a slow, yet gripping, tennis match.

Clint was in no mood for this. Between concern for his sister, worry that they might end up canceling this whole soiree and trying to figure out the rapidly changing mood of the woman before him, Clint figured he was swiftly reaching his outer limits.

"I have a real problem with that," he declared.

Rita blinked at him. "I beg your pardon?"

"I have a real issue with your refusal to tell me where you're going."

Anger flashed through her eyes. Rather than heed the warning, Clint stepped in closer.

"You have an issue with my refusal to tell you something that's none of your business in the first place?"

"That's where you're wrong. I think it's plenty my business."

Her chin lifted with defiance. "I utterly fail to see how."

"Let me explain then," he said, knowing he was being a bit of a heel given his tone and his wording. But he couldn't seem to help himself. She was about to take off in the wee hours of the morning without a word to anyone. Her plan only to drop a text to his sister later. A sister who was plenty distracted and might not even be looking at her phone for countless reasons. "I'm responsible for this event and for the wedding party here to attend it."

"You certainly aren't responsible for me."

"You're here for this wedding aren't you? The one we're having for my sister?"

She leaned back and crossed her arms in front of her chest. "I'm sorry. Does that somehow mean I have given up my free will?"

"What? Of course not. I'd just rather have an idea where my guests may be." *And, in her case, feel assured that they're safe and secure.*

The bellhop cleared his throat behind them. "Ms. Paul, if you'll excuse me. I'm afraid the only cars available are smaller hatchbacks. I wouldn't recommend one of those on the drive to Hana. Would you like me to see if there's a tour I can book you on?"

Rita threw the man a hard glare. "No, thank you. That won't be necessary."

Clint wanted to shake the man's hand. Now he knew where she was going. He just couldn't guess why.

"You enjoy the tour that much?" Clint asked. "Have to go back the next day?"

"Don't be silly. I only want to get to one spot."

"What spot could possibly be so intriguing?"

But she ignored him. "I'll take one of the hatchbacks," she told the bellhop, who now seemed a little afraid, judging by the way he took a step backward.

Was she nuts? She was going to try to drive that rugged terrain in a hatchback? Some of those roads were downright treacherous. Never mind the winding curves that required the stability of a much larger vehicle.

The thought made him shudder. He knew firsthand how a seemingly frivolous decision during a trip could alter one's fate. His parents had made just such a decision and it had cost them their lives.

"Right away, miss." He picked up the tablet.

"What are you doing?" he demanded to know. "Don't you remember all those cars we saw rotted out at the bottom as we drove on some of those mountain roads? What are you thinking?"

"I'm thinking I'm an excellent driver. Please go forward with the car," she directed the bellhop once more.

Clint held up a hand to stop him. "Hold off, please."

Rita practically jumped on her heels in protest. "I am trying to secure a car which I need to get somewhere. You have no say in this."

"Just stop," he told her before she could continue the takedown she was so prepared for. Of him. "That won't be necessary."

Drawing a steadying breath, he focused back on her face. Her lips were pursed, her eyes held a hardened glint. He knew determination when he saw it. She was going to her destination whether he wanted her to or not. "I always make sure to rent a car when I travel. Usually a late-model SUV. I've done so this time. It's available to you if you want it."

That took the wind out of her sails. She visibly relaxed and lowered her shoulders.

"But I'm going to ask to come with you," he added before she relaxed too much. "I'd really rather you not travel that route alone."

"What if I say no? Will you revoke the offer of your car?"

"No, it's still yours if you want it."

A slight softening showed behind her eyes but then swiftly disappeared at his next words. "I'll just follow you if I have to."

Her lips tightened into a thin line once more. "How? You've given me your car."

He shrugged. "Guess I'll have to take one of those death-trap hatchbacks. Just hope and pray I don't plummet to the bottom of Mount Name-I-Can't-Pronounce to my untimely and tragic death." Hard to believe he could joke about such a thing, but there it was.

A smile tugged at the corners of her mouth. He could see her lips trembling in an attempt to control it from fully blossoming. Throwing her hands up, she rolled her eyes. "Fine. Come with me if you insist. But you're probably just going to laugh and call me all kinds of foolish." She looked him over, from his sweaty forehead to the grains of sand on his running shoes. "I suppose you're going to want to get cleaned up first."

"If it's not too much of an imposition," he said with mock seriousness, then bowed.

Rita simply shook her head slowly, then turned on her heel and walked back into the lobby of the hotel. Taking a moment to breathe a sigh of relief, he gave the bellhop a nod of thanks. The other man wiggled his eyebrows at him, his meaning clear. Yeah, Clint had his hands full. With another silent nod of agreement, he turned to follow her.

When he thought about how much of a coincidental fluke it was that he'd run into her in the first place, he cursed out loud. Thank the heavens he'd started his jog early. Or she could very well have been puttering up a mountain right now in a rackety small hatchback.

Whatever her reasons for wanting this so badly, he couldn't even venture to guess. One could only hope they were good ones. But he couldn't help but wonder which one of them was really the fool in all this.

Clint keyed the necessary information into the GPS and pulled the midsize Range Rover onto the road leading out of the resort. He and Rita had decided to take turns driving and he'd won the coin toss to determine who'd go first. Or maybe he'd lost, he couldn't even be sure. He didn't seem to know which way was up when it came to this particular woman.

So why did he find that intriguing when he ought to be downright annoyed about it instead?

He slid his gaze to the passenger seat where she sat next to him, fiercely studying the view from the window. Her legs were crossed, one shapely calve over the other. He'd touched her enough times to know her skin was soft and smooth. Her legs would probably feel that way too under the palm of his hand.

He gripped the steering wheel tighter and pulled his attention to the road.

She was completely different from any woman he'd previously dated. He had thought he preferred blondes, but he seemed to be enamored with her dark silky hair. She wore it up in some type of loose bun at the moment; wispy tendrils framed her face. The effect lent a soft, angelic quality to her features.

Whereas most of his previous dates were curvy, Rita was lithe and toned. And unlike Maxine, his most recent terminated relationship, Rita wore very minimal makeup.

"Are we heading the same way we did yesterday?" she asked, pulling him out of his somewhat inappropriate musings about her body and her hair.

"Yes. But you're eventually going to have to tell me what our ultimate destination is. Unless you plan on blindfolding me at some point."

That notion brought up all sorts of inappropriate thoughts dancing in his brain. He made himself focus on the road; they hadn't even left the city yet. It was going to be another long day. For some reason, that idea didn't fill him with dread the way it should have.

She slowly folded the map, rubbed her forehead. "I'm trying to rectify a mistake I made yesterday. Or think I made. I don't even know."

That made no sense whatsoever. He waited for her to continue.

"I took something I shouldn't have."

She couldn't mean what he thought she meant. The idea was a preposterous one. "Are you saying you took something from one of the souvenir shops? Without paying for it?"

She gasped and shifted in her seat to stare at him, her mouth agape. "What? No! How could you even think that?"

"I didn't really. I mean—I don't know what I mean. I'm just trying to understand what's happening."

"I didn't steal anything, Clint. I'm not a thief!" she declared on a huff.

"Then what are you talking about? Why are we retracing our route from yesterday?"

"I took a rock, okay? I need to get back to Black Sand Beach."

He couldn't have heard her right. A rock?

She blew out a breath. "I think it's my fault Lizzie and Jonathon are fighting."

Okay. Maybe Rita *had* hit her head when they'd jumped off that cliff and he'd missed it. Clint thought about turning around and finding the nearest medical clinic instead of continuing on their current route. But she'd been pretty coherent the rest of the day after that.

"Because the spirits are angry," she added.

Angry spirits…? Understanding slowly dawned as he recalled the waitress from last night and her dire warnings about curses and spirits. Rita was staring at him with expectation.

"Huh" was all he could muster.

"That's it?" she asked. "That's all you have to say to what I just told you?"

"You think you picked up a cursed rock and now you want to return it. In case it has something to do with the sudden threat to Lizzie's nuptials. Does that about summarize it?"

She nodded slowly, still hadn't shut her mouth completely. And what a luscious, beckoning mouth it was. Full lips just slightly pink above a rounded, feminine jaw.

"Yes," she replied. "It's why I want to go back to Black Sand Beach."

Now, why was it so hard for her to have told him that? Honestly, he couldn't figure her out at all.

"All right. Let's hope we make good time. It looks cloudier today than yesterday. We might be a bit chilled."

She gave her head a shake. "You're not even going to try to tell me I'm being silly? That going through all this trouble for a supposed curse is a downright waste of time?"

"Why would I do that?"

She let out a small chuckle. "I know you're not saying you believe it, that something like a lifted rock can have any kind of effect on a wedding." She rubbed her brow. "Sheesh, when I say it out loud, it sounds even more outlandish."

He shrugged. "I know you believe it. That's enough."

"It is?"

"It is for me." He turned onto the Hana Highway.

The thing was, Rita wasn't even sure if she did believe in the curse. In fact, she was almost certain that she didn't give it much credence at all.

She just didn't want to risk it. Not after whatever it was that she'd seen last night. And she still couldn't explain how her shorts had ended up out of the closet and on the floor.

She fingered the object in question inside her jacket pocket. The rock felt smooth and sleek under her skin. As small as a pebble. Hard to believe it could cause any kind of trouble. Well, it was too late to back out now. If Clint thought she was crazy, he was doing a good job of keeping that to himself.

The ride went by in comfortable silence. For the most part anyway. It certainly wasn't comfortable that she was so very aware of him.

He'd changed into navy-blue sailing shorts and a white V-neck tee that brought out his newly tanned skin. A silver-and-gold watch clasped on his right wrist had the most complicated face on it she'd ever seen, with three different dials and four hands. His hair was still wet and combed back to reveal his strong, square jaw.

Even dressed island casual, the man looked like he could grace the cover of *Executive Today* magazine.

Rita forced her attention to the road ahead. It was indeed quite curvy, perilously close to the edge in several spots. But Clint was effortlessly navigating the car in such a smooth way, her stomach hadn't dipped once. So unlike the ride yesterday.

"Are you getting tired of driving yet?" she asked, hoping the answer would be no. For all her protests earlier, she was quite enjoying being able to sit back and enjoy the scenery. No way she'd ever share that bit with him though.

"I think I'm good. No real good spots to stop anyway. Not for a while."

Nodding, Rita turned to stare at the sapphire-blue water beyond the mountain road they were driving on. She'd tried to stay angry, she really had, about the way he'd commandeered the whole endeavor. But how upset could she really be? He hadn't made fun of her. In fact, he hadn't so much as even smirked. He'd provided her with a steady and reliable car for the trip, and spared her from having to make the ride on her own.

Even if he had been a little domineering in the process. No one was perfect, right?

Between her overbearing father and control-loving ex-husband, it was been-there-done-that as far as she was concerned. Regardless of his well-intentioned motivations,

Clint had definitely shown a similar quality earlier today when he'd found her at the bellhop podium.

Moot point. It wasn't like she was committing herself for life to the man. She had just accepted his gracious offer to assist her with her mission. Nothing more.

With what seemed like great time, they finally pulled up to a gravel road. A large wooden sign at the entry said Wai'anapanapa State Park. Rita felt like months had gone by since they'd been here. Hard to believe it had been less than a day. So much had happened since. Clint pulled into one of the parking spots and they both got out of the car. Except, where Rita's limbs felt sore and stiff, Clint seemed to be able to bounce out of the SUV and easily stride to where she stood. Athletic and agile.

"All right. Let's go get uncursed," he said.

She tried to hide her trepidation. What if it didn't work that way? What if the spirits were unforgiving types that didn't care about attempts at restitution after the fact?

She'd never forgive herself if Lizzie and Jonathon broke up for good and there was even the slightest possibility she'd caused it. Even indirectly.

"Let's go." She started walking to the concrete steps that led down to the beach area. "I'll show you where I picked it up."

Clint had been right about today's weather being cloudier and more windy. These waves were definitely harsher than yesterday's. Angry water pounded on the boulders and sent splashes of foam high into the air. A mist of salt water fanned her face when they reached the bottom step.

"I picked it up in the cave," she told him and navigated around two jeans-clad teenagers taking selfies.

"Guess I shouldn't have pulled you in there yesterday," Clint responded.

But he *had* pulled her in. And they'd been merely inches

apart. And she couldn't forget that she'd actually imagined him kissing her, had wanted him to.

"I'm the one who picked up the rock."

"Which is why we're here." He led her toward the crashing waves and to the mouth of the cave in a replay of yesterday. It occurred to her that today there'd be no one to yell at them to come out, to tell them they needed to leave. A shiver of apprehension traveled up her spine. Or maybe it was more anticipation.

She stepped inside and he followed closely behind her. "I guess I should try to put it exactly where I found it on the ground. Or as close as possible."

"Right. So he can be reunited with all his little pebble friends."

"Ha ha." Rita bent down and gently deposited the rock, then straightened. Already, a sense of calm and relief settled over her. Superstition or not, she definitely felt a sense of unburdening.

"Ready?" Clint asked.

She nodded. "Seems anticlimactic somehow."

"You were expecting drama? Or perhaps that the spirits would descend all of a sudden and bestow you with thanks and praise?"

She smiled. "It's the least they could do, you know. They've put us through a lot of trouble."

He fished out his phone. Looked back up at her, eyes wide with shock. "You're not gonna believe this. Lizzie just texted that she and Jonathon have completely made up. Just this very moment."

Rita felt her jaw drop with disbelief. "Oh, my God! You're kidding?"

He waited a beat, then grinned. "Yeah, I am." He slid his phone back in his pocket. "I'm not even getting cell reception."

He was teasing her! Of all times. She reached over and gave him a useless shove. "That was mean."

The laughter died in her throat at his expression. Clint's gaze dropped to where her hand touched his shoulder. To her surprise, he wrapped his fingers around her own. His skin felt warm, strong against hers.

"You almost fell yesterday in here. Remember?" he asked, his voice near a whisper.

Rita's mouth went dry. If he only knew. Yes, she remembered. She'd been thinking about it ever since. The way he'd grabbed her to keep her upright. The solid wall of muscle against her back as he'd held her steady against him. "Guess I should thank you for that too."

His gaze fell to her mouth. "Maybe you can show me."

There it was. A clear invitation. All pretense gone.

And he'd made sure it would be her decision. The ball was fully in her court.

What would he taste like? How would his lips feel against hers? She'd thought so often about kissing him before, when she was merely a besotted coed with a crush. It had never occurred to her back then that she would ever get the opportunity. Yet, here it was. As if she was in some sort of fairy tale or dream. Their time together on Maui had only served to heighten her attraction. She'd grown increasingly more aware of him every moment they spent together. All too often on this trip, her imagination had created scenarios of the two of them together. Intimately. Scenarios, through some miracle, exactly like the one she found herself in now.

Rita had the distinct impression reality would be even better than the products of her imagination. She could guess what he would taste like: masculine and bold. His lips would be firm against hers, just as she'd so often dreamed.

It would be so easy to find out once and for all, to just lean into him and take him up on his tempting offer.

But could she? Could she tune out all the warnings, the red flags? All her life, she'd tried so hard to do what was expected of her, what others told her was the right thing. This one time, did she have the courage to simply do exactly what she wanted?

And she so desperately wanted.

Clint's breath caught as he watched Rita's inner struggle. He knew what she wanted; her eyes had clouded with desire. He had no doubt about that. Whether she would act on it was a completely different question. He willed himself not to move so much as a muscle. As badly as he wanted to lean into her and finally take those lush, tempting lips with his own, the next step would have to be hers. Whatever happened next between them had to be completely on her own terms.

It was only fair.

Not that he was trying to be honorable. The only real honorable thing to do would be to walk away, if he was being honest. Relationships weren't his thing. Not long-term ones. Fallon men couldn't be trusted with real commitment. History told that it never went well. Between his parents' fatal accident and his grandfather's self-inflicted untimely death, Clint determined long ago that he was never meant to be a family man.

He wouldn't lead someone like Rita on. But he could no longer deny his attraction. Nor hide it.

"I don't think that's such a good idea," she finally answered with a breathy rasp. A bolt of disappointment stabbed through his center. He felt the loss like a physical blow. A blow that wasn't the least lessened by the fact that she was right. Of course she was.

"It's not that I don't want to."

Well, that was something at least. It helped, though not much.

"It's just…" She thrust a hand through the hair at her crown. "I'm not sure exactly who I am at this very moment in time. I know it sounds silly."

Clint wanted desperately to wrap her tight in his arms, to kiss away the tension and angst clear in every muscle in her face. "It doesn't sound silly, Rita."

"I wish I could explain."

She didn't get a chance to try. A boisterous family of four appeared in the entryway and made their way inside.

"Ooh, spooky," the teenage girl said, her eyes glancing around the dark cave walls.

"You're a wuss" came the reply from her smaller brother, who stepped around her to go farther inside.

Clint cursed under his breath while Rita smiled politely at the intruders.

"We should go," he told Rita and gently took her by the elbow. "It's getting crowded in here," he added in a lower voice only she could hear.

"You all have a good day," the woman said pleasantly as they stepped out.

It occurred to Clint just how they must have looked, like a besotted couple who'd been interrupted as they stole a private moment in a beachside cavern.

So far from the truth it caused a pang in his gut.

"We've traveled quite a distance. It would be a shame just to turn around and go back." Clint opened the car door for Rita and waited as she crawled inside. It wasn't easy acting like nothing had just happened between them before the family had come in. Although, technically, nothing actually *had* happened.

Entering the car, he shut his door a little too hard. Rita winced slightly next to him.

"What did you have in mind?" she asked.

"A few stops I've heard about that the driver didn't take us to yesterday. Off the beaten path, so to speak. Are you hungry?"

Her stomach answered for her. As soon as he asked the question, he heard a soft grumbling coming from her midsection.

"Take a guess," she said in a giggle.

"There's supposedly a roadside hut that serves the best banana bread on the island. Or so I've been told."

"Sold. But only if it's my treat." She seemed genuinely excited. He hoped at least part of that came from not wanting their private little outing to end just yet. Maybe he was fooling himself. She was simply hungry. Still, he'd take it.

"It's a deal." He put the car in gear and began to drive.

Within minutes, they'd reached the stand and were handed tinfoil-wrapped loaves of aromatic bread that made his mouth water. Rita began tearing at the foil.

"Uh-uh." He stopped her by placing his hand on hers. "Not yet."

She glared at him. "Why not? I want my lunch."

Her outrage made him laugh. "Patience. We can eat it at the next stop."

She reluctantly lowered the bread. "We're still off the beaten path then?"

"Let's go." He'd been thinking about taking her to this next stop all day. Hoped it would live up to expectations. From what he'd been told, the spot was a well-kept secret among the locals who didn't want it overrun with campy tourists the way the state properties usually were.

Rita seemed the type who would appreciate a place like that.

He had his answer when they reached the isolated beach about half an hour later. She gasped as he pulled up along the side of the road and put the car in gear. Before he could turn off the ignition, she'd already exited and started running toward the small stretch of beach.

"Oh, Clint!"

"What do you think?"

"It's pink! I've never seen anything like it. The sand is actually pink! I thought the black sand was impressive."

Before them lay a crystal-blue pool of water surrounded by sand the likes of which he'd never seen before. Rita was partly right as far as he was concerned. He'd describe the color as more of a ruby red, depending on where the light hit it.

"This is otherworldly." She bent down and scooped some of the sand into her palm before letting it slowly sift through her fingers.

"I figured we'd have our banana bread lunch here. Make a picnic out of it."

The smile she flashed him gave him the response he wanted. It also nearly took his breath away. An almost giddy sense of pleasure hit him at how happy she was to be here.

What a schoolboy with a crush he was acting like.

They sat down on a large boulder between the road and water and began to eat.

"Looks like we have company." Clint swallowed the bite he had in his mouth as a large lanky dog jogged toward them. It stopped about six inches away and started sniffing at the food. Clint's food to be more accurate. Rita had impressed him by finishing first.

"Hey, baby." She stood and held her hand to the dog's nose to sniff.

"Is it a stray?"

"I don't think so. No collar but it seems taken care of. Well-fed, no signs of emaciation."

Right. She was a vet after all. The dog licked her finger, then turned back to Clint, eyeing the bread again.

He pulled the loaf back. "This is mine."

Rita squatted in front of the animal. "Are you lost, girl? Let's take a look at you." Placing her fingers along the dog's jaw, she slowly pried its mouth open.

Clint stopped chewing. "Um…is that wise?"

She ignored the question. "Teeth look good. Relatively clean for what I'd guess is her age. She seems to be some type of pit bull–mix breed. Definitely some other terrier in there too."

"So she's not lost?"

Rita looked up to glance at the road behind them. "There are some houses back there. I'm guessing she's just out wandering."

"I think she smelled banana and came looking." He could have sworn the dog actually nodded at that statement. Then it lifted a paw and dropped it onto Clint's knee.

There was barely one morsel left.

"She likes you," Rita declared, clearly laughing at his displeasure.

"She wants my lunch."

Again, he could swear the dog was nodding. He suddenly felt guilty. "Should I give her some?"

Rita seemed to think. "Probably not. It shouldn't harm her but it is pretty sweet. Sugar sometimes upsets their digestive tract."

Guilt evaporated, Clint popped the last piece of bread into his mouth, then leaned over to rub the dog's head. "Sorry, pal. You heard the doc."

He got a sharp bark in response. "Hey, you should be thanking me. I just spared you an upset tummy."

"And diarrhea," Rita added.

Well, now things were getting romantic. The dog gave him one more derisive look, then dropped its paw and started to walk away. Rita followed for a few feet and watched it cross the road.

"She seems to be heading toward that brown house at the turn," she told him over her shoulder.

Sure enough, they both watched as their former visitor walked through the yard and jumped through what appeared to be a puppy door by the side of the house.

Clint heard Rita's sigh of relief. He had the distinct feeling she would have followed that dog until she made sure it had a home and had reached it safely.

"What a cutie," she said and returned to her spot next to him on the boulder. "Do you have any pets?"

Clint shook his head. "I'm never home long enough. The poor thing would starve. I imagine you have a few."

"Not right now. Jay had allergies. He'd react even to the hypoallergenic breeds. So we never bothered to get one."

"Couldn't you have gotten one of those hairless cats or something?"

She bit out a short laugh. "Sphynx cats? Believe it or not, people have reactions to those too."

"My sister wanted one of those, though I'll never understand why. I personally think they look like deflated balloons. With a face." He picked a small pink pebble, thought about throwing it into the water and dropped it back down. In case the curse applied to more than just Black Sand Beach.

And since when did he give any credence to curses and such? He hardly recognized himself on this trip. Now here he was sitting on a magical beach with the most beautiful, alluring woman and so far they'd talked about canine diarrhea and hairless cats.

"But she never got one," he continued. "We didn't have any pets growing up."

"Oh?"

"My grandmother wouldn't allow it. She said she had enough on her hands being strapped with two teenagers to bring up at her late stage in life. Wouldn't budge even though we swore we'd be the ones taking care of any animal she'd let us get." He stared off into the water. "Heck, Lizzie would have settled for a goldfish."

"That's too bad. I think pets serve to teach children a great deal. Particularly a good sense of responsibility."

"Other than that, Grams was all about responsibility." Especially when it came to him. "Our grandmother made no secret of the fact that she'd disapproved of my parents' marriage," he added, not quite certain why he was ready to share so much with her. These were things he'd never spoken out loud about with anyone. Not even Lizzie. "Almost seemed to take it as a personal affront. I got the impression I was somehow supposed to make up for their transgressions to her."

She touched his knee in sympathy. An electric current shot through from the point of contact straight through his chest.

"That's a lot to process for a teenage boy."

"Past history." He shrugged, ready to change the subject. "So what was the last pet you owned?"

"My parents always had one or two dogs. This past year was the first time in my life I didn't have an animal to come home to."

"Good thing you get enough animal contact through your work then, huh?"

She bit her bottom lip, looked out over the water. "I'm not practicing right now."

Whatever the reason, she didn't seem happy about it. He got the impression her sabbatical wasn't by choice. Not her choice, in any case.

"Why's that?"

"Long story. Jay asked me to quit when we first got married. He wanted to focus on a family. I'd only taken the job to make him happy anyway."

"I don't understand."

"My original goal out of college was to try to start my own practice, set up shop somewhere. Or to work with one of the local animal shelters. But both those options would have taken countless grueling hours and total commitment. Jay wasn't too keen on that idea. I let him convince me to try for a clinic instead. He had some help from my parents in the convincing department. They'd never understood my career choice anyway." Her laugh was not a genuine one. "Neither my mother or father could figure out why I'd want to go through all that schooling and training and not become an actual doctor." She used air quotes to emphasize the last two words.

Clint continued to play with the sand at his feet. Staying silent seemed to be the best course of action right now. To just let her continue.

"Anyway, I ended up at a chain practice where they controlled everything from my schedule to the length of my patient visits."

"That doesn't sound like a good fit for you."

"It wasn't. It got to the point where I started spending more time filling out forms to prove profit contribution to the clinic than I did actually treating pets. So when Jay asked me to quit…"

"You quit to make him happy."

"I guess I did."

"And now?"

She tucked a strand of hair behind her ear. "What do you mean?"

He thought his meaning should be obvious, but she was looking at him expectantly. "What's stopping you now from going after that original goal?"

She blinked, then looked away into the distance. "I don't know if I even have the same goals anymore. A lot has happened since I got my degree."

"Sure it has. You've gained even more experience in

your field." He thought of the way she'd handled the wandering dog just now, the pure contentment and energy in her eyes as she tended to it. "You're clearly good at what you do."

She smiled. "I suppose. I just don't know if I have it in me any longer to pursue such grand endeavors. Right now, I just need to settle into a quiet, comfortable routine."

"Sounds a bit boring."

Her chuckle was half-hearted. "I could do with a little boring at this point in time."

More likely, she was scared. Based on the little bit she'd confided, her decisions had been questioned so often and so thoroughly, she was probably hesitant about making any more major ones. Clint would keep all that to himself. Who was he to try to analyze her choices?

"Yet one more thing to figure out, I guess," she added, not tearing her gaze away from the horizon.

He didn't say anything else, though he desperately wanted to. He simply reached for the hand she still had on his knee and gave it a tight squeeze. They sat in silence for long enough that he actually lost track of the time. Five minutes or an hour could have gone by before Rita spoke again.

"Clint." The way she said his name made his heart hammer.

"Yeah?"

"I've changed my mind."

He lifted an eyebrow in question. Then sucked in a breath at her next words.

"I would like you to kiss me. In fact, I'd like it very much."

Rita couldn't recall ever being so bold. She'd asked before she could let herself think too much longer about doing so. And now she couldn't think at all.

Clint's kiss was gentle at first, like a soft breeze on a warm summer evening. But then something turned. He took her by the waist, pulled her closer, her body tight up against his. His mouth grew demanding, delving deeper and asking for more. She was oh, so ready to give it. Shivers ran down her whole body, desire racked her core. She'd never felt such intense longing for a man, simply from his kiss.

A thrill shot through her chest at the knowledge that he wanted her, as well. There was no doubt, not given the way he held her, the way he was plundering her mouth with his own.

So this was what true passion felt like, what all the books and movies and love songs were always referring to. All these years, she'd had no idea until this very moment. With this one man.

Her hands moved up his arms to his shoulders. She wanted him closer somehow, would never get close enough. Her heart hammered in her chest as she molded her body against his. Nothing in her past dreams could have prepared her for the reality of being in his arms, tasting him like this. Her fantasies hadn't done him justice. He was making her burn through to her very soul. An exquisite, enticing burn she'd never get enough of. He tasted like sin and pure masculinity. And banana bread.

That random thought served to pull her out of the spell. Enough to let all the warning cries in. Abruptly, she made herself tear away from his grasp. The loss felt like a bucket of cold water splashed into her face.

She shouldn't be doing this. Couldn't be doing this.

She'd made too many mistakes in these past few years. It would take her years to recover from them.

She couldn't make another one by losing her heart to Clint. There would be no recovering from that.

Clint Fallon wasn't the type of man a girl got over. Ever.

CHAPTER EIGHT

THE RIDE BACK was mostly silent save for the luau music playing on the radio. She'd noticed Clint had gradually turned up the volume higher and higher, as if it somehow refuted the lack of conversation between them. Neither one seemed to know what to say to each other.

Rita felt like a wound-up ball of emotion by the time they returned to the resort and went their separate ways. Her distraction was the reason it took her a minute to realize what she'd walked in on after she opened the door to her room and switched on the light.

She quickly shut if off again as soon as her eyes adjusted and she realized what she was seeing.

"Rita!" Tessa's surprised voice shouted across the room from her bed, immediately followed by the low rumble of a man's chuckle. It appeared Tessa and the groomsman had taken their friendship to the next level.

"It's o-okay," Rita stammered and tried to walk quickly backward out the door. Her jacket pocket caught on the doorknob and yanked her to a halt.

Tessa appeared at the door, wrapped in a sheet. Which had to mean the groomsman wasn't covered at the moment. She made sure to quickly avert her gaze.

"I'm really sorry, Rita. I guess I wasn't expecting you back. You've been gone all day."

"We were exploring the island."

Tessa gave a nod. "With Clint, right? You've both been gone. I just assumed…"

Rita could guess what she'd assumed. "It's okay. I didn't mean to interrupt." It didn't quite feel right that she was the one apologizing but somehow she felt the need.

Tessa blew a tuft of hair off her forehead. "I mean," she said, dropping her voice to a whisper, "Rob and I have been really hitting it off, you know. It's like—I've never felt so attracted to someone. Hasn't that ever happened to you?"

She didn't know how to answer that. It had happened, so very recently. It *was* happening. And she didn't know how to cope with it.

"I'm happy for you," Rita blurted out, not even sure if it was an appropriate response for this moment.

"Thanks. I guess I kinda figured you'd sort of be occupied too."

An image flashed through her mind of exactly what Tessa was referring to. In that picture, it was her and Clint wrapped up in each other under the sheets in a dark room.

She sucked in a breath and forced her mind to focus on Tessa's face.

"Listen, it's okay. You guys…uh…you guys have fun."

Tessa squealed a small laugh. "Oh, we are."

"How about you just drop me a text when it's safe for me to return?"

Tessa leaned over to give her a one-armed hug, the other hand holding tight to the sheet. "Thanks, Rita! You're the best. I'll call you as soon as… Well, you know."

Rita backed away into the hallway as the door shut. The squeal she heard from Tessa in the next instant sounded nothing like the one from before.

Making her way to the ground-floor lounge, she settled on the couch and adjusted a cushion behind her, trying to get comfortable. She almost envied her roommate. To be that bold, to feel that liberated had to be so freeing in so many ways. Tessa obviously didn't give much thought to long-term ramifications. While planning for the future had been a constant theme in the way Rita lived her life. Look how that had turned out. Rita sighed and closed her eyes, willing for at least a few moments of sleep before she could go back to the room.

Tessa's text never came.

He'd become quite the wanderer in Hawaii. Clint made his way down the stairs and past the lobby. He'd gotten tired of tossing and turning, trying to get to sleep. It wasn't early in the evening but it certainly wasn't late by any means. He and Rita had gotten back less than three hours ago.

He couldn't stop thinking about her. Or the way she'd kissed him.

More than that, she'd opened up to him. Though it had been difficult to hear about her former husband. Just the thought that she'd belonged to another man not so long ago made him want to punch a wall. How utterly Neanderthal-like. He wasn't proud of his reaction.

Rita and her ex sounded like two completely different people, totally incompatible. Rita was warm, genuine and fully appreciative of everything around her. Her ex-husband seemed the stoic and serious type. He blew out a frustrated breath. What did he know about it? He'd never even met the man. In fact, he'd never felt such a strong dislike for someone he'd never laid eyes on.

He halted in his tracks as he approached the sitting area by the ground-floor lounge. Great. Now he was starting to see her everywhere. That couldn't really be her sprawled out on one of the couches.

He drew closer to find it was indeed her.

"Rita?" He gently tapped her on the shoulder. Once, twice. Nothing. Leaning in, he gave her arm a gentle squeeze. Finally, she started to stir.

"Clint?"

"Yeah. Hey, what are you doing here? Do you sleepwalk or something?" he asked, not even certain if he was joking.

She winced as she shifted to a sitting position, must have been lying there long enough to have her limbs go stiff.

"I was waiting for Tessa to get back to me."

"About what?"

She arched her back in a stretch, spreading her arms out. Clint had to look away from the scene of her long, graceful neck and the tempting curves under her tank top.

"Tessa had company when I walked in. She said she would call me when they were…you know, finished."

"I see." He glanced down at his watch. "It's past midnight. Way past."

"Guess she forgot."

More likely, they weren't yet "finished." "Do you want to try calling her?"

Nodding, she pulled her cell out of her pocket and dialed. Several beats passed then Clint heard Tessa's voice through the tiny speaker saying she couldn't answer.

"Straight to voice mail." Rita tossed her phone on the coffee table in front of them. "Guess I'll be enjoying the open-air lounge for a while longer."

"Why don't you just go back to your room. Tell them they've had enough time."

Her eyes grew wide. "No way. That was embarrassing enough the first time."

"Embarrassing how?"

"I sort of walked in on them."

Clint slapped a hand to his mouth, but not before he could stifle the burst of laughter.

Rita narrowed her eyes on him; her lips formed a tight line. "Ha ha. I'm glad you think that's funny."

"I'm sorry. It is pretty funny, knowing what I know of

you." No doubt in the world Rita had turned redder than the woman who'd actually been caught in flagrante.

"What's that supposed to mean?"

"Never mind. It's not important."

"I think you might have just implied I'm a prude."

"If the shoe fits…yada yada."

She glared at him. "I'm going to choose to ignore that by changing the subject. How's Lizzie? Have you heard anything?"

Quite a deft way to change the subject, at that. Thankfully, there was at least some good news on that front. "I called her a little while after we returned. Looks like she and Jonathon went to dinner together. Crisis averted apparently."

"Thank goodness."

"Now for your crisis." He motioned to her and then around to the couches.

"I'd hardly consider this a crisis. I can always go ask for another room."

"Are you kidding? This place is continually booked. We had to reserve our rooms months ago."

Her shoulders sagged with defeat. Turning behind her, she punched the seat cushion and leaned back against it. "Looks like I'll have to make myself comfortable here awhile longer."

Like he would allow that to happen in a thousand years. Standing, he offered her his arm. "That's silly. Come with me."

She blinked up at him. He felt a resounding sense of relief when she finally stood up and took his hand. "Where to?"

"Just follow me." He knew she wasn't going to go along with his idea easily, but they could argue along the way.

"Where are we going? I'd like to know," she insisted even as she trailed behind him.

"I'm not going to let you sleep here all night. Not when there's a perfectly good suite we can share."

If she was counting, she would have to acknowledge all the times that Clint had come through for her in the few short days since he'd walked into that airport executive lounge. A nagging voice repeated in her head that none of it boded very well for her newly avowed goal to live more independently, reliant on her own devices.

Clint must have sensed her hesitation.

"It's a two-room suite. One bedroom and one living room complete with a long sofa and a connected door that can be closed."

"I'm not so sure that's a good idea."

"You'll have all the privacy you need."

Rita inhaled deeply as she contemplated his words. It made total sense. Definitely more sense than trying to get any sleep out here in an open lounge area. And frankly, she was exhausted between all the activity of the past few days and her sleepless night. Not to mention, she didn't want to be out here alone in case there were any visitors. Especially incorporeal ones like from the night before.

"It has been a rather long day." Two days, in fact. "And I would kill to wash my face and brush my teeth." Two routine tasks she'd really rather not wait until morning for.

"We can pick up some sundries from the night manager. I'll even let you have the bed."

She shook her head. "No way. If I do this, I insist on sleeping on the couch."

"Suit yourself."

"I haven't actually agreed."

Despite her words, he must have sensed her capitulation, as Clint further pleaded his case. "We have an all-day snorkeling adventure tomorrow. You'll need to be rested up."

Rita rubbed at her forehead, trying to release some of

the tension that had suddenly gathered there and knotted itself under her scalp. She had no good reason to say no. And she was so bone tired. Her only options were to sleep out here, kick a sleeping man out of a warm bed that he was sharing with a warm body. Or she could take Clint up on his offer. Maybe she was too exhausted to think straight, because only one of those options seemed to make sense at the moment. Besides, they were both adults. Technically, she'd known him for years. They'd just spent the whole day together. Quite an enjoyable day, in fact. Well, except for the awkwardness toward the end that came after that soul-shattering kiss.

And that was it right there. She'd be following him to his room right this very minute ready to fall fast asleep, if it wasn't for that blasted kiss. Could she really be that close to him, practically in the same room, all the while knowing what it felt like to be held by him? The way he'd tasted. Her skin tingled as she recalled the way his hands had gripped her around the waist, held her tight up against him.

"Rita. Come on. Show some compassion."

"Compassion?"

"Do it for me. I will get absolutely zero sleep knowing you're out here by yourself. Plus, I think there's some heavy rain due later tonight."

"I'm pretty sure you just made that up. About the rain."

"I might have." He gave her a small smile. "You have to know you can trust me," Clint added, throwing down the proverbial gauntlet and making it almost impossible to say no.

She did trust him. Without any qualms or hesitation. She just wasn't so sure how much she trusted herself.

The man looked like sin. Rita adjusted the waistband of her swimsuit and tried to avert her gaze from where Clint stood on the deck of the boat. Beyond him the water of the

Pacific Ocean gleamed like a sea of blue-green emeralds under the bright, shining mandarin-orange sun.

He'd been right about last night. Despite her heightened awareness of him in the next room, her tiredness had won out in the end and she'd fallen asleep as soon as she'd collapsed on his couch. Hadn't even heard him when he'd come to throw the extra blanket over her. He'd also let her oversleep, so her run to the room to get her tankini for this snorkeling jaunt had been frantic and rushed.

Despite the unexpected lie-in, Rita felt like she could use several more hours of sleep.

No doubt, a set of puffy dark circles framed her bloodshot eyes. Well, it hardly mattered—her face would be under a mask, then submerged in water most of the day. Clint, by contrast, appeared awake and alert. He stood against the railing, bouncing on his heels to the rhythmic reggae music the captain had playing. A jovial crew ran around them, prepping for the first snorkeling stop.

For two people who had spent the night in the same suite, they were doing an impressive job of avoiding talking to each other.

The truth was, she'd been the one avoiding him. But it was for her own self-preservation. Every time she glanced at his face, her gaze fell to his lips and triggered a tingling sensation in hers. Dreams of their kiss yesterday had haunted slumber all night. Images of her locked in his embrace framed against a backdrop of glimmering blue water and sparkling pink sand.

Stop it.

Well, she couldn't keep up the avoidance for long. The wedding wasn't for two more days still. Their paths were sure to cross at some point.

Bending down to reach for her mask, she came face-to-face with a set of sparkling blue eyes when she straightened.

"Hi, Tessa."

"Oh, my God, Rita. I'm so sorry I didn't text you last night. We fell asleep. We were just so tired."

"I kind of figured."

"I'm guessing you found a place to crash." She gestured to where Clint still stood, his tanned muscular back to them.

"Yes, I did," Rita simply replied. There would be no use in trying to correct Tessa's misguided insinuation. Nothing had actually happened between her and Clint overnight. Only in her dreams.

Tessa clapped her hands in front of her chest. "I figured you might." The woman was just too giddy this time of the day. She gave her a sly wink. "So it won't be a problem if Rob and I have the room to ourselves again tonight?"

Was she serious?

"I'm not so sure—"

Tessa's face fell, the smile dropping from her lips. She looked like a wounded puppy. Rita felt her jaw clench as she inwardly cursed. She had no reason to feel guilty. It was her room too.

"What about Rob's room? Perhaps you two can take turns," she offered.

Tessa pursed her lips. "His roommate apparently picked up the perky, smiley waitress at the cabana down the beach. Already told Rob he called dibs on the room."

What in the world? How was everyone in the wedding party so great at hooking up? And here she was, a fluttering, quivering mess just because Clint had kissed her on the beach. In fairness however, she'd never been kissed that way before. And it would probably never happen again. That notion had her heart sinking. Her eyes automatically found him once more. Her breath caught in her throat.

Tessa looked from one of them to the other. "I don't understand. I mean, clearly you two are—"

Rita cut her off. "We're not. Really, we're just friends."

Tessa didn't bother to hide her eye roll. "You could have fooled me. The way you two keep looking at each other."

Rita felt her cheeks flame with heat. Was she that obvious? Could the whole world tell that she was attracted like crazy to the bride's brother? How utterly horrifying.

"I'm sorry for assuming," Tessa continued. "I'll tell Rob he's out of luck tonight. Though I don't know where the poor guy is going to crash if his roommate brings the waitress there with him again."

There was a lounge area on the ground floor that wasn't terribly comfortable but could be considered an option, she almost told her. Rita sighed. It was like a domino effect. She felt herself capitulating. It wasn't like she didn't have a place to stay. Clint's suite did have ample room. And once she shut the door, it was like they weren't even sharing a space.

She studied Tessa's face. Her expression held more than disappointment. Much more. Rita got the feeling she was witnessing more than an island fling.

"You're falling for him, aren't you?"

To her utter surprise, the other woman's eyes started glistening with tears. "I've never felt this way before about anyone. He's gentle and sweet. And he makes me laugh. I can't bear to think about what's going to happen when we leave here. He lives on the opposite coast after all."

Rita took the other woman's hand in her own. "Oh, Tessa. I'm sure you two will figure something out."

"Do you really think so?" Hope shone through her eyes.

"I really do."

"Thanks." She sniffled. "I really hope we can."

"I'll be rooting for you." That comment earned her a wide smile.

Rita sighed with resignation. In the meantime, she could let them have these few remaining nights together. At least one of them had found their chance at happiness and love.

Who was she to stand in the way? Tessa started to stand but she stopped her. "Consider the room all yours."

Clint couldn't really keep up with what Rita was trying to tell him. Something about the waitress from the poolside cabana bar and Tessa living on the opposite coast. And also something about Rob What's-His-Name who was one of the groomsmen and how much Tessa liked him.

In Clint's defense, it was hard to concentrate on her words when the sun was shining on her hair and making it glisten like liquid black silk. Her cheeks were touched by just enough tan that they'd turned an intriguing rosy color he'd be hard-pressed to describe. And don't even get him started on the bathing suit she was wearing. Modest by most standards, it showed just enough of her midriff to scream temptation. The rich scarlet color of the fabric complimented her skin tone in a way that had him losing his train of thought.

A thin gold chain around her ankle made him want to reach down and run his fingers over the charms she wore on it. Then he'd work his way slowly up her calves. Then higher.

He gave his head a shake.

He had to pay attention. She was trying to tell him something important. But all he could focus on was the fact that it appeared she would be staying with him again tonight. That's all he really needed to hear.

They were disembarking off the catamaran after a full day of snorkeling. All in all, not a bad way to spend several hours off the sunny coast of Hawaii. Only it didn't compare to the pleasant enjoyment of yesterday, when he'd had Rita to himself.

"So I guess I'll just come by after dinner sometime. As soon as Rob shows up. You don't mind, do you? I feel kind of awkward asking."

"It's no trouble at all, Rita."

She still looked apprehensive and stopped him as they walked along the beach back to the resort. "Please don't read anything into this."

Something sparked in his chest. After all the experiences they'd shared together so far on this trip, all the ways he'd opened up to her and vice versa, she felt the need to warn him about making assumptions. The notion stung more than he cared to admit.

"Why would I? I'd like to think you're not the type to be coy when it comes to asking directly for what you want from a man."

Her gasp of surprise told him his comment had hit home. Good, he'd meant for it to.

"Maybe this isn't such a great idea after all." Her voice held a plethora of doubt.

What did he expect? Was he also not supposed to read anything into the way she'd reacted to his touch? Or the way she'd moaned softly into his lips as he'd kissed her?

He didn't get a chance to respond as Lizzie stormed past them followed by Jonathon hot on her heels. Lizzie's anger was palpable, the steam rising from her almost a tangible sight.

Not again.

"Huh." Rita spoke behind him. "We returned the rock and everything."

Clint resisted the urge to go after them both and tell them to get it together already, that the attendees didn't have time for this childish behavior from the bride and groom. But he had his own ire to contend with.

"What do you mean exactly?"

She blinked up in surprise. "Clearly Lizzie and Jonathon are fighting again."

"I know that. What do you mean about me not reading into things when it comes to you?"

Rita stomped past him without answering, her footsteps splashing water onto his legs. Well, he wasn't about to let her get away. Catching up to her, he gently but firmly took her by the elbow.

"Care to answer?"

"I don't think I do. Forget about me staying in your suite tonight. Forget I even mentioned it."

"It's a little too late for that, don't you think? You've already told Tessa she could have the room."

She pulled her arm free. "I'll think of something."

Clint rubbed a hand down his face with frustration. "What is it with you?"

"I don't know what you mean."

"It means I noticed how you've been avoiding me the whole day. Barely spoke two words to me even though we've been on the same boat for the past several hours."

"I was enjoying the scenery."

"Sure, you were. You practically pulled a muscle trying to get sunscreen lotion on your back by yourself."

Her jaw dropped. "Are you actually saying you're upset because you wanted to rub lotion on my back and I didn't ask?"

Well, when she put it that way...

He ignored that and continued, "Then as we're disembarking, you finally remember my name and ask about staying in my suite. Only I better not get any high hopes that it might mean something."

"I'm sorry."

"And another thing—wait... What did you say?"

"I apologize. I shouldn't have ignored you. It's just hard to know what to say to you now."

Because he'd kissed her. She was clearly conflicted about it.

Well, so was he. But he refused to regret that it happened and very much hoped she didn't regret it either.

"This is all taking me a bit by surprise." She said it so softly, with such a wistful sadness in her voice. There was no denying the truth in her statement. He suddenly felt like a heel for the way he'd just behaved, making her feel the need to apologize to him.

"Yeah, I know. Apology accepted. And I'd love to have you as a suite mate again."

She finally smiled. "Maybe we can make a whole event of it. Rent a movie and do each other's hair. Like a real sleepover."

As far as jokes went, it was a pretty lame one. But Clint appreciated the attempt to lighten the mood.

He wasn't going to tell her just how impossible it had been to sleep last night, knowing she was only a few feet away. This thing between them, whatever it was, had him spinning and twisting about inside. He'd never felt anything like it.

How in the world was he supposed to ignore that for the next several days until they both went back to their regular, daily lives? He had no doubt Rita was just as bothered as he was. That kiss yesterday in the cave proved it. He wanted to make the most of the time they had here together still. In a way that wasn't awkward or strained.

He watched the remaining members of the wedding party as they slowly strolled past, some holding hands. Tessa and Rob were particularly engrossed in each other as they made their way along the beach. Rita sighed as they walked by.

"You were right yesterday, about everyone coupling up on this trip," Rita stated, echoing his thoughts. "It's not just my roommate and her groomsman."

Without allowing himself to think, he crooked a finger under her chin and lifted her face to look up at him. "Maybe we should too."

He'd shocked her. She visibly retreated as he said the

words. "Oh, Clint. You have to understand. The timing is just so wrong."

Didn't she see that was his whole point? "It doesn't have to be, Rita. We have four more days on this island. We can make the most of it." Boldly, he stepped closer to her. "I know I want to kiss you again. I want to feel what I felt in that cave when you were in my arms. As often as I can before we have to bid our goodbyes once this is over."

The struggle behind her eyes was clear and tangible.

"Think about it." He dropped his hand. "In the meantime, my couch is yours tonight if you need it."

They were both silent as they slowly made their way back to the hotel lobby. Rita dared a glance at Clint's profile. The sleek, stylish sunglasses he had on made it difficult to gauge his expression. Dear Lord, he'd essentially just asked her to consider a mindless fling. He'd just thrown it out there, as if it was the most trivial thing in the world. Like asking her what she wanted to do for lunch later.

To his credit, he was being brutally honest. A heaviness settled into her chest. He wanted nothing more than a light, swift affair. His exact words were *before we have to bid our goodbyes*.

She'd be foolish to read anything more into his proposal.

Did she have the nerve to take him up on it? For just the next few days, could she really put aside her concerns and reservations and just enjoy herself? Live in this fantasy she found herself in?

Think about it, he'd said. As if she'd be able to think about anything else.

CHAPTER NINE

As FAR AS finally getting some sleep, tonight was no different than the previous two.

Clint threw his arm over his head and muttered a curse in the dark. Funny, he'd never been plagued by such relentless insomnia before this trip. Then again, never before had he ever had a woman so close yet so out of his reach.

The timing is just so wrong. The words Rita had spoken to him on the beach echoed through his head.

He grunted out loud. With thoughts like that floating through his mind, it was no wonder he couldn't sleep. A slight movement outside the glass door of the patio suddenly drew his attention. Apparently, he wasn't the only one who couldn't sleep. After crawling out of bed, he tugged the sheer curtain aside to see Rita standing by the railing, staring up at the moonlit sky. He opened the door slowly so as not to startle her.

"Decided to do some stargazing?"

She smiled at him as he walked closer to stand by her side. "It's very pretty. The sky is so clear, the moon so bright."

"Mmm-hmm."

"Why are you up?"

He shrugged. "Couldn't sleep."

"I hope I wasn't making too much noise out here." She reached up, started rubbing the back of her neck.

"You didn't wake me. Stiff?"

She rolled her head back and forth, working out some sort of kink. "No, it's not that."

"You didn't hurt yourself snorkeling, did you?"

He heard her laugh. "Only when I scraped by knee against the rough coral when I foolishly dived under and got too close. Just really wanted a better look."

That didn't explain what was wrong with her neck. Then he realized. "It's the couch. You can't be very comfortable on that thing."

"It's fine, Clint. I just fell asleep at an odd angle. It'll be all right once I knead out the knot at the base of my neck."

"Here." Without giving her a chance to protest, he reached over and started to massage the spot she'd been working. "Better?"

She sighed with satisfaction and Clint felt his mouth grow dry. For heaven's sake, he had to stop reacting to this woman's every movement. What in the world was wrong with him?

"Much better. In fact, I'm gonna go lie down again. Good night," she said with a small wave.

"Rita, wait."

She turned on her heel. "Yes."

Clearing his throat, he decided to just blurt it out. "The bed is huge. Too big for one person. Even with someone my size in it."

"Clint. I'm not sure it's wise for us to share a bed."

The proposal he'd made to her earlier on the beach sat like a proverbial elephant in the room. Maybe he should have never done it. What had he been thinking? Rita wasn't the type to have a meaningless fling. She deserved more from a man than what he'd offered her.

"Listen, if you're concerned that I'll take your sleeping in the bed as some sort of answer to what I proposed earlier, you don't have to worry about that."

"But you did propose it, Clint."

"And now it's totally in your hands. Whatever you decide, whenever you decide it. The ball is completely in your court."

She chewed her bottom lip. "We'll only be sharing the bed in the interest of comfort and practicality?"

He nodded. "I honestly don't see why we can't. I'd offer to take the couch myself if I thought for one instant that you'd allow it." But that was not the way she was wired.

Rita was the type of woman who tried to sleep in a lobby lounge chair so her roommate could have some privacy. She was the type to make sure a wandering dog wasn't a stray and that it made it back to its home safely. She was the kind of woman any man would be proud to have in his life.

Any man who deserved her. And he certainly didn't qualify. She warranted more than he'd ever be willing or able to give. And if that didn't make him selfish for the way he'd casually asked her for a fling, he didn't know what would.

"If it makes you feel better, I can't seem to fall asleep anyway," he told her. "I fully intended to power up the laptop and try to get some work done."

"All night?"

"I've done it before." More often than he could count, particularly those early days when he was getting his business off the ground as well as working ten-hour shifts to lend a hand at the various construction sites.

She glanced behind him into the room. "It does appear rather large."

"A California king they called it when they sold me the package. It would be a shame to let it go to waste."

"Are you sure I'm not kicking you out of your bed?" She remained where she stood.

"You're not," he offered in as reassuring a tone as he could muster.

"All right, then. I could use the rest."

He stepped over to the door and held it open for her, trying to ignore the enticing citrus-and-coconut smell of her skin as she walked past.

The chances of him actually getting any work done were almost zero.

She could hear him breathing deeply in the other room. He'd set up his laptop and gotten to work, all right. But then he'd promptly fallen asleep. She could tell by the steady rhythm of his breath. On the same uncomfortable couch he'd rescued her from.

How was she supposed to relax knowing he was out there and she was in here on a nice comfortable mattress?

Sighing, she lifted away the covers and walked over to the other room.

Yep, out cold. Clint was sprawled on the couch with his legs and arms dangling off the ends. It was way too small for him. His head was bent on the back cushion at the same odd angle she'd woken up in earlier. As it was, she'd barely avoided a nasty tension headache due to the awkward position. She didn't want the same for Clint, especially considering it would be her fault.

She gave him a gentle nudge on the arm and quietly called his name.

He opened his eyes almost immediately. It took a few blinks but eventually she watched as he focused on her face. "What's wrong? Are you all right? Your neck hurt again?"

An odd sensation stirred in the pit of her stomach. His first reaction upon wakening had been concern for her. How many people in her life could she say that about?

Only her mother came to mind. When she wasn't soundly disappointed in her. Which was all too often.

"I'm fine," she responded, touched even further when he blew out a relieved breath. "But I think we should make this a true slumber party."

He sat up and rubbed his eyes. "Huh?"

"We can share the bed. Like a real sleepover. What do you say?"

With a groggy smile, he got up and followed her to the bed.

"Thanks," Clint whispered once they'd both crawled under the covers. She could smell the subtle scent of his aftershave even though it was now hours old. She'd taken a whiff of the bottle in the bathroom earlier, recognized the scent now.

"Please don't thank me for letting you sleep in your own bed, Clint. It makes me feel quite guilty."

"Sorry."

Now he was apologizing; that was somehow even worse. "Good night."

"Good night, sweet Rita."

The endearment evoked a small spark of pleasure in her chest. Would he have ever spoken that way if he wasn't half-asleep? Doubtful. "Get some sleep."

She heard him yawn beside her then turn to his side. Eventually, his breathing seemed to return to the same steady rhythm she'd heard earlier when he'd been asleep. So it surprised her when he spoke again a few moments later. Even more shocking were his words.

"Did you love him, Rita? You must have loved him deeply if you married him, right?"

Clint realized with a start that he'd actually voiced the question out loud. Damn his sleep-fogged brain and the tongue it had set loose. Rita's gasp of surprise left no doubt that she was now stunned and uncomfortable. Probably regretted inviting him into the bed for their "sleepover" as she called it.

They were both wide-awake now.

"That's quite the question."

"I'm sorry," he replied, with genuine regret. It wasn't like he actually wanted to know the answer. "It's none of my business."

"I married him. We both took vows to love and cherish each other."

Her words felt like individual blows to his gut. He'd been right; he hadn't really wanted to know. To top it off, Rita's tone held a strange tightness. He'd insulted her. After all, his question insinuated she may have married a man she wasn't in love with.

Clint wished he'd never even opened the can of worms. "I'm sorry it didn't work out," he lied.

The truth was, he wasn't sorry one bit that she was here solo. This trip would have been a far less memorable experience sans the time they'd spent together. He supposed that made him selfish, considering he had no claim to her. He'd probably only see her in passing, if ever, once they left this island.

"Jay and I grew up as childhood friends. In a way, we've always loved each other."

The blows kept coming. The tightening in his gut had him cringing. He had to acknowledge it as jealousy. As if he had the right.

"But it wasn't the type of love that should have led to marriage."

That threw him for a loop. Was she implying they were just friends? If so, why would they have tied the knot? There didn't seem to be any kind of financial reason, and she didn't seem the type of woman who would let something like a financial concern influence any kind of decision. Let alone a commitment like marriage. He knew about her father's cultural roots. Had that had something to do with it?

The questions hammered through his brain. As much as he wanted the answers, he resisted asking. She would share if she was ready. He'd done enough prying.

Enough time went by that he figured she wasn't ready. But then she surprised him by turning to face him. Her hands cupped under her cheek, the intensity in her eyes shone even through the darkened night.

"Someone like you wouldn't understand."

She was right about that. He didn't understand any of it. Nor could he explain his own reaction to it all. "I'd really like to."

"I didn't grow up the way most American girls do. In many ways, my family was very typical. In others, not so much."

So, it was cultural.

"My father didn't want to leave anything to chance when it came to his little girl, his only child."

"That actually sounds like pretty much any decent American dad."

He heard her inhale deeply. "Yes. And no." She blew out a breath. "He could be confusing as a parent."

Outside the glass wall, the moon slowly faded behind a cloud, casting longer darker shadows through the room.

"How so?"

"Well, for one, he made sure to instill a fierce sense of independence and strength in me. Made sure I knew how capable I was."

That much was clear in her every action, every nuance.

"But by the same token, there were all these decisions he'd made himself that he just wanted me to accept."

"Like marrying the man he'd chosen for you."

"Yes."

"What else?"

"My choice of vocation. He really grappled with the fact that I wanted to spend my life taking care of animals."

"Where was your mother in all this? Did she have any opinions?"

"My mom grew up in the Midwest. A rancher's daughter with five older brothers. Let's just say she made it a life goal to be a dutiful wife. A quality she seemed shocked that I didn't inherit from her."

"Wow. That is shocking."

"What? That I'm so different from my mother?"

"That you have five uncles," he joked, hoping it would lend a little levity to such a serious conversation. To his surprise, the remark earned him a small laugh.

"Yeah, I have like a million cousins. Holidays are fun."

"I guess my holidays will be different going forward too. Now that Lizzie's getting married. Jonathon's also got a large family." Clint only now realized the notion had been on his mind for a while, he'd just never brought it out into the forefront until now. His life was about to change almost as much as his sister's.

"You're going to make a great uncle yourself someday."

He groaned and rubbed a hand over his face. "Not anytime soon, I hope. I need some time to prep my embarrassing uncle game."

Her laugh echoed like a song through the darkness. "Why do I get the feeling you're more likely to be the uncle who shows up with armloads of gifts, spoils the kids rotten, then leaves a ridiculous mess for the parents to clean up after he's left?"

"I shall aspire to such greatness." Clint chuckled. The humor was short-lived.

"Sorry to say, my next family gathering will be as awkward and trying as the last one," Rita said, her voice so low it was barely a soft whisper.

"How come?"

"My father has barely said more than a few words to me since the divorce."

"He's angry?"

"No. Worse. He's disappointed." Maybe he'd imagined it, but he thought she might have wiped at her cheek. The thought of her crying made him wince inside.

"He's convinced I made a foolish decision in ending my marriage. That Jay and I were meant for each other and I blew it. For no discernible reason as far as he's concerned."

"Maybe you should explain your reasons then."

Her response was a long sigh. "My father isn't an easy man to talk to. I'm not sure exactly what I would say."

"I think it will come to you."

"You think so, huh?"

"I do. You still have a chance to try."

She shifted ever so slightly. "You're thinking of your own parents, aren't you?"

"I guess I am. My folks were gone often but when they were around, it was a completely different dynamic."

"In what way?"

"The world just felt whole, complete. Then suddenly it wasn't. And I had to accept the fact that life would never feel that way again."

"You were so strong, Clint."

Touching as it was, he chose to ignore her praise. He'd had no choice but to act strong. "Perhaps your dad just needs a nudge. If he's the man you've described so far, he'll come around."

"I hope so." She shifted closer to him; he could feel her sweet breath against his chin. "I've never discussed any of this with anybody before. I want you to know that."

Clint couldn't help reaching for her. He ran a gentle knuckle down her cheek, then down lower to her long graceful neck, felt her swallow under the tip of his finger. Electricity shot through his arm straight down to his feet.

"I don't know if you and your ex belonged together or not. But I can't imagine being the man who had to let you go."

Her only response was a sharp intake of breath. Clint wanted desperately to pull her to him, to rub the tension in her shoulders, tension so palpable he could see it despite the dark. He clenched his fists; he wouldn't touch her. It would be wrong to do so. She'd confided in him just now. He wouldn't betray that confidence by giving in to the desire he'd felt for her since they'd first laid eyes on each other.

His subconscious must have had other plans.

When they woke up the next morning, she was in his arms, head nuzzled against his neck. Her hair fanned like a dark silk scarf around his chest and shoulders. He didn't move a muscle for fear of waking her.

Unwilling to let her go just yet.

CHAPTER TEN

RITA SEEMED TO LIKE her showers extremely hot, judging by the steam wafting out from the bottom of the bathroom door. He tried not to imagine her behind that door, inside the shower stall, her smooth bare skin under the hot water. Was she lathering up right now, running a bar of soap over her curves?

Oh, man, he had it pretty bad.

He had to step away, before he gave in to the urge to knock and ask if she wanted company. Grabbing the pot of coffee he'd ordered earlier from room service, he poured a cup and walked onto the balcony to take in the early-morning weather. Another gorgeous day it looked like. Was there anything on the schedule wedding related? He couldn't even keep track anymore. Plus, he'd been a little distracted. In the distance, the ocean waves crashed gently along the sand of the beach. The vacant mountain was partially covered in fog, the top quarter not even visible.

The shrill sound of his cell phone in his pocket interrupted his thoughts. He pulled it out and clicked without looking at the screen. Most likely, it was Lizzie calling to give him an update. He'd left her several voice mail messages to check on her yesterday.

He was wrong. A husky, rich feminine voice greeted him when he answered.

"Did I wake you?" Maxine asked with her usual purr.

An urge to disconnect and pretend the call was dropped entered his mind. But he immediately nixed that idea. As much as he wanted to avoid this conversation, running was not his style.

"No. I've been up for a while."

She hesitated before speaking again, perhaps sensing the lack of enthusiasm in his voice. "How are things down there?"

"Fine. Everything's fine."

"And our bride? How's Lizzie faring?"

Our? Clint didn't miss the subtle meaning behind the use of the word. So now Lizzie was somehow her relation, as well. He rubbed his forehead. There was no doubt why she'd called and where this phone call was headed. Not that he'd had any doubt to begin with.

A pang of regret settled in his gut. Maxine wasn't a bad person. She really wasn't. But this thing between them had run its course.

"I've had a nightmare of a week," she told him.

Ah, so that explained the sudden call. Maxine needed a sounding board for the latest professional rejection. And someone to tell her how great she was, that whoever had turned her down was a bumbling fool of an idiot to do so.

He just didn't have the patience right now. "I'm sorry to hear that, Maxie. Hope it gets better for you."

He could almost feel her surprise bounce off the satellite and into the small speaker. "That's all you have to say? Don't you want to hear what happened? It was just awful, Clint."

He didn't have to respond. She continued without giving him a chance to, "The studio said they loved me when I went in and read. But I never even got a call back. Turns out, they've decided to go with that new Australian model who wants to break into the US movie market. I can't even believe they'd make that decision…"

Clint lost focus as she went on. Not that he didn't feel bad for her, he really did. But this was a pattern for her. A complete immersion in melancholy until the next gig came along. She had beauty, talent and connections. The next one always came along. Which is what he would have normally told her back in the United States.

Today, he didn't have the will for it. Nor the desire.

"Sorry, Maxie. You're a talented actress."

"Do you really think so?"

"I do."

He heard her sigh across the line. "You're so good for me, Clint." She paused for several beats. "I miss you."

There it was. He couldn't bring himself to answer, to lie to her. So he did the best he could. "Thank you."

Her gasp of outrage was unmistakable. "Thank you? That's what you're going to say to me?" Her question came through like the demand that it was. Demand that he apologize and thank his lucky stars that she'd deemed him worthy of the contact and this phone call.

Hard to believe a few short days ago he would have gone along, would have played the little game. Now he couldn't believe he'd ever had the patience for it.

"Sorry, Maxie," he repeated, more than ready to have this call over with.

"I accept your apology," she said with a breathless huff. "Now, I have great news for you."

"What's that?"

"I've decided I have to see you. Soon. I'm having my assistant arrange a flight right now."

Damn it. He should have seen that coming. The water shut off in the bathroom and he heard the shower stall click open. An immediate image of Rita dripping wet and naked flashed in his mind and he had to lean over the balcony railing to keep from doubling over.

Whatever Maxine was saying was a stream of static;

he couldn't even focus on her words. "Max, I don't think that's a good idea. I think we both need to move on. Individually."

"I don't understand."

Oh, honey. Sighing, he tried to wrangle his calmest, most soothing voice. "I think you do."

After listening to a stream of curse words and several insults hinting at his questionable heritage, Clint finally figured Maxine was spent for now. He told her goodbye as gently as he could and clicked off the call.

Up until a few days ago, he'd sworn all he'd ever want from a relationship was some idle companionship and a little fun. He couldn't be so certain of that conviction now. He'd shared parts of himself with Rita that he'd never opened up to anyone else. Her face was the first thing he pictured upon wakening in the morning. And the last image he had before falling asleep at night. He heard her laughter in his head and couldn't stop thinking about her when they weren't together.

Now, watching Rita as she stepped out of the bathroom with a thick terry-cloth towel wrapped around her middle and her glorious hair piled high atop her head, a wave of doubt made him wonder. About his feelings for Rita. About what he'd proposed to her on the beach after snorkeling, essentially a short-term, casual relationship for the duration of this trip. Up until now, he'd been all about such casual and meaningless relationships.

When it came to Rita, was that really enough? Or did he in fact want more?

Clint tried for the umpteenth time to focus on the column of figures his administrative assistant had emailed that morning. Rita had gone ahead to breakfast. Having been woefully negligent in answering any business emails, Clint regretfully told her he'd meet her there after responding to the more urgent messages.

A knock on the door waylaid his next attempt at concentration.

Must be the bellhop. He'd asked the front desk to bring all of Rita's stuff to his suite as soon as feasible. So she wouldn't have to keep returning to her room to retrieve various articles of clothing. It occurred to him before opening the door that he'd never actually gotten a chance to tell her about her things being moved. Well, it would be a pleasant surprise.

But the man standing across the threshold wasn't the bellhop. It was his future brother-in-law.

"Clint. We gotta talk, man."

Rita couldn't decide if the steam surrounding her was coming from the pot of hot water at the center of her table or directly out of her ears.

The man had some kind of nerve.

Clint hadn't made it down to join her yet. Which was probably not a good thing for him because the longer she sat here, the angrier she was getting. Finally, she watched him descend down the winding staircase and toward the dining area. He made a beeline when he saw her, his smile wide and cheery.

That wouldn't last.

"Hey, beautiful. Did you start without me?"

"Have a seat, Clint."

The smile faded. Pulling out a chair, he sat and folded his arms in front of him. "Something wrong?"

"As a matter of fact, there is."

"What's the matter? You look mad."

Wasn't he observant. She resisted the urge to sarcastically clap to congratulate him on it. "That's because I am."

"At me? Whatever for?"

He really had no idea. Well, she would explain then. "I went to my room before coming down for breakfast, wanting to drop off my nightclothes."

Understanding dawned in his eyes; his Adam's apple bobbed up and down as he swallowed. "And your stuff wasn't there."

"That's right. Tessa said a hotel employee had come in and asked her to gather everything that was mine. He'd been told to take it elsewhere. By you."

"Yes, I asked them to deliver it all to my suite."

"I caught the man in the hallway before he got to your door," Rita bit out, recalling how flustered the poor employee had been. Torn between following earlier directives or listening to the agitated woman telling him not to.

"I don't see the problem. I was simply trying to spare you from having to run back and forth every morning."

"That wasn't your decision. And it certainly wasn't one for you to make without even discussing it with me."

"It slipped my mind, okay? For what it's worth, it wasn't due to any kind of assumption about what I asked you yesterday."

The sudden further surge of anger had her gripping the table. "It absolutely better not have been."

"I just told you it wasn't. Why is this such a big deal?"

Did he really not see why? For heaven's sake, she'd gone to her room only to find all of her things gone. Without anyone telling her why.

Their server appeared right then, sparing him the reply Rita was about to deliver.

"What can I get for you both?"

Her appetite had evaporated but she needed something to calm the queasy waves in her stomach. "Just toast for me, thanks."

Clint ordered a meat-and-cheese omelet, then turned his attention back to her. "I'm sorry if I made an incorrect assumption," he told Rita after the woman had left. "I just figured you'd be staying with me the rest of the trip."

His words carried an intimacy they weren't quite ready for. She hadn't even given him an answer yet. More accurately, she knew *he* wasn't ready. That's why the whole fiasco with her possessions had her so wound up. He was making assumptions about the two of them, without any hint of awareness on his part. Evidently, he didn't see that.

"I simply would have appreciated some consultation before you went ahead and made decisions on my behalf."

"You are blowing this way out of proportion." His voice was hard, firm. He leaned over, rested his forearms on the table. For a moment, she felt a twinge of apprehension at the hardened glint in his eyes. Right now, he seemed irked, as well. Escalation was never a good thing.

But her point had to be made. She wasn't about to back down.

"They are my things. I decide where they stay. And nothing said I was going to spend another night in your room. I told Tessa we would make that call day to day."

"You don't want to stay in the room, just say so."

She flung her napkin on the table. "This has nothing to do with where I'm sleeping at night. That's not the point. Not at all."

"I guess I'm missing your point. Exactly what is it?"

How much clearer could she be? "Don't make decisions on my behalf. No one gave you such a right nor a claim."

His eyes grew wide. Without an answer, he pushed his chair back and stood to leave. "I've lost my appetite." Well, that made two of them.

"My door is open if you need tonight. Without any expectations whatsoever. Bring your things, don't bring them. Totally up to you."

Rita's jaw clenched with frustration. "That's my whole point."

He shook his head. "Whatever you decide, have a pleasant day."

Turning to leave, Clint only made it about one step from his chair. His sister ran down the stairs at that very moment and made her way to their table, her eyes blazing.

"Oh, no, you don't, big brother. You're not going anywhere." Lizzie pulled his chair back out. "Have a seat. We need to talk."

Okay. Rita glanced from one sibling to the other. This was something of a new, unexpected development. Looked like her own tiff with Clint was going to have to wait.

Things did not appear to be going his way this morning.

She started to get up. "I should probably give you two some privacy."

Lizzie held up a hand to stop her. "No, Rita. Please stay. I'd kind of like a third party here. It might keep me from causing too much of a scene."

Seemed a little late for that, but Rita figured she wouldn't voice that out loud.

Even given her displeasure with him at the moment, Rita shot Clint a questioning look. She wasn't going to stay if it made him uncomfortable. He gave her a small affirmative nod.

"What exactly did you say to my fiancé this morning?" Lizzie demanded of her brother.

"Hey, settle your tone there, sis."

"Just tell me what you said to him."

"He came down to talk to me. Maybe you should be having a conversation with him. Whatever it's about."

Rita found herself fascinated. An only child, she had no firsthand knowledge of sibling angst. Whatever Clint had said to Jonathon, it appeared Lizzie was ready to thrash him for it.

"Oh, I did talk to him," Lizzie said. "It seems he's working for you now."

"So?"

Lizzie slammed both hands on the table. The couple at the neighboring table gave them a startled glance. "So? Why would you offer my fiancé a job? First of all, he's an attorney. You own a construction firm. How blatantly obvious that it's nothing more than a nepotistic gesture."

"I consult with attorneys all the time."

"International law attorneys? You need one of those in-house, do you?"

"Look," Clint began, "he came to me to say he's been edgy and worried. It's why he's been snapping at you. Things aren't going well at work for him. He thinks his days at the law firm may be numbered."

"I know all that."

That seemed to take Clint aback. "You do?"

"Of course, I do. He's my fiancé. We actually share our fears and joys and concerns with each other."

"Then why did he come to see me?"

"Not to ask you for a job!"

"Then what?"

"Nothing. He wasn't asking you for anything. He simply wanted to explain to his fiancée's brother why he might be behaving on edge lately."

Clint squinted against the sun. "Huh."

"But somehow you offered him a job and I'm guessing you didn't take no for an answer."

"Hold on. That's not how it went down."

Lizzie's mouth tightened. "Right. Because you're never overbearing and assuming at all." Sarcasm dripped from her lips.

"If he didn't want the job, he could have just said so."

"Clint. He said he tried. But you just acted like you'd solved everything and showed him the door. Guess what, bro?"

"What?"

"He doesn't want to work for his brother-in-law. He wants to find his own way out of this."

Rita didn't miss the clear sense of pride in Lizzie's voice. Clint must have heard it too. It was hard to miss.

"But now he has all sorts of doubts. Thanks to you."

"What? Why?"

"Now he can't help but think maybe he should take your offer. Because how would he feel if nothing panned out for him and he'd turned you down?"

Clint shrugged, gave his sister a look like she was missing something terribly obvious. "Just tell him the offer stands whenever he wants it."

Wow. Rita wanted to grab his shoulders and give him a hard shake. Not only had he missed the point, it had blown right past him without even entering the strike zone. Lizzie visibly deflated in her chair.

"Oh, Clint," his sister began. "Don't you know what telling him that would do to him? How much worse it would make all this?"

Clint threw his hands up with exasperation. "Fine, go tell him the offer is rescinded. To forget I ever made it."

He really didn't get it, Rita thought. An unwelcome twinge of sympathy stirred in her heart. At this point, she couldn't tell if she felt worse for him or Lizzie. Or even Jonathon. Clint was somehow internally programed to solve any issue he came across. Whether people wanted solutions from him or not.

Lizzie slowly stood, every inch of her dripping resignation. "Enjoy your breakfast, big brother."

She gave Rita a small wave and turned on her heel to leave.

Clint watched her back for several moments before clearing his throat.

Rita scrambled for something to say. Anything. The words failed her. Lizzie was right; she knew that. But there was something so defeated in Clint as he'd watched his sister leave, Rita couldn't help but feel moved by it. Her earlier anger at him notwithstanding.

"You'll have to excuse me," he told her, then stood and walked away in the opposite direction. Away from his sister.

And away from her.

It took all his will not to punch a hole in the wall when Clint got back to his room. Was every female in his orbit put there just to vex him? He plopped himself down on the unmade bed and tried to clear the fog of confusion from his head. Just a few short hours ago, he was lying in this very spot with Rita's soft, supple body nestled against him.

Now he wasn't even sure if they were on speaking terms. And for what? Because he hadn't wanted her inconvenienced.

As for his sister, he couldn't even fathom that one. He really thought Jonathon had come to him looking for help with his next position. How was he supposed to know the man simply needed to vent?

Usually when people came to him directly it was absolutely because they needed something. And unlike Rita, when he did something he thought was considerate, usually they were thankful. Not ready to bite his head off like she'd clearly wanted to.

He needed to get out of here. Out of this room, away from this resort. Though the sun was already bright and hot and it was probably way too steamy for a run, he figured he needed it. Or he really would punch a wall.

Pulling on his running shoes, he made his way out of the hotel and onto the beach. The next forty-five minutes was a grueling stretch of self-torture. Clint was near heaving for breath by the time he made it back. It was worth it. Every ounce of exertion had helped to vent his frustration and clear his head. He'd almost been able to eradicate the image of Rita shooting proverbial daggers at him this morning. Almost.

Despite his good intentions, she was rip-roaring mad at him. And so was his sister.

Clint rubbed the sweat off his forehand with the back of his arm and made his way to the elevator. He had to go see Lizzie. Then he had to clear things up with Jonathon. He couldn't have this hanging over their heads during the wedding. He'd do a mea culpa, even if he couldn't quite grasp exactly what his transgression was.

With reluctance but determination, he punched the floor Lizzie's room was on and knocked on her door moments later.

"Come in. It's not locked."

He wondered if she would be granting entry if she knew it was him. Opening the door, he hesitantly ducked his head in. "You sure I'm welcome?"

His sister sat at a vanity, her arms outstretched in front of her. Several bowls of liquid sat in front of her along with a variety of brushes and colored pencils like he'd never seen before. Lizzie motioned for him to come inside. He did so and shut the door behind him.

Then stopped in his tracks when Rita suddenly walked out of the bathroom. What was she doing here? She carried a glass bowl with some type of reddish pudding concoction.

She quirked an eyebrow at him when she saw him.

"Am I interrupting something?" Clint asked. "You doing each other's nails?" Great, maybe they were bonding over their mutual disgust of all things Clint Fallon.

"Rita's giving me henna tattoos. A bridal design in honor of my wedding."

"A hen of *what*?"

Rita shot an exaggerated eye roll in his direction. "A henna. Tattoo."

As if that cleared it up. "Right."

"Here, I'll show you," Lizzie said and lifted her foot.

He drew closer to see an elaborate array of designs adorning her right ankle. It was a complicated design of swirls and patterns, drawn in some type of orange-reddish ink. He'd never seen anything like it.

"You did that?" he asked Rita, incredulous.

"She sure did," Lizzie answered. "She's going to do my hands next."

He was beyond impressed. Considering the skin on a human foot wasn't the smoothest, particularly around the ankle, the design showed a tremendous amount of detail and a very steady hand. Though, he shouldn't be surprised. After all, part of her profession was performing surgery on small animals. But the pattern on his sister's foot said she also had a striking amount of artistic skill.

"Wow." It was the only word he could summon.

"Amazing, isn't she?"

Yeah, she certainly was. Every time he turned around, she seemed to do something or say something that drove that point home. He studied her now as she sat down on the velvet seat of a short metal stool in front of his sister. She dipped one of the wooden sticks in the bowl of pudding and began to work on Lizzie's right hand.

"You're very sweaty." Rita finally addressed him, throwing the comment over her shoulder without looking at him.

"Yeah, I, uh, went for a run."

"Did it help?"

"Yes. It helped a lot. Which is why I'm here." Clint focused his gaze on his sister's face. "Look, the last thing I want is to have you upset with me as I'm walking you down the aisle."

Lizzie pursed her lips, as if she were holding back a sob. Damn it. He didn't need that. He could handle her anger way better than he could deal with her sadness. "I don't want that either, big brother."

"I'll clear the air with Jonathon. I'll find him later and buy him a beer. Or maybe one of those Hawaiian mai tais."

"The ones they bring out all aflame?"

He grinned, relieved that things seemed to be smoothing over. "Yeah. Those ones. Better yet, I'll make him buy me one."

"I think he'd like that, Clint."

"Good. Don't give the whole job thing another thought, all right?"

"It's a deal." She suddenly smiled wide and looked down to where Rita was painstakingly drawing on her hand. "Hey, I think Clint needs a henna tattoo also. What do you think?"

Uh-oh. What had he just walked into here? Rita stopped what she was doing.

"I suppose. It's not typically something men have done."

"My brother is far from typical. Have a seat," she ordered. "She'll do you as soon as she's finished with mine."

Turned out, that didn't take long. Lizzie jumped up when she was finished and admired the artwork. "I'm going to go find Jonathon and show him. Do Clint's now," she directed before leaving the room.

An awkward silence hung in the air when it was just the two of them. Clint blew out a breath. "I don't know. I've never had a henna tattoo before. Don't think I really want one now. But what the bride wants…"

"The bride gets," Rita finished for him. "Here." She motioned for him to sit.

"That looks really sharp," Clint commented on the wooden stick she'd picked up.

"Don't worry. I'm not planning on stabbing you with it. Though the thought has occurred to me."

"Um…thanks?"

"Let's just say it's a good thing you knew enough to make amends with Lizzie just now."

He tried not to react as her soft, warm fingers moved over his skin while she worked. Sweet heavens. How was he supposed to sit still and resist the temptation to turn around and yank her into his arms when she was touching him like this?

He tried to focus on the conversation. "At the risk of a stab, I'm going to admit that my apology was more to regain the peace than any kind of actual understanding about what I did that was so wrong."

Her fingers stilled. "You honestly don't know?"

"I thought I was helping, Rita."

Her voice was soft when she spoke again as she resumed slowly working on his back. "That's not what Jonathon came to you for. Nor what he needed."

"How was I supposed to know that?"

She leaned closer, her tempting breath hot against his ear. "Perhaps you could have listened."

"I thought I had. And what I heard was that he needed a more secure job. Why would I not offer that to him when I can?"

"Because it only served to make you feel better."

Harsh.

"You're used to taking over," Rita continued. "You're used to exerting control in order to fix things. Whether the situation calls for it or not. You did the same thing when you thought I needed my things to be moved into your suite."

Why was that so wrong? "Yeah, well, I guess I had to learn from a young age that someone had to take the lead when things needed fixing. My parents were gone and the grandmother in charge of us could barely take care of herself." He bit out a curse. The last thing he wanted was to sound defensive. She wouldn't understand. For all their faults, Rita had grown up with two very involved parents—perhaps overly involved—who made sure to give her stability and structure. He'd done his best to do the same for his sister, for better or worse. "Lizzie never fully appreciated what it took to just survive back in those days." Which was fine with him. It was bad enough that one of them was terrified about the uncertainty of their future. Lizzie was too busy grieving to fully comprehend exactly how tenuous their reality had become. He'd had to be the one to plan for their future, to make sure they'd be safe and secure. Their grandmother certainly couldn't be counted on. All the burden had fallen like a ton of bricks securely on Clint's shoulders. No, he'd never talked to Lizzie back then about all the nights he'd lain awake, fighting off near-crippling anxiety. And Lord knew there wasn't anyone else to talk to.

Several beats passed before Rita answered, "Perhaps she would have understood, if you'd bothered to ever tell her."

He hadn't seen any point in that. "She had enough to contend with. I didn't want her bothered with anything more than she had to."

"Hmm. And despite that tendency of yours, Lizzie has still managed to turn into quite a competent and mature young lady."

Clint gave his head a shake. Despite? "What's that supposed to mean?"

She released a deep sigh and he could feel her warm breath against his shoulder and upper back. "It means that you were an incredibly competent guardian for your sister. Anyone can see that, Clint."

"But?"

"But people need room to grow and make their own

mistakes. And often all they're looking for is some reassurance and emotional support."

He couldn't come up with a response to that. Of course she had a point. But he didn't have many choices back then. He could only do what he thought was right. No one had been there to guide him after all. And what did any of it matter now anyway? All past history not worth revisiting.

It took about another half hour for her to finish, where she mostly worked in silence. Half an hour of divine torture and temptation. Her fingers deftly moving over his skin. The warm touch of her hands on his back.

Finally, she stood. "You're done."

"Thanks."

He stole a look in the mirror. His jaw dropped.

"Not what you were expecting?"

She'd drawn an elaborate rendering of...of all things... a butterfly. He groaned out loud. "Great. This will look wonderful on the beach. I'll feel so manly as I sport my fresh butterfly tattoo."

She had the audacity to giggle. "You'll get used to it. Maybe after a year or two."

A year! Or two!

"Whoa. Wait a minute. This is permanent?"

"I thought you knew."

Clint felt a moment of panic, then noticed the smile tugging at the corners of her lips. She was a lousy actress. "Sorry, couldn't resist."

"Ha ha. Can we say we're even then?"

"Even?"

She had to know what he meant. He wanted to put the argument of the morning behind them as well as the whole conversation they'd just had. He wanted to go back to the moment they'd woken up with her embraced in his arms.

A soft sigh escaped her lips. "You're a tough man to stay angry at, Clint Fallon. Yes, I suppose we're even."

* * *

That was definitely her up there.

Clint squinted up into the sun at the top of the rock cliff on the edge of the resort property. The same rock cliff that the resort guests jumped off into the ocean. It had taken him several beats to make sure but that was definitely Rita climbing to the top. Apparently, today was the day she made the jump herself. He couldn't help but recall the afternoon three days ago when they'd held hands and launched themselves together into one of the Seven Sacred Pools.

Looked like she wanted to do this one alone.

He'd been looking for Jonathon, who was supposed to be out on the beach somewhere, soaking up some last rays of sun as a free man before he said his vows tomorrow. But Clint's eyes had inexplicably been drawn to the rock wall, as if he'd sensed her presence there. Now she was gracefully ambling closer to the top. All thoughts of Jonathon forgotten, Clint made his way closer to the wall. There was a line of people waiting on top of it to go before her. Hopefully, that would give him enough time to reach a spot where he could watch her jump from fairly close by. A ridiculous part of him wished she'd asked him to go with her, wished that he was up there right now waiting to take the plunge with her in the way they had that day at the Seven Sacred Pools.

Well, he'd take the next best thing. He'd surprise her by greeting her with a dry, ready towel when she swam out afterward. Taking a quick detour to a resort shack, he grabbed two beach towels. He reached the side of the beach wall just as the person in front of Rita jumped in.

Her turn. Even from this distance he could see her anticipation; excitement was visible in her stance and posture. Taking a step back, he watched as she held her arms in front of her in an arch above her head. In the next instant, she launched herself headfirst into the water. A clean dive that hardly made a splash. If he wasn't worried about looking foolish to the beachgoers around him, he would have actually clapped.

Nothing was going to stop him from giving her a round of applause when she came out. Which didn't seem to be anytime soon. Clint waited as several moments went by. He still didn't see anyone out there who could be Rita. Had she broken the surface further down and he'd missed her?

That didn't seem likely. He'd been watching carefully for her.

A worrisome spike of apprehension stabbed his heart. He knew she was a good swimmer but what was taking so long? Even jumpers who'd gone in after her were already out and swimming to shore.

Deep breaths. He had to get a grip here. She hadn't been under that long. And she'd proven herself more than comfortable in the water both during their snorkeling adventure and when they'd swum at various spots on the Road to Hana.

But the nagging sensation in his chest persisted. He had to do something. He'd never forgive himself if something had gone wrong with her jump and he was just standing here like a dolt.

The wall was rough and jagged. It had to be that way under the water too. Rita could have very well hit her head.

The idea of that possibility and the image it evoked made up his mind. Kicking his sandals off, he dropped the towels and made a mad rush toward the water. He swam several feet faster than he would have thought possible then dived under when he got closer to the diving spot.

No sign of her.

Clint's heart pounded in his chest. He'd waited too long. He should have jumped as soon as it had occurred to him that she might be hurt. Sucking in a deep breath he dived under once more. Salt water stung his eyes and burned his throat as he stayed under too long to keep searching.

This couldn't be happening to him twice in one lifetime. To lose his parents in a boating accident was more than tragic enough. Fate couldn't be so utterly, shatteringly cruel.

He had to break the surface again, needed another lungful of air. There was nothing for it. Panic set in his veins, his heart hammering from exertion and fear.

It seemed to take forever to kick back to the top. A familiar face met him when he finally got there.

"Hey, Clint." She flashed him a brilliant smile. "I thought that was you. Did you see me jump?"

The sudden surge of relief he felt was almost instantaneously replaced with a blazingly intense fury.

"What the hell were you thinking?" Without waiting for an answer, he swam back toward the beach.

She was fast on his heels when he got there. "What exactly is your problem?" she asked.

Clint grabbed one of the towels he'd dropped on the sand earlier and handed it to her. She grasped it none too gently out of his hand even as she uttered a begrudging thank-you.

Leaning down, he grabbed the second one for himself. It was covered in grainy sand now—thanks to the wind—and the chafing sensation as he tried to dry off only served to irritate his nerves even further.

"I asked you what your problem is," Rita repeated. "Is there a reason you came into the water to yell at me?"

"My problem is that I thought you might be floating out to sea about to become a tasty morsel of shark food."

She stalled in the act of towel drying her hair. "What? Why in the world would you think that?"

"Because you didn't come up. Do you have any idea how long you were under?"

She gave a slight shrug. "I stayed under as long as I could."

"Whatever for?" To give him a heart attack perhaps?

Her jaw clenched. "I appreciate that you were worried. But you needn't keep yelling at me. As you can see, I'm perfectly fine. There was no reason for you to come after me. And no reason at all for the way you're behaving now."

Clint sucked in a breath trying to calm himself. It didn't work. She had no idea how much of a scare she'd just caused.

The thought of her hurt, struggling under the water had unnerved him unlike anything else he could recall.

She really had no clue.

"Why would you even do such a thing by yourself?" He realized people were starting to stare but he couldn't seem to lower his voice. The panic still pounded through his system.

"Not that I owe you an explanation. But I've been wanting to do that jump for days and there weren't that many people up there for once." She crossed her arms in front of her chest. "And frankly, I'm starting to feel a little resentful at your tone. It's really none of your business who I jump with, if anyone at all."

Resentful? None of his business?

That was it. Between her inflated reaction this morning to the moved luggage and the vitriol she was feeding him right now, he'd had it.

"You know what, Rita? I believe you're right." He picked up his shirt and sandals. "Feel free to spend the night in the suite if you want. Or not. It's up to you. If not, I guess I'll see you at the wedding."

He didn't give her a chance to respond.

Of all the...

Rita watched Clint's retreating back as he stomped away down the beach. All she'd wanted to do was take a refreshing plunge into the water. Then, as she was under, a glorious sea turtle had swum by, so close she could have reached out and touched it. A truly magnificent, breath-taking beauty of a creature she didn't want to stop admiring. So she'd stayed down there as long as she could. Until her lungs had started to squeeze in her chest and her cells had begun to cry out in protest for oxygen.

Okay, so maybe it had been a little long. But if Clint had just taken the time to listen, she could have explained all that. She might have even asked him to go back in with her so that they could look for it together. Maybe she would have confided that he was the first person she thought of sharing the experience with, had even felt a pang of longing to have him there with her. He hadn't even given her a chance to speak.

Instead, he'd chosen to stand on a public beach, in front of countless people, and loudly chastise her.

In fact, it had been his first reaction. To be domineering and overbearing, two traits she'd had more than her fair share of in her life up until now. Way more than enough.

No more.

She hadn't gone through the trauma of divorce and the sorrow of estrangement with her father to turn around and embrace more of the same from someone else.

So why was she fighting such a strong urge to run and catch up to him? To grab him by the arm and tell him she was sorry he'd been so worried about her.

Why did her eyes suddenly sting and a painful lump form in her throat?

Because she was a fanciful nitwit who'd gone and developed feelings for a man who was utterly wrong for her. At a time when she shouldn't even be entertaining such a notion.

She'd been trying so hard to deny it. But she'd been unable to think of anything or anyone else since she'd woken up in his arms this morning.

The feel of his body wrapped around hers elicited emotions and longings she had no business feeling.

And all afternoon, her mind had replayed the hour in Lizzie's room when she'd drawn on his shoulder. The feel of his skin under her fingers. The woodsy, masculine scent of him mixed with the salty air he'd just been running in.

His surprised and bemused face when he'd realized what she'd tattooed on him. The butterfly had been a whim. He'd spoken of the butterfly effect that night before they'd traveled alone together down the Road to Hana to return the rock.

He hadn't made the connection. And why should he? She'd obviously given it way too much thought. Spent too much time analyzing what would have happened if she'd never walked into that lounge at the airport. Or if he'd flown down in a private aircraft as per his usual routine. So many variables could have been even slightly altered and they would never have even crossed paths until the first wedding excursion. He most likely wouldn't have given her a second glance.

The same way he hadn't all those years ago when she'd first met him as a college coed.

CHAPTER ELEVEN

THE BEACH CHAIR wasn't so bad. At least as comfortable as the couch in Clint's suite. But definitely not as comfortable as his bed. Not that Rita was going to allow herself to think about being in his bed right now. Spending the night there was absolutely not an option this time. Not after their little exchange this afternoon due to her cliff-jumping adventure. Her pride would not allow it.

This was just fine; it wasn't even that cold out here on the beach. Only when the wind blew really hard did it get a little chilly. She could deal with that. For the next few hours she would just lie here with a big beach towel wrapped around her until Tessa's text let her know she could return to their room.

This time, she'd made Tessa promise not to fall asleep and forget.

Who needed Clint Fallon? Certainly not her.

She clung to that thought as the temperature gradually dipped lower over the next hour and a half. Her patience wearing thin, she double-checked her phone in case she'd missed Tessa's message.

Nothing.

All right. That was it. Tessa would get a few more minutes tops. Half an hour at the most. Then she was going to her room whether the other woman liked it or not. At this point, she didn't even care if Rob was still in there with her.

She was so tired and sleepy, she probably wouldn't even be able to stay awake long enough to witness anything.

Somehow, despite the chattering of her teeth, she managed to doze off. She wasn't even sure how much time had gone by when a set of strong, warm arms suddenly reached around her middle. She felt herself being hoisted up, then nestled against a hard, blessedly warm chest. She immediately recognized his scent, even through the haze of groggy slumber.

Clint. Of course. "Hey."

"Hi, sweetheart."

"How did you find me?"

"I checked the lounge area but you weren't there. Then I just knew."

"You did?"

He shrugged, lifting her slightly higher and tighter against him. "Yeah, I don't really know how to explain it. It was like something led me directly to where you were."

"Huh."

"I know it's hard to believe."

Rita recalled the night after she'd picked up the rock. The eerie sensation that someone, or something, was there with her in that room. Trying to tell her something almost. How her shorts had ended up on the floor outside her closet. "I do believe you," she told him.

She leaned into his chest and snuggled further into his welcome warmth.

"Babe, I'm sorry." Clint spoke in her ear, his hot breath warming her cheek. "I want to kick myself that you felt the need to sleep out here."

"I wasn't going to all night. I was going to demand the use of my bed in just a few minutes. As soon as Tessa and Rob are finished." She stifled a giggle, not even sure what she was amused by. Now she was just downright giddy.

"You don't need to do that."

What was he referring to? Between being so cold and half-asleep, it was so hard to focus. "Do what?"

"Demand the use of your bed. You'll be sleeping in mine."

The whole first floor of the resort was deserted when they walked through. Before she knew it, they were somehow in Clint's suite and he was gently depositing her on the bed. She snuggled deep into the soft pillow as he tucked the covers around her.

"I'm sorry," she whispered into the darkness. "For earlier. For scaring you."

"Oh, sweetheart. I should have handled it better."

"You were angry."

She sensed more than saw him shaking his head. "It was more that I was scared."

Something had been nagging at her all evening. She should have thought about Clint's history, the way he'd lost his parents. She felt like a selfish, inconsiderate brat. No wonder he'd been so upset. "Your mom and dad died in a boating accident, didn't they?"

He blew out a breath. "Yeah, they were vacationing off the coast of Greece. Got caught in an unpredicted Mediterranean squall." He flinched as he softly recounted the memories. "They were always off somewhere, exploring the world. Just the two of them."

While their two children were foisted on a grandmother who didn't want them around, Rita thought. Only to be stuck with them permanently when tragedy hit.

"And one day they left and never returned."

"I'm so sorry you and Lizzie had to endure that."

He rubbed a hand down his face. "Ironically, that was the year Lizzie had a starring role in the middle school play. She'd begged them not to go."

Rita felt a surge of tenderness for her friend. The loss of her mother and father at such a critical age must have been unbearable. And what of poor Clint? In many ways, being the older sibling, he had it so much harder. Her heart ached for the young man he must have been. A young man suddenly stranded with more responsibility than he could have dreamed. And he'd accepted it with grace and dignity.

"Lizzie mentioned what happened two or three times while we were at school," she told him. "I didn't push for details. I got the impression she didn't really like talking about it."

"She doesn't. And I can't say as I blame her. We both had to deal with their loss and move on as best we could."

He made it sound so simple. Perhaps deep down, he really believed it actually was.

"The adults you and Lizzie have both turned into despite all that is beyond impressive. Commendable."

"Thank you for saying that, sweet Rita."

Suddenly, Clint stood and turned to go.

She didn't want him to. "Clint, wait."

"Yeah?"

"Where are you going?"

He leaned over her to brush a loose strand of hair off her forehead, let his hand linger at her temple. "I'll go sleep on the couch. You know, in the interest of harmony."

She took his hand in hers before he could pull it away. "Stay."

It was the perfect day and setting for a wedding.

Rita followed the rest of the bridal procession to an archway covered in gorgeous tropical flowers on the beach. A small band behind them consisting of ukuleles and various drums played an island version of the wedding theme. All in all, the scene could have been out of a bridal magazine. Or a young girl's fantasy. When they reached the front, the groomsmen broke off to one side, while she and the other bridesmaids went to stand opposite.

Then Clint walked out with his sister from a covered canopy, leading her down the aisle. Rita had to remind herself to breathe. She hadn't seen Clint since this morning when they'd woken up in each other's arms again after having easily fallen asleep together the night before. Then the hectic pace of wedding preparation had immediately taken hold of them all. Now looking at him in a form-fitting tux with a Hawaiian flower in the lapel, she almost felt light-headed.

He had to be the most handsome, alluring man she'd ever known. And she'd have to say goodbye to him in about forty-eight hours.

Rita swallowed down the lump of sadness that settled in her throat. All fantasies came to an end. There was no use in wallowing. Served her right for letting her guard down and falling for a man who wanted nothing but freedom. On the heels of a failed marriage no less. Well, it seemed to follow a pattern of awful timing she'd somehow fallen into. Her first goal upon returning home would have to be to break out of it.

Lizzie beamed as she approached her groom, her smile as bright as the glowing Hawaiian sun above. Her dress was a delicate lacy piece that seemed to float around her as she walked. A tiara of beautiful flowers adorned her head and framed her angelic face. When they reached the archway, Clint gave his sister a soft peck on the cheek before putting her hand into Jonathon's outstretched one. As he walked toward the other groomsmen, he looked up to catch Rita's eye. The depth of emotion she saw in his gaze almost made her knees buckle.

How in the world was she supposed to go back to any semblance of a normal life after this? How was she supposed to live day to day as if none of this happened? While thinking of him every moment? For she had no doubt she'd be doing just that.

She'd gone and fallen in love with him. Who knew, perhaps it had been years in the making, since she'd first laid eyes on the man all those years ago. Now, with all the time they'd spent together in such close quarters, her feelings had developed into so much more.

She hadn't given him an answer. They still had two more days on Maui. To his credit, Clint hadn't even brought up the proposition he'd so casually made the other day. But she hadn't forgotten. She had no doubt he hadn't forgotten either.

The rest of the ceremony seemed to go by in a daze.

She watched Clint clap as the officiator finally pronounced Lizzie and Jonathon man and wife. He'd done so well by his sister, Rita thought. From a young age he'd taken care of her, made sure she prospered and thrived. Now he'd given her the most dreamlike wedding.

He was sure to make his own bride a very lucky lady one day. Though he swore he wanted to remain single, there was no question that someday someone would come along who refused to let him go. A wise, clever woman would make it her life's goal to figure out how to snare him for good. Rita couldn't help but envy her.

In the meantime, did she have it in her to take the little he was willing to give?

"May I have the honor of this dance?"

Rita looked up to find Clint holding out his arm to her as she sat watching the bride and groom canoodling at the head table. The reception was in full swing now. Even random strangers walking along the beach had joined in the revelry. A couple of local residents were doing an impressive luau dance, their hips moving so fast it made Rita's pelvis hurt just watching them.

Taking Clint's hand, she followed him out to the dance floor. As if by fate, the bouncy rhythmic reggae number that had been playing suddenly switched to a slow Hawaiian love song.

Clint took her gently by the waist and pulled her tight against him. A curl of heat unwound deep in her belly and moved in every which direction.

"Hard to believe they're finally married," she offered by way of conversation.

He laughed against her cheek. "I was really worried for a while there that it might not happen."

"I always had faith," she countered. "In those two and in the spirits."

"Is that so?"

"Mmm-hmm. I knew the spirits wouldn't let us down." Not when it came to the wedding anyway. As far as her heart, the spirits had apparently decided she was on her own. It had been slowly breaking since she'd run into Clint back on the mainland.

She nodded against his neck, resisted the urge to nestle closer and inhale deeply of his scent. She wouldn't be able to enjoy it much longer.

She pulled back to look him in the eye. "Clint, I haven't forgotten what you asked me."

He merely nodded, waiting for her to continue.

"I know I haven't given you an answer yet. I'm not sure that I can, even after all this time."

"Which is in itself answer enough, isn't it?"

Rita swallowed past the painful lump that suddenly formed at the base of her throat. This was so much harder than she'd expected. The truth was, she just couldn't do it, she couldn't have a casual affair. Not with him. Her heart was already lost to Clint Fallon. She couldn't bear to turn her soul over to him, as well. For that's what accepting his offer would do. She would never recover afterward, not when she had to walk away from him as if none of it mattered.

For several quiet moments, they just held each other, swaying softly to the music. Rita didn't trust herself to speak.

"So what's next for you, Sarita Paul?" he surprised her by asking. "Once we all return to reality, I mean."

"I guess I've got a lot to figure out."

"Well, if you're ever in the area," he said against her cheek. "You know the rest."

Something broke in the vicinity of her heart, an actual sensation of snapping that had her struggling for breath. How could he be so casual, so matter-of-fact about whether he would ever see her again? She had to get away before she made a fool of herself by sobbing into his chest.

She slipped out of his grasp and ran toward the crashing waves of the water. It didn't surprise her when his footsteps sounded in the sand behind her seconds later.

"Rita." He spoke her name softly, like a whisper on the wind.

"I'd like to be alone for a while."

"There are some things we should discuss, don't you think?"

She didn't dare turn to face him, afraid of what her face might give away. "Like what? Like how I should look you up when I'm in town? Is that what you'd like to discuss?" she asked over her shoulder.

It was no use. He came to clasp her by the shoulders and turned her to face him.

"You have a lot to figure out. You said so yourself. It would be selfish of me to stand in the way of that."

"Don't pretend that's why you're doing this, Clint. Please give me more credit than that."

He blinked at her.

"Why would you say that?" He seemed genuinely perplexed. For such a smart, accomplished man, he really could be very obtuse. Or he was working really hard at it.

"You're letting yourself off the hook by pretending this is all about me."

He let go of her shoulders and shoved his hands into his pockets. The action had the effect of pulling his shirt tight against the toned muscles of his chest and widening the V at his collar where he'd undone two buttons. The overall look was so devilishly handsome, she wanted nothing more than to forget this conversation and fling herself into his arms.

But that would only serve to prolong the inevitable.

"It's really more about you. And how scared you are."

He didn't meet her gaze, stared at the sand beneath their feet. "What exactly do you think I'm so afraid of, Rita? Please enlighten me."

She ignored the snark in his tone. "Of loving someone and then losing them. It's why you strive so hard to control what's around you. Who's around you. But you can't control human beings, Clint. Nor their feelings."

He looked up, off to the horizon and the setting sun behind her. His next words proved she was right about everything she'd just said.

"You may have a point. It doesn't change anything."

"How can you say that?" she pleaded, hating the sobbing quality of her voice.

"I was clear from the beginning, sweetheart. This was one week on an exotic tropical island. Reality is what it is."

The breaking in her chest she'd felt earlier turned into a violent shatter. "So that's it then? You're going to let fear and uncertainty keep you from moving forward? You're so ready to just turn your back on any feelings that you may find inconvenient."

His eyes narrowed on her face. "And what about you, Rita?"

"What about me?"

"You're not exactly in a position to cast stones."

What was he talking about? She wasn't the one ready to walk away from what they were beginning to feel for each other. Feelings she knew he had to be experiencing also. Or else what did that say about her?

"I have no idea what you mean."

"You really don't see it?"

"See what?"

"Let me ask you something. Exactly how have you moved forward since your divorce?"

What did Jay or her divorce have to do with anything? "What are you insinuating? Maybe you should just come out and say it."

He bit out a curse. "Fine. You're stuck in a holding pattern. Too afraid to move, too afraid to risk another chance at letting others down."

She sucked in some much-needed air. "You have no idea what you're saying. You don't know what it took to sever my marriage, the pain and anguish it caused me and to those around me."

"You're right. It did take a lot of courage. So now what?"

Rita wanted to slam her hands up against her ears. Suddenly, this conversation had turned into one about her. And all her shortcomings as far as Clint was concerned.

The way he saw her was breaking her heart.

He didn't wait for a response. Shaking his head, he continued, "You said you'd thought years ago about opening your own practice. Or maybe working for an animal shelter. Yet you plan on looking for another small office to join when you return. How is that any different than what you were originally trying to get away from?"

"It's very different."

He shrugged. "Is it? Perhaps. I guess I wouldn't know. But it's not what you really want."

"I'm trying to figure out what I want."

"So you say."

She willed the tears that now stung her eyes to keep from falling. He thought she was indecisive and weak. It hurt more than she would have thought.

"And what about your father?" he demanded to know.

"What about him?"

"You've stood up to him. And your relationship suffered. What are you going to do about it now?"

"We just need time," she cried out.

"And it will all miraculously work itself out?" he said with a questioning shrug. "Face it. You're stuck and it's because you've chosen to be. Both in terms of your career and your relationships."

"You have no idea what you're saying."

"I think I do. It's like you've made the climb up onto that cliff. But you're still just standing there, not ready to jump but not willing to climb back down."

So that's how he really saw her. The revelation felt like a physical blow. Lifting her chin, she summoned her voice despite the pain, despite the anger. "At least I made the climb, Clint. Look around you and see if you can say the same."

Something shifted behind his eyes; they suddenly grew darker. She thought he started to reach for her, but it was too late. Rita stepped away and strode past him as far as she could before she had to catch her breath. Maybe it made her a coward but she had to flee. Before he could hurt her anymore.

Clint glanced at his watch and scanned the outdoor reception area once more. There was no sign of her. She'd stormed away from him about two hours ago. And now it was almost midnight and he hadn't seen her since.

He'd already checked her room and tried calling her repeatedly. Man, he really shouldn't have gone off on her like that. Now that he'd cooled down, he figured he should find her and try to apologize. But she was nowhere to be found.

As much as he didn't want to worry his sister on her wedding night, he was going to have to ask her if she knew where Rita was. Either that or he was ready to call the authorities and round up a search party.

He approached Lizzie where she stood by a buffet table feeding Jonathon various pieces of fruit.

"Hey, sis, got a sec?"

"For my big brother? Always."

"You're leaving me here alone?" Jonathon petulantly asked. "It's our wedding night. I thought we might retire soon."

Lizzie gave him a hard kiss on the lips. "I won't be long. You wait right here for me."

Clint bit down on the nausea that little exchange invoked and pulled his sister to the side.

"Sorry for the interruption. And I don't want to worry you, but I haven't seen Rita in several hours. She's not answering her phone. Have you heard from her?"

Lizzie's smile faded and her face fell. "Oh, Clint. You don't know?"

A bad feeling started to bloom in his chest. "Know what?"

"Rita decided she'd been away from home too long. Asked if I'd mind if she left a couple days early."

"She's gone?"

Lizzie nodded; lines of sympathy etched her eyes. "Now that the reception is over, I told her it was fine. Apparently, there are some pressing matters she needs to address back home. She's taking the red-eye out. You two didn't discuss it?"

He could only shake his head.

"I'm surprised she didn't say anything to you."

"Not a thing." Not directly anyway. Indirectly, she'd

told him everything he needed to know. And then she'd just up and left. Without so much as a word of goodbye.

Well, what did he expect? After the way he'd confronted her earlier, she would have had every right to slap him before storming off. And he would have deserved it.

"I'm sorry, big brother." He could barely hear Lizzie over the sudden roaring in his ears. "If I'd realized you didn't know, I would have come to find you right away."

Rita was gone. "It's not your fault. You should get back to your groom."

"What about you?"

He shrugged. "I'll be fine, just need some salty air." Turning, Clint made his way toward the beach, toward the spot he'd stood arguing with Rita. Was that the last spot he would ever see her? The notion sent a painful stab in the area of his chest.

Lizzie was following him. He turned around to give her a questioning look. They'd reached the beach.

"What happened between you two?"

"Nothing you need to concern yourself with. Not now of all times. You just got married for heaven's sake."

"That may be so. But I'll always have time for my big brother."

Clint forced a smile and crouched down in front of the crashing waves. To his surprise, Lizzie dropped down next to him, sitting right on her bottom in the sand. She pulled her wedding dress tighter around her as a small gust of wind carried over from the water.

"I've known Rita for years," she began. "She's one in a million. Whatever went wrong, I'm guessing it was completely the result of you being your usual foolhardy and rigid self."

His sister could be quite blunt. "My only defense is I never tried to lead her to believe otherwise."

"I see. And you think that absolves you somehow?"

He rubbed a hand down his face. "I don't know what I think," he answered truthfully. "This was all supposed to be so simple, so straightforward."

"And all within your control."

He gave her a side-eye glare. "Don't start, Lizzie. I don't want to fight with you too."

"So, you two did have a fight then."

Could it even be called that? Apparently, he and Rita had both been making all sorts of observations about each other. While failing to look within themselves. "More of a heated discussion. Rita felt compelled to point out a few things that she thought I was missing. About my behavior. I sort of returned the salvo."

"I see. What did Rita have to say?"

"I'm sure you can guess."

"That you insist on taking charge because you think if you control as many circumstances as you can, you can spare yourself?"

"Did you two compare notes?"

"You're not exactly an enigma, big brother."

He humphed at that.

She remained silent for a while, played with the sand around her. When she spoke again, the change in topic threw him for a loop. "Jonathon and I decided we'd like a very big family. Like his. And we want to start right away."

Clint didn't bother to stifle his groan. Hadn't he been through enough tonight? "Is that your very uncouth way of telling me that you're going back to your groom now?"

She laughed. "No, I just want you to think about what that means. For you in particular."

"For me?" Where in the world could she possibly be going with this. He honestly had no clue.

"When you become an uncle. Are you going to avoid my children? For fear of growing too affectionate of them?"

"Of course not, especially if they're lucky enough to resemble their uncle."

"Ha ha. The simple truth is that you'll love them and cherish them from the moment they arrive in this world until your very last day. That's just who you are."

"Of course, I will." What was the point of this conversation she was leading him down? Now of all times. And here of all places, on the beach after her wedding.

"And what about me? Did you ever think it'd be easier just to write me off when I became an adult? You never stopped caring about me."

"Are you getting to some kind of point? You're my sister. Your children will be my nieces and nephews. How in the world would I have any choice in the matter when it came to loving them or caring about them? Or you?"

She actually had the gall to throw sand in his direction. He closed his eyes just in time but couldn't avoid several grains landing directly into his mouth.

"You have no clue, do you?"

Clint made an exaggerated show of spitting out the offending sand. "About what?"

"Don't be dense. From where I'm standing, it's patently clear that you have no choice when it comes to Rita either."

Rita pulled out her boarding pass and reconfirmed her seat as she made it to the sitting area of terminal twenty at Kahului Airport. To think, just a few short days ago she'd been in a different airport ready to board a different flight, completely unaware that she was about to come face-to-face with the man she would fall in love with.

For that's exactly what had happened. She could no longer deny it. She'd fallen head over heels for Clint Fallon. But she couldn't manage to figure out a way to reach him. Hard to believe, but this was so much worse than her marriage failing. Her divorce had led to feelings of sadness and profound failure.

When it came to Clint, she felt absolute, sharp, nearly unbearable pain.

Biting back tears, she made her way to one of the many empty chairs to wait for boarding. What was Clint doing at this very moment? Had he even noticed she'd gone?

She felt a small twinge of guilt about leaving him back there without so much as a word. But what was there left to say?

You've made the climb up onto that cliff. But you're still just standing there...

His words were so unkind. So unfair.

She'd taken a giant leap by insisting on splitting from Jay. Hadn't she? Of course she had. Look at the ramifications it had led to, the hit her relationship with her father had taken.

And what had she done about that? Nothing so far. As Clint had made sure to point out.

Without giving herself time to think, she pulled her phone out of her pocket and called up her parents' number. What time was it on the East Coast? Early morning, but she didn't care. Not right now.

Her mother picked up on the second ring. "Rita, is everything all right? It's awfully early."

"I'm sorry. I just wanted to talk to Dad. Is he up?"

"You know he is. He always wakes up at the crack of dawn. What's this about, dear? Are you sure everything's all right?"

No, she wanted to wail out. And it would never be all right again. "Yes, Ma. I promise."

Her mother hesitated a few moments before Rita heard shuffling on the other end of the line. Seconds later, her father's rich baritone and mild accent greeted her with concern.

"Sarita? What's this about? Do you need help? Where are you?"

The concern in his voice brought tears to her eyes. She knew he cared about her; he loved her deeply. But it was no longer enough. She wanted more from him. And she was ready to ask for it.

"Everything's fine, Pa. I just wanted to tell you that I love you."

Dead air. Finally, her father cleared his throat. "I…love you too, sweetheart. You have me quite concerned though, dear one. Do you need to be picked up?"

Rita swallowed down the lump in her throat and forced herself to keep talking. "No, I'm fine. I just need you to talk to me. To be my father."

"I don't understand."

No, he didn't. But she would do everything in her power to make him understand. "And I want you to be proud to be my father. But it can't be solely on your terms, Papa."

Then she could no longer hold the tears back at all.

CHAPTER TWELVE

IF RITA CLOSED her eyes and concentrated long enough, she could easily imagine she was back in Hawaii sitting in a lounge chair on the beach. She could almost feel the salty air against her face and the sun shining bright and hot, warming up her skin.

Hard to believe it was only two weeks since she'd returned. Rather than a sandy beach, she was sitting behind a desk trying to put the final pieces in place to kick off the annual fund-raiser for the Greater Westport Animal Shelter. Not that she was complaining. Somehow, she'd landed her dream job within days of getting back from Lizzie and Jonathon's wedding. Who was she kidding? If it wasn't for Clint and the way he'd confronted her about moving forward with her life, she would have never had the gumption to apply for it.

Even her father was impressed. He'd actually taken her out to lunch to celebrate when she'd told her parents the news last week. Rita's eyes stung as she recalled her father's efforts that afternoon. They'd never, ever sat down together one-on-one just to talk. He'd actually said he was proud of her and her newfound position. She couldn't have been more surprised if he'd jumped on the diner counter and started doing a step dance.

His words echoed in her head still. *You've always had the sheer will and strength to go after what you wanted.*

There was at least one exception, Rita thought. Those qualities her father touted had failed her perhaps when it mattered the most. And she would have to live with that for the rest of her life.

Thank goodness for how demanding the new job was. It was keeping her just busy enough that memories of Clint Fallon only plagued her at night. Except for those moments during the day when a pair of dark brown eyes flashed in her vision, or she thought she smelled the woodsy scent of Clint's aftershave.

Rita threw her pen down on the desk in disgust. Who was she kidding? Hardly a moment went by that he wasn't in her thoughts. Every time her cell rang, her heart leaped to her throat. Until she saw on the screen who it was. Never him.

So far she'd resisted the urge to call her friend under the pretense of asking about her newly married life just to get info on her brother.

But she wouldn't allow herself to stoop to that level.

A sudden knock on the door was followed by her vet technician popping her head in. "I'm really sorry about the interruption, Dr. Paul. But there's a man out here who insists he needs to see you before he'll sign off on his adoption. Refuses to speak with anyone else."

Rita looked up from the paperwork she'd been shuffling. She had to get through it all so that she could start her rounds with the animals. But it had been hard to focus.

"I'd ask him to leave," Val continued. "But he seems really interested in one of the pups. I'd hate for the little fella to miss a chance at adoption."

"That doesn't explain why he needs to see me specifically."

"Should I get Frank from the auto parts shop next door to show him out?" Val asked.

Rita let out a long sigh. Looked like the paperwork and

the animals were going to have to wait a little longer. "No, it's okay. I'll talk to him. Thanks."

She did a double take when the visitor entered the room.

Rita rubbed her eyes. Maybe this wasn't real. Maybe she was simply seeing what she wanted to see. But then he spoke. And all doubt fled. Her heart fluttered like a hummingbird in her chest.

"Hey, remember me?"

"Clint?"

"Hi, sweetheart."

"What are you doing here?"

He shrugged, shut the door behind him as Val stepped away. Rita thought she heard the younger woman giggle. "I wanted to show you something."

This was surreal. All this time she'd been willing the phone to ring. Just to be able to hear his voice would have sent her soaring with happiness. But here he was. In the flesh.

She wasn't sure how her mouth was working but somehow she managed to speak. "Show me what?"

Her jaw dropped when he started unbuttoning his shirt, then shrugged it off. Suddenly, Clint Fallon was standing in her newly gained office, shirtless and smiling. How many surprises could she be dealt today?

"My tattoo," he answered her.

Turning, he pointed to his back above the shoulder blade. Rita's vision clouded as she realized what she was looking at. He'd gone and made her butterfly permanent after all. "I had the tattoo artist trace your design before it could fade."

"Oh, Clint." Without thinking, she flung out of her chair and into his embrace. His strong arms went immediately around her. He smelled the same.

"Does that mean you like it?"

She couldn't summon the words to express what she felt.

"I haven't stopped thinking about you," he whispered as he dropped devastating kisses along her temple, down her cheek. Then he took her lips brutally with his. Rita felt the kiss down to her core. "I missed you."

She pulled away. "Oh, Clint. I missed you too. What took you so long?"

"I wanted to make sure to give you enough time, then I couldn't wait any longer. I've barely been functioning these past few weeks." He paused to look around her office. "Whereas you've clearly been busy. I read about your new post online. Congratulations, babe."

She sniffled. "It was a long shot. I didn't think I was qualified for the director position, of all things."

"Oh, Rita."

"But then I thought about what you said. About just jumping off the rock cliff."

"I'm sorry about that night. I'm so sorry I said all those things."

She hugged him tighter. "Please don't apologize. I needed to hear it all. I needed to hear it from you."

He sniffed her hair. "But I should have also told you how extraordinary I think you are."

"You do?"

"Oh, babe. You're warm, witty, generous. You make sure a wandering dog isn't a stray and that it's well taken care of. You're a staunchly loyal friend. You don't think twice about driving up a harrowing mountain to return a rock which may be jinxing your friend's wedding, just in case it's real."

She had to chuckle at that. "Some men might call that feckless and silly."

"Not this man." He shuddered in her arms. "But please don't try anything like that again. Not without me."

He had no idea. She didn't want to do much of anything these days without him by her side.

"I won't. And as far as loyalty, you have it in spades yourself, Mr. Fallon."

"Huh?" he studied her.

"Oh, Clint. Don't you know how impressive it is? The way you made sure to not only take care of your sister from such a young age but also to help her thrive. And look at all you've accomplished. Completely on your own. I've been in awe of you since the day I met you at school move-in day." She inhaled deeply, decided to make yet another jump. "And now, after all these years, I've gone and fallen in love with you."

He actually lifted her off the ground. Did a mini spin. "Well, that happens to work out, Dr. Paul. Because I've fallen madly, irreversibly in love with you too. We should really do something about that."

He took her lips once more, delved deeply into her mouth. Rita had to catch her breath when he finally pulled away.

"You love me?"

"As sure as the sun rises over that freezing-cold crater every morning."

Rita was certain her heart had burst in her chest. This was beyond any fantasy she'd dreamed up.

"Oh, by the way, I plan on adopting that poor, ridiculously tiny Chihuahua out there."

She couldn't help but laugh. "The Chihuahua? Really? I would have pegged you for a…larger, more rugged breed."

He shrugged and flashed her a smile that sent heat simmering over her skin. "What can I say? You don't seem to have any of those hairless cats."

"They're called Sphynx cats," she reminded him.

"Whatever. The little fella called to me. Plus, your staff told me that he's been here the longest."

A wealth of emotion flooded her chest and threatened to split her heart open. She was completely, steadfastly, head over heels in love with this man. Perhaps she'd loved him since she'd first laid eyes on him as a young college student. Back then, he had seemed beyond her reach, someone to dream about. Now, all these years later, here he was, making her dreams a reality.

"Then he's yours," she vowed, laughing some more when he picked her up and sat her on the desk. "I shall personally vouch for you."

"Good. Guess what?"

"What?"

"You're mine too."

EPILOGUE

One year later

"You know, it's our anniversary too," Clint informed her as he turned onto the roadway leading to Wai'anapanapa State Park.

"Is that so?"

"You bet. It was exactly one year ago that I kissed you for the first time. I don't suppose you remember."

Rita waited for him to park and got out of the car before she answered. "I remember everything about that trip." The statement earned her a deep kiss that had her toes curling. The effect Clint had on her senses had not diminished in the slightest in the year since they'd been on this island for Lizzie's wedding. They'd joined the couple here for a celebratory trip in honor of their first anniversary. Never would Rita have guessed back then that she'd be here with Clint for such an occasion a year later.

A strange sense of déjà vu overcame her as they walked down the steps leading to Black Sand Beach. It was hard not to feel slightly silly when she thought about the superstitious reason behind the need she'd felt to return a silly rock. Superstition could be a powerful thing, it turned out.

Clint held her hand as they made it to the bottom. The waves were quieter today than that morning a year ago. The dark sand was the color of black onyx, just as she remembered. They walked farther toward the water. Though he hadn't come out and said so, Rita knew where he was taking her, touched that he'd thought to do so. He'd obviously been planning.

There it was. The cave where she'd first touched him, where she'd first asked him to kiss her.

"Do you think you'd recognize it?" he asked in a light, teasing voice. "Your rock?"

"I have no doubt. It was a very special one that called to me."

They stepped inside the opening and immediately all the warm memories came flooding back. She wrapped her arms around his neck and gave in to the desire to kiss him.

"I, for one, am glad you picked it up all those months ago," Clint said against her mouth. "Or else I would have never gotten you in here alone."

"Very true."

He winked at her. "See if you can find it."

He was serious. "That's ridiculous, Clint. It was a year ago. It's probably nowhere near here anymore."

"It was magical, remember? Look around. You never know."

Rita let out a resigned groan. Just to humor him, she looked down along the ground, then stood upright. "It's not here."

Clint shook his head. "You didn't even try. Look again. At exactly the spot you left it last year."

Why was he doing this? All she wanted to do was enjoy the scenery and then go indulge in some of that delicious banana bread she'd been thinking about all day.

"If you insist."

Stooping lower, she searched the spot where she remembered dropping the rock so many months ago. Not that she really knew for sure what to look for. All the rocks looked exactly the same.

A small speck of white caught her eye on the ground near the cave wall. She bent to pick it up.

"What is that?" Clint asked, taking her hand to study it.

"A flower. Or half of one. How'd a broken flower get in a beachside cave?"

Clint shrugged. "It doesn't appear to be any old flower."

Rita looked closer. He was right. Upon closer inspection, it appeared the flower hadn't been torn in half at all. "It looks like it somehow bloomed that way, only half a flower. I've never seen anything like it."

"It's beautiful. You know, now that I think about it, I've heard about these flowers. They're native to Hawaii."

"You have?"

"Yes. It's coming back to me. The story behind it. It's called a *naupaka* flower."

Rita narrowed her gaze on his face. Something was up. Clint wasn't normally the type to pay attention to legends or stories. Even if he had indulged her last year when she'd felt the urgent need to return a displaced pebble. And he certainly wasn't the type to remember the name of a flower.

"What's this story?" she asked him.

"More a legend really. About a princess."

"Another sad story about a princess?"

Clint pursed his lips and nodded. "I'm afraid so. Apparently, she fell in love with a man who was already spoken for. He felt the same way about her but the gods decreed they were not meant to be. Since she couldn't give him her heart, she took a flower from her hair and tore it in half. Until their deaths, they each carried half the flower with them always. It's been blooming that way ever since."

Rita didn't know quite what to say. It really was a beautiful, touching story. But it still didn't explain how the flower had gotten here. Or why Clint knew so much about it.

He continued with the rest of the legend. "It's said that

when the two halves of the flower find each other, then true love blossoms."

He hadn't finished uttering the last word when Clint suddenly bent down on his knee before her. Reaching in his pocket, he pulled out two items. One a small velvet box.

The world spun around her head. She forgot to breathe.

And then she realized what the other item he held was— the other half of the flower. He must have been planning this for so long. All of it for her. Tears stung her eyes as she looked into the love that showed in his. How in the world had she gotten to be so fortunate?

"Sarita Ann Paul," he began. He took her hand and opened the box to reveal a breathtaking stone set in a glittering band. It was the most exquisite ring she'd ever seen.

"Would you do me the honor of marrying me?"

Rita barely heard him over the roaring in her ears and the overwhelming joy in her heart. As much as she'd dreamed, nothing could have prepared her for what was happening. Clint Fallon had just asked her to be his wife.

Somehow, she found her voice despite the flood of emotion pouring out of her soul. "Yes. A million times over. Yes!"

* * * * *

THE CAPTAIN'S
BABY BARGAIN

MERLINE LOVELACE

To the one, the only, the handsomest,
the smartest, the kindest, the… Well, you get
the idea. There's no one like you, my darling.
Thanks for all these years of love and laughter.

And special thanks to my sister-in-arms,
the inestimable Lindsay McKenna,
for her firefighting expertise and advice.

Chapter One

"Helluva bash, Swish."

Captain Suzanne Hall, call sign Swish, acknowledged the compliment from her former squadron mate by raising the dew-streaked bottle that had come as a "beer-in-a-bag." She'd never tried this Dutch import before. Then again, that was the whole point of the mystery bag.

"Thanks, Dingo."

The ex-military cop tipped his beer to hers while keeping an arm looped around the shoulders of the woman next to him. Personally, Swish thought the hold was more possessive than cozy. With good reason. The moment Dingo had walked in with the long-legged, *extremely* well-endowed showgirl, every male in the place had locked onto her like a heat-seeking missile.

To her credit, Chelsea Howard had ignored the

goggle-eyed stares and only occasionally put up a hand to twirl a strand of her rainbow-hued hair. "I've never been to a place like this," she commented as her gaze roamed the fun-and-games indoor-outdoor restaurant.

Neither had Swish. Lively, laughing groups sat elbow-to-elbow at picnic tables or clustered around fire pits or swapped after-work horror stories with coworkers at high tops arranged in conversational squares. Others conducted raucous battles at miniature golf or bean-bag bingo or darts or skeeball. A four-piece band thumped out country-western crossover, carrying over the clink of cutlery and buzz of conversation. In a separate section well away from the happy-hour crowd, families enjoyed the same fun atmosphere. There was a third section, a glass-enclosed, sit-down, linen-on-the-table restaurant for those more serious about eating than fun and games.

What made the whole complex so amazing, though, was the menu! Swish had almost drooled over the pictures online. Appetizers included pretzels and provolone fondue. Homemade chips with a deservedly world-famous onion dip. Cheddar and potato pierogis. BBQ pork belly nachos. Thai chili chicken wings. The dinner menu was equally exotic, but even without the rave reviews from previous guests, Swish had decided The Culinary Dropout was the perfect spot for this year's Badger Bash.

The annual Bash took place whenever two or more troops who'd served under Colonel Mike Dolan, call sign Badger, happened to be in the same general vicinity at the same time. Since Swish and two additional Badger protégées were currently stationed at Luke Air Force Base, located some miles to the west of Phoenix, they'd opted to hold the reunion here. Eight more of their former squadron mates had flown or driven in from other locales.

And since the once stag-only Bash had expanded to include spouses and/or dates, Swish had insisted on adding some couth to the event. Or, at least, ramping it up from previous years' venues. Like the New Orleans "gentlemen's" club where the performers all turned out to be drag queens. And the wolf- and moose-head decorated bar in Minot, North Dakota, that they'd had to shovel their way out of after a late May blizzard. And the off-off-the-Strip Vegas lounge featuring really bad Dean Martin and Frank Sinatra wannabes. Then there was last year's gathering at the Cactus Café, a smoke-filled dive on Albuquerque's old Route 66.

Although…even reeking of spilled beer and stale sweat, the Cactus Café had produced at least one un-expectedly happy surprise in the person of the brown-eyed blonde currently sitting across the table from Swish. At last year's Bash, Alexis Scott had walked smack up to Major Ben Kincaid, call sign Cowboy, and offered him a fat wad of cash to marry her. Ben had turned down the money but accepted the proposal. And damned if he didn't now act even more stupid about his wife than Dingo did about his showgirl. Of course, the fact that Alex was pregnant might have something to do with Ben's goofy grin.

"Where do you suppose they came up with the name Culinary Dropout?" Alex mused as she sipped her club soda and soaked up the ambiance.

"No idea." Swish speared a chunk of lobster from another appetizer, this one served in an old-fashioned glass canning jar. "Maybe the genius who created these succulent delights decided he didn't need culinary instructors to unleash his artistry."

"If that's the case, I agree with him!"

"Yo, Dingo!" The call came from a sandy-haired communications officer seated near the middle of their long table. "You think you can still hit a target?"

"Blindfolded and backwards," the former military cop turned electronics engineer drawled.

"With a bean bag?"

"Blindfolded and…"

"Ha!" His challenger clambered off his stool. "You're on!"

Chelsea went with Dingo to cheer him on. Hips rolling, her lithe body a symphony of long-legged grace, she once again popped half the eyes in the place out of their sockets.

Alex noted her best friend's impact on the crowd with a wry smile. Cowboy with unfeigned admiration. Swish with a sigh.

"I wish I could believe it was the hair," she murmured.

"Trust me," Alex answered with a laugh. "It's not the hair. Or the legs or the boobs or that wicked smile. I roomed with the woman for two years before I left Vegas for Albuquerque. Chelsea is…"

She circled a hand in the air a few times. Grinning, her husband supplied the answer.

"Chelsea."

"Exactly. And now I have to pee," she announced, easing off the high-backed stool. "Again. Good thing I didn't go through all this the first time I became a mother. I might've thought twice about this pregnancy business."

Although that might've sounded strange to an outsider, everyone at the table knew Alex had adopted her deceased sister's stepdaughter. Correction. She *and* Ben had adopted the seven-year-old. The little girl had subsequently charmed everyone in their wide circle of friends.

"How is Maria?" Swish asked.

"Smart. Stubborn. Independent. Developing an attention span that lasts about five seconds longer than your average flea." Alex patted the mound of her tummy. "And sooo excited about having a baby sister or brother."

"You don't know which yet?"

"Don't want to."

The smile she shared with her husband started a slow ache under Swish's ribs, one she'd been so damned sure she'd finally vanquished.

"That's half the wonder," Alex said softly. "Not knowing and being so totally in love with this little somebody anyway."

The ache lingered as Swish watched Alexis thread her way through the crowd toward the ladies' room. Ben tracked his wife's progress with a look that twisted the knife even more.

Dropping her gaze, Swish poked a finger at the little pile of maple-roasted wannabe nuts on the napkin in front of her. The music and laughter and thunk of beanbags hitting targets faded. The strings of lights blurred as her thoughts narrowed, turned inward, and summoned the image of a face she knew as well as her own.

Her husband had looked at her like Ben did his wife. Back when she'd had a husband.

She played with the wannabe nuts as the memories

crept in. Of she and Gabe growing up together in the same small Oklahoma town. Of how they'd progressed from fifth-grade puppy love to high school sweethearts to being an inseparable couple through all four years at the University of Oklahoma.

They'd married the day after graduation. The same day they'd been commissioned as Air Force second lieutenants. Then spent the next five years juggling short-notice deployments, assignments to separate bases and increasingly strained long-distance communications. Their divorce had become final three years ago, on their sixth wedding anniversary.

The hole in Swish's heart was still there but shrinking a little more each day. That's what she told herself, anyway, until Ben—who'd known them both, had been friends with them both—took advantage of the band's break between numbers to share a quiet confidence.

"I talked to Gabe last week."

"Yeah? He call you or did you call him?"

Dammit! She wished the words back as soon as they were out of her mouth. What difference did it make who initiated the conversation? Divorce was hard enough without expecting your friends to take sides and remain loyal to just one of the injured parties.

"He called me." Ben circled his beer on The Culinary Dropout's distinctive coaster. When he looked up at her again, his blue eyes were shaded. "To tell me he's thinking about getting married again."

Swish swallowed. Deep and hard. Then forced a shrug that felt as though it ripped the cartilage from her shoulder blades. "It's been three years."

She dug deeper and managed a smile. "I'm surprised he's held out this long. Last time I talked to my mom, she said every unattached female under sixty in our hometown was after him. Did Gabe mention which one snagged the prize?"

"No."

"Oh, well. No matter, I guess."

Unless it's Alicia Johnson.

The nasty thought plowed into her head like a runaway troop carrier. Gritting her teeth, Swish jammed on the mental brakes. She had no right to question Gabe's choice for a second trip down the aisle. Absolutely none! Even if Alicia was a pert, bubbly pain in the ass.

"He called from California," Ben was saying.

"California? What's he's doing out there?"

"Someone died. A great aunt, I think he said. He had to go out to settle her estate."

"Aunt Pat? Oh, no!"

The regret was sharp, instant, and so, so painful. She'd lost more than Gabe in the divorce. She'd lost his family, as well. They'd sided with him, of course, after the ugly details surfaced. She didn't blame them, but she'd missed his folks and his sisters and their families. And his feisty old aunt, who could spout the most incredibly imaginative oaths when the spirit moved her.

"He's driving back to Oklahoma from San Diego," Ben related. "If the timing's right, he might stop in Albuquerque to meet Alex and Maria. I told him we'd be home late tomorrow afternoon." He paused, his eyes holding hers. "Unless something unexpected came up."

"Like me throwing a world class hissy fit about you consorting with the enemy?"

"Is he? The enemy?"

Her breath left on a sigh. "No, of course not. Gabe's your friend, too. You don't have to take sides or choose between us." She hesitated several painful beats. "Did he, uh, ask about me?"

"No."

Disgusted by the hurt that generated, Swish gave herself a swift, mental kick. For God's sake! She was a captain in the United States Air Force. A combat engineer with two rotations to Iraq and one to Afghanistan under her belt. She'd built or blown up everything from runways to bridges. Yet here she was, moping like a schoolgirl who hadn't been asked to the dance because her ex chose to get on with his life.

"Well," she said briskly, "if you and Gabe do connect in Albuquerque tomorrow, tell him I wish him the best."

"Will do."

"Great. Now why don't we see how Dingo's doing blindfolded and backward?"

As one of the organizers of this year's Bash, Swish was among the last to leave when The Culinary Dropout finally closed its doors at 2:00 a.m. Even then, she provided taxi service to one of her buddies who'd flown in for the occasion.

She hung with him at his hotel room for a while, sharing black coffee and memories of the legendary Special Ops colonel who'd spawned their annual Badger Bash. She'd worked for Colonel Dolan only once, when she was a brand-new second lieutenant. The colonel could blister the paint off you with a single glance and did *not* suffer fools gladly. But Swish had learned more about leadership and taking care of her troops from him than from any of her bosses since.

Dawn was starting to streak the sky above the Superstition Mountains when she strolled out of the hotel and clicked the locks of the Thunderbird soft-top convertible she'd treated herself to when she got promoted to captain. She stood beside the merlot-colored sports car for a moment, breathing in the scent of honeysuckle and piñon while debating whether to put down the top.

The fact that she was wearing the traditional Badger Bash "uniform of the day" decided her. The generally accepted attire included boots, jeans and T-shirts sporting whatever quirky message the attendees wanted to impart. Swish had opted for a black, body-sculpting tank with a whiskered, green-eyed tiger draped over one shoulder. It had been designed and handcrafted by Ben's wife, who insisted the tiger's eyes were the exact same jungle-green as Swish's. The matching ball cap sported the same glittering black-and-gold-tiger stripes and caught her shoulder-length blond hair back into a ponytail. The perfect ensemble for tooling through a soft Arizona dawn, she decided.

Mere moments later she had the top down and the T-bird aimed for the on-ramp to I-10. Luke AFB was a good thirty miles west of Scottsdale. The prospect of a long drive didn't faze her. Having learned her lesson from previous Bashes, she'd arranged to have the rest of the weekend off. She could cruise through the dim, still-cool dawn, hit her condo, shower off the residue of the night and crash.

But first, she realized after only about fifteen miles, she had to make a pit stop. She shouldn't have downed that last cup of coffee, dammit. For another few miles she tried the bladder control exercises she'd resorted to while operating at remote sites with only the most primitive facilities.

But when she spotted a sign indicating a McDonald's at the next exit, she gave up the struggle. Flipping on the directional signal, she took the ramp for Exit 134. The iconic golden arches gleamed a little more than a block from where she got off.

Unfortunately, a red light separated her from imminent relief. She braked to a stop and drummed her fingers on the wheel. She might've been tempted to run the light if not for the vehicle stopped across the deserted intersection. It was a pickup. One of those muscled-up jobbies favored by farmers and ranchers. Older than most, though. And vaguely familiar. Narrowing her eyes, she squinted and tried to see past the headlights spearing toward her in the slowly brightening dawn.

Suddenly, her heart lurched. Stopped dead. Kicked back to life with a painful jolt.

Locking her fists on the wheel, Swish gaped at the cartoon depicted on the pickup's sloping hood. She recognized the needle-nosed insect dive-bombing an imaginary target. She should; she'd painted it herself.

Her gaze jerked from the hood to the cab. The headlights' glare blurred the driver's features. Not enough to completely obscure them, however.

Oh, God! That was Gabe. Her Gabe.

Fragments of the conversation with Cowboy rifled through her shock. California. A funeral. Gabe driving home. Visiting with Cowboy and his wife in Albuquerque.

Her precise, analytical engineer's mind made the instant connection. Phoenix sat halfway between San Diego and Albuquerque. A logical place to stop for the night, grab some sleep, break up the long drive. The not-as-precise section of her brain remained so numb with surprise that she didn't react when the light turned green. Her knuckles white, she gripped the wheel and kept her foot planted solidly on the brake.

The pickup didn't move, either. With no other traffic transiting the isolated intersection, the two vehicles sat facing each other as the light turned yellow, then red again. The next time it once again showed green, the pickup crossed the short stretch of pavement and pulled up alongside her convertible.

The driver's side window whirred down. A tanned elbow hooked on the sill. The deep baritone that used to belt out the hokiest '50s-era honky-tonk tear-jerkers rumbled across the morning quiet.

"Hey, Suze."

He'd never used her call sign in nonoperational situations. The military had consumed so much of their lives that Gabe wouldn't let it take their names, too. That attitude, Swish reflected, was only one of the many reasons he'd left the Air Force and she hadn't.

She craned her neck, squinting up from her low-slung sports car. "Hey yourself, Gabe."

"I thought I was hallucinating there for a minute. What're you doing in Phoenix?"

"I live here. I'm stationed at Luke."

"Oh, yeah? Since when?"

The fact that he didn't even know where she lived hurt. More than she would ever admit.

Swish, on the other hand, had subtly encouraged her mother to share bits of news about her former son-in-law's life since he'd moved back to Oklahoma. Mary Jackson had passed on the news that the high school tennis team Gabe coached had won state honors. And she gushed over the fact that the voters of their small hometown elected him mayor by a land-slide. Somehow, though, her mom had neglected to mention the fact that Cedar Creek's mayor was getting married again.

"I've been at Luke a little over four months," Swish answered with as much nonchalance as she could muster, then let her gaze roam the dusty, dented pickup. "I see you're still driving Ole Blue."

He unbent his elbow and patted the outside of his door. "I rebuilt the engine a last year. Spins like a top."

"Mmm-hmm."

The memories didn't creep in this time. They hit like a sledgehammer.

Swish had surrendered her virginity in Ole Blue's cab. Impatiently. Hungrily. Almost angrily. She'd teased and tormented Gabe until he finally toppled her backward on the cracked leather seat and yanked down her panties. Even then, as wild with hunger as they both were, he'd been gentle. For the first few thrusts. Once past the initial startled adjustment, Swish had picked up the rhythm and climaxed mere moments later, as though she'd only been waiting for his touch to ignite those white-hot sensations.

She'd still been floating back to earth when he pulled out of her and started swearing. At himself. At her. At the incredible stupidity of what they'd just done. What if her parents found out he'd violated their trust as well as their daughter? What if he'd let himself come and gotten her pregnant! What about her scholarship to OU? The bridges she wanted to build. The exotic lands they both wanted to travel to!

Still soaring on that sexual high, Swish had kissed and stroked and nipped the cords in his neck until he cursed again, shoved the key in the ignition and drove her home.

Other, less sensual memories involving Ole Blue swirled like a colorful kaleidoscope. The night they spread an air mattress in the truck bed and stretched out to watch a gazillion stars light up the sky. The times they'd pulled into a space at the only still-operating drive-in movie in the area to munch popcorn and watch the latest action flick. The load of manure they'd loaded and hauled to fertilize the garden belonging to a friend of his mother.

A flash of headlights in the rearview mirror yanked her from the past to the present. They were still blocking the intersection, with Ole Blue hunched like an oversize panther beside Swish's red mouse of a car.

She glanced in the mirror, back at Gabe. "Well, I guess…"

"Why don't we get a cup of coffee?" He hooked his thumb at the golden arches behind him. "I obviously need to catch up on your career moves."

She opened her mouth to refuse. The memories she'd just flashed through were too raw, too painful. She'd be a fool to resurrect any more. Then again, she *did* have to make a pit stop. Like reeeeally bad now.

"Okay," she heard herself say. "I'll meet you inside… after I hit the head."

She cornered into the parking lot, killed the engine and was out of the T-bird before Ole Blue had made a U-turn at the intersection. This early in the morning the ladies' room was empty and clean as a whistle, with the pungent tang of disinfectant taking precedence over the scent of deep-fried hash browns and sausage coming from the kitchen.

When she emerged, she found Gabe lounging against a booth with a coffee cup in either hand. A smile crinkled the squint lines at the corners of his hazel eyes as he tipped his chin toward the restroom she'd just vacated.

"You must've been on the road for a while if your iron-bladder exercises failed you."

"Hey! I made it, didn't I?"

Anyone overhearing the exchange would've wondered at the subject matter. Or assumed she and Gabe shared a history that included an intimate knowledge of each other's bodily functions. Which they did.

Feeling like a total idiot for mourning the loss of that particular history, Swish reached out a hand. "Which coffee is mine?"

"Take your pick." He held out both cups. "They're the same."

She blinked, startled. Her husband had always been a two-sugars-one-cream kind of guy. "When did you start drinking undoctored coffee?"

"When I added too many extra inches to my waistline."

Her gaze made a quick up and down. If Gabe had put on extra inches, she sure as hell couldn't see them. The chest covered by his stretchy black T-shirt tapered to a still-trim waist. The snug jeans emphasized his flat belly. His lean hips. The hard, muscled thighs she'd traced so often with her hands and her mouth and her...

"You sure you don't want more than coffee?" he asked, gesturing to the illuminated menu. "I'll be happy to stand you to a Number 3."

The fact that he remembered her preference for a Big Breakfast with Hotcakes made her throat ache. "This is good," she murmured, sliding into the booth he'd staked out.

The silence that followed was short but awkward. And obviously painful, as they both rushed to break it.

"What are you…?"

"So sorry about…"

They both broke off, and he gestured for her to go on.

"So sorry to hear about Aunt Pat. What happened?"

"An aortic aneurism. She died in her sleep. One of her spin-class buddies found her the next morning."

Swish wasn't surprised that the feisty seventy-six-year-old had been into spinning along with all her other fitness pursuits. She and Pat had once run side by side in a 5k Race for the Cure with the older woman decked out in flashing sneakers, cotton-candy-pink leggings and a cropped tank that announced she was One Fast Oldie.

"How's your mom taking her sister's death?"

"Hard. She flew out for the funeral but couldn't stay to help settle the estate. Her hip's been giving her trouble."

The reply plucked at Swish's hurt again. She'd been so close to his family. His dad before he died, his mom, his sisters. To cover the ache, she switched subjects.

"*My* mom told me about the election. Ninety-four percent of the vote. Pretty impressive for a high school history teacher-slash-tennis coach."

"Yeah, well…"

The grin that had haunted her dreams for too many months slipped out. As self-deprecating and sexy as she remembered. She felt its all-too-familiar impact wrap around her heart.

"Hard to bask in the glow of victory when my cousins constitute at least half the electorate."

Swish had to laugh. "I know most of those cousins.

They're as stubborn and hardheaded as you are, Mr. Mayor. They wouldn't have voted for you unless they believed in you."

"Maybe. Or it might've been because I ran against Dave Forrester."

Her jaw dropped. "You're kidding! Freckle-faced Forrester overcame his shyness enough to run for public office?"

"Freckle-faced Forrester now owns the largest oil and gas franchise in the county," Gabe returned drily. "Lucky for me—but not for my constituents—he's been slapped with a half-dozen lawsuits for property damage due to fracking. He's not the most popular guy around Cedar Creek these days."

Wow! The skinny, gap-toothed kid who'd traded spitballs with her? An oil and gas executive? She was still trying to get her head around that when Gabe broke into her thoughts.

"What about you? What are you doing at Luke?"

She shook off the tendrils of her past and leaped gratefully into the present. "I'm assigned to the 56th Fighter Wing. Would you believe I head up the Base Emergency Engineer Response team?"

"Prime BEEF? Now I'm impressed."

The designation didn't begin to describe the scope of her team's duties. The mission of Luke AFB was to train the men and women who flew and maintained the F-16 Fighting Falcon and the F-35 Lightning, the world's newest and most sophisticated fighter. The base population included more than ten thousand active duty, reserve and civilian personnel, plus their families. Another seventy thousand retirees lived in the local area. Swish's job was to make sure the facilities were in place to support all these people in both peacetime and wartime.

"That's quite a responsibility," Gabe commented.

"It's what you trained for. What you've worked so hard for. And why you were awarded that Bronze Star after your last deployment."

"You know about the Bronze Star?"

She couldn't keep the surprise out of her voice. He couldn't keep the bite out of his.

"Know that my wife…?" He stopped. Took a breath. Started again. "Know that my *former* wife and her team risked their lives to repair an abandoned runway outside Mosul? That they opened the airstrip despite heavy enemy fire so US aircraft could use it as a base to repel an ISIS attack? Yeah, I know about it."

Okay, that gave her a warm buzz. Almost warm enough to mitigate the fact that he hadn't known she was now assigned to Luke. Not quite warm enough to erase the news Ben had imparted last night, though. She looked down at her now sludgy coffee. Looked up. Took her courage in both hands.

"Cowboy told me you're getting married again."

"I'm thinking about it."

"Anyone I know?"

He hesitated, shrugged. "Alicia Johnson."

Dammit all to hell!

Somehow, someway, she managed to keep from crushing her cup and slopping coffee over the table. A bitter realization stayed her hand. As much as she disliked the nauseatingly effervescent pixie, she had no right to castigate Gabe for his choice of partners. God knows, he hadn't castigated her when she turned to someone else out of desperate loneliness.

"Whatever you decide," she got out, despite lungs squeezed so tight she could hardly breath, "I hope you find the 'forever' we were so sure we had."

He stretched out a hand, covered hers. "Same goes, Susie Q."

It was the silly nickname that did it. His pet name for her from the fifth grade on. Forever associated in both of their minds with the package of cream-filled chocolate cupcakes she'd brought to his bedroom when he fell out of a tree and broke his collarbone.

She tried, she really tried, to keep her smile from wobbling. Twisting her hand, she gave his what she intended as a companionable squeeze. His fingers threaded through hers. So strong. So warm. So achingly familiar.

He raised their joined hands. Brought the back of hers to his lips. Brushed a kiss across her knuckles. Once. Twice. Swish didn't even *try* to pull away.

Until he gently, slowly, lowered his hand and eased it out of hers.

Chapter Two

"I...uh..."

Gabe smothered a curse as his wife—his *former* wife!—stammered and tried to shrug off the impact of their brief contact.

One touch. One friggin' touch, and she looked ready to bolt. He should let her. God knew it wouldn't be the first time. Instead, he soothed her obvious nervousness with a safe, neutral topic.

"I didn't get to talk to Cowboy much over the phone. It sounded like he's enjoying his foray into fatherhood, though."

"He is."

She relaxed, bit by almost imperceptible bit, and Gabe refused to analyze the relief that ripped through him. He'd think about it later. Along with the ache in his gut just sharing a booth with her generated.

"Did you know his wife, Alex, designs glitzy tops and accessories for high-end boutiques?"

"No." He gestured toward the tiger draped over her shoulder. "Did she design that?"

"She did."

"Nice."

Very nice. Although…

Now that he'd recovered from the shock of their unexpected meeting, Gabe wasn't sure he liked the changes he saw in the woman sitting opposite him. She was older. That went without saying. But she'd lost weight in the three years since they'd said their final goodbye. Too much weight. She'd always been slim. With a waist he could span with his hands and small, high breasts that never required a bra when she wasn't in uniform. Now her cheekbones slashed like blades across her face and that sparkly, stretchy black tank showed hollows where her neck joined her shoulders.

And those lines at the corners of her eyes. Gabe knew most of them came from the sun. And from squinting through everything from high-tech surveying equipment to night-vision goggles. But the lines had deepened, adding both maturity and a vulnerability that tugged at protective instincts he'd thought long buried.

The eyes themselves hadn't changed, though. Still a deep, mossy green. And still framed by lashes so thick and dark she'd never bothered with mascara. The hair was the same, too. God, how he loved that silvery, ash-blond mane. She'd worn it in a dozen different styles during all their years together. The feathery cut that made her look like a sexy Tinker Bell. The chin-sweeping bob she'd favored in high school. The yard-long spill she'd sported in college. How many times had he tunneled his fingers through that satin-smooth waterfall? A hundred? Two?

He liked the way she wore it now, though. Long enough to pull through the opening at the back of her ball cap, just long enough for the ends to cascade over her right shoulder. Gabe had to curl his hands into fists to keep from reaching across the table and fingering those silky strands.

He sipped his coffee, instead, and tried his damnedest to maintain an expression of friendly interest as she brought him up to date on other mutual friends. Pink, getting ready to ship across the pond again. Dingo and the showgirl he'd been seeing off and on for over a year now. A real wowzer, if even half of the adjectives Suze used to describe the buxom brunette were true. Cowboy's wife, Alex, expanding her clothing design business even faster than they were expanding their family.

Strange, Gabe thought. He always associated their friends with their call signs. Yet he never thought of Suze as Swish. There were several different explanations of how she'd acquired that tag. One version held it resulted from the detailed analysis she'd sketched on a scrap of paper during a fierce, intrasquadron basketball game. In swift, decisive strokes she'd demonstrated the correct amount of thrust and proper parabolic arc to swish in a basket.

Another version was that she'd gained the tag after one of her troops mired a Swiss-made bulldozer in mud. Suze reportedly climbed aboard, rocked the thirty-ton behemoth back and forth, and s*wished* it out.

There was another version. One involving beer, a bet and a camel, although Suze always claimed the details were too hazy for her to remember.

Gabe knew his reluctance to use her call sign was only one small indicator of the rift that had gradually, inexorably widened to a chasm. He hadn't resented sharing her with the Air Force or with the troops she worked with. Not at first. Not until they became her surrogate family. But she always was, always would be, Suze to him.

Or *Susie Q.* The pet name came wrapped in so many layers of memories. Some innocent, like the time he broke his collarbone and she'd perched on the side of his bed to feed him bits of her cream-filled chocolate treats. And some not so innocent. Like the time…

Without warning, Gabe went tight. And hard. And hungry. Smothering another curse, he shoved the image of his wife's nipples smeared with whipped cream out of his head. But he had to drag in long, slow breaths before his blood started circulating above his waist again.

"I can't tell if Dingo's serious about Chelsea or not," Suze was saying. "He hooks up with her whenever he's in Vegas. And they spent a week together in Cabo a few months back. But neither of them seem to be talking about long term." She cocked her head. "Gabe?"

"Sorry. I was thinking of something else."

"Right."

She fiddled with the tab on the lid of her cup. They'd covered every banal topic they could while dancing away from the only one that mattered. Silence stretched between them. Gabe was reluctant to break it, and even more reluctant to end this strange interlude. Suze finally took the lead.

"Well, if you're going to make Albuquerque this evening, you probably should hit the road."

"Probably should."

"Unless…"

She flicked the tab. Up. Down. Didn't quite meet his eyes.

"Unless?" he prompted.

"Unless you'd like to swing by my place for breakfast first. It's out of your way but…" The barest hint of a smile flitted across her face. "I still can't cook worth a damn but I *have* learned to concoct a relatively passable Mexican frittata."

It was an olive branch. A tentative step toward putting the past behind them and becoming friends again. That's all it was, Gabe told himself fiercely. All it could be. Yet he snatched it with both hands.

"You're on."

Even before he snapped his seat belt and keyed Ole Blue's ignition, his thoughts had done a one-eighty. This was a mistake. Possibly one of epic proportions. There was no way in hell either of them could back to being just friends. But as Gabe trailed her maroon sports car through the now-bright Arizona morning, he came up with a dozen different explanations for his temporary insanity.

Neither of them had tried to deny that their frequent separations while they were both in uniform had created the first cracks in their marriage. The cracks had gotten wider every time Gabe suggested they choose different career paths, ones that wouldn't put them on opposite sides of the globe so often. The fissures had become a yawning crevasse when he'd issued a flat ultimatum.

Looking back, he knew he shouldn't have forced her to choose between him and the Air Force. Or hung up his uniform and headed for Oklahoma while they were still struggling to balance the deep, visceral satisfaction she got from her job with his gnawing need to get back to his roots.

And he sure as hell shouldn't have let her admission that she'd turned to someone else for comfort eat like acid on his pride. They'd been separated for six months by then. Already talking around the edges of divorce, when they talked at all.

That was when he'd heard the rumor. Third hand, passed via a friend of a friend of a friend. It hadn't meant anything, the well-meaning pal had assured him. Suzanne had already given the guy his marching orders.

Gabe knew then he should've swallowed his rage at the thought of Suzanne, *his* Suzanne, in another man's arms, jumped on a plane and tried one last time to heal the breach.

Which is exactly what he would've done if she hadn't called back while he was in the process of throwing a few things in an overnight bag. Every word icy and clipped, she'd told him she'd applied for two weeks' leave. She needed to get away. Think things through. And, like a fool, he'd let her go. Didn't ask where. Didn't try to track her down. Just stubbornly, stupidly believed deep in his heart they'd find a way back to each other. He'd continued to believe it right up until she FedExed him the divorce papers.

As the memories flashed by with the same speed as the miles, his mind went to a place he knew it shouldn't. Maybe Suze had offered more than an olive branch back there at McDonald's. Maybe these past three years had been as lonely for her as they had for him. Maybe, just maybe, she was giving him the chance to correct the most colossal blunder of his life.

If she was, and if he did, all ten levels of hell would freeze over before he let her go again.

The fierce vow probably explained why she'd barely closed the door of her condo behind them before he made his move. That, and the fact that a swift glance around her airy living room revealed no reminders of their broken marriage. Even with the wood shutters tilted against the morning sun, enough light slanted in for Gabe to see the furniture was new. So was the triple panel of bold, slashing color mounted above the sofa. Even the oversize area rug that looked like it had been woven from fabric scraps in dozens of different colors and patterns.

She must have caught his frown as he studied the rug. Tossing her keys and small clutch purse on the tiled counter that separated the living room from the kitchen, she addressed the issue head on. "I'm only renting this place until I decide where to buy."

He answered with a shrug that added an edge in her voice.

"It came furnished, so I put our Turkish…" She stopped, restarted. "So I put the Turkish carpets in storage with the rest of my things."

For some reason that deliberate midcourse correction pissed Gabe off. She couldn't admit they'd ever shared a home? Couldn't cherish the small treasures they'd collected from all over the world?

Conveniently forgetting that he'd boxed up pretty much every item he'd carted back to Oklahoma and stashed them in the attic of *his* home, Gabe forced a grin. "Seems like I remember us rolling around naked on those Turkish carpets a few times."

The surprise that flashed across her face gave him a dart of fierce satisfaction. It also provided a chance to dig the spur in a little deeper.

"More than a few times, now that I think about it. Often enough for one of us to get a little carpet burn on her ass, anyway."

When he waggled his brows, she laughed and shook her head.

"That was you, big guy. After which, you threatened to tell folks you'd been wounded in the line of duty."

"At which point *you* threatened to pin a purple heart on said wound."

"Would've served you right if I had!"

They were both grinning now, and Gabe moved in for the kill. Lifting a hand, he brushed his knuckles down her cheek. "We had some good times, didn't we?"

Her laughter faded. The twin emerald pools he'd seen himself in so many times stared up at him. Gabe waited, his heart slamming against his ribs, until her breath left on a whisper of a sigh.

"Yes, we did."

He opened his palm and cupped her chin, then feathered his thumb across her lower lip. His pulse was drumming in his ears now. And in that instant, he knew he wouldn't—*couldn't*—take Alicia up on her increasingly unsubtle hints that she was ready to move in with him. Permanently.

This was the only woman he'd ever loved. The one he'd ached for with the fumbling, frantic passion of youth. The one he'd promised to share his life with. There wasn't room in his heart for anyone but her.

"I've missed you, Suze."

"I've missed you, too." Tears dimmed the luminescent green of her eyes. "So much I hurt with it."

His palm slid to her nape. His other hand came up to ease off her ball cap. With it out of the way, he tugged at the squishy elastic band that held her hair. The wind-tangled strands came free and framed her face.

"There," he said, his voice gruff. "I've been aching to do that since the moment we walked into that McDonald's."

"Gabe..."

It was half sigh, half plea. Heat roiling in his belly, he tightened his hold on her nape.

"I've been aching to do this, too."

He fully intended to keep the kiss gentle. To stoke her hunger carefully, slowly, until it matched the fire now smoldering in his blood. But she fitted herself against him with a familiar intimacy that sparked searing pleasure at every contact point. Her mouth, her breasts, her hips. All straining against him. All filling him with a raging need that made him whip an arm around her waist and haul her even closer.

Swish reacted instinctively. The feel of him against her, of the hard press of his mouth on hers, shattered the dam. Hunger, hot and urgent, poured through her. Panting, gasping, her lungs burning, her lips frantic under his, she hooked her arms around his neck. The last shreds of sanity screamed at her to pull back. Now! While she still could! But the rest of her, every atom of the rest of her, wanted Gabe with a ferocity so intense it seared her soul.

She wasn't sure who attacked whose clothing first. She might've yanked up his black T-shirt to get at the hard, tanned muscles of his chest. Or maybe he whipped her tank top up and off. She didn't know. Didn't care. She was too busy heeling out of her half-boots to think about it.

She kicked the boots away at the same instant his hands went to the zipper of her jeans. He shoved them down over her hips. She shimmied the rest of the way out. She hadn't bothered with a bra. She never did when not in uniform. So all she had on when he scooped her up was the thin layer of her black lace hipsters.

"That way," she gasped, pointing to the arch that led to the two bedrooms. Unnecessarily, as it turned out, as Gabe was already halfway there.

The master bedroom suite echoed the same eclectic style and bright colors as the living room. Red, yellow and turquoise pillows in varying shapes accented the sage-colored comforter. The collage of desert sunrises and sunsets arranged above the headboard picked up the same colors.

Gabe didn't so much as glance at the gorgeous display. He almost dumped her on the bed and dragged off her panties before stripping off the rest his own clothes. Boots. Jeans. Jockeys.

Jaw taut, nostrils flaring, he turned back to her. His eyes, those green-brown eyes flecked with bits of gold, raked from her neck to her knees. Suze could see herself reflected in the dark irises. Her arms flung up beside her head in wild abandon. Her breasts bare, the nipples already hard and aching for his touch. Her stomach hollowing as the muscles low in her belly clenched in greedy anticipation.

Then, just as she opened her legs to welcome him, he turned away. She lay frozen, unable to move or think or understand why he reached for the jeans he'd just discarded. She whipped her arms down and pushed up on one elbow. She was all set to torch him like one of the commercial high-pressure propane flamethrowers her fire protection troops used when he faced her again, a crumpled foil packet in his hand.

"I have no idea how long I've carried this in my wallet," he said with a wry grimace. "A year maybe."

Which implied, she thought on a surge of primal satisfaction, he hadn't delved into his secret stash for prissy missy Alicia Johnson.

She dismissed as totally irrelevant the possibility that Alicia might have supplied the necessary protective measures herself. The only thing that mattered to her now was that Gabe, her Gabe, apparently hadn't *initiated* a sexual encounter.

Until now.

"Let me."

Her heart stuck in her throat, she rolled onto her knees and held out her hand. She squeezed every ounce of pleasure she could out of tearing open the packet and sheathing his now rigid erection. The veined shaft rising hard and pulsing from its nest of wiry chestnut hair triggered atavistic instincts as old as time. This was her mate. The man she'd given her heart to years before she gave him her virginity.

She'd never looked at another man during their years together. Never wanted another man's hands on her. At least, not until the hurt and the loneliness had got too much to bear. Even then, she'd taken only one other man to her bed.

The experience had left her so empty, so heartbroken that she'd never repeated it. But word had gotten back to Gabe. How, she never knew, not that it mattered. His raw fury had leaped from the email he'd sent asking if it was true.

The anger still simmered, she discovered. Not as raw. Not as livid. But she could see it in his eyes when he tunneled his hands through her hair and tipped her head back.

"Do you have any idea how many times I've thought about you doing this with someone else?" he asked, his voice low and rough.

"I can guess."

"That damned near killed me, Suze."

"I know," she said, her throat tight. "I was sorry then. I'm sorry now."

The reply did little to take the edge off his hostility. He toppled her back, splaying her on the sage-green spread, then followed her down. His body was rock hard, his muscles taut and his tendons corded as he kneed her legs apart.

She welcomed him, craving a cleansing as much as he did. Yet for all his seeming anger, he took time to make sure she was primed. His fingers found all the triggers. Started the pinwheels spinning and the juices flowing.

She didn't have to tell him that she was wet and ready. He knew her body's responses as well as she did. Better. She was panting when he positioned himself between her thighs. Groaning when she lifted her hips and rose up to meet his thrusts. She ground her mouth against his, more than matching his savage hunger.

Her climax slammed into her with almost zero warning. One moment she was straining against his hips.

The next, she arched her spine, groaned deep in her throat and exploded.

She had no idea how long she drifted on those dark, undulating waves of pleasure before she realized he was still rock hard and buried inside her. When she pried her eyes open, the worry in his green-brown eyes melted her heart.

"You okay?"

The question was as tight and strained as his body. Swish slicked her palms over his taut shoulders. "More okay than I've been in three years."

The reply didn't seem to reassure him. Still frowning, he propped himself up on his elbows and framed her face with his palms. "I didn't mean to be so rough."

"Do you hear me complaining?"

"No, but…"

"We need to get that old hurt out of our systems, Gabe. We're halfway there."

"Halfway?"

"Yep."

She gave the muscles low in her belly a tight, hard squeeze. A flush rushed into Gabe's cheeks, and she squeezed again. Reveling in his response, she rolled onto her hip, then up to her knees.

"All right, fella. My turn to get rough."

By the time they finished, Gabe felt drained of all bodily fluids and Suze lay across his chest like a bag of bones. When he eased her to the side to cradle her in the crook of his arm, she nuzzled her nose into his neck.

"Gimme a few minutes," she grunted. "Then I'll get up 'n' make you that omelet."

"No hurry. I'm good."

Christ! As if that bland adjective came anywhere close to describing how he felt at that moment.

"Okay," she muttered against his throat. "I was up all night last night. I'll just snuggle here for a little bit."

Snuggle forever.

Gabe caught the suggestion before it slipped out. But the words hung there in his mind as she dropped into a light doze. Not five minutes later, she was out like a brick.

That was fine with him. He wasn't on a tight schedule. School was over for the year, he wouldn't start coaching summer tennis clinics for another week and his deputy mayor could handle any minor crises that might erupt. He could lie here as long as he wanted, his wife sleeping beside him, her breath warm on his neck and the overhead fan gently stirring the ends of her hair.

He teased the loose strands with an absent, hazy concentration. They slid through his fingers, still wind-whipped but not dry or dusty. As he twisted a skein around his thumb, his thoughts segued from the familiar feel of her hair to what their unexpected encounter might mean in terms of their future.

Grimacing, he reinforced his silent decision to end things with Alicia. She'd still been stinging from her own divorce when she'd turned to Gabe for companionship. Somehow their casual encounters had morphed into dates, then to an "understanding" that Alicia had begun to take more seriously than Gabe did. She'd been pushing for them to move in together. Her place or his, she didn't care, and he'd been edging close to saying what the hell.

Now...

He scrunched a few inches to the left so he could

look down at his wife's face without going cross-eyed. He always got a kick out of watching her sleep. Those ridiculously thick lashes fanned her cheeks. Her breath soughed in and out through half-open lips. And every once in a while her nose would twitch and she'd make little snuffling noises.

God, he loved this woman! She'd been in his blood, in his heart, for almost as long as he could remember. Maybe now they could put all the hurt and separation and loneliness behind them. Maybe their chance meeting at that deserted intersection wasn't chance at all, but a...

The sudden, shrill notes of a xylophone clanged through the quiet. Gabe jerked and Suze's head popped up.

"Wha...?"

She blinked owlishly, then muttered a curse when the xylophone clanged again. Rolling onto her opposite side, she slapped her palm against the nightstand until she located her iPhone. She flopped onto her back and squinted at the screen. Evidently she recognized the number because she scowled and stabbed the talk button.

"Captain Hall," she croaked, her voice still hoarse with sleep. As she listened for a few moments, her scowl slashed into a frown. She jerked upright and gripped the phone with a white-knuckled fist.

"Casualties?"

Gabe went taut beside her. The single word brought back stark memories of his own time in the Air Force. He'd begun his career as a weapons director flying aboard the Air Force's sophisticated E3-A, the Airborne Warning and Control System. AWACS aircraft averaged hundreds of sorties a year. Flying at thirty thousand feet, they provided the "eyes in the sky" for other aircraft operating in a combat environment.

After four years in AWACS Gabe had volunteered to transition to drone operations in an effort to remain on the same continent as Suze for at least a few months out of the year. He'd been transferred to Creech Air Force Base, just outside Las Vegas, and trained to remotely pilot the MQ-9 Reaper. With its long loiter time, wide-range sensors and precision weapons, the Reaper provided a unique capability to perform conduct strikes against high-value, time-sensitive targets.

Turned out Gabe was good at jockeying that joystick. Good at locking onto even the fastest-moving targets. Good at launching his laser-guided missiles from precisely the right angle and altitude to destroy those top priority targets.

It was the secondary casualties that churned his insides. He could see them through the unblinking eyes of high-powered spy satellites. The bystanders hurled fifty or a hundred yards from the impact site. The wounded leaving trails of blood in the dirt as they crawled and begged for help. The parents keening soundlessly as they cradled children who'd run to or been hidden near the target.

Collateral damage. That was the catchall phrase for noncombatants caught in the cross fire. Gabe had never taken a shred of pride in his body count, never wanted to know the numbers. Even now he couldn't relax until he heard Suze expel a relieved breath.

"No casualties? Thank God for that. I'm on my way." She tossed aside the rumpled sheet and almost tripped over his discarded jeans on her way to her closet. "ETA twenty minutes."

She tossed the phone on the dresser and yanked open a drawer. With one leg in a pair of no-nonsense briefs, she offered a quick explanation. "Sorry, Gabe. There's been an accident. I have to get to the base."

"Aircraft?"

"Pipeline break." She dragged on a sports bra followed by the regulation brown T-shirt. "Evidently we've got the mother of all fuel spills."

Gabe knew that meant getting a hazmat team on-scene ASAP. Spilled aviation fuel was not just a fire and explosion danger, but also a potential environmental disaster. The FEMA Emergency Management course he'd attended after being elected mayor had offered some excellent tips on exactly this kind of crisis.

Tucking the sheet around his waist, he waited while Suze yanked on her desert-colored BDU pants and shirt, then plopped down on the side of the bed to pull on her socks and boots.

"I went to the FEMA Disaster Response course in Baton Rouge last month. They're recommending a new sorbent for fuel spills that…"

"Sorry, Gabe, I don't have time."

She stood up, grabbed her phone and a leather trifold he knew contained her ID, her driver's license, a credit card and some cash.

"I'll call you when I can."

He was still sitting in bed with the sheet bunched around his waist when the front door slammed behind her.

Chapter Three

The spill was even worse than Suzanne had feared.

As the designated training base for the F-35 Joint Strike Fighter, Luke AFB had awarded a multi-million-dollar contract to a civilian construction firm to modify the aviation fuel bulk storage tanks, feed lines and manifold system. The intent was to improve the new fighter's refueling turnaround and thus increase the number of sorties that could be flown during a training cycle. Suzanne had participated in the multi-organization review and final approval of the contractor's construction plan. She'd also assigned one of her troops to monitor the construction on a daily basis.

The project had gone smoothly to date. Or so they'd thought. When she arrived at the coordination point, the quick briefing she got from Hank Butler, the Base Fire Chief, in his role as acting on-scene commander, told another story. An experienced civilian with more than thirty years of firefighting and disaster response under his belt, Butler had shared valuable tips with Swish and her team during their training exercises. He'd also worked with her on several smaller spills.

"You're gonna have your hands full with this one, Captain."

According to the chief, the contractor had breached an underground fuel line. That was bad enough. What made it worse was that the breach hadn't been detected until a ground-water monitoring well more than half a mile from the storage facility recorded significant levels of contamination. Her mind clicking a hundred miles an hour, Swish took both mental and physical notes as the chief ran through the actions taken so far.

All personnel evacuated from the fuel tank farm. Check. All feeder lines shut down. Check. All refueling and flying activity within a designated radius halted. Check. Fire and explosive potential from leaked fumes being monitored. Check.

Relieved that the most immediate danger to both people and facilities had been addressed, Swish geared up for the long, tough job ahead. Although Logistics procured and stored the fuel, the loggies shared responsibility for containing and cleaning up spills with the civil engineers. In close coordination with the EPA, of course. And the Arizona Department of Environmental Quality. And the Staff Judge Advocate. And a half-dozen other agencies and concerned parties.

Right now her most pressing priorities were to first locate the breach in the underground line, then block further flow into the groundwater. Thankfully, every member of her Spill Response Team had trained for just such emergencies. Several had experience with similar incidents. One, thank God, had been part of the Luke AFB team that identified hazardous waste sites resulting from disposal methods that were approved back in the '50s and '60s but didn't meet modern EPA standards.

Mike Gentry was a bioenvironmental engineer and key member of her Spill Response Team. Almost as senior as the fire chief, Mike had been talking retirement. Swish could only murmur a fervent prayer of thanks that he'd held off—although this mess might well convince him to put in his papers sooner rather than later.

"Okay, Mike, with the feeder line shut down, we can use reports from monitoring wells along the line to help pinpoint the leak, right?"

"Right. I've already requested immediate status reports from wells eleven and twelve, Captain."

Using hard data from the monitoring wells and on-site samples, they pinpointed the probable point of the leak. Swish's heart twisted when she drove out to the site and surveyed the greasy oil slick on the long, narrow lake. The scorching May heat didn't help the situation. With the afternoon temperature nudging close to a hundred degrees, toxic fumes danced with heat waves to form shimmering, iridescent clouds above the water's surface. Breathing heavily through her respirator, Swish knew a single spark could set the whole damned lake on fire.

Sweat poured down her temples and stung her eyes, making each breath she sucked in through the respirator a Herculean chore, but she didn't remove the mask until the booms were in place, the skimmer operating.

* * *

It was midafternoon when Swish grabbed a few minutes to scarf down the sandwiches and chips that Food Service personnel delivered to her and the rest of the team. Close to seven in the evening, she finally took a long enough break to call Gabe. Stepping away from the dig area, she thumbed her contacts listing. His cell phone number was still there. Even after all this time apart, she hadn't been able to bring herself to delete it. She had no idea if it was still good but tried it anyway.

"Hey, Suze," he answered after a few rings. "Got everything under control?"

"More or less." Puzzled, she cocked her head. "I'm hearing a funny buzz. Where are you?"

"Cruising along in Ole Blue."

A figure waved to her. Holding up her index finger, she pantomimed "Be right with you" to the EPA rep who'd been sweating alongside her and her team all afternoon.

"Cruising where?" she asked, her gaze on the excavation in progress.

"Home."

The succinct reply jerked Swish back to the conversation. "Home, like in Oklahoma?"

"Roger that."

She tried not to feel hurt. But she did, dammit. She did. "Nice of you to take off without bothering to say goodbye."

"I left a note."

Now she wasn't just hurt. She was pissed. "Oh. Well. That's okay, then. A note makes you rolling out of my bed and hitting the road without a word just fine and dandy."

"Christ, Suze!" A matching anger rolled back at her.

"What the hell did you expect me to do? Sit around for two or three days, twiddling my thumbs until you remembered you left a husband in that bed?"

"*Ex*-husband."

"Yeah," he snapped, "and that's pretty much the reason why."

She couldn't believe he was ripping at her for doing her job! Okay, she should've called sooner. But she was damned if she'd apologize or, worse, grovel. She'd done both often enough in the past.

"Drive safe," she snapped back.

He didn't bother to reply. She was left with a dead phone in her hand and another ache in her chest.

The note was right there, propped against a coffee mug, when she finally got back to her condo a little past two in the morning.

Maybe we'll pull up at the same intersection again sometime.

That was it. No *It was great seeing you again*. No *Call me*. Not so much as a hint that they'd reconnected in the most elemental, mutually satisfying way. And it *was* mutual, Swish thought as she crushed the note in an angry fist. He'd wanted her. As much as she'd wanted him.

Still wanted him.

The realization was as unwelcome as it was irritating. They'd tried the happily-ever-after once. It hadn't worked then. It wouldn't work now. Nothing had changed.

The next few weeks kept Swish up to her eyeballs with work. As busy as she was, though, she couldn't seem to regain her usual energy and equilibrium.

The spill containment and recovery efforts proceeded on track. Reps from the EPA and the Arizona Department of Environmental Quality fully endorsed her team's efforts. The booms contained the oil slick on the lake and the skimmers removed the surface contaminants, while the soil vapor extraction system scooped up and vacuumed the contaminated subsoil.

Yet she'd flash on the memory of those few hours in Gabe's arms at the craziest moments. In the middle of a boring staff meeting. Or in her office, while staring sightlessly at some report. More than once she got all mopey, even teary-eyed.

She had to remind herself that she'd lived through separations and a final bust-up before. She'd live through this one, too.

An unexpected visit from Dingo in early June raised her spirits. He was passing through Phoenix on his way to Tuscon. Some kind of business meeting, she gathered, although Dingo tended to be as vague about his life after the military as he'd been while wearing a uniform. They agreed to meet at one of her favorite Mexican restaurants just a few miles from Luke's main gate.

A call from the Staff Judge Advocate working the spill claims delayed Swish, so she got to the restaurant fifteen minutes late. She waved off the hostess with the explanation that she was meeting someone, took a half-dozen steps into the popular eatery and stopped dead.

Good grief! Was that Dingo in a charcoal-gray worsted suit and red power tie? The military cop whose lethal security forces had protected Swish and her team five or six years back, when they'd been ferried into a highly classified location to lay down a runway for the air assault to follow? He'd been Captain Andrews, then. Captain Blake Andrews. His face smeared with camo paint, his weapon at the ready, he'd looked as tough and scary as they came.

He still looked tough. And, yes, a little scary, but so damned handsome. Swish could certainly understand why Chelsea Howard had latched onto him. She was no slouch herself in the looks department. The two of them, Swish mused, made a striking couple.

Returning his wave, she wove her way through the tables. Her sand-colored BDUs caught more than a few glances. They also generated a good number of smiling nods. Americans in general—and the folks in the various communities surrounding Luke AFB, in particular—took pride in their military, which only added to the pride Swish herself took in the uniform she wore. And that led to the question she posed to Dingo when he commented on the ripple her appearance had stirred.

"Do you miss it?" she asked curiously.

"The uniform? Or knowing you're a small part of something big and really important?"

"Either. Both."

"Sometimes. But there are other ways to serve the public."

He didn't mention Gabe. Or the fact that his buddy was now mayor of Small Town, America. He didn't have to. But she was half relieved, half disappointed when he aimed the conversation toward another mutual acquaintance.

"I stopped by to see Cowboy and Alex last week."

Swish accepted the menu the waiter handed her and waved off anything but water. As much as she would've loved an icy margarita, she didn't drink while on duty.

"I haven't talked to either of them since the Bash. How're they doing?"

"Good. Alex's stomach is in the overripe watermelon range now." He paused, gave her an assessing stare. "Cowboy said he'd talked to Gabe."

And there it was.

"Supposedly," Dingo said, "Gabe's deep-sixed his half-formed plan to get married again."

Her reaction was instant and visceral. A brief flicker of sadness for her ex. A surge of guilty relief. And stupid, irrational, completely selfish joy. She wallowed its incandescent glow for several moments before guilt pushed front and center again.

"Did Cowboy say why he called it off?"

"No."

Dingo knew, though. Or guessed. She saw the speculation in the look he leveled at her. To deflect it, she waited until the server took their order, then turned the tables.

"What about you and your oh-so-delectable Vegas showgirl? Last I heard, you and Ms. Chelsea were heading right for hot and heavy."

"We're there. Or we were."

The slow tide of red that darkened his cheeks surprised Swish. In all the years she'd known Blake Andrews, she'd never seen him flustered or fidgety. Until now. He shifted in his seat. Crossed his knee. Uncrossed it again. Returned her gaze with a scowl.

"That woman has me wrapped six ways to Sunday. Every time I think I've got a handle on her, she goes off in a totally different direction. Like the last time I flew into Vegas to see her."

His tone vectored toward petulant. Fascinated, Swish

watched his facial expressions follow the same downward trajectory.

"I bought a ticket for the show at the Wynn. Paid top dollar for a VIP seat, right up front. I was going to surprise her with dinner and…well…whatever afterward."

"From the sound of it, I'm guessing 'whatever' didn't happen."

"The show didn't happen! Or Chelsea's part in it, anyway. Took me three calls and a face-to-face with the production supervisor before I found out she damned near drowned in her last appearance. He fired her. So what does she do?" he demanded fiercely.

"I can't even begin to imagine."

Swish couldn't. She really couldn't. She'd met the flamboyant, long-legged dancer for the first time at this year's Badger Bash, a mere three weeks ago.

Three weeks since she'd driven home in the early dawn. Three weeks since she'd spotted Ole Blue across a deserted intersection. Three weeks since she'd come to the bitter realization that she still loved her husband. *Ex*-husband, dammit. *Ex!*

"She goes to work at Treasure Island, that's what happened!"

"I hear they have a great magic show," she commented, scrambling to catch up.

"They do, except Chelsea's not in it. She's one of the outdoor pirates who swarm the English warship. She swings across the lagoon on a damned rope. Every hour on the hour."

"Not a great gig for a dancer," Swish agreed weakly.

"Ya think?" He leaned forward, his gray eyes shooting ice chips. "The fool woman can't swim."

"So why do they keep hiring her for these aquatic gigs?"

"She's got friends. Lots of friends."

"Well…"

"Well nothing. She's an idiot, as I tried to point out last time we were together."

"Uh-oh."

Last, Swish bet, being the operative word. Dingo confirmed that with a frustrated slap of his menu on the colorful tile table.

"Uh-oh is right. She axed me, just like Gabe axed his almost-fiancée."

And me, Swish wanted to add. *He axed me, too.* She couldn't put *all* the blame for their last split on him. Still…

"Enough about Chelsea and me," Dingo said, recovering his customary cool. "What's going on with you?"

"Not much, aside from a massive fuel spill, an around-the-clock recovery effort and feeling totally wiped most of the time."

"Wiped? Captain Superwoman? What happened to the inexhaustible energy that made the rest of us groan and beg for relief while you were just getting wound up?"

"Guess I just don't wind as tight as I used to."

He sat back, studying her with the beginning of a frown. "You look a little wiped, too. Still gorgeous, of course, but tired. Maybe you should see a doc."

"Nah." She forced a smile. "It's just the spill. It had me going day and night there for a while. I'll be fine now that we've got a handle on it."

Except she couldn't seem to reclaim her usual levels of energy and enthusiasm. Even Mike Gentry commented on it when he and Swish drove out to check on the removal of the last of the booms the following week. May had melted into a June that was as hot as only Arizona could bake it. The lake surface was diamond-bright, the fumes that had formerly hovered above it gone, thank God.

"Breathing through a respirator would've been torture in this heat," she remarked, leaning a hip against Mike's vehicle.

"It's pretty well torture anytime." The bio-environmental engineer slanted her a quick look. "You okay, Captain? You look tired."

"You're the second person who's told me that." She made a face and tucked a loose strand of hair back into the bun at the nape of her neck. "I'd better start taking vitamins or gulping down some Power Red."

"You might want to have the doc run a few tests," Mike commented. "You may have sucked in some fumes."

She hadn't exhibited any of the classic symptoms, like irritation of the eyes or nose, coughing or blood in her sputum. But she couldn't deny feeling a little out of breath at times. Especially in this heat. And she was too smart to brush off the possibility that she *had* sucked in some toxic fumes. Back at the office, she made an appointment with her primary care manager at the base hospital.

When she walked up to the entrance of 56th Medical Group's sand-colored two-story facility the following morning, the sun burned in another blistering blue sky. The fat, prickly pear cactus that stood sentinel beside the hospital's front door was taking the heat better than Swish was.

"I don't understand it," she told Dr. Bhutti. "I pulled two deployments to Iraq, one to Afghanistan. The heat didn't bother me half as much at either place."

The dark-eyed physician looped her stethoscope around her neck. She and Swish had formed a tight bond at their first meeting, having both served in combat zones.

"Are you hydrating adequately?"

"Forty-eight to sixty-four ounces every day, although lately I seem to be more thirsty than usual."

"Alcohol intake?"

"Minimal. I haven't even felt like a beer after work."

"How much time do you spend in the sun?"

"Three or four hours a day when we have construction or environmental projects underway. Other times, not so much."

"Any chance you could be pregnant? A woman's basal temperature elevates during pregnancy, which makes her more prone to dehydration, heat exhaustion and heat cramps."

"No, I..."

Swish stopped, her breath blocking her throat. An image of Gabe digging a crumpled foil package out of his wallet leaped into her head. How long did he say he'd been carrying the damned thing around? A year? And she'd been so tickled by the fact he hadn't used it with Miss Priss.

"I guess I *could* be."

The doc rolled back her stool. "Well, we'll know soon enough. I'll write an order for a lab test. You may want to cut back on your exposure to the heat until we get the results. And keep drinking plenty of water."

Shock eddied into the first wavelets of panic. "Can't I pee on a stick or something? Find out now?"

"Hang loose. I'll get a kit."

Swish edged off the exam table, her boots thudding on the floor. Too agitated to sit, she paced the tiny room. She couldn't be pregnant. The odds couldn't be *that* stacked against her and Gabe!

A chance meeting at a traffic light. One hot and heavy session between the sheets. Okay, two. Three? No, just two. She'd climaxed first. She was sure she had. Then she'd straddled Gabe's hips and pumped him for all she was worth.

She'd been so eager, so impatient. He hadn't been exactly gentle, either. The condom could've popped anytime during their straining and rocking and thrusting. Ha! Who was she kidding? The roof could've fallen in on them and they wouldn't have noticed.

Dammit all to hell!

She was standing with her arms crossed, boots planted wide, glaring at a chart depicting the pulmonary system, when Dr. Bhutti returned.

"Here's a home pregnancy kit and the lab slips for your blood and urine tests. But be advised that the results from these kits are unofficial as they're not always reliable," she cautioned. "There's a restroom next to the lab. Pee in one of the cups and leave the sample to be analyzed. The home kit is yours to use whenever."

No way Swish was going to wait for the Air Force to do its thing. Clutching the lab slip and the home kit, she threaded her way through a large area crowded with uniformed personnel, retirees and their families, some waiting for prescriptions to be filled, others waiting to called in to see a doc. With almost twenty-six thousand folks eligible for care at the Luke Hospital, it was always a busy place.

She handed the tech at the lab desk the doc's order. "Urine sample first, Captain, then we'll take your blood. You'll find the necessary supplies and instructions in the restroom next door."

It wasn't her first time having to pee in a cup. Every active-duty member had to do a random urinalysis at least once a year. Once every two years for Guard and Reserve members. There were all kinds of safeguards built into the process. An observer had to be present. The donor had to write his or her name on the plastic bottle in the presence of that witness, making it, in essence, a legal document. A rigorous chain-of-custody record was completed by every person at every step of the process. Consequently, Swish had filled her share of little plastic cups. And for at least the tenth or twelfth or twentieth time, she wondered why the hell someone hadn't invented a better way for women to hit the target.

She finally got the cup half full, set it on the edge of the sink and ripped open the home kit. Her palms got clammy as she extracted an eyedropper and a test strip encased in plastic wrap. She closed her eyes for a moment, the dropper gripped between thumb and forefinger. What if the test was positive? What if she was carrying the child Gabe had always wanted? What would she do? What would he do?

They'd work it out, she decided fiercely. One way or another. Jaw set, she suctioned up a small sample of pale gold urine and dropped it on the test strip.

She no idea how long she stood staring at the bright

purple splotch that blossomed on the strip. Long enough for someone to rattle the door handle once, then rattle a few moments later. A third, distinctly impatient shake tore her gaze from the lavender bloom.

"Hey! Anyone in there?"

"I'll be out in a sec."

She collected the home kit elements and stuffed them back in their box, then tossed it in the trash. Capping the urine cup, she used the Sharpie provided by the lab to write her last name on a label, slapped it on the cup and placed the sample on the shelf as instructed. A brief twirl sent the sample into the lab. She emerged and yielded the restroom to a beefy, irritated lieutenant colonel.

"All yours, sir."

Not until she'd rolled up her sleeve and stretched out her arm for the blood test the doc had ordered did the possible ramifications hit her. If she *had* breathed in toxic fumes... If her blood had contained residual gases when the egg fertilized by Gabe's squiggly little sperm had worked its way to her uterus... If those gases had impacted the baby's subsequent cell formation...

"Captain!"

She turned a wild, unseeing stare on the lab tech who'd just stuck a needle in her vein.

"Don't faint on me, Captain! Look up at the ceiling. Breath deep. Slow. There, we're done."

Chapter Four

When Swish drove to work early the next morning
she carried the effects of a long, worried night. Her
eyes ached, her skin felt drum tight and her thoughts
continually skidded off track. Not even putting the top
down on her T-bird and cruising along with the sparse
early traffic could blow out the cobwebs. Her stomach
stayed knotted until Dr. Bhutti's call at zero-eight-forty.

"Congratulations, Captain. It's official. You're pregnant."

"What about the blood tests?"

"They came back clean. No evidence of any damage
to your respiratory system. Your heart and lung functions are normal."

"How about the baby? Could it have been affected
by toxic fumes even if nothing showed up in the tests?"

"Unlikely, in my professional opinion, but why don't

we talk about that when you come in to discuss your pregnancy profile. Does this afternoon at sixteen hundred work for you?"

"I'll be there."

Swish hung up, careening wildly between relief and the knowledge her life had just veered off in an unplanned and totally scary direction. Somewhere in the dark reaches of the night she'd eliminated any thought of an abortion. Even with the fear hanging over her like a double-bladed ax that the fetus might've been affected by fumes, she knew she'd see the pregnancy through.

Her mother was a deacon in their church, her dad a retired county assessor. They never talked politics or religion outside the house, but they'd raised their daughter with a very traditional set of values. They'd also been broken-hearted when Swish and Gabe divorced. Aside from losing a son-in-law they both adored, they had to at least temporarily shelve their hope for a brood of noisy, boisterous grandchildren.

They'd be surprised but supportive at the news that Swish was pregnant. In the meantime, she'd have to make major changes in her personal life *and* her career. A pregnancy profile dictated limits on physical training, body weight requirements and environmental exposures. It also disqualified her for worldwide duty and took her off mobility status during her pregnancy and for at least six weeks afterward.

Damn! She'd worked so hard to achieve command of her rapid response engineering team. If the team had to deploy now, it would go without her. Cringing at the thought, Swish went down the hall and rapped on the door of her boss's office.

Lieutenant Colonel Spence Hawthorne had commanded the 56th Civil Engineering Squadron for less than a month. Hawthorne had barely had time to get to know his people—or they him—but what Swish had seen so far impressed her. She had no idea how he'd take the news that the leader of his Prime BEEF team was about to come off mobility status for the next year, though.

He reacted pretty much the way she anticipated, given that he knew she was divorced. Very cautiously. "You're pregnant?"

"That's what the tests say."

"Are, uh, congratulations in order?"

For the first time since Dr. Bhutti suggested she might be pregnant, Swish felt her lips curve in a grin. "Yeah, they are."

"Okay, then." Stretching out a bear-sized paw, he came around from behind his desk and pumped her hand. "Congratulations, Captain. Now, who do you recommend to take over for you as Prime BEEF commander?"

Wham! Just like that she was displaced. Although she'd come in prepared for exactly that question, it still hit hard. "Captain Donaldson's my designated alternate. And Lieutenant Harbaugh would be a good backfill for him."

"I'll take a look at their records. What's happening with the spill?"

"We're on track with the cleanup. EPA's promised to sign off on it this week."

"Good job, Swish."

"Thanks. There's one more thing."

"I'm listening."

"I'd like to take some leave." She drew in a breath,

let it out. "I need to go home and tell my ex-husband that the weekend we spent together last month has produced some unexpected consequences."

"That should be an interesting conversation."

"No kidding."

"How long do you need?"

"I've racked up so much leave that I'm in use-or-lose status. So I'm thinking two weeks, starting after my prenatal check."

"Go." He approved her request with only one caveat. "Just be sure you come back."

Dr. Bhutti had told her that most initial prenatal appointments weren't scheduled until after the eighth week. Swish was just hitting her seventh, but the doc understood her concerns and got her in with Dr. Evans the following Monday.

The visit was a long one, with more urine and blood samples; checks of blood pressure, height and weight; a pelvic exam and pap smear; and an ultrasound that confirmed a due date based on Swish's encounter with Gabe. The doc took a detailed family and genetic history and went over her deployment record in some detail. He also assured her the blood test would verify the RH factor, hemoglobin and hematocrit, as well as check for hepatitis B, HIV, rubella and syphilis and do another screen for any toxic blood gases.

"Given your concerns, Captain, I suggest we do another, noninvasive blood test at about ten weeks to check for genetic abnormalities like Down syndrome or other chromosomal problems."

Gulping, she agreed.

* * *

With the prenatal visit behind her, Swish debated whether to fly or drive back to Oklahoma. It was only a little over fourteen hours by car. Easily doable in a day.

Or she could break it up with an overnight stop in Albuquerque to visit with Cowboy and his very pregnant wife. Just as Gabe had been planning to do when he'd spotted his ex idling at a red light across an intersection.

The irony wasn't lost on her, but she figured Alex might have some good advice on what to expect in the coming months. More to the point, two easy days on the road would give Swish time to figure out what long-distance parenting arrangements she should propose to Gabe. She didn't doubt for a moment he'd want to be involved in their child's life. They'd just have to work out how much and how often.

A call to Alex that evening resulted in a warm invitation and a rueful explanation. "Ben's not here. He got hit with one of those short notice, I'll-have-to-kill-you-if-I-tell-you-where training exercises. So Maria and I would love some company."

"Great. I should be there by five tomorrow afternoon, if that works for you."

"Works perfectly. See you then."

She left her condo just as dawn was coloring the sky and hit I-10 well before it turned into a one long stop-and-go. The rising sun was in her face this time, instead of the rearview mirror, and the glorious red-and-gold sunrise gave her spirits a decided lift.

Her good mood took a temporary dive when she saw the sign for Exit 134. The same exit she'd pulled off on that fateful morning to hit the ladies' room. As the

McDonald's sign flashed by, she couldn't help thinking how different her life would be right now if she'd crossed her legs and held it. Or, once off the interstate and stopped at the traffic light, if she'd waited for the light to turn green, zipped through the intersection, waved to ex and continued on her merry way.

Right. Like life gave anyone do-overs. Shrugging off the useless shouldda, wouldda, coulddas, she put the exit behind her. Twenty minutes later she turned onto I-17 and headed for the mountains.

She stopped for coffee in New River and lunch in Flagstaff. As always, the majestic San Francisco peaks painted a palette of colors that ranged from hazy green at their base to stone-cold granite near the jagged peaks. Even this late in June she could see a trace of white on the distant Humphrey's Peak.

By the time she'd cruised past Gallup and hit Albuquerque's outskirts, she was ready to take a break. And pee! It was probably purely psychological, but now that she knew she was pregnant the need came even more urgently. Refusing to think about how Gabe would tease her about her bladder battles now, she tracked Mapquest to Alex and Cowboy's address.

Their casita looked like an earth-toned adobe box on the outside but Swish detected an artist's flair in the chilis dangling from raffia ropes and the cactus branching fat arms strung with twinkling white lights and a cloud of colorful, fluttering butterflies.

Alex met her at the door with a hug that she made her angle sideways to accommodate her now bulging belly. Swish battled an instant stab of envy for the mom-to-be's cotton tunic sporting an arch of colorful spangles.

"You look like a giant rainbow."

"I'm certainly a giant something," Alex returned, laughing.

The casita's lush interior was another celebration of Alex's artistic talents. The desert-toned walls, the sofas and chairs covered in green cactus and red chili patterns, the Native American prints and baskets on the walls all delighted Swish. But it was the magnificent Eagle Dancer occupying a place of honor on the mantel above the fireplace that drew her like a magnet. She'd only been assigned to Luke for four months, but she'd spent enough time in and out of other bases in the Southwest to recognize the exquisite workmanship that had produced this carved wooden kachina with its feathers and intricate turquoise beading.

"This is gorgeous!"

"I think so, too."

With a misty smile, Alex rested her arms on the tummy Dingo had described as an overripe watermelon. A slight understatement, Swish decided.

"It was my wedding present to Ben."

Her use of Cowboy's given name was a little jolt. A small but subtle reminder that she was, if not an outsider, at least not lodged at the epicenter of that tight, inner military circle. With her thriving business, Alex maintained a life and an individuality independent of her tangential connection to the military.

Gabe had cut even that tangential connection. He lived a life apart from her and the Air Force now. Was it fair of Swish to pull him back into the periphery of that circle? She was still wrestling with that question.

"Maria's over at her friend Dinah's house," Alex announced as she led the way into the kitchen. "So I made two pitchers of margaritas. High-test for you, virgin for me."

She picked up a frosted green pitcher and was ready to pour when Swish shook her head. "Better make that virgin for both of us."

"Why? You're staying the night, aren't you? Not driving anywhere until... Oh!"

Alex's dark brows shot up, and Swish nodded in response to the unspoken question.

"Yep, me, too."

"Since when?" Plunking the pitcher back onto the tiled counter, she answered her own question. "Wait! You were drinking at the Bash last month so you must've just found out."

"I did."

Alex glanced down the counter, looked up. Swish guessed immediately what was coming. Cowboy's wife was as fiercely loyal to her friends as any of the Badger's protégées were to theirs.

"Chelsea told me Blake Andrews stopped by Phoenix to visit you," Alex said, her voice several degrees cooler than before.

"We met for lunch. Just lunch."

The other woman held her gaze for a moment longer, then nodded. "Good to know."

"But what's with Chelsea's new gig at Treasure Island? Dingo says she swings across the lagoon on a rope every hour on the hour."

Her loyalty to her former roommate satisfied, Alex laughed. "Not anymore. All it took was one dunk. She's unemployed again."

Not for long, Swish bet. If those mile-long legs and generous boobs didn't wow some other producer, the dancer's infectious laugh and sparkling personality would. Wishing Dingo the best of luck with his on-again, off-again girlfriend, she turned to more immediate concerns.

"This whole pregnancy bit is so new, I haven't wrapped my head around it yet. You mind if I pick your brain about what to expect?"

"Pick away!" Alexis poured two virgin drinks, waved Swish to a counter stool and plopped onto the one next to her. "Where do you want to start? The bloating? The gas? The swollen ankles or the fact that one whiff of sizzling fajitas makes me puke?"

"Actually, I was hoping you'd clue me in to some of the legal ramifications. I know you and Cowboy adopted Maria over her natural father's objections. I'll have to work out a custody arrangement, too."

"Ummm, I can see that might be an issue since you and the father aren't married."

"Actually, we were. Once."

"Gabe?" Alex tried her damnedest to choke back her surprise. She didn't quite get there. "Are you telling me Gabe's the father?"

"Yep."

"Where? How?"

"He was driving east on I-10. I was driving west, back to the base."

"You mean the day after the Bash? When he was going to stop by to see us?"

"Yep," Swish said again. "We hooked up by chance, then went our separate ways."

"So that's why he was so late getting here! Wait till I tell Ben." Her eyes danced. "Are you two planning to get back together?"

"No. Well. Maybe. At least, as far as it involves the baby." Her shoulders slumping, Swish admitted the truth. "Oh, God, Alex, I don't know *what* we're going to do. I haven't even told Gabe I'm pregnant yet. That's why I took leave and am heading back to Oklahoma."

"Well…" Her hostess used the excuse of topping off their drinks to gather her thoughts. "There are several single moms and military couples in Ben's squadron. I know they have to sign some kind of document detailing who'll take care of their kids if they get deployed."

"I know. A Family Care Plan."

Air Force regulations required that all single parents and military couples with children name a non-military Short-Term Care Provider who could assume care of their child in the event the parent or parents were deployed on short notice. They also had to designate a Long-Term Care Provider willing to assume full responsibility for the child if the parent or parents were deployed for an extended period of time, selected for an unaccompanied overseas tour or assigned to a ship at sea.

Swish didn't doubt for a minute that Gabe would agree to be their child's designated care provider. Assuming, that is, he didn't push for full custody. The possibility had been buzzing around in the back of her mind for most of the day's drive.

"Our situation probably isn't all that unique but it will require some negotiation."

"How so?"

"We got a quickie, no-contest divorce. We'll have to go back to court to address legal custody of our baby."

She'd done some research. The Service Member's Relief Act protected military personnel from having to defend themselves from civil suits—including divorces and child custody hearings—while overseas and not able to defend themselves. The Uniform Deployed Parents Custody and Visitation Act passed in 2012 was a more comprehensive attempt to balance the rights of service members, the other parent and the best interests of the child involved. Her situation with Gabe fell somewhere in the middle of all that legalese.

"I'm sorry, Suze. I wish I could help. Our petition to adopt Maria sprang from a completely different set of legal circumstances. I can refer you to a really good family practice attorney, though. He's licensed here in New Mexico, which wouldn't help if you have to petition an Arizona court, but he's one of the best in the field."

"Thanks. Hopefully Gabe and I can work all this out amicably. If not, I may take you up on that referral."

"Good enough. Now let's talk maternity tops. I'm developing a whole new line of tanks and tees celebrating big bellies."

"If they're all as gorgeous as that rainbow you're wearing, I'll take one of each."

"No way. You, my friend, will get a one-of-a-kind Alexis Scott design."

The lively, bright-eyed Maria and her black-and-white cat entertained Swish at breakfast the next morning while Alex darted over to her workshop. She returned just as her guest was getting ready to leave and presented her with a stretchy, cap-sleeved royal-blue top that featured the Air Force insignia in sparkling silver and darker blue crystals. Above them, Alex had emblazoned Warrior Mom in bright, bold red.

"Best I could do on short notice. Try it on and see if it fits."

Swish ducked into the powder room off the hall and exchanged her sun-faded 56th Fighter Wing T-shirt for glittering blue and red crystals.

"This is fantastic, Alex. Thank you!"

The designer tapped a finger against her chin. "It'll do for a rush job. But I'm working on more elaborate designs for each of the four military services. I should have the prototypes ready when you come back through. You'll have to give me your honest opinion."

"Will do," Swish promised.

With the morning sun once again in her face, Swish hit I-40 and headed east through Tijeras Pass. Even in high summer, wind whistled through the narrow pass with enough gusto to rock the car. Once through the canyon, the Sandia Mountains fell behind her and the landscape flattened to high desert plateaus scarred by zigzagging washes. Triple-strand barbed wire defined widely scattered ranches. Angled snow fences were positioned to keep the interstate clear come winter.

She stopped to pee twice that morning. Once in Tucumcari. Again just over the Texas state line. Lunch was chicken and dumplings at the Cracker Barrel in Amarillo. She made another pit stop when she hit the Oklahoma state line. Fifty miles later, the rugged mesas of the Panhandle gave way to rolling plains that tugged at something deep inside her. This was the land that had nourished her. Nourished Gabe. Their baby's roots went deep into the red Oklahoma soil.

She exited I-40 some thirty miles outside Oklahoma City and had to smile at the oversize water tower proclaiming Yukon as the birthplace of Garth Brooks. Gabe had saved his earnings as a pizza delivery boy for months to buy tickets for Brooks's big concert at the Chesapeake Center in Ok-City the week Swish turned eighteen. She still had every song the country star had ever recorded in her iTunes library.

Once through Yukon, she followed a spear-straight county road nine miles south to the town of Cedar Creek. Born and bred in this sleepy, tree-shaded town, she knew its history backward and forward. Not surprising, since she'd worked one entire summer at the town's musty records office and history center.

From prehistoric times, hunter-gatherers had camped alongside the creek lined with stunted, twisty-limbed cedars. The same creek she and Gabe used to swim in. And go skinny-dipping in. And…

Biting down on her lower lip, she blanked the memory of those hours splashing in the sun-dappled creek and let her gaze roam over broad, flat fields. The area's primary industry had always been agriculture. Early settlers had planted huge orchards and plowed acre after acre of rich soil. Swish and almost every other kid she knew had earned spending money picking asparagus, carrots and strawberries in the spring, cantaloupe and watermelon and sweet corn in the summer, apples and pears in the fall.

Which was how Gabe had busted three ribs, she remembered with a wry smile. He'd had to show off. Demonstrate to her and his pals what a fast picker he was by reaching too far out on a limb. His subsequent tumble off his ladder had scared the dickens out of Swish. It had also made him miss most of his junior year football season and almost cost him his scholarship to OU.

And that, she acknowledged grimly as she forced yet another vivid scene out of her head, was why she'd made such infrequent visits to her parents in the past few years. Every street, every dusty storefront, even the elementary school, held too many memories.

Fighting those memories, she eased off the gas and made a slow drag down Main. The changes were all too noticeable. A depressing number of antique and second-hand shops had moved in when the original businesses relocated to properties closer to the Walmart on the east side of town. The local bank that had passed out lollipops to every kid who came in with their parents was gone, replaced by a drive-through chain branch.

To her delight, though, Ruby's Cafe still occupied a prime spot at the corner of Main and 3rd Street. And a hand-printed placard said the bandstand at the center of Veterans' Memorial Park still hosted summer Saturday evening concerts.

She noticed even more changes when she turned off Main onto the street that followed twisty, turning Cedar Creek. Yards that had been dappled with weeds when she'd last visited her folks were neatly mowed, their edges trimmed. Homes that had looked a little run-down had new coats of paint. Even the junker on the corner of Cedar and 5th had undergone an amazing metamorphosis. The awful clutter on its front porch had disappeared. So had the three rusty vehicles that used to roost on cinderblocks in its drive.

She spotted a surprising number of new homes, too. Classy brick-and-river-stone facades. High-pitched

roofs. Two- and three-car garages. All set on a bend of
the creek previously occupied by an abandoned mill.

That had to be Gabe's doing. All of this! As she knew
all too well, her ex-husband had an extremely low tol-
erance for clutter. His years in the military had only
exacerbated his type A personality. From all appear-
ances, it looked as though Cedar Creek's determined
young mayor had demolished the crumbling mill and
opened all those pretty lots with their sloping views of
the creek to a new wave of settlers. She guessed they
probably were probably spillover from the sprawling,
ever-expanding Federation Aviation Administration's
training center less than fifteen miles away. Looking
at the manicured lawns and elegant facades, she'd bet
her next paycheck that Gabe intended to turn their once
sleepy farm town into one of OKC's more desirable
bedroom communities.

She would've won her bet, as her parents confirmed
a mere half hour after they'd joyously welcomed their
only chick back to her childhood home. He dad was
older and grayer but still trim and energetic. Her
spritely, gregarious mother now sported glowing turquoise tips at the ends of her silvery bob.

Swish's open-mouthed astonishment at the bright
color delighted her mom. Almost as much as when they
took up their favorite positions on the front porch and
her daughter bit into a raisin-pecan-oatmeal cookie with
an ecstatic sigh.

"Iced tea. Fresh-baked cookies. I'm home."

As easily, as naturally as that, she slipped back into
her Cedar Creek skin. She was a daughter, a neighbor,
a friend to so many who still lived here. Luke AFB, the
fuel spill, her Prime BEEF Team all belonged to another

world, another person. As they had so many times, she and her mom shared the porch swing. Her dad sat in the ratty, high-backed wicker fan chair that Mary Elizabeth Kingfisher Jackson had been threatening to get rid of for the past ten years.

"What's with all these new houses?" Swish asked. "Where's everyone coming from?"

"I don't know," her number-cruncher dad said. "And I don't care. You wouldn't believe it, Suze. With all the newcomers, we could ask two or even three times what we would've asked a few years ago for this property."

She planted a foot on the floor and stopped the swing's gentle motion. "Are you guys thinking of selling?"

"Probably not for a few years yet. But we're feeling our age more with each passing day. If the value of the house keeps rising due to Gabe's clever outreach pro—ow!"

Wincing, he yanked his ankle out reach of his wife's sharp-pointed mule. He couldn't miss her warning scowl, however. "Sorry, Suzanne. When you called to tell us you were coming home, your mom made me swear I wouldn't mention Gabe."

"It's okay." She took a sip and let the sugary-sweet tea give her courage. "As a matter of fact, Gabe and I sort of…uh…reconnected last month."

Hope sprang into her parents' eyes. So obvious. So painful that she almost blurted out that she was pregnant. She couldn't, though. Not until she'd told Gabe.

"Whooo-wheee!" Hooting, her dad slapped his thigh. "Are you two are getting back together?"

"Oh, baby!" Her eyes filming with tears, Mary shot an arm around her daughter's shoulders and hugged her joyfully. "You don't know how long and hard we've prayed for this. You and Gabe belong together. You always have."

Acutely uncomfortable, she explained as gently as she could. "We're not *back* together, Mom. We just spent a few hours together last month."

"But you came home. All the way from Arizona just to see him again. Those hours had to mean something."

Oh, they did! Much more than she could share at this particular moment. She dodged their hopes with a bright smile.

"I came home to see you *and* Gabe. Right now, though, I'm more interested in our chances of getting dad to fire up that new grill I saw on the back patio without singeing his eyebrows off."

The oblique reference to a long-ago family camping trip had her mom laughing and her dad huffing indignantly.

Hours later she drifted toward an exhausted slumber in her old bedroom. The same daisy-splashed comforter draped her bed. The same ancient iMac sat on her desk. And the same posters decorated the walls.

God, how she'd crushed on Linkin Park. Looking back, she realized the rock band had showcased her induction into the bewildering mysteries of adolescence. Menstruation. Weird sensations low in her belly every time Gabe walked her home from school. The startled glance he aimed at her chest that hot spring day they skipped World History to skinny-dip in Cedar Creek.

Whoa! She could still see his surprise. Still hear the indignation. *When the hell did you get boobs, Susie Q?*

The past swamped her, and she gave up thinking of

herself as Swish. To everyone here, she was *Suzanne*, the obnoxiously inquisitive kid who'd delved into those dusty archives at the Cedar Creek records office. *Suze*, the baton-twirling majorette who'd pranced ten paces ahead of her high school band in every hometown parade and state competition. *Susie Q*, the eager bride who'd married the only man she'd ever loved.

And *USAF Lieutenant Suzanne Hall*, she tacked on with a small pang. So thrilled with her construction engineering degree from OU. So eager to raise her hand and be sworn in as a second lieutenant. So freakin' proud of her shiny gold bars. And so damned eager to shake off Oklahoma's red dust.

Scrunching her eyes shut, she blocked the colorful reminders of her past that surrounded her. She might be stretched out in the same bed she'd dreamed in for so many years, but she was *not* the same hopelessly idealistic teen who'd believed in happily-ever-after. She'd come home for one reason and one reason only.

She would call Gabe first thing in the morning and arrange a meeting. She'd have to give him time to get over the shock. God knew she was still dealing with it. Once he'd recovered, they would calmly, rationally work out a child custody agreement. One that recognized the rights and desires of both parents. Then they'd go their separate ways.

Again.

Fighting a stupid rush of tears, Suze dragged the sheet up over her head.

Chapter Five

Suzanne Jackson Hall was back in town.

Gabe heard about it when he dropped into Ruby's for the Thursday evening meatloaf special. Three different people couldn't wait to let him know they'd spotted his ex-wife cruising Main in a berry-red T-bird earlier that afternoon.

He got another confirmation of the news when he stopped to fill up Ole Blue up at Jerry Dixon's Gas 'N' Go on his way home. While Jerry ran his credit card, he oh-so-casually let it drop that when his wife, Janice, had gone out to water her hydrangeas, she'd waved to Suze and her folks from across the street.

So Gabe wasn't surprised when his mother and two of his three sisters called that evening to report additional sightings. None of them could cite the reason for the visit, however, although Gabe suspected someone would nose it out before much longer.

To his surprise, he even heard from Alicia Johnson. The petite, perpetually upbeat Realtor had handled their breakup surprisingly well. She admitted that she'd pretty much given up on him deciding to take their relationship to the next level. But she'd also let him know she was still available if he changed his mind. For a while, anyway.

Actually, her easy acceptance of the split had dinged Gabe's pride a little. At least until he heard through the grapevine that Alicia had attended some black-tie charity function in Oklahoma City on the arm of oil-and-gas magnate Dave Forrester while Gabe was out in California.

Tonight's call, she informed him, sprang from the fact that she still cared about him. Enough to want to be sure he'd heard about his ex. "I know how small towns are," she said with one of her rippling laughs. "You've probably already received a half-dozen reports that Suze is home. But just in case...?"

"I got the word."

"Okay, then." A pause. "Tell her hello from me when you see her."

Yeah, sure. Like *that* was gonna happen.

Gabe never claimed to be the sharpest pencil in the box, especially when it came to understanding the female psyche. Growing up with three sisters had hammered home the unshakable conviction that men and women really did inhabit different emotional planets.

But even he understood why Suze and Alicia had never developed a shred of rapport. A sixth grade Sadie Hawkins dance shortly after Alicia and her folks had moved to Cedar Creek had ignited the initial feud with Gabe caught squarely in the middle.

Then there was the infamous band-room incident in junior high. No one, Gabe included, knew who said what to whom. Neither of the principals involved would discuss it. But Suze quit band and never went back. In his heart of hearts, Gabe suspected the dustup might've had something to do with the fact that she was tone deaf and couldn't play the trumpet worth squat. Even her mother had gently suggested she wasn't a good fit for the church's youth orchestra. Thankfully, Gabe had managed to avoid getting caught in the middle of that one.

"It's too bad Suze and I ended up rivals," Alicia admitted. "I would've liked to be her friend. She's so darn smart and a natural-born leader. Not to mention the fact that she had the hottest stud in three counties dangling at the end of her line."

Gabe returned the only safe answer he could come up with. "I'll tell her you said hey."

Then he waited. All the rest of that evening and a good chunk of the next morning.

With school out for the summer, he didn't have classes to prepare for. No searching for new ways to pound the relevance of history into high schoolers whose hormones had taken possession of their brains. Even the tennis clinics had been put on hold in this 100-plus degree heat. Nor did he have a city council meeting to stretch his patience and diplomatic skills to the breaking point. So, right up until nine-forty-five on that hot, steamy June morning, it was just him and Doofus.

"What do you think?" he asked the chocolate-eyed, lop-eared mutt. "Is she gonna call or not?"

The hound lifted his head from his outstretched

paws. Angled his head. Then huffed out a distinctly dog-flavored breath, his dewlaps quivering in ecstasy as Gabe scratched behind his ears.

"You're a big help," Gabe chided with a wry smile. He still hadn't figured out how he'd come to share his life with this oversize mutt with a wiry, corkscrew coat, the instincts of a hunter and the personality of an over-eager puppy.

Gabe had found him shivering under Ole Blue, every rib plainly visible and his coat a tangled mess. He'd brought the dog in for the night, intending to take him to the shelter if no one responded to the notices he put out. That was last November. Seven months later they were still housemates.

The size of a small horse, the dog ate like there was no tomorrow and went nuts at the sound of a bell or buzzer. *Any* bell or buzzer. The phone. The front door. The micro-wave. The washer dinging the end of a cycle. So when Suze finally called, Doofus reacted with typical hysteria.

Gabe was in his beat-up leather armchair, feet propped on the hassock, reviewing Cedar Creek's re-vised five-year budget on his laptop while the dog sprawled, paws in the air, on the floor beside him. Jerked from his sleep, the hound leaped up and raced for the front door, woofing his fool head off and dem-onstrating yet again how he'd earned his name.

"It's the phone," Gabe shouted over his ear-shattering barks. "Hey! Doofus! It's the phone! Oh, for…! Hang on a sec, Suze."

He pushed out of the chair and made for the front door. As soon as it opened, the hound leaped out, ready to take on any and all hostiles. Thoroughly disappointed to find not even a squirrel to chase, Doofus barked out a loud warning just for the heck of it before wheeling back inside. His claws clicked on the hall tiles as he pranced back to the den and plopped down beside Gabe's chair.

"What in the world was that?" Suze wanted to know when Gabe got back on the phone.

"My self-appointed greeting committee. Any sudden noise sends him to the front door in a frenzy of excitement."

"When did you acquire a greeter?"

"About six months back."

She hesitated, then plunged in. "I'm assuming the jungle drums have already telegraphed the news."

"That my ex drove into town yesterday afternoon? Yeah, they have. You took your time getting around to telling me yourself."

He tried, honestly tried, to keep the bite out of his voice. Probably would've done a better job of it if he hadn't lain awake half the damned night wondering why she'd come home so suddenly.

Gabe kept in touch with her folks. He never thought of them as his *ex*-in-laws. Last time they talked a few days ago, both Mary and Ed Jackson were doing well, and Gabe would've heard immediately if they'd suffered some kind of emergency since then. So, if it wasn't her folks who bought her home, it had to be him. Him and their unexpected, unresolved last meeting.

The fierce hope that thought stirred scared the crap out of him. Their separation and divorce had left a mile-wide crater in his heart but he'd recovered. Slowly, painfully, he'd forced himself to adjust to LSS. Life sans Suze.

Hooking up with her last month had ripped the wound open again. For those few, wild hours that he'd cradled her in his arms, Gabe had actually let himself think they could erase the mistakes and hurts of the past and start over. Then she'd leaped out of bed and yanked on her uniform and hadn't bothered to call until seven hours later, when he was already on the road.

He understood she loved her job. He also understood that she was good at it. So freakin' good she'd probably end up as the three-star commander of some joint task force or another.

He also understood about emergency responses. Hell, even here in sleepy Cedar Creek, he and his first responders dealt with their share of disasters. The damage was generally small scale—a vehicle accident or kitchen fire or a tragic drowning—but the impact on people's lives was immediate and too often devastating.

If Gabe hadn't learned anything in the past, tumultuous few years, it was that life didn't hand out any do-overs. No starting from scratch again. Not for him, for Suze, for his constituents or his former targets. Yet damned if his pulse didn't do a quick roll when she requested a face-to-face.

"I need to talk to you. Can we get together for coffee?"

"Sure."

She waited for more, but he refused to make it easy for her.

"Mom said you bought the old Schumann place. That you've been fixing it up. Should I come there?"

"That works."

"Now?"

He was just irritated enough at her for taking so long to call—and at himself for being so anxious to hear the sound of her voice—that he enjoyed the snap in her reply.

"Okay. I'll brew up a fresh pot."

* * *

Suze used the short drive to rein in her temper. She knew exactly why Gabe had pushed her buttons. She would've been pissed, too, if she'd been waiting for her ex to explain why he'd suddenly dropped into town. Assuming, of course, he'd been waiting and not doing the dirty with Miss Priss.

Thank God Dingo had told her Gabe had called it off with Alicia. The relief that Prissy Missy wouldn't become stepmother to the child Suze now carried occupied her thoughts all the way to the Schumann place.

It was one of the older homesteads, set in a curve of the creek, with a natural windbreak provided by a stand of ancient pecan trees that had no doubt yielded their succulent harvest to the hunter-gatherers who'd roamed this area for thousands of years. The first Schumanns to settle in Cedar Creek claimed this choice plat during the land run and put up a wood-framed, two-story house. One of their grandkids—great-grandkids?—had added an L-shaped addition. Another had slapped on some puke-green aluminum siding and lived there until he and his wife passed away. *Their* kids had put the house on the market immediately but it had sat vacant for as long as Suze could remember.

As she turned onto 8th Street, memories of the Schumann place crowded in. How many times had she and Gabe and their pals ignored the *No Trespassing* sign to swim in the shady creek behind the deserted homestead? How many bright September afternoons had they waded through knee-high weeds to reach the pecan orchard and fill gunny sacks with ripe nuts? They'd picked most of the harvest off the ground, although Gabe often attached a hook to a long broom handle so he could reach the lower branches and shake down a golden-brown rain. She could almost taste the luscious chocolate-pecan pies Gabe's mom baked from their harvest.

She would swing by to visit her former mother-in-law in the next day or two. Gabe's sisters, too. Once she and Gabe had worked out a plan for how...

Good God!

Her foot hit the brake. She jerked the convertible to a stop midblock, staring in stunned surprise at what used to be a decrepit, empty shell. The sea of prickly weeds that had surrounded it was gone, replaced by a sweep of tree-shaded lawn and a curving drive. The wraparound porch, once sagging and all but invisible behind a screen of scraggly, overgrown bushes, now sported new railings and support beams painted a clean, inviting white. The nauseating green siding was gone, too. Suze almost didn't recognize the old homestead with those wide windows, river-rock trim and double-wide front door.

And the crepe myrtles. Dear Lord, the crepe myrtles! That huge Dynamite Red at the corner of the porch had been so clogged with strangler vines it had never put out more than a few blooms. And the hedge of Twilight Lavenders alongside the detached garage... She ached to bury her face in those fragrant blossoms and breathe in the scent she always associated with home.

Still marveling at the old homestead's transformation, she took her foot off the brake and turned into the drive. The front door opened just as she glided to a stop. Gabe came out onto the porch, a coffee mug in one hand and the other gripping the collar of a shaggy hound.

The self-appointed greeter boomed a welcome while

his ragged tail sliced the air a mile a minute. Bright-eyed and eager, the dog strained against the hold on his collar until Gabe issued a sharp command. "Sit!"

He obeyed, but his butt continued to wiggle furiously on the varnished porch planking. Suze approached the dog cautiously and held out her hand for him to sniff. After one perfunctory whiff, he drenched her palm with eager, slobbering kisses. Smiling down at his liquid brown eyes and goofy grin, she fell instantly in love.

"Looks like he's part Lab," she commented.

"He is. But the vet thinks he's mostly wire-haired pointing griffon."

"What the heck is a wirehaired pointing whatever?"

"A sporting breed supposedly developed toward the end of the nineteenth century to flush, point and retrieve water fowl and game birds. God knows, he spends more time in the creek than out of it."

"Never heard of a griffon."

"Me, either, until Doofus barreled into my life. He's pretty good at not jumping on folks but when I release him, better be prepared."

Suze dutifully planted both feet and let the hound dance around her a few times. He certainly looked like he wanted to jump up and lick her chin. She could see the eagerness in his quivering, shivering excitement. But he confined his attention to the hand she kept extended until the flick of a bushy tail across the lawn snagged his attention. He whirled, locked on his prey, then took off, barking ferociously at the squirrel who dared invade his domain.

"That'll keep him occupied for a while," Gabe said drily. "C'mon in."

He held the door for her, and Suze took the few steps

onto the porch and into the air-conditioned cool of an entry hall paneled in whitewashed wood.

"There's a powder room," Gabe said with a nod at a nearby door, "if you want to wash off the dog slobber."

"Thanks." She glanced around in genuine appreciation. The interior's transformation was as startling as the exterior's. "I can't believe what you've done with this place. It was still an abandoned wreck last time I was home."

"Fixing it up kept me busy. And," he added on a flat note, "it helped me get my life back on track. I needed something other than teaching and city council meetings to fill my evenings and weekends."

Riiight. That put her squarely in her place.

"I'll wait for you in the kitchen. Straight back and to the left."

Suze took her time in the powder room, her nervousness returning. She used the natural light streaming through the row of glass blocks set above the door to freshen her lip gloss and rake a hand through her hair. She'd worn it down today, with only the sides clipped back to keep it out of her eyes. *Not* because Gabe always liked it that way. And she hadn't chosen her slim white jeans and clingy red tank with him in mind, even if they did mirror their high school colors of cream and firehouse red.

"Okay," she instructed her image in the mirror. "Go do this."

It wasn't hard to find the kitchen, considering that Gabe had knocked out most of the walls on the ground floor. The short entry hall led to a sweeping, sunlit open space that flowed from great room to dining area to kitchen. The great room was all male—oversize leather sofa and chairs, giant flat-screen TV, a walk-around bar in one corner. The dining area boasted a gray plank table and eight upholstered chairs with a centerpiece that stopped Suze in her tracks.

They'd found that gnarly piece of driftwood on their honeymoon! It had washed up on the beach at Galveston and Suze had insisted on lugging it home. She'd always intended to do something with it. Someday.

"I was helping your folks clean out their basement," Gabe explained with a shrug. "They asked if I wanted it."

Her breath hitching, she smoothed a finger over the undulating curves and admired the clever silver candleholders drilled into the wood at various points. "This is gorgeous. Who did it?"

"An artist friend of Alicia's."

Suze's hand dropped to her side. She kept her expression blank. She was sure she had. But Gabe could read her like an old, dog-eared book.

"It's over between Alicia and me," he said evenly, his hips propped against the butcher block island that ran almost the entire length of his open, airy kitchen. "We shifted our friendship back into neutral when I got home last month."

She had to bite down on the joy that leaped through her. It was too fierce and hot and primitive to think about at the moment. It was also extremely shallow. As much as she disliked Alicia, she had no right to take such selfish delight in a breakup that must have been difficult for Gabe.

"I'm sorry if our interlude in Phoenix messed things up for you."

"No, you're not. Do you want some coffee? Then you can tell me what this unexpected visit is all about."

Oooo-kay. This was how he'd played it on the phone earlier. Short. Abrupt. Not yielding an inch. She couldn't really blame him. She would've been pissed if he'd breezed back into *her* life without warning or explanation.

"Coffee would be good."

While he filled a mug and topped off his own, she moved to stand at the French doors that gave access to a covered flagstone patio. Beyond the patio was another slope of lush lawn. Beyond that was the tree-lined creek.

Doofus was still chasing squirrels, she saw, as the hound streaked across the backyard in full hunt mode. His prey made it to the pecan orchard and darted up a tree, only to perch on a lower limb and jeer at its wildly leaping pursuer.

"Remember how you used to knock ripe pecans down from those branches?" she asked as Gabe passed her a mug.

"I do."

"Does your mom still bake those sinful chocolate-pecan pies?"

"She doesn't bake much of anything anymore. She's had a hard time since the hip replacement."

"I plan to stop by and see her." She raised her gaze to his face. "If it's okay with you?"

The question ignited a spark of anger. "Hell, Suze. You're as much a daughter to her as any of my sisters. You don't need my permission to visit her, any more than I needed yours to help your folks clean out their basement."

"Hey, back off! I was just trying to be polite."

"Screw polite. Why are you here, Suzanne? What's going on?"

"All right! Okay!" She puffed her cheeks and blew out a long breath. "Brace yourself, Mr. Mayor. Your life's about to get knocked off track again."

His brows snapped together. He didn't say anything, though. Just waited with that tight, unreadable expression for her to drop another bomb, like the one that had ended their marriage.

Suze had to do it quick, before she lost her nerve. "I'm pregnant."

His expression didn't change. He didn't so much as blink.

Dying a little inside, she realized she'd been stupid to imagine he'd greet the news with at least a semblance of delight. He'd been so ready to put down roots, so ready to begin their family, but her unwillingness to even negotiate a start date for his dreams had started them down the painful path to divorce. That, and their frequent separations. And her reluctance to put her career on hold. And the brief affair she'd had during their final separation.

Given all those factors, Gabe had to be asking himself some very ugly questions. Like who the father was. And how far along his ex-wife was. And what the hell she intended to do about the pregnancy.

Suze waited for him to unload but he still hadn't broken his silence when Doofus loped up to the French doors and let loose with a roof-rattling woof. Gabe smothered an oath, twisted the door handle and kneed the overjoyed dog aside.

"Cool it, mutt."

Taking Suze's elbow in a fierce hold, he steered her toward the kitchen counter. Eyes smoldering, he thunked down his mug, plucked hers out of her hand and stabbed a finger at one of the high-backed stools. "Sit."

"Gabe, I…"

"No!" He cut her off with a fiery glare. "Me first."

Okay, she deserved this. After all the heartache, all the talk of a baby, she owed it to him to sit and listen while he spilled his anger. So she damned near toppled backward off the stool when he shoved a hand under her hair, gripped her nape in a hard vise and held her steady while he plundered her mouth.

The kiss combined the kick of dark, rich Colombian coffee and unbridled male exuberance. She could taste both, feel both, and responded in kind. Her arms whipped around his neck. Her mouth molded to his.

This was Gabe. Her Gabe.

An achingly familiar joy flooded her heart. It was followed almost instantly by an entirely new sensation. One wrapped in a hundred different shades of happy.

This was Gabe. The father of her child.

Tears burned behind her closed eyelids. She tried to blink them back, but when he broke the kiss and spotted then leaking from the corners of her eyes, he muttered a low curse.

"Hell, Suze. I'm sorry. So damned sorry."

Her lids fluttered up, and she blinked a question from tear-blurred eyes.

"That condom must've been a year old," he said in disgust. "We shouldn't have trusted it. *I* shouldn't have trusted it."

The gruff apology spurred a quick, almost hysterical laugh. "Funny, I was thinking pretty much the same thing for most of that drive from Phoenix to Cedar Creek."

He kept his palm around her nape, his gaze gentle on hers. "That must've been one helluva long drive."

"I broke it up with an overnight in Albuquerque. I wanted to talk to Cowboy's wife, Alex."

"Because she's pregnant, too?" His mouth curved. "You could've waited and talked to any one of my sisters. Between them, they've racked up at least ten years of big bellies, aching backs and room-clearing farts."

Laughing, Suze eased out of his hold. Trust Gabe to tease her through this weepy hormonal moment. "Actually, I wanted to talk to Alex about the custodial agreements. She couldn't offer much help, though, except to suggest we consult a good family practice attorney."

Gabe withdrew, slowly, almost imperceptibly. Suze sensed the wall that came down between them even before he tilted his chin and narrowed those gold-flecked hazel eyes.

"Custodial agreements, huh? As in, how many weeks a year I'm allowed to spend with my child?"

She should've been grateful for his unquestioned acceptance of the fact that the baby was his. Would have, if his tone hadn't alerted her to rocky shoals ahead.

"As in," she replied with deliberate calm, "whether you'll assume full legal responsibility for *our* child if I'm deployed or assigned to a remote locale."

He backed away. Leaned against the island again. Crossed his arms. "So you intend to stay in uniform?"

"That's the plan right now."

"I see." His eyes went as hard as the agates they used to dig out of the creek bank. "Guess we'd better make an appointment with Shirley Stockton."

"Who?"

"She and her husband moved into town from LA

a few years back. He's a supervisor at FAA. She's a lawyer. We don't get all that many child custody cases here in Cedar Creek, but those we do, Shirley usually handles."

Miserable, Suze understood all too well why the air between them had gone from sizzling to frigid in a few short sentences. For a few, unthinking moments, Gabe had equated her pregnancy with a complete change in direction for both of them. He'd assumed the baby would heal the breach of the past three years. That Suze would separate from the Air Force. That the two of them would pick up where they'd left off, and their separate, complicated lives would once again merge.

She'd wanted that, too. For that same, unthinking moment when his mouth covered hers. God, how she'd wanted that!

"We probably should also talk specifics," Gabe said, interrupting her chaotic thoughts. "Like when you're due and how we're going to break the news to our families."

She grimaced. "My folks already jumped on the fact that we hooked up in Phoenix last month. They keep hoping we'll get back together."

"Yeah, well, doesn't sound as though you've considered that as an option."

The cold, dismissive comment brought her off the stool.

"The hell I haven't!" Tears stung her eyes again, and she cursed her out-of-whack hormones. "You think the divorce has been any easier on me than it has on you? I've ached for you, you idiot. I've missed your laugh, your homemade chili, your stupid jokes."

She flung up both hands, palms out and stopped him as he surged toward her.

"I have *not* missed the arguments. Or feeling guilty

about the hours I have to put into my job. Or the pressure you laid on me to separate from the service and spend the rest of my life here in Hicksville, Oklahoma."

She winced, instantly regretting her outburst. "Okay, I didn't mean that last part."

Gabe slumped against the counter again, his face tight and angry. "Oh, yeah, Susie Q, you did. You couldn't wait to shake loose of Cedar Creek."

"And you couldn't wait to get back."

He broke the silence that followed with a curt, "So here we are."

"Here we are," she echoed.

As if sensing the resentment and unhappiness hanging as thick as a cloud in the kitchen, Doofus crowded against Gabe until he dropped a hand and scratched behind a wiry, tufted ear. Eyes closed, the hound succumbed to quivering ecstasy.

"Okay, look. I need a little time to assimilate the fact I'm going to be a father. Why don't we have dinner at Ruby's tonight? Five thirty? We can talk it through then."

"Neutral ground? That works for me. Especially since this is sour cream chicken enchilada night."

Oh, God! She'd dreaded this part but knew if she didn't tell him now, she might not find the courage to do it later.

"While you're assimilating this business of being a father, there's one other bit of information you need to factor in. The day we got together in Phoenix... When I responded to that fuel spill..."

"Yeah?"

"My guys and I were on respirators the whole time we worked the spill."

"But?" he asked, suddenly wary.

"But I felt so tired and draggy for weeks afterward, I was afraid I might have breathed in some toxic fumes."

He stiffened and she rushed on. "The doc ran all kinds of tests. She found no evidence of toxic infiltration in my blood or lungs. None!"

"Did she know you were pregnant?"

"*I* didn't even know! She's the one who told me. She also said she's a hundred percent confident the baby's okay but I thought should… I felt I'd better…" She lifted a hand, let it drop. "I thought you should know."

When he didn't respond, she beat a hasty retreat.

"I'll see you at Ruby's."

Chapter Six

"Doofus! Let's go!"

Gabe needed to run. Hard. Fast. Slamming the dirt with everything in him.

He'd run track in junior high. Been pretty damned good at it, too. Took home All State honors at both 800 and 1500 meters. In high school, his speed made him a local star on the football field and won him a scholarship to OU. He hadn't racked up as many TDs in college as he had in high school, but he'd more than justified his scholarship.

He'd fallen off his competitive pace in the years since, of course, but could pound some serious pavement when he wanted to. And right now, he wanted to.

Although he knew he'd regret it later, Gabe didn't bother to warm up. No stretches. No starting slow and working up to full stride. With Doofus loping joyfully beside him, he cut across the back of his property, jumped the creek at its narrowest point and hit the two-lane, little-used Farm Road that took him from town to country in less than a mile.

The Endicotts' cornfield was on his left, the Stuarts' okra and sweet potato patches on the right. This late in June the sweet corn stood only waist high and the okra was just beginning to put out shoots. But Gabe's thoughts that late June morning were about as far as they could get from calculating the economic impact of a good crop season for his constituents.

He'd managed to hang onto his cool when Suze calmly announced she intended to remain in uniform, give birth to their child, then flit in and out of its life for the next twelve or fifteen years. Or longer, if she made senior rank, as Gabe knew she would. She could extend her career to twenty-eight or thirty years, for God's sake!

While he sat here, in Cedar Creek. For the next twenty-eight or thirty…or fifty…years. That last number put a hitch in his stride. He almost stumbled as he squinted through the heat waves and saw his future stretch as straight and unchanging as the road ahead.

Doofus was sniffing at a dead crow on the side of the road but caught the sudden change in Gabe's rhythm. He contorted into a U, unwilling to abandon the fly-blown carcass but obviously wondering what his human was up to. When Gabe picked up his pace again, the dog unbent and happily resumed poking his nose into the rotting entrails.

By the time they'd circled around the Prestons' peach orchard and hit County Road 122, they were both swimming in sweat. Their route took them past a new development Gabe had worked his ass off to push through the zoning and planning committees. With five-acre lots and a sweeping view of the open fields to the south, Stony Brook Estates offered homeowners the wide-open spaces associated with country life but none of the rural inconveniences. All but two of the lots had sold, and the two- and three-hundred-thousand-dollar homes that had sprung up all had access to county and state-wide utilities. The tax revenue coming into the town from these new homes wasn't too shabby, either.

Another two miles brought them into older and more familiar territory. When they cut back across the creek behind Gabe's place, Doofus chose to splash and paddle to cool down, but Gabe opted for heeling off his running shoes and turning the garden hose on himself. Thinking his human was having more fun than he was, the dog danced around Gabe until they were both drenched.

To dry off, Gabe stretched out in one of the loungers on the vine-shaded flagstone patio. The same stones he'd damned near broken his back hauling in and muscling into place. With Doofus already on his back, belly exposed, legs splayed, Gabe thought about the next fifty years.

Since Ruby's was only a few blocks from her parents' house, Suze walked to her dinner meeting with Gabe. The moment she opened the front door, though, she almost turned and scooted out again. The place was jammed. Not surprising, considering how popular—and inexpensive—Ruby's specials were. Yet any hope that the café would constitute "neutral" ground evaporated when she faced a phalanx of curious stares.

Fighting the cowardly impulse to flee, she let the door whoosh shut behind her. A quick glance confirmed the café hadn't changed since her last visit two years ago. Hell, it hadn't changed all that much since her high school days. Granted, the Free WiFi sign taped to the old-fashioned cash register was a surprise. So was the Taylor Swift crossover hit competing with the dinner hour chatter. But tattered, leather-topped round stools still offered seats at the chipped Formica counter and the same square tables crowded the space between the counter and the row of booths lining the far wall.

Her throat tight, Suze remembered the times she and her friends had plopped down at the counter to stuff themselves on burgers and fries that beat the crap out of every fast-food spot within fifty miles. She remembered, too, all the occasions her family and Gabe's had pushed two or three of those tables together to accommodate an impromptu gathering. But the most vivid memories were of the times she'd huddled with Gabe in "their" booth. The last one in the row, just before the entrance to the kitchen and restrooms.

With the arrogant confidence of youth, they'd been so sure that the noise from the kitchen would drown out conversations that tended more and more toward X-rated as they progressed from adolescents to preteens to sex-hungry high schoolers. Looking back, Suze guessed those conversations had probably provided the folks around them with grins and outright guffaws.

She almost groaned when she spotted Gabe waiting for her in their booth. Before she could join him, though, she had to run the gauntlet.

"Suzanne! Heard you were back in town, girl. You gonna stay this time?"

She smiled at the owner of the only bookstore in town. The polar opposite of any rational being's image of a literary aficionado, Madelyn Winston was crude, rude to her customers and downed gin like it was water. But she'd kept Suze supplied with her favorite paperback novels all though school, many of which her mother would've been horrified to know she'd read.

"I'm on leave, Madelyn. Just taking a break."

"Will you be here this coming weekend?"

That came from Harry Peterman, the chubby, round-faced dentist who'd filled her cavities.

"I think so."

"That's great! We'll add you to the parade lineup. We love to include our very own hometown hero."

Too late Suze remembered that Dr. Peterman had headed the Fourth of July organizing committee for the past ten or fifteen years.

"I'm on leave," she told him. "I didn't bring my uniform."

"No problem. You can ride in the same convertible with Gabe. Everyone in town knows the two of you served in combat zones. Unless…uh…" Red flooded his chubby cheeks. "Sorry. I guess that might be a little uncomfortable for you."

"Just a little," she drawled.

"For pity's sake, Doc. Try for some class."

That came from Ruby herself. Suze couldn't begin to guess the café owner's age. Although a new crosshatch of wrinkles seemed to appear in her leathery skin every year, she sported the same red-orange hair and hoarse cigarette croak she'd always had.

"Hey, Ruby."

"Hey, Suzanne. Good to see you, girl."

"Thanks. You, too."

"Gabe's waiting for you." The proprietress angled

her chin toward the back of the café. "He's having the special. You?"

"Yes, please."

"Whadda you want to drink?"

"Try the featured cabernet," Madelyn advised. "It not bad for a Texas label. Not bad, at all."

"I'll stick to iced tea," Suze said with a smile…and immediately realized her mistake.

Heads turned. Brows rose. Glances zinged from patron to patron.

She observed the unspoken communications with a silent groan. She wasn't a boozer. Despite several notable youthful indiscretions, she'd never racked up anything even *close* to Madelyn's record of alcohol consumption. But apparently everyone from her book supplier to her dentist remembered that she enjoyed a glass of wine with dinner.

"Just tea," she reiterated. "Wouldn't be cool for the mayor's ex to get hauled into court for a DUI."

Keeping her smile plastered on, she skirted the tables and headed for the back of the café. When the occupant of the second booth jumped out and blocked her forward progress, she had no clue who he was. With a mumbled "'Scuse me," she tried to go around him.

"Suzanne! My God! Haven't seen you since high school."

"I'm sorry, I…"

"Dave Forrester. We sat next to each other in Advanced Physics."

"Dave? Good Lord, I wouldn't have…"

"Recognized me?" he finished on a laugh when she faltered. "I'm not surprised. I've put on a few pounds since then."

More than a few, she thought in amazement, although he carried the weight well. He'd been a skinny, freckle-faced runt in high school. His freckles were now almost lost in a deep butternut-tan attractively accented by sun-bleached blond hair and white squint lines at the corners of his eyes. Belatedly, Suze remembered Gabe telling her that Forrester was now a big honcho in the oil and gas business. Judging by his surprisingly rugged out-door appearance, the executive must still spend a good part of his time in the field. She gave him points for that.

"I heard you head your own company now, Dave."

"I do. Don't want to brag, but we made the Fortune 500 list last year."

"Good for you," Suze said, meaning it.

They'd been friends in high school, feeding off each other's passion for math and physics. Although Suze had sensed that her lab mate wanted to share more than a bench clamp and stringed cylinder, she'd been care-ful to signal neither interest nor encouragement. Only later did she learn that Gabe had underscored her effort with a direct and extremely blunt warning to Forrester to back the hell off.

She wasn't surprised that subliminal male rivalry had spilled over into a competitive race for mayor of Cedar Creek. And, she discovered a moment later, an apparent competition for the same woman.

Moving aside, Dave gestured to his dinner compan-ion. "You remember Alicia, don't you?"

Damn! Crap! Sonova-freakin'-bitch.

Steeling herself, Suze pivoted to face her pixieish, violet-eyed nemesis. "Hey, Alicia."

"Hey, Suzanne." The smile was Colgate Ultra–bright.

"I asked Gabe to tell you hello from me when he and I talked last night."

"Oh, darn. He must've forgotten to give me the message."

The saccharine sweet reply shaved a few kilowatts off Prissy Missy's smile, but she never stayed dim for long. Her lips pursed into a dimpled pout that belied the bright glint in her eyes.

"I'll have to let him know what I think about that next time I see him."

"You do that." Hoping to hell there was no steam coming out of her ears, Suze nodded to Forrester. "Good to see you, Dave."

"You, too. Hey, listen. Last time I talked to Gabe, we were on opposite sides of the negotiating table 'bout cleanup at one of our wells. He let drop that you just worked a major spill at your base out in Arizona. If you've got time while you're home, I'd surely like to talk those pesky environmental issues with you." He fished in his hip pocket and extracted a heavily embossed business card from his wallet. "Give me a call. Maybe we can have lunch sometime."

"Maybe."

She tucked the card in her jeans pocket and was stopped twice more on her way to the back booth. Once by a friend of her father's, once by one of the servers who happened to be the grandson of her seventh grade math teacher, Very Scary Mrs. Lee.

"Gram is so proud of you," Tyler gushed. "She brags all the time about how you were her star pupil."

Suze blinked. That was news to her. Sharp featured and even sharper tongued, Very Scary had been relentless in her determination to pound advanced algebra into her students' heads. Everyone in her class had lived in dread of being called on to provide the answer to a homework problem.

"You should've seen Gram's face when she told me about that article," her teacher's eager grandson was saying. "The one in the *Daily Oklahoman* about you getting a Bronze Star medal. She said it's, like, a *big* deal."

"Well..."

"She's in the Gray Cedars Nursing Home now. If you have time while you're here, I know she'd love a visit."

"I'll sure stop by," Suze promised, meaning it. As intimidating as the math teacher had been, she'd pushed and prodded her students to their limits. Suze owed her scholarship to OU in no small part to the dedicated teacher's determination to see her students achieve their full potential.

By the time she finally reached the back of the diner, her mouth ached from forced smiles. "Lord," she muttered when she slid into the booth. "Looks like everyone in town still comes in for Ruby's sour cream chicken enchiladas."

"Pretty much. Did Doc Peterman tag you for the Fourth of July parade?"

"He tried, but I'm not ready to assume the hometown hero mantel."

"Why not? You earned that Bronze Star."

"Cedar Creek can boast more genuine heroes than me. You, for instance. Do I need to remind you that you logged more combat hours than I did before you separated?"

He didn't alter his lazy slouch against the back of the booth, but Suze could see the skin tighten across his cheekbones. "Let's not get into another debate over whether toggling a joystick to take out a target three thousand miles away qualifies as combat. I saw Dave Forrester give you his card. What's up with that?"

"He said you told him about the spill back at Luke. He wants to talk about those 'pesky' environmental issues involved in cleanup."

"About damn time he talked about them with someone who has some smarts!"

He shot a frown at the man now exiting the café. Suze craned around the edge of the bench in time to see Forrester loop a casually possessively arm around Alicia's waist.

She swung back around, her gaze locked on Gabe's as she heard the echo of his cool, flat comments this morning.

It's over between him and Alicia. They shifted their friendship back into neutral.

His decision? Or Alicia's? Suze couldn't help wondering as disgust underscored his next comment.

"The town council and I are fed up with his stall tactics. We're about two depositions away from suing his ass off."

"Whoa! That serious, is it?"

"I'll take you out to the Jones place, if you want. You can see the oil seepage on their property and…"

He broke off, wincing. "Hell! I can't believe I suggested that! Last thing you need is to risk the health of our baby by breathing in more toxic fumes."

Suze braced herself. Not the smoothest transition to the reason for this face-to-face but, abruptly, here they were.

Or not.

Smothering another curse, Gabe leaned toward her.

"Meeting here at Ruby's has to rank up with one of my stupidest ideas of all times. What do you say we get our dinners to go?"

"Okay by me."

He hooked a finger at their young server. "We'll take our two specials to go, Tyler."

"Sure thing, Mr. Mayor. I'll bag 'em right up for you." He turned a shy smile on Suze. "It was sure good to see you again, Captain. You won't forget to stop by and see Gram, will you?"

"I'll try to visit her tomorrow."

"She'll be totally jazzed to see you."

He was back within minutes with the two boxed and bagged dinners. "I put your drinks in the bags, too."

"Thanks. Tell Ruby to add the dinners on my tab."

"Sure will." He pocketed the generous tip Gabe passed him. "And thanks again for getting Shelby that summer job as a lifeguard. She's totally hyped about it."

"You're welcome."

"We're hoping this lifeguard job will help her turn the corner."

Suze waited until she and Gabe had rerun the gauntlet and exited into the evening heat to ask. "What corner does his sister Shelby need to turn?"

"She hooked up with the wrong crowd last year. Got bad into meth"

"Oh, no!"

The thought of the lively, inquisitive Shelby Lee glassy-eyed and stupid from drugs made Suze's heart hurt. It must have done the same to her steel-spined grandmother, the very scary Mrs. Lee.

"Shelby can't be more than, what? Sixteen?"

"Fifteen." With a light grip on her elbow, Gabe

steered her toward Ole Blue. "Jeff Hendricks found her stumbling along Route 9 three months ago and took her into custody. The kid was high out of her mind. Her folks can't afford private rehab, but we worked with DHS to get her into a state-sponsored program."

Suze didn't have any trouble substituting "I" for "we." That was Gabe to the core. Every one of his constituents, no matter how young or how old, could expect 150 percent from their mayor.

"How's she doing?"

"So far, so good."

When he opened Ole Blue's passenger door and she hoisted herself into the front seat, the cracked leather greeted her like an old friend. She refused to let herself think about the times she and Gabe had tussled on this same seat. Or the countless hours they'd steamed up the front windshield. Despite her best efforts, however, the memories wrapped around her like Saran Wrap as he deposited their dinners on the floor between them and backed out of the parking slot.

"Where are we going?" she asked, slanting him a quick look.

"Beats the hell out of me." He shifted into Drive. "You know any place we can escape our past and focus on the future?"

The question nicked an unexpected nerve. Stung, Suze had to remind herself that focusing on the future was the reason she'd driven all the way from Phoenix to Cedar Creek. Yet the fact that she was now carrying Gabe's child seemed to add to, not detract from their shared past. She didn't want to escape it. Not anymore. This small town with all its triumphs and tragedies formed a major part of their baby's heritage.

Thrown off-balance by the thought, Suze had no answer to his question. "I can't think of any place within a hundred miles."

They cruised Main with the scent of the spicy sour cream sauce tickling their nostrils. When Gabe cut right on 5th, then left on Poplar, she guessed where he was heading even before he made another turn. A short drive from there took them to the small park carved out of a bend in the creek. The tiny green space was just big enough for a swing set, two picnic tables and a pebbled walk along the creek bank. A historical marker indicated that the town's first settler, Jacob Neumann, had registered a claim to this quarter section on April 22, 1889—the same day of the land run—and subsequently donated the land for this stamp-sized little park.

The tiny retreat was far enough off the town's main streets to give at least an illusion of privacy. As an added plus, the park's thick canopy of trees provided cooling shade from the early evening sun. Buzzing cicadas and the sluggish ripple of the creek sounded familiar refrains as Suze and Gabe claimed a table tucked under a massive, scaly-barked sycamore.

"This is better," he said as he opened the sack. "*Much* better."

"Still neutral territory," Suze agreed, "but at least we can talk without interruption. And eat," she added as Gabe extracted a half-dozen takeout containers, along with plastic utensils, straws and paper napkins.

Once the cartons were opened, drinks distributed, and utensils unwrapped, she dug in. The special was even more delicious than she remembered. Soft, still-warm flour tortillas wrapped around spicy shredded chicken and cheese and onions. A creamy white sauce flavored with red and green chilies topped the fat enchiladas. The accompanying beans were done Okie style, whole pinto instead of mashed and refried, and Ruby always seemed to throw half a garden's worth of chopped carrots, corn and green onions in each serving of Spanish rice.

Suze downed almost half her enchilada before glancing across the picnic table to see Gabe watching her with a glint of amusement in his hazel eyes. "You always did like the Wednesday special."

"It's my fave."

He gestured toward her stomach with his fork. "Hope the baby likes all that spicy stuff, too."

"He's been pretty tolerant so far. I've been tired and draggy at times, but no morning sickness."

"He?"

"Or she. I alternate genders at will."

"That's what my sisters did, too, until they learned the sex. Sometime around the third or fourth month, I think."

"That's the normal time frame." Suze poked at her beans, then forced herself to meet his eyes. "The doc talked to me about a noninvasive prenatal blood test at ten weeks. They check for Down syndrome and a few other chromosomal conditions. They can also look for bits of Y chromosome in my blood to see if I'm carrying a boy or a girl."

"Let's talk about that."

He was so calm. So steady. So *Gabe*. Just being able to share all this with him almost got Suze hormonal again.

"You said your family practice doc found no evidence of toxic infiltration in your blood or lungs."

"Right."

"And you've been to a GYN for a prenatal check?"

"Right. And all tests came back normal."

"But you're still worried."

"Hell, yes, I'm worried. No, make that scared. This whole baby business has pretty well rocked me off my rails. I haven't quite figured out all the necessary accommodations and changes to my lifestyle yet."

"*Our* lifestyles, Suze. We have to figure out the necessary changes to *our* lifestyles. I want to be part of it, start to finish."

"Well, you were certainly there at the start."

She stabbed at the last of her enchilada but a need to lay the truth bare stilled her hand. She laid the fork down, slowly, carefully, and met her husband's eyes.

"It's your baby, Gabe. In case you were wondering,"

"I wasn't."

"We can do a blood test."

"No."

"That way you won't ever doubt it."

"No."

"Just think about…"

"Dammit, Suze. I don't need a blood test. You said I'm the father. That's enough for me. It's always been enough."

The air went out of her with a soft whoosh. Her shoulders slumped, her chest caved. And the stupid, *stupid* tears burned her eyes again.

"Sorry," she muttered. "No morning sickness so far, but my emotions are jumping up, down and every way but sideways."

"Hey, I've got eleven nieces and nephews, remember? My brothers-in-law can tell stories about out-of-whack hormones that would make any sane man run for the hills."

"So, why aren't you running?"

"My kid. My wife. My life."

"Ex-wife." She sniffed. "Ex."

"Yeah, well…"

He swung a leg over his bench, came around to her side of the table. When he sat down again and opened his arms, Suze fell into them as naturally as if she'd never left them.

"Here's the thing," he said, his chin rubbing back and forth against her temple. "I took Doofus for a long run after you left this morning. All the way out to the Endicotts' place and back again."

That had to be eight or nine miles. Suze would've commented on his endurance if she wasn't still swimming in hormonal soup.

"I did some heavy thinking after the mutt and I hosed down."

"And?"

"And every thought circled back to the only thing that that's ever mattered to me."

He curled a knuckle, tipped up her chin. The sun had slanted well down below the tree line now. Shadows played across his face, made even more hazy by the stupid tears that still blurred her eyes.

"I think we should undo the *ex*."

"What?"

"Marry me, Suzanne. Again."

Stunned, she jerked upright. "You're kidding!"

"Never been more serious in my life."

The magic of the moment dissolved in a hard, sharp hurt. As quick as that, they were back to where they'd been three years ago. The only game changer was the baby. Gabe had itched to put down roots. She'd thrived on the excitement and fulfillment of her job.

And never the twain shall meet.

"So we get married again," she said, her voice thick with unshed tears. "We add another room onto your house for a nursery. Raise our little prince or princess and their brothers and sisters here in Cedar Creek. You'll coach their T-ball games and teach them history. And I'll... I'll... Hmm. I guess I could work for Dave Forrester. He needs someone to help clean up his environmental messes."

"That's one scenario," Gabe said gruffly, refusing to let her pull out of his arms. "Here's another. We get married again. I go back to Phoenix with you. We have this baby together and any others that come along. Then, someday, if it's right for both of us, we may—or may not—come back to Cedar Creek."

For the second time in as many minutes, he'd yanked the rug right out from under her. Stunned, Suze leaned back in the circle of his arms. "How can you move to Phoenix? Your teaching job is here. And in case you've forgotten, you're the mayor of Cedar Creek."

"Remember Joanna Hicks?"

"Who's Joanna...? Wait! Isn't she the bodybuilder? The one who competed for Mrs. Oklahoma some years back?"

"That's her."

Suze could still remember the publicity stills Ms. Hicks's proud husband had plastered all over town. Joanna Hicks must've been in her fifties at that time, and according to Suze's mother, she and every other woman in Cedar Creek would've killed for those rippling deltoids and flat abs. To the entire town's delight, Ms. Hicks walked away with the crown.

"Joanne's the senior member of the town council," Gabe related. "She can step in as mayor without missing a beat."

"But... But you're so good at it. Everyone says so. They also say your next step should be to run for state or national office."

He brushed that off with a careless shrug. "Maybe I will. Someday. Right now all that matters is you and our baby."

"What about your job? You love teaching."

"Last I heard, they had high school teachers in Arizona. And they pay them a damn sight more than they pay here in Oklahoma."

"Right. As if you do it for the money!" Her mind whirled. "What about certification? And afterward? When the baby's born? If I get transferred to another state?"

"You'll be on restricted duty, so for at least a year you won't be deploying or pulling remote duty. Plenty of time for us to figure out what happens afterwards."

She struggled to gather her chaotic thoughts. "Gabe, you don't really mean this. You can't."

"Yeah, I do."

He brushed his mouth over hers. Once. Again.

"I won't lie to you. I love Cedar Creek. Almost as much as I love living within shouting distance of our families. But they haven't been able to patch the jagged hole in my heart these past three years. You're the only one who can do that, Susie Q. You and our baby."

Chapter Seven

When they'd finished their dinners and bagged the trash, Suze was still in a daze. She'd driven all the way from Phoenix hoping to work out an amicable custody sharing agreement. Her ex's astounding offer to jettison his home, his family and both his careers had turned her world upside down.

He'd meant it, though. Every word. If his dead-serious expression hadn't convinced her, that achingly tender kiss would have. As light as the touch had been, her lips still tingled and her heart fluttered thinking about the promise behind it.

She struggled to gather her chaotic thoughts as they drove out of the park. The plan was to break the news about the baby to their respective families. But Suze needed more time. More thought.

"Let's go to your place," she suggested. "We can

talk to our folks tomorrow. We should keep tonight just for us."

"I was wondering how long we'd have to make nice before I could waltz you away from our respective families and into bed."

Whoa! There was nothing light or tender about that declaration. Or the quick, fast grin he shot her way. Her hormones took off again, and this time they catapulted her straight out of confusion and into lust.

By the time they pulled into Gabe's front drive, heat was racing through her veins. Even with her pulse tripping a mile a minute, she had to battle a sudden wave of guilt as she took in the gorgeously renovated homestead.

"Oh, Gabe. You've put so much work into this place. How can you give it up?"

"We'll rent it out. Or sell it. It's just a house, Suze. A place."

They heard Doofus's sonic booms before they climbed out of Ole Blue. Gabe slammed the truck door, frowning. "We'll have to figure out what to do with him, though. I doubt the neighbors at your condo would appreciate his vocal tendencies. Maybe one of my sisters can take him."

He meant that, too, Suze realized with another jab of guilt. He was really serious about packing up and leaving his life here behind. The reality of it humbled her.

"We're not going to palm Doofus off on your sisters. He's weird, but a fun kind of weird. My condo lease is up in six months. We can find another place to live. Somewhere with several layers of soundproofing inside and plenty of space for him to run outside."

That potential problem resolved, she accepted the hound's ecstatic welcome. "We're going to be besties," she informed him. "And when the baby comes, you'll have to pull extra shifts on guard duty."

The prospect didn't appear to worry Doofus. Suze and Gabe waited at the screen door while he made a rapid circuit of the front yard, watered four of his favorite bushes and bounded back. His claws clicked a happy staccato as he pranced down the entry hall ahead of them. Suze's heart thumped to the same beat, then kicked into double-time when Gabe caught her elbow and tugged her around.

No soft brush of his lips this time. No gentle acknowledgement of their recommitment to each other. His mouth locked onto hers. Hard and hungry and demanding an instant response. She gave it eagerly, fiercely, and barely noticed when the dog charged back down the hall to get in on the action. Gabe pushed him away, or tried to. Finally gave up and admitted temporary defeat.

"The bedroom's upstairs. I'll feed this guy, which should lower his energy to a more manageable level, then come on up."

Suze had no trouble locating the master bedroom suite. The oak-tread staircase opened directly onto it. Gabe had knocked out the walls up here, too, she saw with an admiring glance. Gone were the dime-sized bedrooms that characterized most early Oklahoma territorial homesteads. What was left was a clean, uncluttered space with skylights that opened the sloping roof to the swiftly darkening night sky and a king-size bed positioned for a perfect view of the stars.

The master bath was just as spacious, Suze saw when she ducked in to use the john and wash off the residue of the dog's effusive greeting. Another skylight let in the light and would sound a noisy tattoo during Oklahoma's frequent hail storms, she suspected. Still, the prospect of lying beside Gabe and watching lightning flash across the sky above them was almost as seductive as the idea of curling against him under a blanket of stars.

The guilt rushed back. This was his home. He'd put so much of his heart and soul into it. How selfish, how *wrong*, was she to give up so little when he proposed to give up so much?

Then Gabe came up the stairs, shedding his shirt and barking a stern command over his shoulder in the process. "Stay! Right where you are. I mean it, Doofus!"

Suze flipped off the bathroom lights and met him in the middle of the room. Enough moonglow now spilled through the skylights to wrap him in soft light and dark shadows. Hunger curled in her belly as she ran her palms over his shoulders, his upper arms, his chest. His biceps bunched at her touch. His pecs went rock hard.

Did that deep-throated purr come from her? That low, vibrating hum? She didn't know. Didn't care. Hunger for this man, for *her* man, consumed her. This was her mate. The man she'd chosen. Claimed as her own before God and their families and damned near half the town. She'd claim him again, Suze thought fiercely. Tomorrow. But tonight there was just Gabe and her and the bed that beckoned like a safe port in a storm.

They took their time. Heeling out of sandals and shoes. Unsnapping and peeling down jeans. Disposing of extraneous items. And exploring each new patch of bared skin with eyes and hands and mouths.

Gabe forced himself to go slowly. Gently. His sisters had once embarrassed the hell out of him with an impromptu discussion of their heightened sex drive during their pregnancies. He did his damnedest to block their respective spouses' too-frank comments from his mind by focusing on the fact that this was Suze. His Suze. And it was their baby she was carrying. He'd cut off both arms and a leg before he'd do anything that might harm either of them.

Still, his lungs burned with the effort of holding back. He gritted his teeth. Waited until she opened for him and rose to meet his slow thrust. His jaw still locked, he harnessed his hunger until she clamped her calves around his and drove to a shuddering, spine-arching climax. Then he tangled his fingers in hers, pinned the backs of her hands to the mattress beside her head and let the pleasure sweep over him in hot, dark waves.

Wrung dry and damned near catatonic, he collapsed beside her. His breath was harsh and rough, hers a soft, ragged sigh. They lay side by side while the sweat cooled on their skin and the sky above them darkened to night.

"Gabe."

He could barely manage a grunt when she poked an elbow into his ribs.

"Gabe, wake up. I need to call my folks and tell them I won't be home tonight. Unless…"

"Unless nothing." His brains hadn't totally un-scrambled but he had no trouble interpreting the question behind her hesitation. "We're back where we belong, Susie Q. In bed. Together. Tell your folks we'll explain tomorrow."

"I doubt they'll need much of an explanation but…" She poked him again. "Pass me my phone."

With another muffled grunt, Gabe rolled onto his

side. Her jeans were too far away to reach so he retrieved the phone from his. At which point he discovered Doofus crouched at the top of the stairs. The dog's eyes gleamed in the moonlight and his snout was flattened against the hardwood flooring. When he saw his human show signs of life, he gave a pitiful whine.

"Stay where you are," Gabe commanded sternly as he snagged his jeans and fished out the phone. "Right where you are."

Another whine, even more desolate that the last, brought Suze up on one elbow. "Am I usurping his side of the bed?"

"You are, but he'll have to get used to it."

"Poor baby," she cooed to the mournful watcher.

"Don't give him any encouragement!"

The warning came too late. Translating her sympathy into an invitation, Doofus launched himself across the room and took a joyful leap. When he landed in the middle of the bed, Suze laughed and scooted over to make room for him.

"I warned you," Gabe said in mock disgust as he handed her the phone. "Your folks are on speed dial. Just hit five."

When her mom answered, she didn't comment on the fact that Gabe's number must've come up on caller ID but she almost choked when Suze said she wouldn't be home that night. Then staunch, upright, church deacon Mary Elizabeth Kingfisher Jackson chuckled and issued a delighted invitation.

"Why don't you and Gabe come for breakfast?"

Suze mouthed the question at the man beside her. His response was to tug the phone out of her hand.

"We'll be there, Mary. And if you should feel in-

clined to make your world-famous blueberry pecan pancakes, I'd be real grateful."

"I think I can manage that."

"That went well," Suze commented drily when he cut
the connection. "If she makes you pancakes for fooling
around with your ex-wife, just think what she'll cook
up when we tell about the baby."

"We'll eat extremely well for the foreseeable future,"
Gabe said smugly. "Speaking of which…" He propped
himself up and aimed a stern finger at the foot of the
bed. "Off, Doofus. Now."

The dog tried to burrow in but Gabe was relentless.
"Off. The. Bed."

Looking aggrieved, the hound wiggled backward on
his haunches and just sort of slithered off the end, taking the rolled-back comforter with him.

"Back to the foreseeable future." Still propped on
one elbow, Gabe rested a hand on Suze's sheet-covered
belly. "How long can we let your mom feed us?"

"How long can I stay, you mean? I'm on two weeks'
leave but I took my time getting here." She laid her
hand atop his. "So we have another eight days, Gabe.
Nine at most."

"Plenty of time for your mom and mine to get a head
start on fattening you up. The baby and I will take it
from there. Now we'd better get some sleep. We've got
a busy nine days ahead."

Suze's parents took the news that their daughter and
her former husband were getting back together exactly
as she'd anticipated. Her dad whooped and pounded
Gabe on the back. Her mom laughed and cried at the

same time. They greeted the news that they were going to be grandparents even more ecstatically.

"Oh, Suzanne! You can't imagine how happy this makes us. When are you due? I need to start planning a baby shower."

"Not until February."

"Perfect. We'll have it in January and do a snowflake theme. I saw the cutest decorations on Pinterest the other day. Have you told your mom yet, Gabe? I want to get her and your sisters in on the planning, too."

"Not yet. We're going to see her after we leave here."

"Well, then, my gracious. Let's feed you so you can get over there!"

Still beaming, she led the way into the kitchen. The round glass table was already set with cheerful yellow placemats and her mom's favorite mishmash of china. A lone sunflower poked its head from a chipped pitcher.

With the ease of long habit, the four of them divided the labor. Suze popped slices of wheat bread in the toaster, her dad pan-grilled thick slices of Canadian bacon and her mom poured the prepared batter onto a griddle. Gabe did his part by filling the juice glasses.

Once they were all seated and digging in, her mom wanted to know about the wedding. "When do you want to have it and who shall we invite?"

Suze and Gabe exchanged glances. They'd tossed around various options and had agreed on one that worked best for them, given the circumstances.

"We did the big church wedding last time, Mom. This time around we're going for quick and easy. We plan to detour to Vegas on our way to back to Arizona and get married there."

"Oh, no! You're not going to go through one of those tacky, drive-up chapels."

"No, ma'am. Suze has a friend who works out there. Since we've got so little time, we thought we'd call her and ask her to set it up for us."

"Why so little time?" Her mother angled her head with its turquoise-tipped bob. "You've got months to do this right. Why not wait a few weeks and have a nice, quiet celebration with your families when Suze gets out of the service and moves back to Cedar Creek?"

"I'm not separating from the service, Mom, or moving back. Gabe's moving to Arizona."

Confusion blanked the faces of both her parents. They exchanged surprised glances, and it was her hard-working, traditional, nose-to-the-grindstone dad who posed the inevitable questions.

"But your job, Gabe? Your responsibilities as mayor?"

"School's out for the summer. The school board has plenty of time to find a replacement. And Joanna Hicks can handle the town council until or unless they decide to hold a special election."

"What about your house? You've worked so hard on it. Surely you're not going to let it just stand empty?"

"I'll rent it out until we see what happens after the baby comes."

Her folks were raising the same objections Suze had, and Gabe was answering with the same calm certainty. But the guilt came back and made the blueberries in her pancakes suddenly taste too tart.

Still, she'd offered him the chance to be part of their child's life without completely uprooting his own. Getting remarried and moving to Arizona had been his idea, after all.

"What *will* happen after the baby comes?" Her mom wanted to know. "I'm assuming you won't have to deploy while you're pregnant, Suzanne, but what about afterward?" Her anxious glance went from her daughter to her former son-in-law and back again. "You two split up because of all the separations and, well…all those separations. How is adding a baby to that mix going to make it any easier?"

"I've changed," Gabe answered calmly. "So has Suze. We're different people now, Mary, with very different priorities."

Suze knew he'd never told his in-laws the precise reasons behind his decision to separate from the Air Force. Only she knew how much launching lethal drone strikes from thousands of miles away had played on his conscience. Her folks had just assumed, as had the rest of their friends and family, that since his marriage had fallen apart just as he was finishing his service commitment, he'd come home to heal.

Now he was thrusting himself back into the military environment. Not as an officer this time. Not as a war fighter. As a military spouse. It would be a completely different and challenging role for him.

A new role for her, too. She'd worked with enough other military woman to know how tough it was to combine wife, mother and warrior. Suze would need to adjust her career goals and assignment preferences to accommodate her family.

Gabe sure was right about different priorities.

His mom pretty much mirrored her parents' reactions. Violet was thrilled that Gabe and Suze were together again, overjoyed to hear about the baby and shocked that her son's life was taking such an abrupt one-eighty.

She didn't question their decision, though. Violet had lost her husband when he was in his forties and pretty much raised her four children on her own. If nothing else, she'd taught them to make their own choices in life.

"She looks so frail." Suze worried when they left. Her mother-in-law's limp had added to her growing guilt. "The hip replacement must've taken a lot out of her."

"It did. I've tried to talk her into moving in with me. So have Jill and Dave. Penny and Lyle even offered to build one of those snazzy mother-in-law retreats behind their house. But mom's determined to remain queen of her own castle."

A little more of Suze's joy had seeped away with each of these encounters. Dinner at his middle sister's house that evening pretty well drained it. Penny and Jill and their spouses were there, along with Kathy's husband, Don. Kathy was pulling midnights at the big new healthplex that served Mustang, Cedar Creek and surrounding communities. Of all Gabe's family, Kathy had been the most unforgiving. She'd made no secret of the fact that she blamed the demands of Suze's military career for the divorce—totally ignoring the long hours she herself put in and the many emergencies she responded to as a critical care nurse.

The sisters and spouses present voiced the same hearty congratulations at the news that Gabe and Suze were getting back together. And the same incredulous surprise that he intended to leave Cedar Creek to take up duties as a househusband. By the time Suze and Gabe left, her emotions were all over the place again.

"Dammit!" She gripped her hands in her lap and

glared through Ole Blue's windshield at the leafy oaks twisting and bending in the breeze. "I woke up so happy this morning. Now all I want to do is run away from home. *Again*."

"No running this time, kid. For you or for me."

She angled in her seat. "We screwed up so badly last time, Gabe. How do we know we're not screwing up again?"

"We don't."

"It's not just us this time," she said with a touch of desperation as he turned in to the curving drive. "As everyone we've talked to today has pointed out, we're adding a baby to the equation."

"We're adding more than a baby," he said wryly as the twin spears of Ole Blue's headlights initiated a booming chorus from Doofus.

"I'm serious. Maybe we need to rethink this whole thing. Maybe we're making another mistake and... Whoa!"

She slapped a palm against dash to brace herself as Gabe hit the brakes and jammed Ole Blue into Park. Without saying a word, he killed the engine. Then he shouldered open his door and marched around the hood. Yanking open her door, he reached across her to unclip her seat belt and almost dragged her out of the truck.

"This is not a mistake."

This being the hard kiss he laid on her.

"Neither is this."

Scooping her up, he took the front steps in two swift strides. He had to balance her on his knee to unlock the front door, then scoot sideways when Doofus burst out. The dog was still emitting a vociferous welcome when

Gabe let the screen door slam and kicked the front door shut behind him.

His muscles were taut, his stride swift as he hit the stairs. Moments later, Suze was stretched on the bed where she'd wakened to such sleepy, all-pervasive joy a mere fourteen hours ago.

"Forget Vegas," he told her, popping the buttons on his shirt. "We're heading to the county courthouse tomorrow and forking over fifty bucks for a marriage license. Since Oklahoma doesn't require blood tests or a waiting period, I'll get Judge Porter to marry us."

"And I don't have any say in this plan?"

"Yeah, you do. Two words. I do. Now shut up and kiss me, Captain."

So she did.

And would've done a whole lot more if Doofus hadn't chorused his eagerness to rejoin the party. Gabe muttered an oath and went downstairs to let him in. When the two of them came back upstairs, Suze welcomed her soon-to-be husband with open arms.

The Canadian County Courthouse was housed in a low, sand-colored building on Choctaw Avenue in El Reno, Oklahoma. Part of the Oklahoma City Metropolitan statistical area, the county ranked as the fifth most populous in the state. As such, it did a booming business in marriage licenses. The clerk was friendly and efficient. Gabe's driver's license and Suze's military ID satisfied the age and identification requirements. Since Gabe knew the question of their current marital status would come up, he also presented their divorce decree.

"As you may know," the clerk explained, "divorced persons can't marry anyone other than their previous spouse for a period of six months. But," she continued as she skimmed the court documents, "it looks like you're good on that count. As you also know, the normal fee is fifty dollars. Only five if you had premarital counseling."

"Our pastor did the counseling the first time around," Suze confirmed. "The certificate should be on file."

"Hang on, let me scroll back to the original license."

Now that she thought about it, Suze had to admit that premarital counseling should probably be an even more stringent requirement for couples who failed miserably the first time around. Luckily for her and Gabe, it was not.

"Yep, there it is. Okay, folks, five dollars and you're on your way."

When Gabe handed her the bill, she printed out the license and passed it across the counter with a pointed reminder. "It's good for ten days."

"Ten days," Suze echoed as she and Gabe crossed the sun-baked parking lot. "That's two more than we have left in Cedar Creek. Think we can do everything that needs doing in just over a week?"

Gabe slanted her an amused glance. "This from the woman who maintains three separate go-kits and can clamber up the ramp of a C-17 with less than five hours notice?"

"That's different."

"What's different? You get the word, you pack up, you go." Grinning, he dropped a kiss on her nose. "Besides, we're not exactly charting unfamiliar ground here, woman. You. Me. A marriage license. A promise to hang on. This time," he added, his expression and his voice going dead serious, "forever."

"This time forever," she echoed.

Yielding to her mother's fervent pleas, they'd asked their pastor to conduct the marriage ceremony. Suze had spoken to him personally, explained it would be a private ceremony with only immediate family in attendance. They'd settled on four o'clock the same afternoon they obtained the license.

That presented Suze with another dilemma. She hadn't packed anything suitable for a re-wedding, and she didn't think her folks would appreciate the irony of her sparkly, one-of-a-kind Warrior Mom T-shirt. So, after she and Gabe got back to the house, she jumped in her T-bird and made a quick excursion to Penn Square Mall in Oklahoma City.

The mall catered to the wealthy, oil-money suburbs that surrounded it and included plenty of high-end stores. With time so short, however, Suze zipped into Dillards and took the escalator to the second floor. Luckily, she spotted the perfect dress on an end cap right as she got off the escalator. A soft, summery chiffon in misty blue, it featured a wide belt in supple, cream-colored leather. The matching floppy-brimmed hat trimmed with white roses was an added bonus. She grabbed the hat, found the dress in her size and darted into a dressing room. Her purchases in hand, she hit the shoe department and scored a pair of Donald Pilner sling-backs in the same creamy leather as the belt.

She kept to the speed limit on the way back to Cedar Creek and got home with just enough time to shower, blow-dry her hair and slap on some lip gloss. Wearing her wedding finery, she went downstairs to find Gabe waiting for her. He'd gone with a dark suit, a gray shirt with a satiny sheen and an amber tie that made his hazel eyes look more gold than green.

As they drove to the church, Suze couldn't help thinking that the contrast between this occasion and their first wedding. She and her mom and her best friend had spent months planning and organizing that one.

It took place the day after she and Gabe graduated from OU and been commissioned as second lieutenants in the Air Force. So, so proud of their bright, shiny lieutenant's bars, Suze had chosen to wear her formal mess dress uniform instead of a wedding gown. The starched, pleated white blouse. The midnight-blue jacket with its silver officer's braid banding the cuff. The matching long skirt slit up to her knee. Gabe had worn his uniform, too. And their friends from OU's Reserve Officer Commissioning Program had raised their sabers to form an arch when the bride and groom exited the church.

No uniforms this time around. No arch. But the church was the same. Still small, still painted a blistering white, its steeple standing proud against a bright, searing sky. The congregation was minuscule compared to that of Oklahoma's huge cathedrals, Suze knew. Only about two hundred worshipers, most of whom knew or were related to each other. And the pastor's sermons often took a tilt to the left…surprising considering how deep they were in the Bible Belt.

Roses had filled every niche and cranny of the sanctuary for their first wedding. Friends and family had crammed the pews. Her bridesmaids wore shimmering lilac silk, and Gabe's groomsmen had formed solid phalanx. Their flower girl had tripped, Suze recalled with a smile, and spilled her basket of rose petals. The four-year-old's heartbroken wails had brought Gabe from his post at the altar, and his teary-eyed niece was still clinging to his hand when Suze floated down the aisle.

She didn't float this time. Her footsteps dragging, she approached the church door with a touch of dread. The thought of standing at the same altar, repeating the vows they'd already broken once, suddenly struck her as tempting fate just a little too much.

"Why did I let my mom talk us into this?" she muttered.

"Because you love her, and she loves you."

She pulled him to a stop. "There's still time, Gabe. We could delay this. Head for Vegas."

"We could. Or we could share this moment with our families, like we've shared every other significant event in our lives."

She made a face. "Have I ever told you that you really piss me off sometimes?"

"Yeah, babe," he answered, laughing. "You have. So are we going to do this or not?"

"I guess so."

Still grinning, he opened the door. Suze took one step inside and stopped cold.

The small sanctuary wasn't crammed. Flowers didn't burst from dozens of vases. No lilac-robed maids of honor or uniformed groomsmen waited for them at the altar. But family and their closest friends filled at least half the pews. Gabe's sister Penny waited at the door to hand her a small bouquet of white roses. And little Tildy gave a delighted yelp.

"Uncle Gabe!"

The girl wiggled off her mom's lap, snatched up a

wicker basket and promptly spilled its contents. When she scooped up a handful of petals and threw them at the new arrivals with the force of a future left fielder, Kathy sent her once and future sister-in-law a droll glance. "Déjà vu all over again."

The perfect theme for the occasion, Suze thought with a wry grin.

She and Gabe. Second time around. Firmly suppressing her last flickers of guilt and doubt, she re-joined her life to his.

It all seemed so surreal until she slid his ring on his finger—again. He'd taken it off after the divorce but kept it. She'd kept hers, too. The wide band of etched white gold was in her safety deposit box back in Phoenix. To her surprise, Gabe had somehow found the time to purchase a circlet of channel-cut diamonds set in the same white gold.

"You can wear it above your original ring," he said as he slipped the circlet over her knuckle. "Seems pretty appropriate for a twice-married bride."

A moment later it was done. They were husband and wife.

Again.

Suze should've been lost in the sweeping joy of the moment. Instead, she found herself folding her left hand into a fist and making a fierce, silent vow. Despite the uncertainties and challenges ahead, this ring wasn't going into any safety deposit box.

Chapter Eight

Their first honeymoon had been a week at an all-inclusive resort in Mexico, a gift from their collective family members. Their second consisted of a celebratory supper at Ruby's with family and friends, followed by a quick trip to move Suze's things from her parents' house to Gabe's.

Their second wedding night, however, more than matched that of the first. They were older, wiser and much more appreciative of what they'd let slip through their fingers. The loving was slow, sweet, each kiss a reminder, each touch a promise.

Stars winked above the skylights when they were done, but it was still early enough for Gabe to take Doofus for the run he so desperately wanted and Suze to indulge in an extended soak in the modern version of a claw-foot tub that dominated the master bath. With its slightly inclined back and extra-long length, it fit her perfectly.

After her soak, she pulled on a pair of shorts and her Warrior Mom T-shirt, then stretched out on one of the patio loungers while she waited for Gabe to return. Bullfrogs bellowed their love songs from the creek, and the distant boom and pop of firecrackers signaled that folks were getting a head start on the upcoming Fourth of July weekend.

Gabe and Doofus joined her on the patio, both sweaty from their run. He was chugging from a bottle of water and took time to splash water into the hound's outdoor bowl before plopping down in the lounger next to Suze's.

"Damned idiots," he muttered as a starburst of red, white and blue exploded above the tree line. "We've banned firecrackers inside town limits. Outside, though, there's plenty of open space to shoot off Roman candles and spinners. And plenty of idiots who'll end up at the ER when the things explode in their faces."

"C'mon," Suze teased. "How many bottle rockets did you and your pals shoot off when you were kids?"

"Too many. It was pure dumb luck that none of us lost fingers or an eye. But they were legal back then."

He frowned as another boom carried through the trees. Seconds later a rocket trailing green stars arced across the night sky.

"The problem is, it's been so dry lately. We were close to record low precipitation for the month of June. Half the county is a tinderbox just waiting for a spark. The chief's got all of his full-time and most of us volunteer firefighters on standby."

"You're one of the volunteers?"

"I signed on when I moved back home. The training was brutal," he admitted. "Probably not as bad as what you combat engineers go through, but I must have sweated off a good ten pounds in that turnout gear."

Firefighters in Air Force units were integral members of the Civil Engineering Squadron. Suze had participated in enough training exercises and emergency responses with them to appreciate the grit and determination it took to qualify, even as a volunteer.

When another starburst lit the sky, Gabe swore again. "I wish our state legislators had the balls to outlaw sale of fireworks to individuals. God knows I've harangued enough of them about it."

"Maybe you should've run for state senator instead of mayor," she joked.

"I thought about it. Might still do it someday."

The answer didn't surprise her. She knew Gabe was passionate about politics on the national level. They both were. But their military duties precluded any kind of active participation in political campaigns or issues.

So when her mom relayed the news that he'd been elected mayor, Suze had realized she should've expected Gabe to get involved. He was too smart, too active, to channel all his energy into teaching and coaching. Especially, she thought on an inner grimace, with no wife or kids to otherwise distract him.

He made a good mayor. Everyone said so. He'd make a good state senator. And maybe, in time, lieutenant governor or governor. The thought that he was shelving the idea took some of the sparkle from their starlit wedding night.

He put it back in after he abandoned the evening to the bullfrogs, adjourned to the shower and joined her in bed. Suze would never again take for granted the simple joy of having her husband lean over her, his shoulders blocking the moon's glow and his eyes dark pools as he stroked her tummy.

"Guess we need to start thinking about names," he murmured between strokes.

"Mmm. Better leave it to me. You're not exactly a wizard in the name department."

"Hey. Jill liked Matilda when I suggested it."

"Right. Jilly and Tildy. Obviously, Jill didn't think that one all the way through. And Doofus?"

The dog's ears shot up at the sound of his name. Once again, he'd been banished from the bed but was only waiting for anything that sounded even remotely like an invitation to reclaim his half of the mattress.

He remained banished, however, and no grass or roof fires erupted during the night to launch Cedar Creek's volunteer fire department into action.

Suze and Gabe used the next couple of days to inventory the house and sort out what would stay, what would go into storage and what would go with them. They were ready to start packing the boxes stacked in various rooms but had decided to hold off until after the Fourth of July celebrations. Gabe had too much to do to get ready for the parade, their family picnic afterward and the fireworks display that night to focus on packing.

The call came just as he and Suze were finishing breakfast. She was still in the oversize T-shirt she used as a sleepshirt. Gabe was in sweats and getting ready to take Doofus for his morning run. He answered, listened for a moment, then told the caller he'd be right there.

"What's happening?" she asked when he disconnected with a smothered oath.

"The crew setting up the reviewing stand for the parade somehow managed to puncture the K-6."

It had been a while since she'd submitted a study of central Oklahoma's water treatment and distribution systems as part of her hydraulics engineering course. She remembered enough, however, to know Cedar Creek's K-6 was one of two major arteries leading from the primary pumping station to a network of secondary mains. With the K-6 shut down, half the town wouldn't be able to wash their breakfast dishes or water their lawns. Or, she thought grimly, raise enough water pressure to respond to fires at the far ends of the branch.

"I did that hydraulics study in college," she reminded Gabe. "It's probably way out of date now, but...do you want me to come check out the break with you?"

"Yes! No," he amended in the next breath. "My guys alerted the county water management board. Their emergency response crew is on the way. Much as I could use your expertise, one of us needs to be here for the walk-through with Alicia."

"Riiight."

Gabe had already grabbed his keys and green ballcap with Mayor embroidered across the crown.

"She's the best Realtor in the area, Suze, and she's heading out of town this afternoon to spend the rest of the weekend at some posh resort with Dave Forrester. If we're going to get the house listed for rent before we head to Arizona, we need to get the walk-through done this morning."

Like Little Miss Priss needed a walk-through, Suze thought snidely. She probably already knew everything from the alarm system code to which side of the bed the owner slept on. Smothering the nasty thought, she flapped a hand.

"No problem. I've got it covered. Go!"

Still, it left a funny taste in her mouth when Gabe rushed off to handle an emergency that fell smack into *her* area of expertise. She hadn't just studied water distribution systems in college. Air Force Prime BEEF teams dug wells, repaired pipes and, in their humanitarian response role, had to handle all kinds of disasters. Suze remembered all too clearly jumping into a sewage-filled trench in earthquake-ravaged Ecuador to help her grunting, straining troops wrestle a new section of pipe into place. It had taken them days to scrub the stink from their boots and uniforms.

No stink for her today, she decided. No baggy uniform, either. By the time Alicia rang the bell an hour later and catapulted Doofus into a frenzy, Suze had washed and dried her hair, liberally applied the few cosmetics she'd brought with her and wiggled into jeans that clung to a butt that was still pretty damned trim, if she did say so herself. Her yellow 56th Fighter Wing T-shirt was a little faded from wear but, she thought smugly, sent an unmistakable signal.

Alicia had pulled out all the stops, too. How someone so diminutive could manage to look so damned sophisticated escaped Suze. It might've been the three-inch wedge sandals that tied around her ankles. Or the linen sundress that swirled flame red at the hem, transitioned to flamingo pink at the waist, and ended in black and white polka dots at the bodice. The oversize white Jackie O sunglasses added another, undeniably chic touch.

Fending off the ecstatic Doofus with one hand, Alicia slid the sunglasses down her nose with the other. Since her eyes were pretty much level with Suze's boobs, they couldn't miss the red unit patch.

"Is that your unit?"

"The 56th Fighter Wing," Suze confirmed.

With some effort, she managed to refrain from shooting the traitor now slavishly twining himself around the other woman's legs an evil glance.

"It dates back to 1947, when it was part of SAC and provided defense of our northern tier. Now we're part of Air Education and Training Command and are the initial training base for F-35 aircrews."

"I have no clue what any of that means," Alicia admitted with one of her tinkling laughs, "but it sounds pretty impressive to a small-town Oklahoma girl. Oh, I meant to *this* small-town Oklahoma girl."

Your choice, Suze wanted to say. Nobly, she refrained. "Would you like something to drink? I can make a fresh pot of coffee. Or there's water and iced tea in the fridge."

"Iced tea would be good."

Once in the kitchen, the Realtor plopped her Kate Spade bag and leather briefcase on the counter. She accepted the tea and helped herself to a packet of sweetener before trying to bridge the gap between personal and professional.

"Look, I know this is as awkward for you as it is for me…"

"Not quite," Suze drawled.

She was tempted, *really* tempted, to flash her new diamond band but surprised both herself and her guest with an apology.

"Sorry, Alicia. I didn't mean to sound so catty."

"Well…"

"And while we're at it, I guess I should say I'm sorry we never clicked in school."

Alicia's delicately feathered brows soared. After a startled moment, she acknowledged their long-standing rift with a rueful smile.

"Me, too, although we both know the reason why. I fell for Gabe, like, two days after my family moved to Cedar Creek. He was such a hottie and so sweet to the new girl in school. I guess I wasn't exactly subtle about it."

"Subtle, no. Persistent, yes."

"Lot of good it did me." She folded her elbows on the briefcase and propped her chin in her hands. "I won't lie to you, Suzanne. When you and Gabe divorced, I went after him with every weapon in my arsenal. Almost succeeded in nailing him, too."

"I know. He told me."

"He should've been such easy pickings. He was so lonely when you two separated."

He wasn't the only one. Suze cringed inside, wondering if Gabe had told Alicia that his wife had turned to another man for comfort.

No. He wouldn't do that. The hurt would've been too deep, too personal. Still, she had to take a quick swallow as Alicia surveyed the kitchen with a proprietary eye.

"Did he tell you I started my campaign by helping him with the renovations?"

"He seems to have neglected to mention that."

"You may be the construction engineer, but my degree's in interior design. I suggested these smooth-planed planks for the floor and the river stone for the fireplace. Gabe liked the idea of incorporating the key elements of Cedar Creek's environment."

Since Suze was once again wearing his ring, she could afford to be generous. "I like it, too, Alicia. I especially love all the windows and skylights. They bring the outside in. You did an amazing job."

"I did, didn't I?" Looking smug, the Realtor unclipped her briefcase. "You'll have to tell Dave Forrester next time you see him. I've been pestering him to turn me loose in that mausoleum he built out in Stony Brook Estates."

"I didn't know he'd built out there."

"Six-thousand square feet's worth. I'm going to meet him there at noon, so we'd better get to work."

Once she had her iPad in hand, flighty, flirty Alicia transformed into SuperRealtor. She clicked picture after picture, added dimensions, laid on the superlatives.

"You know," she said as Suze and Doofus walked her to the front door, "Gabe could make twice what he put into the house if he decided to sell instead of rent."

"Renting is good for now. But don't offer more than a year's lease. We're not sure where we'll be after the baby's born."

"So the rumor's true?" Alicia's gaze dive-bombed to Suze's middle, zinged up again. "You're pregnant?"

Suze didn't bother to ask where she'd heard the rumor. With three ecstatic grandparents-to-be and six siblings-in-law, some version of the news was bound to leak.

"It's true."

Alicia's smile didn't convey quite its usual brilliance, but her congratulations were heartfelt. "That's great, Suzanne. I'm happy for you and Gabe. Honestly. But renting for just one year with no option to extend may restrict your customer base."

"We'll take that chance."

"Okay. Well…" She held out a hand. "Congratulations again. I sincerely hope you and Gabe make it work this time."

"That's what she said?" Suze's mom asked an hour later. "She hoped you two would make it work *this* time?"

They were in the kitchen, preparing their contribution to the family picnic to come later that afternoon. Mary sprinkled bright red paprika over two trays of deviled eggs while Suze turned the last of the sizzling chicken in the cast-iron frying pan.

"That's what she said."

"If I didn't believe in saying no evil," her mother muttered with a determined shake of the paprika container, "I'd have a name for that woman. I probably shouldn't tell you this but…well…" Another vigorous shake. "Someone told Kathy she stripped naked and went skinny-dipping in the creek out behind Gabe's house. Just her bad luck he'd gone over to Ok-City and didn't get back until she was shriveled up like a…"

"Mom! That's enough paprika. We'd better shove this stuff in the fridge and get downtown. The parade starts in twenty minutes."

Her mother abandoned the spice and dusted her hands on her navy-blue slacks. She'd topped them with a round-necked red T-shirt, and, to her daughter's delight, she'd also gone in for a new do. The turquoise tips were gone. Her chin-length bob now sported streaks of red and blue amid the snowy white.

Given the limited wardrobe Suze had brought with

her, she opted to go with white jeans and her royal blue Warrior Mom T-shirt. If Alicia had heard a rumor about the baby, it had to be all over town anyway.

"Are you going to ride in the parade with Gabe?" her mother wanted to know.

"He's participating as mayor. I don't think…"

"Well, I do! You're the mayor's wife. You should be there with him."

She might've still held out if Gabe hadn't called her just as she and her folks joined the herd of excited kids and indulgent parents streaming toward downtown.

"Where are you?"

"On 5th, about to turn onto Main."

"Cut across to 3rd. And hurry. We're in the third slot, right behind the VFW color guard and Colonel Amistad's car."

He hung up before she could ask him whether his crew had plugged the water main. Yielding to the combined pressure of her husband and her parents, Suze cut through the alley between the pharmacy and Dottie's Antiques & Collectibles.

She found Gabe standing beside a vintage convertible with a magnetic placard on each door identifying the passenger as Cedar Creek's mayor. She guessed he'd come straight from the leak site. His jeans were wet from the knee down, no doubt from hosing off layers of mud, but he must've swung by his office to grab a sport coat.

He was standing next to a uniformed Air Force officer who had racks of ribbons climbing almost all the way up to his shoulder. Although Suze hadn't met Colonel George Amistad before, she knew him by reputation. He'd risen through the ranks from wrench bender to officer candidate to hotshot pilot to commander of the Air National Guard unit that shared a runway with Will Rogers Airport.

His wife accompanied him. The petite, blue-eyed blonde was a direct descendent of the Choctaw chief who'd led his tribe over the Trail of Tears. The Amistads lived on the south side of Oklahoma City but given Cedar Creek's close proximity to the FAA and Will Rogers Airport, Gabe interacted with the colonel frequently on community matters and had asked him to act as grand marshal of the parade this year.

Suze's salute was automatic, unthinking, a junior officer's tribute to an officer, a gentleman and a hero. He returned it with the same courtesy.

"I read about your Bronze Star, Captain Hall. Sounded like you took some heat down range."

"Just a little, sir."

"Proud of you."

"Thank you."

"Proud of your hubby, too." He clapped a hand on Gabe's shoulder. "I hate that the Air Force lost someone with his smarts, but he's done a great job as mayor. Sure would like to see him run for national office before I die. Senator Hall has a ring to it, don't you think?"

His comment was so close to Suze's previous thoughts that she blinked. "Yes, sir."

"How about you come see me tomorrow. You and Gabe? We're the first Guard unit to bed down the new MC-12. I think you'll both be interested in its capabilities."

They'd planned to get serious about packing tomorrow but both recognized a politely veiled order when they heard one.

"We can do that," Gabe confirmed.

"Good. Make it around ten. We can…"

A shrill, ear-piercing screech made them all wince. It emanated from the toy whistle blown by a sweating Dr. Peterman. The chubby, round-faced dentist wind-milled his arms at the various lead elements.

"Showtime, everyone!"

The band formed into neat lines. The volunteer fire-fighters jumped aboard their pumper. The still incredibly hard-bodied Joanna Hicks adjusted her rhinestone crown, twitched her Mrs. Oklahoma sash into place and ascended to the throne mounted on the bunting-draped trailer being towed by her adoring husband. The floats and bands behind them scrambled into position.

Harried, Doc Peterman rushed over to shoo the grand marshal, the mayor and their wives to their vehicles. Suze joined her husband in the backseat of the vintage Corvette. The band launched into John Philip Souza's "The Stars and Stripes Forever." The VFW honor guard stepped out. Colonel Amistad's vehicle followed at a sedate speed. The Corvette kept a respectful distance behind him, and Cedar Creek's Fourth of July celebrations were officially underway.

The family picnic that followed the parade was quintessential Small Town, America. For all Suze's youthful eagerness to shake off the dust of Cedar Creek and explore the world, she cherished her memories of occasions like this.

The Hall and Jackson clans congregated at Gabe's place so the kids and Doofus could splash in the creek. Shrieking and woofing, they frolicked under the watchful eyes of assorted grandparents, parents, aunts and older cousins.

Hot dogs and hamburgers sizzled on the grill. Foil-wrapped sweet corn steamed. Suze nuked the chicken she'd fried that morning at her mom's house while Gabe's brothers-in-law dumped ice into chests crammed with beer and soft drinks. Their wives loaded portable picnic tables with Jell-O salads, deviled eggs, potato salad, baked beans, fried okra and an assortment of chips.

A stranger surveying the mounded platters and Saran-covered bowls might doubt the feast could all be consumed at one sitting, and it wasn't. Everyone made several passes over the next few hours, however. A lively game of volleyball later in the afternoon revived appetites enough for the homemade ice cream to make an appearance to a round of applause, along with the iced watermelon and angel food cake topped with strawberries, blueberries and whipped cream.

When the sun slid behind the tree line, the tables were cleared, the kids corralled and the lawn chairs folded for easy carrying. Then the whole group traipsed the few blocks to Veterans' Memorial Park. Although it was just coming on to dusk, tiny white lights outlined the roof and posts of the newly painted Victorian bandstand. The Combined Senior Adult Choir and orchestras from the four churches in town were assembling for their traditional patriotic concert. Suze's mom abandoned the family to take her place among the sopranos, while her dad went to help with the speakers and mics.

Half the town was already in place, their lawn chairs and blankets riding the gentle slope in front of the bandstand. As Suze and Gabe and the rest of their family wove their way to a vacant spot, friends and neighbors she hadn't seen in years congratulated her and Gabe on their remarriage. Several also offered congratulations on the baby.

"The village tom-toms must've been thumping non-stop," she commented drily.

"Comes with the territory. How's this spot, gang?"

With the enthusiastic approval of the rest of the clan, Gabe helped unfold lawn chairs, then went to make sure his crews had everything in place for the fireworks.

"Be back when I can."

When he strode off, his mother crooked a finger. "Here, take this chair next to mine, Suzanne. You've been so busy, we haven't really had a chance to just sit and chat since you got home."

"I know, Violet, and I'm sorry for that."

Suze settled in the woven green-and-white chair and yielded to little Tildy's demands for a cuddle. With the toddler wide-eyed and nested comfortably in her lap, Suze surveyed choir and orchestra.

"How many of these Fourth of July concerts have you attended?" she asked her mother-in-law.

"Dan and I made about every one."

Violet lowered her eyes, her thoughts turned inward for a moment. Even after all these years, she still missed her husband. Suze remembered him as a big, bluff, generous-hearted man who loved to play dominoes with his pals from the VFW.

"We couldn't come the year Penny was in the hospital, so sick with meningitis. I had to take a pass last year, too, because of this danged hip replacement."

"You're still limping pretty badly. Did you do physical therapy?"

"Three months of it." She made a face. "Getting old is not for the faint of heart."

"So my mom and dad keep telling me."

Tildy spotted her older siblings and demanded to be set down. Her chubby legs pumping, she chased after the others under the watchful eye of her parents and aunts and uncles. Her grandmother kept an eye on her as well, before turning to her daughter-in-law.

"I'm so happy about the baby, Suzanne."

"Me, too."

She really was. Coming home had vanquished her initial doubts and fears. Coming home and falling in love with Gabe all over again.

Except…

As she and Gabe had discussed, she would be on restricted duty until after the baby was born. Then it would be another six months before she became eligible for worldwide duty again. Her unit at Luke would have to work around her during that long stretch.

She couldn't quite quash a niggling feeling of guilt at leaving her team in the lurch. And wondering just how she and Gabe would handle the separations once she was eligible to deploy again. Being apart so much had wreaked havoc on their marriage before.

He was determined this time would be different. That *they* were different. She had to believe he was right.

The orchestra began to tune up. The choirs shifted into place. Under the cover of squeaky reeds, sliding trombones and shuffling feet, Violet said softly, "I've had time to think about Gabe going back to Phoenix with you. I admit I didn't much like the idea when the two of you told me."

Suze flicked a glance at her sisters-in-law. Penny and Jill sat next to each other, their heads together as they laughed over some private joke. Kathy was adjusting her eldest daughter's headband, an elaborate affair that sported an array of blinking, bobbing, red, white and blue stars. Their husbands stood in a loose cluster, no doubt assessing the latest acquisition by Oklahoma City's pro basketball team.

"You weren't the only one who didn't like the idea."

"Yes, well, I've changed my mind. I think you're doing the right thing."

Suze felt her jaw sag. As the orchestra's only flautist trilled in the background, she stared at her mother-in-law in surprise. Smiling, Violet reached for her hand.

"Cedar Creek is your home. Your roots go bedrock deep. So do Gabe's. But this town may be filled with too many memories for you both, and too many people who want a piece of your lives. So it could be that you need to build a new life together, just you and Gabe and the baby. Then, when you're ready, come home again."

Before Suze could reply, the conductor rapped his baton on his music stand and called for quiet. The talk and laughter buzzed down, the conductor turned back to face his silver-haired performers and the concert kicked off with "This Land Is Your Land," a much-loved favorite by Oklahoma's own Woody Guthrie.

Suze joined in the singing but Violet's comments kept circling in her head. They were still there when Gabe rejoined the group.

"Fireworks all set to go?" his mother asked.

"All set. It's going to be a heck of a show."

He repeated the same promise when he was called to the stage. He also thanked the orchestra, the choirs and the volunteers working the lighting, sound, safety and cleanup.

He stood so tall and handsome and at ease beside the podium. He used no notes while he reminded his listeners about the men and women who'd fought for and defended the country's independence. And were still fighting to defend it, he said with a deliberate glance in his wife's direction.

Suze flushed at the spontaneous applause and faces turned in her direction. Gabe waited for it to die down before emphasizing that gatherings like this were taking place all across America.

"Celebrating our fundamental freedoms with friends and family is what keeps this community and this country strong. Whatever happens in Washington, we stand together in Cedar Creek."

He stepped down to hearty applause, topped by a shout from an appreciative female constituent. "Justin Trudeau and that Macron dude got nothing on you, Mayor! You just keep on doin' what you're doin'."

Hoots and laughter followed him back to his seat. As the choir began a stirring medley, Suze leaned closer. "You must not have told anyone about moving to Arizona. The jungle drums would've been working overtime."

"I gave Joanna Hicks a heads-up but asked her to keep it quiet until after the Fourth. I'll present my formal resignation at the town council meeting tomorrow afternoon. Tonight is just for having fun, not saying goodbye."

Despite his easy slouch, Gabe kept his eyes on his watch as he counted down to the fireworks display. The town's pumper and crew were parked right at the edge of the dirt lot where the contractor providing the pyrotechnic display had set up. His fellow volunteer firefighters were monitoring their phones, prepared to respond instantly. An ambulance from the regional hospital was five minutes away.

When tragedy struck, however, it didn't happen at the carefully controlled site. The first indication was a loud *ka-boom* that jerked everyone around. The second was a wild burst of fireworks gyrating like corkscrews through the sky to the east. Gabe was already shoving out of his chair when his phone shrilled. He answered, then took off at a run.

"Stoney Brook Estates," he threw over his shoulder. "Chuck Osborne's place. Be back when I can."

Suzanne was only a half-step behind him. She knew the Emergency Action Checklist for On-Scene Commanders backward and forward. If nothing else, she could help at the command center, work the communications or coordinate relief efforts. Whatever Gabe or his on-scene commander needed.

Chapter Nine

Gabe, the fire chief and the medical examiner pieced the sequence of events together after the fact. Tragically, the Osborne fire had resulted from one of those freak accidents people read about but never believe could really happen.

Chuck Osborne and his two young sons had decided to hold their own Independence Day celebration. In preparation, Chuck had almost bought out one of the fireworks tents that sprouted up like mushrooms throughout Oklahoma in late June. He and the boys had shot off parts of their cache the previous couple of nights but saved the biggest and best for the Fourth.

Then Chuck, a savvy avionics systems instructor at FAA who damned well should've known better, leaned over to light the fuse of a rocket mounted on a launcher stuck in the ground. The rocket exploded prematurely and rammed straight into his chest. The force of the hit had stopped his heart and fiery sparks set his shirt alight.

One of his frantic sons had tried to douse the fire by rolling him in the dirt but the boy was too young and his dad was too heavy to roll. The other son raced for the garden hose. By the time he'd tugged the hose as far as it would reach and arced a stream of water at his father, flames were devouring the tinder-dry grass around him.

When Gabe and Suze arrived, it was a scene right out of their worst nightmares. Thick black smoke blotted out the evening sky. Flames formed a seemingly impenetrable wall stretching from the Osbornes' home to the fields behind it. The blazing backdrop illuminated the two- and three-hundred-thousand-dollar homes scattered at wide intervals through the development.

The fire chief gave Gabe a quick sit rep. "Chuck Osborne's dead. His son said a rocket augured into his chest and exploded. Wife says she saw his body enveloped in flames. The boys suffered burns, don't know how bad yet. Donna, too. They're on their way to the regional hospital."

Gabe squinted at the roiling smoke and dancing flames. "We need help with this, chief."

"Already put out the call for aid from our surrounding communities. Mustang's pumpers and tanker are five minutes out. Yukon and OKC are responding, too."

"What about a Hot Shot cadre?"

"I've notified the Forestry Service," the chief confirmed. "They're sending a team. They'll also call in air support."

The taut reply knotted Suze's stomach. It stayed bunched as her husband pulled on the turnout gear he'd picked up at the station on their mad race out of town—bunker pants, jacket, boots, gloves and helmet with its protective visor.

Just rigging out in the scorching July night drenched him in sweat. As he strapped on his single-harness chest-radio pack, Suze had to bite back the suggestion that he should direct the effort, not put himself on the front line. Gabe might be the town's mayor, but he was also a volunteer firefighter. She knew there was no way in hell he'd keep a safe distance from those vicious flames while his fellow volunteers were battling them.

The fire chief didn't argue, either. He'd trained these men and women. Put them through hell before he certified them. And he needed every damned one on the line.

"I've sent the A team to work the Osborne house," he advised Gabe tersely. "I have two other teams clearing a firebreak between it and the Forrester place. Might save it, if the wind doesn't pick up."

Gabe was assigned to A team. Her heart in her throat, Suze watched him hurry down the road to join the group aiming a fat inch-and-a-half stream of water at the flames engulfing the Osbornes' home.

"What can I do?" she asked the chief.

His narrowed, smoke-reddened eyes cut from the fire to her. She'd known him for most of her life. More to the point, he knew her.

"Every damned TV and radio station in central Oklahoma wants an update and Hal Jorgenson, our Public Affairs officer is down with colitis. Our deputy PA's on her way. Until she gets here…"

He jerked his head toward his command vehicle.

The driver's door hung open. Suze could hear the shrill squawks and tinny requests for status from where she stood.

"You know what to tell 'em, Captain. And what *not* to tell 'em. Take care of it."

Suze took care of it until the deputy PA screeched up in a mud-spattered pickup.

"Thanks for covering for me," she panted. "You start a log?"

"Right here."

The farmer's wife skimmed the log and let out a low whistle. "Can you stay? Looks like I might need some help."

"You got it."

The two women acted as the central point of contact for news crews and concerned officials for the next two hours. They shared information on the teams that had raced to the scene from the mutual aid townships, relayed updates provided by the chief to include the arrival of the Hot Shot team and an incident commander specially trained to combat wildfires, and coordinated with Will Rogers World Airport tower to keep the air space clear for the tanker that flew in to drop fire retardant.

Suze was guzzling down bottled water when a Mustang City crew radioed a terse report.

"The heat got to our bulldozer operator. We're retreating to our fallback position to cool him down."

The water bottle crunched and crinkled in her fist. The Mustang crew had been plowing up cedars to keep the fire from jumping the creek toward the west boundary of the development. The flames had to be getting perilously close to their position. If the cedars ignited, the fire could whip along the entire creek, maybe even snake though town.

While the deputy PA briefed the chief, the urgency of the situation ripped at Suze. One dozer could clear more brush and vegetation in ten minutes than a full crew hacking and axing for several hours. She wasn't a trained firefighter but she could operate a variety of heavy equipment, including some earth movers.

Years of training and experience warred in her mind with the possible risks to her baby. She'd already exposed her unborn child to one potentially toxic situation during cleanup of the fuel spill. Did she dare risk exposing it to another?

The escalating situation forced her choice. One life had already been lost. Other folks stood to lose all they owned. She couldn't stand by and just watch.

"I can drive a dozer," she told the chief. "I might be able to help."

He didn't waste time arguing. "Go!"

Spinning, she headed for Ole Blue. Three miles and a racketing drive over unpaved roads later, she screeched to a halt at the Mustang crew's fallback position.

Sweat drenched and smoke stained, they'd propped their woozy dozer operator against a rear tire of the flatbed trailer that had transported his machinery. They'd removed his protective gear and had hosed him down and were now waiting for his body temp to lower enough for him to take in some liquid.

"I'm Suzanne Hall," she told the team leader. "Captain Suzanne Hall. I command an Air Force Prime BEEF crew and have hands-on experience operating a bulldozer."

The firefighter looked her up and down. What he saw obviously didn't reassure him but before he could question her qualifications the man beside him widened his red-rimmed eyes.

"Hey! Aren't you the captain from Cedar Creek who got the Bronze Star?"

"That's me."

"I read about her in the paper, Mike. If she says she can operate a dozer, I believe her."

She understood the team leader's skepticism even as she yanked on the dozer operator's gear. Firefighting bulldozer drivers were a rare breed. She'd read one report indicating that of the more than fourteen hundred firefighters in Orange County, California, only two were bulldozer operators. The Mustang fire department was damned lucky to have a volunteer operator. Even luckier that he happened to own a construction company and could haul in crawlers and backhoes in a crisis like this.

Although officers in charge of Prime BEEF teams weren't expected to get down in the trenches, Suze had decided early in her career to acquire at least a basic familiarity with her team members' unique skill sets. Consequently, she'd learned the intricacies of emergency airfield lighting systems, had wrestled with mobile arresting barriers, and had a working knowledge of HVAC and sanitary systems.

She'd also learned to operate various items of heavy equipment. The dump trucks were a breeze. The graders and backhoes took a little practice. Surprisingly, the dozers with their hydrostatic transmissions and GPS machine controls were also relatively easy to operate. Still, her team had held their collective breath when she'd dropped the blade and attacked a heavily damaged runway during a deployment at a remote base in Iraq—then whooped when she plowed up an entire section of cratered concrete in the first pass.

She felt that same grim determination now. She was fierce. Focused. Straining to hear every word gasped out by the heat-stricken dozer operator.

"Come at the bank…from an angle. Watch for washouts and cuts. Don't let 'er tip…into the creek."

"Got it."

"Make sure…you have an escape plan. If the…fire burns over you, unfurl the curtains and…plow through to the black."

The thick, reflective curtains would cover the dozer's window and provide a protective cocoon if the flames surrounded it. But even with the shield down and the built-in air-conditioning blasting, she knew temperatures inside the cab could still reach upwards of a hundred and seventy degrees. The black, she guessed, was the charred land behind the fire line.

As she started for the dozer parked down at the creek, the team leader was still dubious. "You sure you know what you're doing, Captain?"

"Guess we'll both find out quick enough."

As she approached the crawler, the fire-fed heat sucked the air from her lungs. Panting, she swung into the cab and slammed the door. She kept one foot braced against the floor and the other on the deceleration pedal as she hit the starter. The hundred-and-fifty horsepower engine rumbled under her and the air gushing through the AC vents went from hot and acrid to cool and acrid. Keeping her hands on the throttle, she squinted at the tree-lined bank ahead.

Smoke, dust and darkness threatened to obscure her visibility. The fire retardant dropped by the tankers had splattered the cab's windows with red splotches. Jaw locked, she raised the blade, dropped it again and dug it into the red Oklahoma dirt at a shallow angle. With grim determination, she throttled forward.

The twisted, stunted cedars lining the bank went down like dominoes. Their trunks crunched under the blade. Branches whipped at the crawler's sides. Perched eight feet above the fallen trees, Swish rolled along at a blinding five miles an hour while doing her damnedest to keep the tractor from tipping into the creek. Her insides squeezed when the left tread slipped and seemed to lose traction. The cab swayed, but she got it righted and kept plowing.

It was after midnight before the more than two hundred firefighters who'd responded finally tamed the beast. It had consumed over a thousand acres, most of them the open fields that stretched from Cedar Creek toward the FAA center a dozen miles to the east. The Osbornes' home was a total loss. Dave Forrester's newly constructed mansion had sustained some smoke and water damage and would need extensive repair.

Gabe hadn't seen his wife since they'd parted some five hours ago, but he'd heard via the chief that she'd joined forces with a crew from Mustang. He'd connected with her once by phone to make sure she was okay. He could tell her adrenaline was still pumping as she described the firebreak they'd established. But when she called him to let him know the Mustang crew had shut down operations, he could hear the weariness in her voice.

But that was Suze. The woman gave 200 percent to every task, every challenge. It was what made her so good at her job. And what put her squarely in line to shoot up the ranks.

Guilt nagged at him for forcing her to choose between him and her career three years ago. He could only swear a silent oath that they would do better this time around.

"Where are you now?" he asked her.

"On my way back to the command center."

"We've got things under control here. Go home. Take a cool shower. Crash. I'll get a ride home from the chief."

"Have you heard how Mrs. Osborne and the boys are doing?"

"The youngest, Danny, is in bad shape. He's been evacuated to the burn center at Integris Hospital in OKC. Donna and the oldest weren't burned as badly, but they're both pretty traumatized."

"I feel so, so sorry for them."

"Yeah, me, too. Go home," he repeated, scrubbing the heel of his hand across his chin. "Get some sleep. I'll try not to let Doofus wake you when I roll in."

Suze didn't argue. She was hot, sweat-grimed and totally whipped. She managed a smile for Doofus's ecstatic greeting and hung loose on the back patio while he made his usual mad dash around the yard, watering everything that caught his fancy.

His duty done, he bounded up the stairs ahead of her and leaped onto the bed. She didn't have the energy or the inclination to order him off. Leaving him in gleeful possession, she peeled off her clothes and left a trail all the way to the shower.

The pelting water revived her enough to shampoo her hair. That helped get most of the grime out from under her nails. Still, toweling the thick mane dry just about sucked out her the last of her energy. Head bent, towel still working, she padded back to the bedroom.

Suddenly, she stopped dead. Her discarded jeans lay in a heap, her panties next to them. The dark blotch staining the panties started her heart hammering in her chest.

"Oh, God!" Her fists tightened on the towel ends. Her legs went rubbery. "OhGod, ohGod, ohGod."

Doofus jerked up his head. His ears pricked forward, and he gave a low whine when Suze dropped to one knee. He was beside her, nosing her arm, when she snatched up the panties. She shoved him away and sat back on her heels.

The stain was dry. Rust colored. She stared at it for what felt like ten lifetimes, then shoved to her feet and rushed downstairs. With Doofus clicking at her heels, she cut straight for the laptop on Gabe's desk. He'd shared the password so it took her only a few seconds to power up, log on, and Google *pregnancy, spotting.* She read at least a dozen articles before her heart stopped hammering.

"Okay," she told the anxious hound who'd plopped his head onto her thigh. "Okay. It's not uncommon in the first few weeks. As long as the blood isn't bright red and I didn't experience any cramps, we don't need to worry."

She hadn't cramped. Had she?

Her pulse skittered. With the bulldozer's engine rumbling under her and the blade chewing up cypress after cypress and her adrenaline pumping a gallon a minute, would she have felt a cramp if she'd had one?

She considered calling her mother. Or Gabe's mother. As late as it was, she ruled them out and called his oldest sister, instead. Kathy had more than six years as a neonatal intensive care nurse under her belt. Suze hated to wake her on one of her rare nights off but knew she could trust her judgment.

Her voice clogged with sleep, Kathy demanded an update on the fire first, then echoed the articles her sister-in-law had pulled up. "Yeah, it's not unusual. I spotted with two of my kids. I wouldn't worry about it, unless it continues or you start cramping."

Reassured, Suze thanked her and disconnected. For her own peace of mind, though, she walked the floor for another twenty minutes. Doofus watched every turn and foray she made to the bathroom to check for additional spotting. When none appeared, she fell into bed, too relieved and exhausted to stay awake for Gabe's return.

Gabe and the chief swung by the station to clean and stash their protective gear before heading home. Half the company had already stood down but a team would remain on-site to watch for flare-ups. They would also secure the scene for reps from the Oklahoma State Fire Marshall's office, which was charged with investigating any fire involving loss of life and/or property damage above a certain level.

Gabe had the chief drop him off at the end of the drive, hoping he could walk up to the house and slip inside before Doofus went nuts. The plan almost worked. He got through the front door and was halfway up the stairs before the hound launched into full alert mode.

The sudden, startled barking rattled the windows. His claws scrabbled on the wood floor. And when he appeared at the top of the stairs, the acrid stink of smoke clinging to the shadowy figure coming up apparently confused the heck out of him.

"Yeah, it's me."

Reassured by the sound of his human's voice, Doofus went from confused to ecstatic. He danced beside Gabe as he went into the bedroom and dropped a kiss on Suze's cheek.

"Whattimeizzit?"

"Coming up on 3:00 a.m. Go back to sleep. I'll join you shortly."

"Shortly" stretched out for a good twenty minutes. His back against the shower tiles, he lifted his face and tried to let the lukewarm stream wash away some of the horror of the night.

But try as he might, he couldn't shut down the chaotic sounds and sights that kalidescoped through his mind. The flames leaping into the night sky. The charred bodies. The utter weariness in Suze's voice when he'd talked to her.

Christ! The woman was incredible. She'd jumped aboard a bulldozer and plunged into a raging fire. Yet now, with the adrenaline drained out of him, a nasty little niggle of doubt picked at the edges of his weariness.

Flattening a palm against the tile, Gabe let the water pound his head and shoulder. He'd told Suze he would support her. That he would jettison the job and the home that he loved to move to Phoenix. That once the baby was born, they would work out their future together, one day at a time.

And as long as she wore an Air Force uniform, the

odds were the future would include more toxic spills. More aircraft accidents and explosions and raging fires. More deployments to dangerous forward locations.

Could he handle saying goodbye to her again? Stand by while she packed her go-kit, kissed him and the baby, and left?

He'd convinced her he could. Convinced himself he could. But now, with the horror of the night still smoldering in his mind, Gabe couldn't help wonder if he was deluding himself.

His mind as tired as his body, he pried his shoulder blades from the wall, shampooed, soaped down, dried off and slid between the sheets. Suze mumbled something that sounded distinctly grumpy and bucked her butt against his hip. Gabe rolled onto his side and spooned her body with his.

The feel of her, the scent of her, his provided an instant counter to his doubts. He settled her closer and repeated what he suspected might become his personal mantra. The months and years ahead wouldn't be easy. For him, or for her. But this time they'd make it, dammit. They would!

He fell asleep with that fierce vow echoing in his mind and his wife in his arms.

His side of the bed was empty when Suze woke the next morning. She shuffled to the bathroom, still groggy. The sight of the panties she'd rinsed out last night draped over the side of the tub brought her fear crashing back. She didn't draw a whole breath until she made sure she hadn't spotted again during the night.

Relieved, she followed the scent of coffee to the kitchen. A note propped on the counter informed her that Gabe had an early morning meeting with the state fire inspectors. It also reminded her of the ten o'clock meeting with Colonel Amistad. Gabe would have to cancel but encouraged her to make the meeting.

She stood at the counter, undecided. The breakfast table was covered with empty packing boxes and wrapping paper. So was the dining table. Since Alicia was sure she could rent the house furnished, they'd decided to leave the big stuff and basic necessities like dishes and pots and pans. But they still needed to pack the personal items that Gabe wanted to put in storage.

Suze's gaze swept the empty boxes. What the hell. Both she and Gabe had packed up and moved often enough before. Still plenty of time left.

Since she'd run through the limited wardrobe she'd brought with her, she called the sister-in-law nearest to her size.

"Penny, I need to borrow something suitable for a meeting with Colonel Amistad."

"Who?"

"He was Grand Marshal of the parade."

"If you say so. Come on over. *Mi* closet *es su* closet."

Twenty minutes later, Suze left her sister-in-law's house wearing a pair of black slacks and a sleeveless, amber-colored linen tunic. Since her feet were two sizes larger than Penny's, she slipped into the sling-backs she'd bought for the wedding and belted the tunic with the matching, cream-colored belt.

She clipped her hair up as a concession to the heat but couldn't bring herself to put up the T-bird's top. As a result, she had to make herself presentable again when she pulled into a visitor's slot outside the headquarters of the 137th Special Operations Wing. She sat in the vicious sun, raking her fingers through her hair, twisting it up again, while her gaze roamed the buildings and hangars visible from where she'd parked.

She had a feeling she knew what had prompted this invitation to meet with the 137th commander. He knew her background. Knew, too, that his unit could make use of her training and hard learned experience.

She'd taken a few minutes to Google the 137th before leaving for her meeting with its commander. The wing's long and distinguished history stretched back to 1947, when it began life as a fighter group flying the F-51 Mustang.

Now the 137th was transitioning to a new platform. Smaller, sleeker and crammed with the world's most sophisticated avionics, communications and surveillance equipment. Suze could see several of the MC-12 Liberties parked on the apron. From where she was standing they looked like corporate turboprops, which is precisely how the modified Hawker Beechcraft Super Kings had begun life. She couldn't wait to get an up close and personal tour. When she was ushered into the colonel's office, however, Amistad suggested a chat before he had one of the MC-12 pilots show off his baby.

"I'm sorry Gabe couldn't make it," he said when they'd settled at the small round table against a wall that displayed all the unit awards the wing had won. "I understand why, though. Our fire crews didn't return to base until well past midnight. I image Cedar Creek's mayor stayed on scene for hours after that."

"He did, and he said to tell you how much he appreciated your engines responding as quickly as they did. He'll send an official thank-you as soon as he can."

"No problem. And actually, you're the one I really wanted to talk to this morning."

At her questioning look, he flicked a glance at her wedding band. "You know how the rumor mill works. Word is, now that you and Gabe are back together he's moving to Phoenix with you."

"The rumor mill has it right." She hesitated, then filled in the rest of the blanks. "We're also going to have a baby."

"I heard that, too. Not that it makes any difference for what I'd like to propose."

She'd guessed what was coming before he laid the offer on the table.

"Our civil engineering chief plans to retire next year. He's an Air Reserve Technician, with more than thirty years under his belt."

Suze's knowledge of Air National Guard operations was sketchy but she understood that an ART combined two worlds. As a civilian, an ART worked the same job in the same place, generally keeping fairly normal duty hours, until retirement.

At the same time, ARTs were members of the Air Force Reserve Command. As such, they wore their uniforms and rank. And like all members of the Guard and Reserve, they were subject to mobilization and deployment.

"The position is competitive," Amistad confirmed, "so we'll advertise it Air Force–wide. But with your background and experience, you'd have a real shot at it."

When she started to reply, he held up a palm.

"You might not deploy as often as you do now, but I can't make any promises. Last year we sent various elements of the wing to a half-dozen hot spots around the world. The difference is, you'll home base here, in Oklahoma City, between deployments."

Suze's first thought was that this could be the best solution for both her and the Air Force. If she requested separation due to pregnancy, her unit at Luke could fill her vacancy. No work-arounds, no tagging someone else to deploy in her place.

Separation due to pregnancy would also allow her the time and the leisure to experience the full spectrum of motherhood. A time, her sisters-in-law warned, stretched from gestation to delivery to that scary postpartum period that would have her swinging from "Isn't the baby the most precious thing you ever saw" to "I need out of this freakin' house *now*!"

And, as the Colonel had stressed, she would home base here, in Oklahoma, instead of moving from assignment to assignment and base to base for the next thirteen or fourteen years. And that kind of stability meant Gabe could explore higher public office, as everyone seemed think he should.

Balancing all the potential positives was the prospect of working the same job in the same place for the next twenty or thirty years. She'd joined the military in the first place for the travel and excitement and adventure it offered. She loved the challenges and the fact that every transfer, every assignment meant new challenges, new adventures.

Except…she had to think of more than just herself now. And having a baby would certainly offer all kinds of challenges and adventures.

"I don't want an answer now, Captain. Think about it. Talk it over with Gabe. Get back to me when you're ready. And in the meantime…" He pushed away from the table. "How about an up close and personal tour of the MC-12 Liberty?"

Her escort was standing by. Like many Air National Guard pilots, Captain Marv Westbrook was older and more experienced than most of his active duty counterparts. He was also just back from the ten-nation NATO operation to retake Mosul.

"Flying so low and slow got a little hairy at times," he admitted in what Suze knew was a monumental understatement, "but we provided real-time intelligence, surveillance and recon to the coalition forces. You'll be impressed as hell when you see the comm and sensors packed into the Liberty."

She certainly was. She was even more impressed when Marv wrapped up his part of the tour and turned her over to the 137th's Chief of Civil Engineering. For the next hour she happily immersed herself in the world of rapid runway repair, explosive ordnance disposal and emergency humanitarian relief projects.

Seriously impressed by the 137th's operation, Suze said goodbye and made her way back to the T-bird. She'd put up a protective windshield screen but still eased onto the hot leather of the driver's seat *very* carefully. It took some maneuvering to keep the backs of her arms from making contact with the hot leather but she keyed the ignition and soon had the AC blasting.

She was still parked and waiting for the steering wheel to cool enough to wrap her palms around when her cell phone chimed. Caller ID showed "unknown caller" but the area code was local. Thinking it might be someone she'd just talked to at the 137th, she answered.

"Captain Hall."

"Hey, Suzanne. It's Dave."

She went blank for a moment before connecting the voice to her former classmate, Freckle-faced Forrester. "Hi, Dave."

"I got your mobile number from Gabe. Hope you don't mind."

"'Course not."

"I called him to let him know I'm on my way home and will bring a damage assessor out to check out the house this afternoon."

"Be prepared," she warned. "From what I could see, it looked pretty bad."

"That's what I heard. Listen, I heard you've got a meeting with Colonel Amistad. Sure wish you'd come talk to me before you sign on with the Guard. Like I told you, I could…"

"What makes you think I'm joining the Guard?"

"Hey, this boy ain't as stupid as he looks. First, Alicia tells me you're renting out the house but restricting it to a short-term lease. Then Gabe lets drop that you drove over to talk to Colonel Amistad despite the wild night I know you both had. So I figure it's about something pressing and made a few calls."

She barely heard his eager prattle. Her mind was still wondering if Gabe had known the Colonel wanted to recruit her.

"And speaking of wild nights… I heard what you did, Suzanne. Climbing aboard that dozer was pretty slick. And exactly why I want you working for me. I'm telling you, girl, the oil and gas business has done a one-eighty since the slump a few years ago. You could make four, five times what you're making now."

She shook herself out of her whirling thoughts. She

didn't bother to tell Forrester it wasn't about the money. For her *or* for most of the men and women she served with. Hell, many of the junior enlisted troops in her squadron qualified for food stamps.

"Sorry, Dave," she replied. "Not interested."

"Just think about it. Talk it over with Gabe."

Which was exactly the same advice Colonel Amistad had offered.

Feeling as though she was being yanked in a dozen different directions, Suze put the convertible in gear. To her disgust, she'd barely reached the front gates before her bladder reminded her that she'd once again downed too much coffee. Her stomach chimed in to suggest that a bacon cheeseburger wouldn't be out of order. Yielding to their urgent demands, she pulled into a conveniently located Braum's just a short distance from the base.

She hit the ladies' room first. Mere seconds later, the dark stain in her underwear sent her running out of the fast food restaurant. Big, sprawling Tinker Air Force Base to the east of Oklahoma City maintained a fully staffed medical clinic. But Tinker was a good thirty minutes away.

Shoving the T-bird into gear, she headed for the new healthplex closer to home.

Chapter Ten

Gabe got the text while he and the fire chief still had their heads together with the state inspectors. He'd put his phone on vibrate so as not to interrupt their discussions and had let several calls go to voice mail. Then *Call me. Now!* popped up on his screen.

"'Scuse me, I need to take this." Frowning, he cut away from the others and stabbed Suze's speed dial number. "What's up?"

"I'm at the ER at the healthplex. I had some vaginal bleeding."

"Are you okay?"

"Mostly."

"The baby?"

"I'm… I'm not sure. They're going to run some tests."

"I'm on my way."

He made a quick excuse to the others and hit Ole Blue on the run.

The healthplex was only minutes away, thank God. Yet the drive seemed to take a lifetime. Gabe's stomach churned with every hiss of the wheels on the pavement. All their hopes, all their newly devised plans, had centered on the unexpected, unanticipated, miraculous result of their night together in Phoenix.

If Suze lost the baby…

If they didn't have the child to help stitch their marriage back together…

Jaw locked, knuckles bone white where he gripped the steering wheel, Gabe tore into the hospital parking lot.

Opened just a few years ago, the ultramodern facility looked and felt more like a gleaming hotel than a medical center. Even the freestanding ER offered unique lighting, soothing colors and a long, curving row of spacious exam rooms that minimized the clinical setting and maximized patient comfort.

Suze was in exam room three. She was wrapped in a hospital gown and sitting on the edge of the bed as a lab tech unsnapped the rubber tie banding her upper arm. Gabe's heart squeezed at the emotions that flashed across her face when she saw him. Relief, worry, guilt all rolled into one.

"The bleeding's stopped," she related, stretching out her free hand to take his. "The doc doesn't think it presages a miscarriage but…" She stopped, bit her lip, forced herself to continue. "But he's ordered several tests."

"This one checks your hCG," the tech confirmed as she matched the information on the label attached to blood-filled vials with the data on Suze's wristband. "That's a hormone produced by the placenta during pregnancy. Doc Terry's also ordered an ultrasound.

They're waiting to take you down now. I'll let them know you're ready."

She snapped off her gloves and tossed them in the trash, then picked up her plastic carrier with its rack of samples. Gabe had his arms around his wife before the tech was out the door.

"Oh, God." She buried her face in his shoulder. "I was so scared. Still am. I should've come in last night."

The whisper was so low and muffled Gabe wasn't sure he'd heard right. "You were bleeding last night?"

"A little, but I checked a dozen sites on the internet and…"

"Christ, Suze! You checked the internet?"

She pushed back a little. "I also called Kathy. She said spotting is fairly normal this early in a pregnancy."

"Why didn't you call me?"

"You were working the cleanup from the fire and I…"

"Are you ready, Mrs. Hall?"

A cheerful young orderly in cinnamon-colored scrubs rolled in a wheelchair. Gabe was still trying to digest the fact that Suze hadn't told him about the spotting as he walked with her down several long, spotlessly clean corridors.

The radiology tech was ready for them. "Hello, Ms. Hall. I'm Hector Alvarez. Doctor Terry's ordered an ultrasound of your abdomen. Have you had one before?"

"Yes, a few weeks ago."

"Then you know what to expect." He helped her get situated on the table, draped a sheet over her upper thighs and rolled the hospital gown up to bare her belly. "When was the last time you ate?"

"I had some instant oatmeal around eight-thirty this morning."

"Nothing since?"

"No."

"How about liquids?"

"Coffee. But it's pretty well flushed out."

"Great. We should get some clear images. Okay, here we go."

He squirted the warm gel on Suze's still-flat belly and began to move his wand. Like Suzanne, Gabe kept his focus on the screen. He'd seen copies of his various nieces' and nephews' ultrasounds stuck to his sisters' fridges with magnets. But when the tech pointed to the tiny, curled form nestled in his wife's belly, he experienced a swift, hard jab of delight.

"That's it?" he asked the tech. "That little peanut?"

"Yep, that's your baby."

Suze kept a death grip on Gabe's hand. "Is it okay?"

"The radiologist will have to review the scans but I'm not seeing anything to concern me." He worked the wand in a slow circle. Dropped it lower. Stopped and worked over the same spot again. Suze was watching the screen and missed his slight frown.

"Would you turn a little onto your left side, Ms. Hall? There. That's good."

With quick efficiency, he placed a series of electronic markers and clicked several images. Gabe leaned closer, straining to see whatever had caught the tech's attention but he'd already moved the wand to a different angle. He clicked several more images, slid the wand lower, clicked again.

"Okay, that should do it. The radiologist will review the images and zap a report to the ER toot-d-sweet. I'll just clean off that gel, and you'll be good to go."

The same cheerful orderly wheeled Suze back to

the ER. A nurse followed them into the room. "Doctor Terry's reviewing your lab results now. He'll be in as soon as he gets the radiology report."

"Good, in the meantime…" She nodded to the bathroom. "I need to go."

"No problem. Just ring if you need help."

While his wife emptied her bladder, Gabe leaned his hips against the marble windowsill. His glimpse of the ultrasound tech's small, quick frown had churned a gallon of acid in his gut. It had also kept him from letting Suze know how pissed he was that she hadn't told him about the spotting.

Granted, she'd been asleep when he got home last night. But she'd stirred enough to ask him what time it was. At the very least, she could've called him when she got up this morning.

Hell! Maybe she had. He whipped out his phone, checked the calls that had gone to voice mail and saw one from her. Cursing himself for not taking it, he listened to the short message.

Nothing about spotting. Nothing about calling Kathy. Only that she was heading for the meeting with Colonel Amistad and would see Gabe when she saw him.

There was no message from his sister, either. Jaw tight, Gabe vowed to have a discussion with Ms. Kathleen Hall Sheppard about that when he got Suze home.

But that, they discovered when the ER doc came in a few moments later, wouldn't be today. Terry looked more like a cage fighter than a physician. His shaved and shiny bald head gleamed even in the ER's subdued lighting, and his shoulders strained at the seams of his white coat. His approach matched his appearance. He was brusque and to the point, which both Gabe and Suze appreciated.

"Your tests look good, Ms. Hall. Your hCG level is elevated, as it should be. That and the ultrasound confirm your placenta hasn't abrupted."

"So I'm not losing the baby?"

"I don't think so. A lot of women experience bleeding during their pregnancies."

Suze collapsed against the raised bed back. "That's what Kathy told me. My sister-in-law," she explained. "She's a neonatal intensive care nurse here."

"Kathy Sheppard?"

"That's her."

He turned his cool, penetrating gaze on Gabe. "You're Kathy's brother? The mayor of Cedar Creek?"

"Right."

"We treated your fire victims here in the ER last night. One of the boys was transported to the burn unit at Integris. The other kid and his mom are upstairs."

"I know. I'm going up to see them before I leave."

Terry nodded and turned back to Suze. "Spotting is common, but heavy bleeding like you had this morning concerns me. Did you overexert yourself and lift something heavy in the past twenty-four hours?"

Her mouth twisted in a grimace so full of guilt that Gabe supplied the answer.

"My wife's a combat engineer. She can operate just about every piece of heavy equipment in the Air Force inventory. She helped us last night by climbing aboard a bulldozer and plowing a firebreak."

The doc's eyes narrowed. "Damn! I just made the connection. You're the Captain I read about in the paper some weeks back."

"There's something else," Suze confessed, worrying her lower lip with her teeth. "Last month, before I knew I was pregnant, my team and I responded to a fuel spill. I wore a respirator and the tests the doc at my base ran indicated no toxicity in my lungs or blood gases. But…" She chewed on her lip again, harder. "I thought you should know."

"Well…" Terry tapped his pen against the lab report. "I'm going to level with you. If you do miscarry, there's nothing we can do for you here in the ER. Nature will take its course. But if it does happen, you're in the right place. We'll watch to make sure you don't hemorrhage."

He hesitated just a second too long. The color drained from Suze's cheeks, and Gabe went still.

"There was something that popped up on the ultrasound. Nothing involving the baby," he said swiftly. "Just an anomaly we need to scope out."

"What kind of anomaly?"

"It's called a uterine mass. Could be a cyst. Could be a fibroid. Neither one is anything to worry about, but the radiologist wants another pass at it. So I'm going to admit you to the hospital and order more tests."

When Suze's eyes went wide, Gabe saw the incipient panic in their forest-green depths. Saw, too, the iron will that shut it down.

"Thanks, doc," she said, forcing a calm he knew she was far from feeling. "Run every test in the book. I'd rather err on the side of caution."

"Same here. I'll put in the admit order."

For the next few hours, Gabe had to throw up a firewall to block his chaotic thoughts from his wife. She was up to her ears in her own vicious stew of guilt and worry. He was damned if he would add to it as he accompanied her to the surgical unit, where a resident performed a needle biopsy on the uterine mass. The fact that they'd have to wait until the next day for the biopsy results only added to their combined stress.

His sister Kathy relieved some of their tension when she showed up at the healthplex several hours before she had to go on duty. She'd talked to Suze's doc before joining her brother and sister-in-law, and was quick to share what she'd learned.

"Dr. Terry's still waiting for the biopsy results," she reported after fierce hugs all around. "He's pretty convinced the mass is a uterine fibroid, though. A noncancerous growth in the muscle tissue. The technical term is leiomyoma. They're more common in older women but could certainly cause the bleeding you've experienced."

"Could it have hurt the baby?"

"I doubt it. Not at this stage. But it might crowd the fetus as it grows and presses against the mass. You should probably have it removed."

"Removed?"

"It can be done laparoscopically. Don't worry about that right now. Just relax and think happy thoughts. Which," she added with a wry smile, "is what my loving husband always advises when I'm fat and leaking and ready to take an ax to him for convincing me that we should have one more kid."

Suze laughed, which was exactly what Kathy had intended. Gabe shot her a grateful smile, then braced himself as the rest of the family followed in waves. Suze's parents. Gabe's mom, accompanied by his sister Jill. Penny and her husband and kids. Once Suze got moved to a regular room, Gabe consigned her to their collective care while he took the elevator up two floors to check on Donna Osborne and her son.

Twenty minutes later, he jabbed the down button. The brief visit had ripped him apart. Hell, the past twenty-four hours had just about shredded him. Needing some time to pull himself together, he exited the elevator and paused by the wall of windows in the family waiting area.

Despite the panorama of rolling, sun-kissed hills outside the window, his thoughts seemed to swirl in a dark vortex. He'd served in combat. Both on the ground and as the operator of an RPV armed with lethal missiles. He knew better than most that death and destruction could come at you without warning, without mercy. Now it had happened to Donna Osborne and her family.

And could happen to his *wife*!

The impact was searing. Visceral. Wrenching. The sense of having failed both Suze and the Osbornes ate at his gut. As if to counter it, the anger he'd so rigidly suppressed earlier slipped its leash.

Suze shouldn't have climbed aboard that dozer yesterday, dammit! And she should've told him about the spotting when she'd first discovered it last night. What the hell did the fact that she'd called Kathy but not him say about the state of their marriage?

The small spark of anger gathered heat. Hadn't they learned their lesson the first time around? Yet here they were, married again for all of three days, and already the lines of communication had fractured. Despite everything else going on—the wedding, the parade, the fire—she could have, *should* have called him.

He wanted to put one of his fists through the wall. He settled for jamming them in his pockets. Then he dragged in several long breaths and unlocked his jaw. This sure as hell wasn't the time or the place for *could've, should've*. His only priority right now was to be here for his wife.

Suze's parents were the last of the family to leave their daughter's spacious hospital room.

"You just rest." Mary leaned over the bed to kiss her cheek. "Hard to do in a hospital, I know, but try."

"I will."

"And you…" She wagged a stern finger at Gabe. "Call us when you know the test results. Whatever and whenever you hear."

"Will do."

When they left a silence settled over the room, broken only by the beep of a monitor from across the hall. Suze welcomed the unaccustomed quiet but roused after a few moments to tell Gabe he should go home, too.

"You need to go let Doofus out and feed him. Feed yourself, too."

"Penny's husband said he'd take care of the mutt." He dragged a chair over closer to the bed and reached for her hand. "I'll grab something at the cafeteria when they bring your supper."

Suze lay there, her fingers twined loosely with his. Despite the contact, she sensed a subtle withdrawal, as if he'd pulled into himself.

Or not. She had so much going on inside her own head she couldn't seem to get over the storm of emotions that had racked her since she hit the ladies' room at Braum's. The storm had wrung her out. She was so tired. So drained. The adrenaline that had pumped through her yesterday was a distant memory. All she had left now was a small, steely core that refused to give way to panic.

Her glance drifted to the window with its view of the parking lot below and the hills beyond. Then to Gabe. His head was bowed, his gaze on their loosely clasped hands. He was in the jeans and blue knit polo shirt he must've worn to his meeting with the state inspectors this morning. The shirt still looked trim and neat, but the face above it showed the effects of a long night and its aftermath. The white squint lines at the corners of his hazel eyes cut deep grooves. Those bracketing his mouth looked permanently etched.

He couldn't have slept more than a few hours last night. Although he slouched in the chair with his usual careless grace, his shoulders had a tired slump to them Suze couldn't remember seeing before. And even as she watched, his eyes closed for a brief moment.

"Gabe," she said quietly. "Go home."

He blinked awake instantly. "Not gonna happen, babe."

"I know you must have a stack of incident reports to review. Calls you should make. Go do what you need to do, then get some sleep. I'll be fine."

"I don't need to do anything or be anywhere or talk to anyone except you."

She sighed and let the silence spin out for another few moments.

"I guess…" She tried to keep the tremor out of her

voice but couldn't quite get there. "I guess we should talk what-ifs."

What if she lost the baby? What if their primary impetus for reconnecting disappeared? What if Gabe quit his job, resigned as mayor, moved to Arizona and hated being her military dependent when he'd previously been active duty himself. What if...?

He jerked forward, his fingers going tight on hers, and his fierce retort cut off her incipient panic. "No what-ifs. I'm not ready to play that game and you're in no condition to. Let's just take whatever happens a step at a time."

She couldn't help it. Her throat clogged. Tears burned behind her lids. Her nose got drippy. Sucking air up it, she glared at him.

"Damn these hormones! I can sure understand where Kathy was coming from."

Something flickered in his eyes at the mention of his sister, quickly came and quickly went.

"Better watch out," Suze threatened, only half in jest, "or I'll take an ax to you for turning me into this snuffling, sniffly bundle of stupid."

"You, wife, are as far from stupid as any woman I've ever known."

It sounded like a compliment. The words certainly stroked her. But was there a faint edge to his voice? Suze cocked her head, unsure.

Gabe must have sensed her puzzlement. He responded to it with a little shake of his shoulders and pushed out of his chair. "But just to be sure you don't act on any homicidal impulses..." He heeled off his shoes. "Scoot over."

"Gabe! You can't crawl in with me."

"Why not? It's not like you're hooked up to anything vital."

"True, but…"

"Scoot over."

Oh, God! She needed his arms around her. Needed his breath warm against her temple and his fierce assurance that all would be right with the world. Still snuffling, she scooted over.

She woke with a start when a white-coated physician rapped lightly on the door to her room. Blinking, she tried to guess what time it was. Late, she realized with a glance at the now-dark windows. Very late, she surmised when she squinted at the dinner sitting congealed under transparent plastic domes on her bedside tray.

She hadn't heard the food service folks deliver the dinner tray. Hadn't heard any of the nurses who must've checked on her in the hours since she'd crashed. But Gabe's murmured "We've got company," prodded her to semi-wakefulness.

"Huh?"

"We've got company."

She blinked awake to find a small, slender and obviously amused female physician observing their conjoined status. The doc's assistant stood behind her, equally amused.

Suze shifted, and Gabe vacated his half of the bed. He raked a hand through his hair, although the dark brown pelt was too short to show either the hours in the sack or any attempt to tame it.

"I'm Doctor Le," the trim young physician said as she came forward to offer Suze her hand. "I'm the hospital attending. Your case was transferred to me when you were admitted."

Her glance cut to Gabe. "And you are?"

"Her husband."

"I was certainly hoping that was the case." She shifted her attention back to Suze. "I have the results of your biopsy, Captain Hall. Dr. Terry asked me to share them with you as soon as they came. Is it okay with you if we discuss them in your husband's presence?"

Suze's arm snaked out. Gabe gripped her hand again. Harder this time.

"Yes," she said, her mouth dry.

"The biopsy confirms Dr. Terry's initial diagnosis. The mass is benign. What we call a uterine fibroid, also known as a…"

"Leiomyoma," Gabe cut in on a huff of relief.

The doc's brows rose. "Not many people are familiar with the technical term. Are you in the medical profession?"

"No, but my sister is. Kathy Sheppard. She's a nurse in the…"

"Neonatal ICU. I know Kathy. She's one of our most outstanding nurse practitioners."

Gabe and Suze exchanged glances. Apparently Kathy was well known in her sphere of operations.

"I'll tell her you said so," Gabe responded.

"And you must be the brother she's always bragging about. The mayor of…?"

"Cedar Creek."

"Right. Well…"

Suze's throat went dry, but the doc's smile worked magic on her sudden and unbelievably vicious attack of nerves.

"The mass is just large enough to press against your uterus. Your baby must have squeezed it, which is what caused the bleeding. I don't see any cause for alarm yet, but your OB/GYN needs to watch it."

"Is the baby okay?"

"Looks fine. I'll make sure you get copies of the lab report to take to your OB. Is he or she local?"

"No. I'm active duty, stationed at Luke Air Force Base in Arizona."

"A hard copy it is, then. In the meantime…" Her smile kicked up another notch. "Just relax and go back to whatever you were doing. We'll keep an eye on you tonight, Ms. Hall, but we'll probably send you home tomorrow."

When the door swished shut behind her and her PA, Suze collapsed against the pillows. To her profound disgust, a new rush of tears burned her lids.

"This is ridiculous." Thoroughly irritated, she scrubbed the back of her hand across her eyes. "How the heck am I supposed to command the respect of my troops if I go all female and weepy at the drop of a hat?"

"Jeez! We just got terrific news. You're entitled to go all weepy." Gabe gave a rueful laugh. "I'm a little soggy myself."

He was!

Biting her lip, Suze tried to remember another time when her husband's emotions had been pared down to the nub. He hadn't cried when his dad died, she recalled. Not in front of her, anyway. His mom and sisters had gone through several boxes of Kleenex at the funeral but Gabe had sat like a stone.

And he'd acted anything but maudlin at their wedding. Their first wedding, she amended. *Her* folks had shredded the Kleenex that time, but Gabe had grinned through the entire ceremony. Which made the way he dropped his chin to his chest and stared at the floor for several stark moments all the more poignant.

"Gabe," she said quietly. "Go home now. Fix something to eat, then crash. One of us, at least, should get a good night's rest."

He resisted but eventually yielded. Before leaving, though, he called her folks to share the biopsy results. Relieved and happy, they promised to swing by first thing in the morning. Suze tried to dissuade them but they silenced her protest with a promise of homemade cinnamon-raisin rolls.

"I'll be here for that, too," Gabe said with smile as he bent to kiss her goodbye. "See you in the morning."

"Let's just hope it's considerably less eventful than today's."

She was thinking of all that had happened in the space of twelve hours when she remembered the call from Dave Forrester.

"Gabe?"

She caught him halfway to the door. He turned, a question in his tired eyes.

"Yeah?"

"Did you know Colonel Amistad wanted to talk to me about a civil engineering vacancy coming up at the 137th?"

"He mentioned something about a vacancy at the parade. I assumed that was part of the reason he invited us to meet with him."

"You didn't tell me that."

"Didn't I?"

He looked at her with an expression she couldn't quite interpret, then rolled his shoulders.

"Sorry 'bout that. Guess we both need to work on our communication skills. See you in the morning."

Chapter Eleven

Once visiting hours were over, the hospital entered that twilight world of dimmed lights and hushed voices where even the night crew's rubber-soled shoes sounded like bats squeaking in the corridors.

Kathy came by when her shift ended. She'd already tapped the nurses on Suze's floor for the biopsy results and endorsed Dr. Le's recommendation that her sister-in-law follow up with her OB when she got back to Arizona. She'd also brought some clean underwear and a pair of turquoise scrubs decorated with teddy bears for Suze change into.

"More comfortable to sleep in than that gown."

"Thanks, Kath." Suze poked her head through the V-neck top. "For the scrubs and for being so supportive about Gabe and me getting back together. I know you were pretty pissed at me after the divorce."

Her sister-in-law acknowledged that with a unapologetic nod. "I thought you put your career ahead of your husband."

"You don't think I'm still doing that by letting Gabe give up his job and move back to Arizona with me?"

Kathy didn't reply for several moments. When she did, Suze caught a glimpse of pain in the hazel eyes so like her brother's.

"I've learned the hard way not to judge what goes on in anyone else's marriage. Don and I... Well, we've had some problems." She shook her head, as if to rid it of bad memories, and resumed her usual, brisk manner. "We're working through them, though, just like you and Gabe have had to work through yours. So you guys do whatever's right for the two of you, and to hell with what anyone else thinks."

Surprised and grateful, Suze returned her hug and thanked her again for the scrubs and the encouragement.

When Kathy left, Suze tried to rest. After the emotional upheaval of the day, she should've folded like a floppy-brimmed boonie hat. Instead she was restless and too wired to even doze.

The long nap with Gabe probably accounted for part of that restlessness. She picked up her cell phone but a glance at the clock showed it was almost ten, so she decided not to call. Hopefully, Gabe was already in bed and zoned out. She, on the other hand, had to get up and pee. Again.

Once up, she decided to wander down to the nurses' station in search of conversation and comfort food. The two females and one male on duty supplied her with both.

"I read about you in the paper," one of the nurses related. "I'd guess not many women get a Bronze Star."

"More than you think these days. Women account for close to twenty percent of Air Force, not quite as much in other branches of the service. They're pulling combat tours right alongside their male counterparts."

"My brother's a Marine," she volunteered. "He's with the 2nd Marine Expeditionary Force in Kandahar."

"Tough area," Suze commented with deliberate understatement.

The Taliban had regained a big patch of Kandahar. The province included the majority of Afghanistan's opium-producing poppy fields, which the terrorists used to fund their operations. Although the US-led coalition of NATO forces in Kandahar served as "advisors," they were right there, side by side with their counterparts, when the crap hit the fan.

The second female was more interested in Cedar Creek's hot young mayor.

"Is he as sexy as he looks?"

Suze laughed. "Sexier."

"Wow!"

She chatted with the evening crew for another ten or fifteen minutes. One Diet Dr Pepper and two ice cream cups later, she was still restless.

"What floor is the maternity ward on?"

"This floor, east wing. The nursery's viewing window will probably be curtained for the night, though."

Suze decided to take her chances. After her morning scare, she felt an undefined but deeply visceral need to connect with other mothers, other babies. Dropping her sister-in-law's name at the east wing's central station helped. The viewing window was, indeed, curtained, but the flick of a switch opened it for a few precious moments.

The interior of the nursery remained dim, sheathing the plastic bassinets in soft light. Suze rested a palm on her stomach and let her gaze roam the high-tech cradles. Only three were occupied. The scrunch-faced occupants were all asleep. She watched them until Kathy's friend signaled that she needed to close the curtain and get back to her station.

Suze waved her thanks and meandered back to her own room. Still restless, she clicked on the TV and was watching an old movie with the soundtrack on low when she got a late visitor. The stranger didn't knock on the half-closed door, just poked her head inside.

"I heard your TV, Ms. Hall. May I come in?"

"Sure."

Suze understood why the woman hadn't knocked when she nudged the door open with one shoulder. Both arms were bandaged up to the elbow.

"I'm Donna Osborne," she said, confirming Suze's instant guess. "Your husband came to visit me earlier. He said you were here."

Suze clicked off the TV and swung her feet off the bed so she could sit up and face her visitor. "I'm so sorry about your husband."

Tears filmed the woman's tired eyes. "I still can't believe he's gone."

Suze was searching for the right words in the face of such raw grief when Donna Osborne showed she had a core of steel.

"I could've lost my boys, too," she said, blinking back her tears. "I almost did. So although all I want to do is howl and scream and pound my head against the wall, I have to be strong for them."

"How are they doing?"

"The oldest's burns are superficial, thank God. My mom flew in from Chicago this morning and will stay here at the healthplex with him. I'm transferring to Baptist tomorrow to be closer to my baby."

"I'm so sorry," Suze said again.

"Me, too." Donna let down her guard for a moment, and her face took on a haunted look. "It was such a stupid, stupid accident."

Suze could've said that, in her experience, most accidents were pretty damned stupid. Instead, she gestured to the chair beside her bed.

"Would you like to sit down?"

Donna pulled herself together again and shook her head. "No, I need to get back upstairs. I just wanted to thank you. Your husband told me what you did. To help put out the fire. I couldn't sleep wondering if you're in the hospital because of…because of us."

"No. It's something else entirely."

Donna nodded, obviously relived. "Well, that's one less guilt I have to carry on my heart. Whatever the problem is, I hope you're better soon."

"Thank you."

"And please tell your husband that I appreciate everything he's done for me and the boys more than I can ever say. I can't believe he's accomplished so much so quickly."

"He has?"

"He didn't tell you? He notified the insurance company for me. And talked to our church about organizing a clothing and toy drive. He's also assured me…" her eyes blurred again "…that someone from the medical examiner's office will contact me about when we can make funeral arrangements." She managed a wobbly smile. "He's a good man, Captain."

"I think so, too."

"Cedar Creek's lucky to have him."

Gabe was right, Suze thought when her unexpected visitor left. They *did* need to work on their communication skills. He hadn't told her about any of his activity on behalf of the Osbornes. Then again, she hadn't asked. Probably because she'd been so wrapped up in her own worries that she hadn't given any thought to his.

She lay awake as the clock ticked toward midnight, then one. Her body still sagged with residual tiredness but her mind swirled with everything that had happened in the past few days. The past few weeks, actually. In that short space of time, her world had turned upside down. So had Gabe's. And until this moment, they'd both been operating from their individual but separate perspectives.

Those searing few moments with Donna Osborne now had Suze reviewing every decision and questioning every step in the process. She finally dozed off and slept as well as anyone could in a hospital until her mom rapped lightly on her door.

"Hi, sweetie."

A quick glance at the clock showed it was barely six thirty. "Hi, Mom. What are you doing here so early?"

"Delivering the fresh-baked cinnamon-raisin rolls I promised. I wanted to be sure the night crew got some before they went off duty at seven. Dad's distributing them now. He'll be here in a minute."

"Hope he saves some for me!"

"Of course." She tipped her daughter a worried glance. "How did last night go? Any more spotting?"

"No."

"Thank God! Dad and I said some heavy prayers for you and our grandbaby."

"I said a few myself."

"Does Gabe know?"

"Not yet. I didn't want to call and wake him this early."

"Uh-oh. I called to tell him about the cinnamon rolls. He's on his way in. And I thought you might want to freshen up before he gets here." She dug into a tote splashed with embroidered hollyhocks almost as colorful as the streaks in her hair. "I brought you a hairbrush and a toothbrush. Some clean underwear, too, although it looks like you've already had a change of clothes."

"These are Kathy's scrubs. She brought them by before she went off duty last night."

"She's got a kind heart, even if she did say some rather disparaging things about you after the divorce."

"We talked about that."

Suze wanted to ask her mom if she'd heard anything about Kathy and her husband but refrained. That flash of pain she'd spotted in her sister-in-law's eyes made the topic too private, too personal.

Once she'd washed her face and brushed both her teeth and her hair, though, she did ask about Cedar Creek's community activities in support of Donna Osborne and her boys.

"The whole town's rallied," Mary Jackson reported. "For the Osbornes and the other families whose homes were damaged. The Kellys and the Sugarmans have moved into the Comfort Inn temporarily. We're having a bake sale at our church today to cover the cost of their rooms. The Methodist Church is soliciting contributions for Walmart gift cards so they can buy what they need in the interim, and Ruby's offered free meals until they get settled. Oh, and Alicia Johnson's been a whirlwind. As soon as she and Dave Forrester got back from Texas, she lined up rentals for both families and arm twisted the owners into giving the first three months rent free. I have to tell you, Suzanne, I could never warm up to Alicia when you were girls. And," she added with a sniff, "I certainly didn't like the way she threw herself at Gabe after the divorce. My opinion's changing, though."

"Mine, too."

"Really? What…? Oh, good. Here's your dad."

She jumped up to relieve him of an extra-large Tupperware carrier so he could give his daughter a kiss. "Cute teddy bears," he said, eyeing her borrowed scrubs. "Where'd you get them?"

"Kathy. She stopped by when she got off work last night." Suze twitched her nose, closed her eyes and floated on a heavenly scent. "Oh, my Lord, Mom. Those rolls smell incredible. Do we have to wait for Gabe?"

"Hell, yes, you do," her husband answered from the door.

He elbowed the door open, double-stacked coffee containers in both hands. He yielded the top ones from each hand to her parents before dropping a kiss on Suze's nose.

"Morning, wife."

"Morning, husband."

His gaze raked her face. "You look a little better than when I left you last night."

Suze wished she could say the same. He'd obviously showered and shaved, but the lines at the corners of his eyes and mouth seemed to have taken up permanent residence.

"Did you get any sleep last night?" she asked.

"Some. How about you?"

"Off and on."

"How's our little Peanut?"

The worry in his eyes belied the flippant question. A smile spread across her heart as she reassured him. "Still holding his or her own."

"So we're celebrating," her mom announced as she popped the top on the Tupperware container. "Sugar all around."

"Oh, Mary. Bless you."

Relief etched in every line of his face, Gabe closed his eyes and dragged in the scent of cinnamon, raisins and hundred-proof sugar icing.

"If I wasn't married to your daughter and your husband wasn't standing three feet away, I'd beg you to run away with me. All you'd have to do for the rest of your life is flip blueberry pecan pancakes and bake cinnamon rolls."

"Don't be so ridiculous." The scold didn't match her mom's delighted smile. "You don't need to suck up to me. You've already got my vote."

Suze knew her mother had tossed out the comment carelessly, without thinking. Yet the barb dug deep. She popped a soft, doughy bite studded with raisins and dripping with sugary frosting into her mouth, then reached for her coffee to wash it down. The brew was strong and black, just the way she liked it. Just the way Gabe always fixed it for her.

Without warning, her mind flashed back to their chance meeting in Arizona. The unplanned stop at McDonald's.

Her husband waiting with a coffee in each hand when she'd come out of the ladies' room. He'd remembered how she liked her coffee then, too. He'd remembered everything.

The confused, conflicting thoughts that had tumbled though her head during the sleepless hours last night coalesced. The brief, middle of the night talk with Donna Osborne had added a sharper focus to choices facing her and Gabe.

Like the bits of a thousand-piece jigsaw puzzle, they fell into place. And for the first time since she'd come home, Suze caught a clear, unclouded glimpse of her future.

She eased into it slowly, carefully. Between sips of the life-giving caffeine. "Donna Osborne came to see me last night."

"Seriously?" Gabe frowned. "She didn't look strong enough to get out of bed when I saw her yesterday afternoon."

"She was still in pretty bad shape. Both hands and arms were bandaged, and her grief seemed as though it was tearing her apart."

Her mom *tch-tched* in sympathy. "She and the boys will have a long road to recovery, emotionally and physically. Yesterday at the church we were talking about how we could help."

"Mom mentioned that Alicia has lined up rentals for the two families whose homes were damaged," Suze told Gabe. "Do you know if she's found anything for the Osbornes?"

"As a matter of fact, I was going to talk to you about that today." He polished off his roll and swiped his hands on a napkin. "I'd like to offer Donna my place until the boys are both well and she decides whether she's going to stay in Oklahoma or move back to Chicago to be closer to her folks. We'll be on our way to Arizona this time next week, so the timing should work."

"I thought of that, too, and it seemed like a perfect solution. There's just one problem."

"What's that?"

"You won't be going to Arizona."

The hand holding Gabe's coffee cup stopped halfway to his mouth. "You want to run that by me again?"

"I'm putting in my papers as soon as I get back to base."

Gabe went completely still, his eyes locked with hers. "When did you decide that?"

"Last night. After I talked to Donna Osborne."

"You don't think that's something we should discuss and decide together?"

The terse question turned her mom's expression from puzzled to worried. She glanced at her daughter, then her son-in-law and back again.

"What papers?" she wanted to know. "What are you talking about?"

They ignored her.

"I said last night we needed to improve our communications skills," Gabe said, each word clipped. "Maybe we should start with yours."

Flustered by the sudden tension in the air, her mom fisted her hands on her hips. "What papers, Suzanne?"

"C'mon, Mary." Her husband hooked a hand in her elbow and tugged her toward the door. "I'll explain outside. Let's get some fresh coffee and give them some privacy."

She went, but they could hear her wail from halfway down the corridor. "*What* papers?"

"Okay," Gabe said, his eyes still cool and flat. "It's just us, Suze. How about telling me why you've decided to separate from active duty and, oh, by the way, unilaterally reverse the course of our lives."

"Would you buy super-ultra-hyper hormones?"

"Suzanne…"

"Hey, it was worth a shot."

"Dammit!" His growl was all the more effective for being low and furious. "First you don't bother to tell me about the spotting. Now this?"

"I'm sorry, Gabe. I am, really. It was just so late, and Kathy said not to worry. And you were gone when I got up the next morning."

"Don't give me that bull. We both have cell phones, don't we?"

"Okay, I screwed up on that one." Sighing, she tipped her chin toward the chair pulled up next to the bed. "Can we at least sit down while I try to unscrew this one?"

She perched on the edge of the bed. Gabe faced her, his knees spaced between hers. His expression wasn't quite as taut as it had been a few moments ago but hadn't completely thawed yet.

"When I drove home to Oklahoma to tell you about the baby," she said slowly, trying to reduce her thoughts to an understandable logic, "I figured we'd work out amicable custody and visitation terms. And I knew you well enough to feel sure you'd take over as custodial parent if and when I deployed."

His lip curled. "Good to know you had such confidence in me."

"Okay, I deserve that. But I swear, Gabe, I never imagined, never *dreamed*, that you'd want to be such a big part of our baby's life that you'd quit your teaching job, resign as mayor and move to Arizona. Looking back, I think I was so surprised that I just grabbed at the offer with both hands."

"So what's changed?"

"Lots of things, but mostly my perception of the kind of the life we could build together in Cedar Creek."

She slicked her palms over her knees, then bridged the short distance from her thighs to his. His muscles were hard to her touch, his jeans stretched taut across them.

"You're a natural at your elected position, Mr. Mayor. You care, you're not afraid to get down and dirty, and you make things happen. Everyone says the next step is the state legislature. Then maybe the governor's office. But what's even more important to me is how you shape young minds."

She smiled at the memories.

"I kept thinking of the teachers who pushed and prodded me. Very Scary Mrs. Lee. Remember her?"

"Our seventh grade math teacher? Like I could forget."

"And my advanced physics prof our sophomore year at OU. If not for him, I wouldn't be an engineer—or be wearing captain's bars."

"Yeah, well, let's talk about those captain's bars. You said you intended to put in your papers. Does that mean you're quitting the Air Force completely? Or are you thinking about the Guard or Reserve?"

"I'd like to apply for the full-time vacancy coming up at the 137th. There's no guarantee I'll get it. I'm pretty junior compared to some of the folks out there. And if I do, I'll probably have to deploy at times, depending on the world crisis or natural disaster."

Gabe searched her face. He knew how much this intrepid woman thrived on challenges, the tougher the better. "What if you don't get the job at the 137th? What if you're stuck playing mommy in Cedar Creek for the rest of your life?"

As soon as the words were out, he realized how stupid they were.

"Oh, hell! Of course you won't stay stuck in Cedar Creek. If the 137th job doesn't pan out, you'll go to work for Dave Forrester and end up managing his entire conglomerate. Or get appointed to an international commission chartered to extract water from hot air in Africa. Or, hey, join the NASA team that wants to construct a laser highway to the moon."

Laughing, she didn't deny any of possibilities. "I'm thinking I could also lobby for the director of the EPA position when my husband wins a seat in the US Senate."

Gabe leaned forward and framed her face with his palms. "Tell me the truth, Suze. If the 137th job doesn't come through, can you really hang up your uniform with no regrets?"

"No regrets at all? Probably not. I love the camaraderie. And the sense of being part of something bigger than myself. You and the baby will just have to push me down a career path that provides that same level of satisfaction."

He blew a soundless whistle. "Looks like the kid and I have a job cut out for us."

"Yeah, you do." She angled her head and pressed a kiss on his palm. "So…are we good?"

"About staying in Cedar Creek? You know the answer to that. About how we got to that point? Not hardly."

His hand slid from her cheek to her chin. Curling his knuckles under her chin, he brushed his thumb across her lower lip. The touch was soft, sensual, but the look in his eyes was dead serious.

"It's not going to work if either one of us makes unilateral decisions on major issues like this one. We have to keep the comm lines open and humming."

She started to respond but his thumb pressed against her lips, halting her reply.

"We talk, Susie Q. About the baby. Our jobs. The price of a half gallon of Ben & Jerry's Cherry Garcia. Deal?"

"Deal."

Chapter Twelve

Air Force regulations allowed Suze to request separation from active duty no earlier than ninety days and no later than thirty days prior to her expected delivery day. That meant she'd have six months yet at Luke AFB to train her replacement, apply for transition to the Reserves and get ready for another move. None of which, she insisted, was any big deal.

Nevertheless, Gabe requested a six-month leave of absence from his teaching and mayoral duties to accompany her. The school board was thrilled that he intended to return for the spring semester instead of quitting outright and happily approved the temporary absence. The members of Cedar Creek Town Council were just as accommodating. They approved Joanna Hicks as mayor *pro tem* but extracted a promise from Gabe to be immediately reachable by phone or computer if necessary.

When Suze tried one last time to suggest he wait for her here in Cedar Creek, Gabe shut her down. "We're not going through any more separations than we have to. Especially when you also have that uterine fibroid to take care of."

"Kathy says it's a simple outpatient laparoscopic procedure."

"Simple or not, I intend to be there. Besides, Doofus and I could use a break, right pal?"

The wire-haired griffon woofed his agreement.

"Ooooh boy," Suze laughed. "It's gonna be fun driving halfway across the country with Doofus occupying the back seat of my convertible, going crazy every time we pass a car or a truck."

"Ole Blue's got a trailer hitch. We'll tow the convertible and let Doofus reign supreme in the truck's jump seat."

"Like I said," Suze drawled, "it's gonna be fun."

Surprisingly, it was.

Before departing on their odyssey, they helped Donna Osborne, her mom and her oldest boy settle into the house. Donna still hadn't decided whether to remain in Cedar Creek or move closer to her parents. She had to put off thinking about that until her youngest had recovered and she'd sorted through the bewildering business of insurance claims for her home and her husband's death. The offer to live rent-free in Gabe's house for the next six months relieved her of one crushing problem.

They showed Donna through the house and gave her the keys late on a Thursday afternoon. The next morning they loaded up Ole Blue. Gabe had stashed most of his personal effects at Penny's house, so all he had to toss in the truck's lockable storage container was one duffle containing his clothes, the weekender roller bag Suzanne had brought for what she'd thought would be a short visit and a thirty-pound sack of dry dog food.

He stuffed his laptop and a thick wad of folders in a soft-sided briefcase. The case joined Suze's tote in the truck's air-conditioned cab. So did Doofus. Deliriously happy at the prospect of an outing, he left nose smears all over the narrow windows on both sides of the jump seat. As Suze had predicted, he took vocal exception to every moving object as they cruised down Main Street and headed for the interstate. Gabe finally shot him an evil look in the rearview mirror and warned of dire consequences—up to and including a visit to the vet for a too-long delayed snip—if he didn't lie down and shut up.

They hit I-40 and headed west. With each mile of undulating prairie, another boulder seemed to roll off their shoulders. Gabe, because this was his first hiatus from work since his election. Suze, because each passing moment confirmed the rightness of her decision.

They stopped to let Doofus do his thing in the dog-walking area at the rest stop just over the line into Texas. They stopped again for lunch in Amarillo. Since they couldn't leave the dog in a hot car, they drove through a Taco Bell and took their lunch to another highway rest stop. Two tacos each for Suze and Gabe, one as a treat for Doofus mixed in with his healthy-bones Purina chow. While they were stopped, Suze asked Gabe if he'd mind making a brief detour in Albuquerque.

"To visit Ben Kincaid and his wife?"

Suze nodded. "Ben wasn't there when I went through on the way out. I know he'd like to see us both."

Gabe readily agreed. Divorce, he'd discovered, tended to strain loyalties. He'd found it even more difficult to keep up with friends and acquaintances after he'd separated from the Air Force. Major Ben Kincaid was one of the few who'd made an effort to at least stay in touch.

"Yeah, sure, we can stop if they're going to be home." His grin slipped out. "I have to admit, I'd like to meet the woman who brought Love-'em-and-leave-'em-happy Ben Kincaid to his knees."

Alex Kincaid not only confirmed that they'd be home, the busy entrepreneur was thrilled to hear Suze was a bride. Again.

"Omigosh! You and your ex? Back together again? Wait until I tell Ben! He was bummed that he missed you on your way out to Oklahoma, and he said then that he wouldn't be surprised if the two of you hooked up again. He'll be *so* smug when he hears he was right."

"Are you sure it's convenient for us to stop by? I would've called earlier but…well…it's been kind of hectic. We just made the decision to pack up and head west two days ago."

"Heck, yes, it's convenient. You have to stay with us tonight. I want to hear every detail, Swish."

After almost ten days in her hometown, surrounded by family and friends who knew her only as Suzanne or Suze, hearing her military call sign again gave her a little jolt.

"We can't stay the night, Alex. We have a very large, very noisy hound accompanying us, so we booked a room at a pet-friendly hotel west of Albuquerque."

"At least stay for dinner," Alex pleaded. "Ben can

throw some steaks on the grill and share his latest war stories with you while *I* get acquainted with the guy who's so hot you married him twice."

Suze had to laugh. "And he's looking forward to meeting the gal who shot Cowboy down in flames."

"Great! Call us when you hit the outskirts of town and we'll fire up the grill. Oh, and bring the dog in with you. Our backyard isn't all that big but it's enclosed. Maria will love playing with him."

"But her cat probably not so much."

"So Sox can stay inside. See you soon."

The evening was one of the most relaxing Suze had spent in months. Make that years. She and her husband, together again, seated at a table with a view through French doors of a backyard landscaped in gorgeous high-desert style, sharing laughter and lusciously marinated steaks and the company of another couple obviously devoted to each other. Cowboy had stopped on his way home to buy a couple of bottles of nonalcoholic sparkling cider to celebrate both the remarriage and the baby. The four of them lingered at the table, enjoying the bubbly, long after the dishes were cleared.

Outside, Maria shrieked in delight as Doofus frolicked with her in the sprinkler Ben had set up for them. Delirious with joy, the dog barked his fool head off and did a leaping, contorted jig as he tried to plant his huge paws over the water spouts. Maria's cat was not amused. She sat on a windowsill in the kitchen, her tail twitching back and forth and her eyes narrowed to slits as she monitored the outdoor activities.

The adults had kept the conversation general while Maria was with them. Once the girl went outside, Cowboy turned the talk back to Suze's surprise announcement that she intended to separate from active duty, move back to her hometown and go into the Reserves. Not unexpectedly, his reaction was mixed. He was still Special Ops. Still gung-ho. But marriage and a ready-made family had given him a decidedly different perspective on the demands of a military career. After some back and forth, he reluctantly admitted that being a full-time Air Reserve Technician and member of an Air Guard unit with a distinguished combat record like that of the 137th would make use of Swish's training, experience and leadership skills.

Alex endorsed his opinion. "Looks like a win-win situation to me," she said as she grimaced and shifted on her cushioned chair. When she caught Swish's glance, she laughed. "I thought the second trimester was a pain in the you know what. It's got nothing on the third."

"Bad, huh?"

"Just your average backaches from hell, spider veins, swollen ankles and heartburn. Which is exactly what I tried to tell Chelsea."

"Has she been up to visit lately?"

"No, but I talk to her at least once a week."

"Who's Chelsea?" Gabe wanted to know.

"Oh, sorry. She was my roommate when I lived in Vegas," Alex explained. "I forgot you weren't at the last Badger Bash. You would've met her there. She's a dancer. A good one, although she's currently between gigs."

"She won't be unemployed long." Her husband grinned. "The woman is five nine, most of it leg, and built like the proverbial brick…"

"Care…*ful*!"

"Let's just says she's built."

"She's the one who's got a sort of on-again, off-again going with Dingo," Suze put in.

"Okay, got it," Gabe said. "I remember you mentioning something about that. So is it on now or off?"

"We're not sure. Chelsea hasn't said, and no one's heard from Dingo."

Suze and the lively dancer hadn't spent all that much time together at the Bash but she'd admired her liveliness and outspoken personality. Chelsea Howard was out there, literally and figuratively.

"So, what's she up to if she's not working?" she asked between sips of sweetened iced tea.

Alex threw a quick glance at her still-splashing daughter, then heaved a sigh. "She's decided to have a baby."

Suze snorted into her tea. "Good grief! This baby thing is spreading like a virus!"

"She read some article about inherited genetic traits in *Scientific American*," Cowboy said with another grin.

"*Scientific American?* Really?"

"Hey, she's not all hair and long legs," Alex put in loyally.

Cowboy picked up the narrative again. "She figures with her talent and undeniably spectacular looks, she could mate her DNA with that of a certified genius and hit the baby jackpot."

"Is that all she wants to mate? Their DNA?"

"Apparently." Cowboy's blue eyes glinted with laughter. "She's drawn up a list of candidates and plans to start interviewing them between auditions for another gig."

"Are you serious?"

"As a mortar attack."

"I need to meet this woman," Gabe commented to no one in particular.

"She's going to fly up for a visit when she narrows the list to the final three. To get Alex's input."

"Is she talking artificial insemination?"

"I'm not sure. I'm almost afraid to... Oh!"

She sat up, her eyes wide, and flattened both palms on her belly. Stiffening, Cowboy went on full alert until Alex slumped against her chair again.

"Whew! That was a good one. Braxton Hicks contractions," she explained to her startled guests. "I've had them intermittently for a while but they're getting more frequent. My doc says that's common in pre-labor. The cervix is preparing for delivery."

Her husband was already on his feet and cupping his wife's arm. "Let's you into a more comfortable chair. Swish, how about you keep Alex company in the other room while Gabe and I pull kitchen duty, then get Maria and the hound dried off?"

She was only too happy to agree. After her own scares with spotting, she intended to pump Alex for any and all information she wanted to share about this life-altering condition.

She and Gabe and Doofus said goodbye just a little more than an hour later. They weren't about to overstay their welcome in the face of their hostess's obvious discomfort and the hissing hostility of Maria's cat to the canine invasion of her territory.

Before they left, Alex presented Swish with another of her personally designed tees. This one was done in camouflage colors and featured a glittering American eagle with wings folded to shelter its chick. Its talons clutched a banner with a fierce warning: Don't Mess with an Air Force Mom.

"I've designed one for each branch of the service," Alex related. "I put the designs up on my website two days ago and we're already swamped with orders."

"I love it! But you have to let me pay for it."

"Just wear it around your base. We'll consider the free advertising as payment in kind."

"You got it."

Doofus, who'd bonded with Maria, vociferously protested being herded into Ole Blue. Over his mournful howls at being separated from his new best pal, Swish gave Alex a final hug and a strict order.

"Call us if those fake contractions turn real and you guys need babysitting or hand-holding service. Gabe or I or both can jump a plane and be here in a few hours."

"Thanks. I'll remember that. And same goes for you, Warrior Mom. One call, and either Ben or I will be there."

It took close to forty minutes to navigate Albuquerque's traffic, pick up I-40 again and reach the hotel situated just across the Rio Grande. By then, Doofus couldn't wait to get out and explore the empty acres behind the hotel. Gabe kept him on a long, retractable leash, which he strenuously objected to. So much so that they were both hot and bothered when they returned to the hotel room.

"I've already hit the shower," Swish said while the hound slurped water from his dish.

She stretched out on the bed and was half dozing when Gabe emerged. He'd wrapped a towel around his hips, giving her a bird's-eye view of several interesting inches of pale belly below his tan line. His dark-brown hair still glistened with damp, and the glint in his hazel eyes started her heart humming in her throat.

Oh, God, he was gorgeous. Not the *GQ* kind of gorgeous, all suave and slick and styled. Or the muscled-up Navy SEAL kind. Just your average lean, tanned, smart, funny, thoughtful, kind type of gorgeous.

She wanted him so bad she hurt with it. But they'd decided to take it slow and careful until she consulted her doc. That decision was now slapping smack up against the desire coiling in her belly.

"Here's the deal," she told him, her voice husky. "You can drop that towel and make cautious, careful love to your wife. Or…"

"Or?"

"Or you can drop the towel and let me make wild, crazy love to my husband."

"There's a third option." He waggled his brows in an exaggerated leer. "How about you lie back, close your eyes and let me demonstrate the various ways a husband can pleasure his wife using only his hands, his tongue and his imagination?"

She wasn't going to argue with that!

Her pulse kicking into overdrive, she threw aside the light comforter she'd drawn over herself after the shower. The abrupt movement sent an unmistakable signal to Doofus. He'd been snoozing in a corner but now, sensing action, he charged across the room. Snagging a corner of the comforter, he dragged it completely off. His tail slashed back and forth. His teeth showed in a goofy grin as he waited for his humans to initiate his favorite game. When they ignored him, he whined once. Twice. Raked the mattress with an insistent paw.

He rocked back on his haunches, preparing to join

the fun on the bed, but Gabe sensed what was coming and paused in his imaginative efforts long enough to bellow a warning.

"No! Do not even *think* about it!"

Deterred but not completely cowed, the hound circled a few times, pawed the comforter into an acceptable nest, settled in and glared at his humans from the floor.

Suze was totally oblivious to their audience of one. True to his word, Gabe had exercised his very inventive imagination. She was writhing. Panting. Gripping the pillow with both hands. As the exquisite sensations rose and fell and rose again, she tried to hold back. Tried to spin them out. But the high, wild waves crested. One after another. Then came crashing down.

When her mind reinhabited her body, Gabe had eased up beside her. His right arm snaked under her shoulders. His left palm flattened on her belly.

"Wonder what Peanut thinks just happened?" he mused.

"Please," she groaned. "Don't go there. I won't be ready to explain what just happened until the kid is in his or her teens."

"Better not wait that long. My crush on you went from bashful to excruciating the first week I hit puberty. I spent that entire damned school year trying to disguise my hard-on every time you sashayed by."

"Ha! You wouldn't know bashful if it hit you in the face. But since we're being honest here, I'll come clean, too." She curved a palm against his cheek and answered his questioning look with a sly smile. "Why do you think my hip swing kicked into fourth gear every time I caught you watching me?"

"C'mon. You couldn't have known the agonies I was going through. Not at that age."

"Shows what you know. That bulge in your jeans fueled more erotic fantasies than any of the steamy novels I snuck out of the library."

"Christ, Suze." He curled his arm, drawing her closer. "With two oversexed parents like us, Peanut doesn't have a chance."

Laughing, she laid her hand atop the one resting on her belly. After all the months and years apart, after all the loneliness and regrets and stress, she and Gabe were right where they were supposed to be. Wrapped in each other's arms. His breath warm on her heated skin. Her hand coupled with his.

Whatever happened, whatever bumps and detours they had to face in the years ahead, this was exactly where they would stay.

Chapter Thirteen

Almost a year later, Suze grinned as she skimmed the text message that popped up on her iPhone screen.

From: Gator
To: Swish
Hey, girl! Cowboy, Kojack, Barbie, Dingo & Elvis already here. Where U at?

"Gator wants to know where we are," she relayed to her husband.

Gabe glanced her way, sunlight glinting off his aviator sunglasses. His left elbow rested on the open driver's-side window while he steered their rented Jeep Wrangler along California's fabled Highway 1. Big Sur splashed and crashed far below on their left. The rumpled, drought-parched Santa Lucia Mountains crowded close on their right. Thankfully, the massive landslide that had shut down a twelve-mile section of the highway south of Monterey last year had been cleared. They'd made good time since picking up the Jeep at LAX and heading north.

"Tell him we're about ten miles out."

Her thumbs worked. X-Man says 10 miles out.

The answer came back a few seconds later. Beer's on ice. Haul ass.

Still grinning, she clicked off the phone and dropped it in the armrest's cupholder. She could hardly believe another Badger Bash had rolled around. Or that she'd left the last one, spent what was left of the night shooting the breeze with her Air Force pals, then driven home through the just-breaking Arizona dawn, only to pull up at a red light and spot her ex-husband's truck across the intersection.

Her ex-ex now. The designation had tickled her. So much she'd started calling him XX, which quickly morphed to X-Man. Their family and friends had quickly picked up the tag. His students loved it, too, although none would dare use it to his face. Even the members of the town council had taken to calling him Mayor X-Man.

She stretched in her seat, enjoying the breeze from the open window and trying not to worry too much about Ellie, aka the Peanut. This was the first time they'd left their three-month-old for longer than one night. Granted, her parents had plenty of backup with Gabe's sisters and their husbands close by. And, as Suze's mother reminded her when she'd shooed her daughter out the door, Doofus would remain on duty. The hound was totally, completely goofy about the baby. And so fiercely protective no stranger got within twenty yards of Peanut until they'd been thoroughly vetted.

Suze had quashed her maternal doubts and told herself that this short weekend jaunt would be a good first step in dealing with any incipient separation anxiety. It would also help condition her for an upcoming two-week deployment to a classified location that she and a small cadre from the 137th had been tapped for.

Her transition to full-time Air Reservist had come faster and gone smoother than she'd anticipated. The slot Colonel Amistad had discussed with her had opened up less than two months after Ellie's birth. The competition for it had been fierce, but Swish's training and experience during her years on active duty gave her an edge. She was back in uniform again, doing what she loved and going home most evenings to her husband and daughter.

Life was good. Very good.

The breeze tugged at the hair she'd pulled through the opening in the back of her cap. It was another Alexis Scott creation, bling-studded and sparkling in the bright sunlight. She and Alex had become close this past year, communicating regularly via text, email and Facebook on the joys and challenges of motherhood.

"It'll be great to see Alex and Cowboy again," she commented to Gabe. "I was surprised when she told me they weren't bringing either Maria or little Ben with them, though."

"Guess they needed some adult time." Gabe glanced her way again and waggled his brows above the rim of his sunglasses. "I have to admit, I'm looking forward to it, too. Particularly the part that comes after this beach bash Gator's organized."

"The hotel's right on the beach. Nothing says we can't slip away whenever the mood strikes us. Or..." She matched his leer. "I seem to recall getting lost in the sand dunes with you once or twice when we were stationed in North Carolina."

"Either option works for me."

The Bash was in full swing by the time they checked into their hotel room, dumped their bags and changed into cutoffs and tank tops. Following the sound of laughter, they took the wooden stairs leading to the half-moon cove that thousands of years of pounding waves had carved out of the cliffs.

A dozen or so people now laid claim to the narrow stretch of pebbly beach fringing the cove. Wooden Adirondack chairs weathered to a silvery gray had been arranged in a circle around a stone fire pit, already lit and dancing with flames. Buckets and trays of appetizers provided by the hotel were being passed around. As Suze and Gabe descended the stairs, they caught snatches of raucous laughter as the chairs' occupants vied with each other to recount ever more improbable exploits of Colonel Bob Dolan, aka Badger.

The organizer of this year's Bash caught sight of them first. Interrupting the tales, he called a greeting. "Yo! Swish. X-Man. 'Bout time you two got here."

Gator lifted his wife off his knee and heaved out of the low-slung chair. After enveloping Swish in a bear hug, he pounded Gabe on the back and gestured to the others with his dew-streaked beer bottle.

"Y'all know everybody."

Almost everybody, she corrected with a quick sweep of the small crowd. There were a few unfamiliar faces. Kojack's new wife was one. Barbie Doll's fiancé was another. After quick introductions, Gabe went to retrieve two beers while Swish perched on the arm of Dingo's chair. He was sprawled next to Alex and Cowboy, his legs thrust toward the fire pit. Despite his lazy slouch, though, Swish picked up a tense vibe.

"You okay?" she asked, nudging his knee with hers. "You look a little tight around the edges."

"I'm good."

The terse reply arced her brows. She looked a question at Alex, who answered it with one word. "Chelsea."

"Uh-oh."

From her conversations with Alex over the past twelve months, Suze knew the vivacious showgirl's on-again, off-again relationship with Dingo was currently off. She also knew Chelsea had become a fierce advocate for a new cause. She no longer aspired to join the ranks of single mothers. In one of those too-weird-to-be-believed encounters that had even the Vegas police shaking their heads, she'd accidentally rescued a fifteen-year old sex slave. Horrified by the girl's situation, Chelsea had now turned her formidable energy to busting up human trafficking rings.

Drawing Swish a little way apart, Alex relayed the latest news in a soft murmur. "Chelsea's decided to go undercover. And she wants Dingo to pose as her pimp or procurer or whatever the heck they call it in the trafficking business."

"Oh, God! Please tell me you're kidding."

"I wish I could."

"Dingo *can't* have agreed to go along with that crazy scheme."

"Chelsea says he threatened to wring her neck first. But you know how…"

"Whoa!"

The startled exclamation cut through their quiet conversation and jerked them around. Like everyone else on the tiny slice of beach, they gaped at the woman descending the wooden stairs.

Her cutoffs were probably illegal in at least a half-dozen states. Their ragged fringe had to tickle her crotch. But they also showed off disgustingly trim thighs that other women would kill for. The V of her stretchy, sleeveless top revealed a deeper crevass than the Grand Canyon, and its rib-kissing hem displayed even more skin, including a diamond belly button stud that caught the setting sun and flashed fire with every step.

For several frozen moments, the awed silence was broken only by the sputter and hiss of the fire and the wash of waves against the pebbled shore. Then Dingo bolted out of his chair and made for the stairs.

Suze was still transfixed by the scene when Gabe appeared at her side to murmur, "That, I presume, is Chelsea."

"You presume correctly."

In a quiet undertone she related the dancer's hopes to draw Dingo into undercover work with her.

Gabe's lips pursed in a soundless whistle. "I sure as hell don't envy him the next few months."

He handed her an icy bottle and clinked his own against it. A shift of his shoulders blocked everything else from her view. The fire. The shadowed cliffs surrounding the cove. The small drama currently taking place at the bottom of the stairs.

"Did I ever thank you, Susie Q?"

His voice was a soft, erotic caress backed by the murmur of the sea. She shivered and smiled her delight. "For?"

"For being sane, sensible, uncrazy you. And for loving me."

"You have, actually. But if you want to express your

appreciation again, we could slip away for that quality adult time we talked about earlier."

Grinning, he plucked her beer out of her hand and plunked it down next to his on the arm of Dingo's vacated chair. Since everyone else's attention was still riveted on the showgirl and the ex-cop, he drew her away from the circle of chairs.

They picked their way along the rocky shore until the cliffs towered a hundred feet or more above them. The nooks and crannies carved by the relentless sea provided a good measure of privacy, but not enough for either one of them to risk a public indecency charge.

Gabe settled for propping his shoulders against a rocky wall and tugging off his wife's sparkly hat. Her ash-blond hair tumbled over her shoulders, and her green eyes were as deep and beguiling as the ocean.

She leaned back against the circle of his arms and smiled up at him. "I still can't believe everything that's happened since last year's Bash. You. Me. Ellie. Alex and Maria and the two Bens, big and small. If the next year is as hectic as this last one, I don't know if I can handle it."

"You can handle anything." He raked back the hair at her temples and framed her face with his palms. "Now, how about you forget Ellie and Alex and the two Bens and just kiss me, Captain."

* * * * *